Lucky
Stiff

Annelise Ryan

KENSINGTON BOOKS
http://www.kensingtonbooks.com

KENSINGTON BOOKS are published by

Kensington Publishing Corp.
119 West 40th Street
New York, NY 10018

All Kensington titles, imprints and distributed lines are available at special quantity discounts for bulk purchases for sales promotion, premiums, fund-raising, educational or institutional use. Special book excerpts or customized printings can also be created to fit specific needs. For details, write or phone the office of the Kensington Special Sales Manager: Kensington Publishing Corp., 119 West 40th Street, New York, NY 10018. Attn. Special Sales Department. Phone: 1-800-221-2647.

Kensington and the K logo Reg. U.S. Pat. & TM Off.

ISBN-13: 978-0-7582-7275-1
ISBN-10: 0-7582-7275-8

First Mass Market Printing: March 2013

10 9 8 7 6 5 4 3 2 1

Printed in the United States of America

Praise for Annelise Ryan and the Mattie Winston Mysteries

FROZEN STIFF

"Ryan mixes science and great storytelling in this cozy series . . . The forensic details ring true and add substance to this fast-paced and funny mystery. Good plotting and relationship drama keep the mystery rolling, while Mattie's humorous take on life provides many comedic moments."

—*Romantic Times Book Reviews*

"[Mattie's] competence as a former ER nurse, plus a quirky supporting cast, makes the series intriguing. Ryan has a good eye for forensic and medical detail, and Mattie gets to be the woman of the hour in her third outing."

—*Library Journal*

"Absorbing . . . Ryan smoothly blends humor, distinctive characters, and authentic forensic detail."

—*Publisher's Weekly*

SCARED STIFF

"An appealing series on multiple fronts: the forensic details will interest Patricia Cornwell readers, though the tone here is lighter, while the often slapstick humor and the blossoming romance between Mattie and Hurley will draw Evanovich fans who don't object to the cozier mood."

—*Booklist*

"Ryan's sharp second mystery . . . shows growing skill at mixing humor with CSI-style crime."

—*Publishers Weekly*

WORKING STIFF

This one is dedicated with much love to my sisters:
Cathy, Laurie, and Amy.

Chapter 1

There are few things in life that smell as bad as a burnt human body. You'd think with all that flesh, which is really just another form of meat, it might smell like a pig roasting on a spit. But you'd be wrong. Your average roasting pig doesn't have hair, intact organs, and vessels filled with blood. Unfortunately, the person whose death I now have to investigate comes with all those things, and the stench is nauseating.

Adding to the biological odors are the various household items that have burned: plastics, Styrofoam, building materials, and a variety of fabrics. This is a smell I know well, because I've been living next to another burnt-down building for the past couple of weeks: the house I used to share with my ex-husband, David Winston. The only person who was in my old house when the fire struck was my ex. Despite the fact that I've imagined him being tortured or dying in hideous ways many times over the past few months, he escaped from the fire unharmed. Unlike the person before me, who is burned so badly I can't tell if the body is that of a man or a women, David is alive and healthy. And if his recent behavior is any indication, he's also well into "manopause."

My ex is a surgeon. He cuts people open in an effort to better or save their lives. My name is Mattie Winston. I'm a nurse, and I used to do the same thing, working side by side with David in our local hospital's OR. But after catching David using his pocket rocket as a tongue depressor on one of my coworkers, I left my job, my home, and my marriage rather abruptly. Fortunately, my best friend and neighbor, Izzy, threw me a lifesaver by offering me both a job and the mother-in-law cottage behind his house. Since Izzy is the county medical examiner, my new job as a death investigator still involves cutting people open, but with two significant differences: all of my patients are a certain distance past their freshness dates, and rather than trying to save their lives, I'm trying to figure out how they lost them.

The ME's office is located in the small Wisconsin town of Sorenson, where we cover deaths for a county-wide area. I grew up in Sorenson, and that makes my job very difficult at times, since I know most of the people I have to autopsy. Today the death I'm investigating is right here in town—a body discovered in a home that is now little more than a burnt-out shell. As a result, I'm not sure yet if our victim is someone I know. Adding to the tragedy is the fact that it's Christmas Day, as evidenced by the empty tree stand and a dozen or so broken glass ornaments in one corner.

Very little in the room I'm standing in is recognizable. Heat from the flames melted the foot or so of snow that was on the roof. The melt-off, combined with the fire damage and all the water from the fire hoses, brought down most of the modest ranch's upper structure, leaving the scene a soggy, exposed, piled-up mess. An early-afternoon sun is shining down on us, and the outside temperature is already 48 degrees—very atypical for December here in Wisconsin. Fortunately, there was plenty of snow on the ground before today, allowing us some semblance of a white Christmas.

Izzy is beside me as we carefully pick our way through the charred remains, which are still smoking in places, despite the heroic efforts of the fire department. It's a bit easier for me to maneuver than it is for Izzy, because I'm six feet tall and have very long legs. Izzy, on the other hand, stands right around five feet tall; his legs aren't much longer in their entirety than my shinbones.

Several of the firefighters are still working on-site, spot-quenching little flare-ups and guiding us through the debris field. They were the ones who called us when they found the body. Also here are several cops, including Steve Hurley, the tall, dark-haired, blissfully blue-eyed homicide detective I lust after, but can't have.

"Are you guys sure this is arson?" Hurley asks a woman firefighter standing nearby.

"Positive," she says. She is a cute blonde, with a large, fluorescent name label across the back of her fire coat that says: KANE. Her cheeks are flushed and there are smudges of ash on her face, but they're not enough to hide her prettiness. If anything, they enhance it, giving her an impish, pixie look. Even with all her fire gear on, it's easy to tell she has a trim, petite figure. I want to hate her on sight, especially when I see Hurley give her the once-over . . . twice. My figure has never been petite, not even in the womb. My mother once described giving birth to me as akin to crapping out bowling balls for twenty hours straight. I have what Izzy's life partner, Dom, calls a Rubenesque figure—a comment that makes me both want to hate Dom and ask him to make me a Reuben sandwich. Dom is a killer cook.

Speaking of cooking, Kane points over toward the couch and says, "There's a pour pattern over there. If you look at the alligator pattern on the wall above it, you can tell that's where the fire started, even though someone tried to make it look like it started here by our victim. There's this other, smaller pour pattern next to the body leading from this overturned drink glass. Judging from the empty vodka bottles we found in the trash, and the ashtray beside this glass, I'm guessing someone wanted us to think the victim caused the fire by reaching for a drink, spilling it, and tipping over in the wheelchair while holding a cigarette."

"Any idea who our victim is?" Hurley asks.

"For now, we're assuming it's the man who lives here, a thirty-eight-year-old paraplegic by the name of Jack Allen."

"Oh, no," I mutter, looking aghast at the blackened mass.

"You know him?" Izzy asks.

"I do. I've taken care of him at the hospital several times. In fact, I took care of him when he had the car accident that paralyzed him. It was back when I was working in the ER, about seven, maybe eight years ago. I also saw him when we took his gallbladder out last year, and again more recently when he came in to have a bedsore debrided."

Kane cocks her head to one side. "I'm sorry, I thought you were with the ME's office," she says, eyeing me with a puzzled expression.

"I am. I've only had this job for a few months. Before that, I worked at Mercy Hospital as an RN."

"Ah," Kane says, and I see a glimmer of recognition on her face. "You're that gal who was married to the surgeon—the doctor who was doing it with that OR nurse who ended up murdered."

"Yep, that's me."

"And you also worked in the OR?"

I nod.

"Now I know why you look so familiar." I'm thinking she's going to mention some surgical procedure she had recently, but no such luck. "You were the one who was pictured on the front page of that tabloid, standing by the Heinrich car crash in your underwear."

My face grows hot. "Yes, that was also me," I say, my smile tight. Izzy and Hurley snort with laughter; I give them a threatening look as I silently curse my recent claim to fame. There are many perks to living in a small town like Sorenson. Unfortunately, anonymity isn't one of them. Infamy comes cheap and lasts a long, long time.

"I'm sorry, I don't remember your name," Kane says.

"I'm Mattie Winston. Nice to meet you," I lie.

"I'm Candy Kane. Today is my birthday and my parents had a warped sense of humor."

"Happy birthday," Hurley says with a smile that makes me want to step between him and Candy to block his view.

"Thanks," Candy says, smiling back. "After I'm done here, I get to go home and open all those lovely happy-merry-birthday-Christmas presents. We holiday kids tend to get the short end of the stick when it comes to gifts."

This seems only fair to me, since she clearly didn't get the short end of the genetic stick.

I look back at the floor and try to make sense of the fact that the burnt corpse lying there might be Jack Allen. The body is lying on its side in a fetal position;

the blackened arms are bent up like a boxer's trying to block a punch. I know from my recent studies that this pugilistic positioning is characteristic of severe burn victims, caused by shortening of the muscles and tendons as they heat up. I can't see the victim's face because the head and shoulders are covered with a pile of debris—ceiling tiles and old vermiculite-type insulation. The only thing about the body that fits our tentative ID is the wheelchair that's tipped on its side and positioned behind the body.

Candy says, "The neighbors say he was a smoker, as well as a drinker, though they fell short of describing him as an out-and-out drunk. One other interesting tidbit mentioned by the neighbors is the fact that our victim apparently won a very large jackpot at the North Woods Casino a few months ago."

"How large is very large?" Hurley asks.

"Five hundred thousand and change," Kane says.

Izzy lets out a low whistle.

"Sounds like motive to me," Hurley says. "And it might help us narrow down the list of suspects. All we have to do is follow the money."

"First we need to verify that this is Jack Allen," Izzy says. He steps forward, reaches down, and lifts one corner of a ceiling tile that's covering the victim's head, exposing the face. I can only see one half of it, as the other half is against the floor, but the entire head is relatively untouched by the ravages of the fire. Izzy turns and gives me a questioning look.

"That's Jack, all right."

Izzy stares down at him. "Interesting how the debris protected his face from the flames."

"It would," Candy says. "That vermiculite insulation contains asbestos."

"Asbestos?" I echo, looking concerned.

"Don't worry," Candy says. "Right now, everything is so saturated it would be nearly impossible for any fibers to become airborne. But it will require a special crew with the proper equipment to clean up the place."

Izzy nods solemnly. "Well, at least we have a tentative ID. We can verify things later with his dental records." He cocks his head to one side and stares at the body with a puzzled expression.

"What is it?" I ask.

"Look at the position of his head. His chin is tucked in close to his chest. If the head had been exposed to the fire, I might think it was because of tendon shrinkage from the heat. But the head was protected from the fire, and that makes me think it was forced into that position. The presence of the glass and the ashtray suggest there was a table of some sort here, like a coffee table."

"There probably was," Candy says. She points to several burnt pieces of wood that look like long, skinny cinders from a fireplace. "These look like the legs on a wooden structure of some sort."

"If so," Izzy says, "it's possible Jack died from positional asphyxiation. If he fell out of his chair and his head became wedged between it and a table, it could have blocked off his airway. I'll get a better idea of how feasible that theory is when I open him up."

Candy looks at Hurley and says, "There's one more thing I think you should see." We follow her through the debris into what appears to be the dining room. She stops in front of a charred piece of furniture and points to the melted, twisted remains of a stereo on top of it. As I look closer at the burnt mess, I see what looks like a large stereo speaker, relatively intact despite evidence of intense heat and flames.

"There's only one speaker," Hurley says.

"And it didn't burn," I add.

"Good eye, both of you," Candy says, though she directs her smile at Hurley. She points to some melted plastic and wires. "It looks like there was another speaker here, but it was destroyed in the fire. There's a reason this one survived." She reaches over and flicks her finger against the front of the intact speaker, eliciting a metallic ping. "This is a false front. It's constructed out of metal and made to look like a speaker, but it's actually a safe." She pulls on the speaker front and it opens, revealing an empty metal box. "There's a key lock on the back that operates a little spring device to open it."

"Was there anything in there?" Hurley asks.

"Nope, it was unlocked and empty when we got to it, and no sign of the key. But we did find this." Candy points down at the floor near the corner of the buffet and I see the edges of a hundred-dollar bill poking out from beneath some debris.

After snapping a picture, Hurley reaches down with his gloved hand and pulls the bill loose. Though its edges are singed, the main body of the bill is intact.

Candy says, "A lot of people don't know that paper money isn't really made out of paper. It's made out of cloth—linen and cotton, to be precise. And that means it doesn't burn so easily, especially if it's wet."

"You're thinking there was more of this in there," Hurley says, gesturing toward the safe.

Candy shrugs, but she gives us a knowing smile, which makes it clear she does think that.

Hurley sighs. "Well, if our casino winner was stashing wads of cash in his house, our list of suspects is going to be a hell of a lot bigger than I thought."

"Sorry to make things more complicated for you," Candy says with a cutesy little grin.

Hurley holds her gaze a bit longer than I like. "No need to apologize. You did some great investigative work here. I appreciate it."

"You're welcome. And if there's anything else you need from me, don't hesitate to ask." She takes a card out of her pocket and hands it to him. "That's my personal cell number on there. Call me anytime," she says with a suggestive tone. Then she gives Hurley a flirtatious wink and adds, "If you're nice to me, I just might give you a candy cane."

I have a few suggestions for what she can do with her candy cane, but I keep them to myself.

"Ahem," Izzy says, eyeing me with a worried expression. "I suppose we best get to securing the body so we can get it back to the morgue before all this water destroys our evidence. What do you guys say to doing this autopsy today?"

"Fine by me," I say. After years of employment at the hospital, I'm used to working on the holidays. "You'll be giving me the perfect excuse for avoiding the remainder of the celebration at my sister's house. My mother was already having a conniption about all the germs that might be lurking in my sister's live Christmas tree. When I left for this call, she was bleaching the tree ornaments." My mother has a few mental quirks, not the least of which are her hypochondria and her OCD. I'm pretty certain that by day's end she'll be at home consulting her impressive medical library in search of tree-borne diseases, imagining symptoms to fit.

"I'm fine with it, too," Hurley says. "I have no plans for the rest of the day and I'd like to get this wrapped up as quickly as possible."

"Wrapped up?" I echo. "Interesting choice of words, given the holiday."

Izzy rolls his eyes and heads back to the living room. I follow reluctantly, leaving Candy and Hurley alone in the dining room together. I force myself to focus on the immediate tasks at hand, but part of my mind imagines me holding a giant candy cane with the curved end looped around Hurley's waist, dragging him away from Candy in vaudeville style.

Chapter 2

Izzy and I manage to scoop up the remains of Jack Allen's body and get it back to the morgue some two hours later. We spend most of that time photographing and documenting the scene as the arson investigators collect their evidence.

Also documenting the scene outside is Alison Miller, Sorenson's ace reporter and photographer. She is lurking about, snapping shots and talking to anyone who's willing. I've known Alison for years. It was right after our high-school graduation that she went to work for our local paper, which comes out twice a week. I once considered her a friend, but our relationship these days is somewhere between animosity and outright loathing. That's because she became my chief competition for Hurley's affections not long ago, until Hurley made it clear he wasn't interested. Alison didn't take the rejection well and blamed it on me. I'm probably the only person from whom she won't try to get a quote.

Candy, the person who seems to be my new competition, doesn't stay long. While her absence relieves me a little, I can't help but notice that Hurley still has her card tucked safely inside his jacket pocket. I remind myself that I have no right to be jealous of what—or whom—Hurley does, because we don't have that kind of relationship. It's not from a lack of desire, however. There is a definite attraction between us that became evident early on during cases we worked together. But my lingering ambivalence over my marriage—and the tiny fact that I was still married—put a bit of a kibosh on things.

The marriage thing has recently been resolved. After I rejected David's repeated pleadings to give our marriage another chance, he finally got the message that I was done with him . . . right around the time he met up with Patty, the very attractive and single insurance agent who is handling the claim for our house fire. Now the two of them are an item. My divorce became final two days ago; and along with my freedom, I also received a tidy little settlement of nearly three hundred thousand bucks—my portion of the insurance claim on our house, minus the amount David gave me for the car I totaled some time ago that was in his name. The settlement wasn't as much as I'd hoped, because David, who handled all our financials, apparently neglected to update our homeowner's policy two years ago when we added on several hundred square feet of house in an addition off the back. While the house was once estimated to be worth close to a million bucks, in the current housing market, which stinks worse than what's left of Jack's house, that value has dropped to around seven hundred grand. And the insurance policy was for the original amount of the purchase, which was only five hundred grand, plus another hundred thousand for the contents. David had at one time offered to let me have a larger portion of the settlement in order to make up for the value of the land, which is now in his name only. However, after listening to him bitch about how much it was going to cost to rebuild and refurnish the place, I decided—in the spirit of idiocy—to settle for an even fifty-fifty split.

Still, my portion of the settlement has made for a nice early Christmas present; and for the first time in months, my bank account is flush while I try to decide how to invest the funds. David is using his half to rebuild the house, albeit a smaller, scaled-down version of the original.

Unfortunately, my newfound freedom doesn't help my situation with Hurley. Thanks to cuts in the Wisconsin state budget, and a few shady dealings by some cops and evidence techs in Milwaukee, a lot of job titles and duties were eliminated, merged, and otherwise shuffled recently, mine included. Instead of being a deputy coroner, I now bear the hefty title of medicolegal death investigator. Though it sounds fancier, it's basically the same job I was doing before, except now our office works more closely with the police department: both with the collection and processing of evidence, and with the overall investigation. We each provide oversight to the other. In a way, this is a good thing for me because it means I get to spend more time with Hurley and I can legitimately do what I've always done—be nosy and get into everyone else's business. But because we're basically serving as watchdogs for one another, it also means there can't be any hints of fraternization or situations that might cause conflicts of interest. Bottom line, in order to keep my job, I can't date Hurley. And despite my recent windfall, I want to keep my job. I enjoy it; I'm good at it; and the majority of my money from the divorce settlement needs to be earmarked for retirement.

While I can't date Hurley, there's nothing that says I can't continue to place myself in strategic positions for observation whenever he has to bend over. And I do so as often as I can during our scene processing, admiring the long, lean lines of his back and a pair of buns that look like they could crack open an oyster.

I know these musings aren't healthy and I'll have to pick myself up, dust myself off, and get back into the dating scene at some point. It's not something I look forward to. The one date I've had so far turned out to be an unmitigated disaster, and the man is now living and sleeping with my mother.

Speaking of dusting off, I feel and look like a chimneysweep by the time we get Jack's body back to the morgue. I opt to take a quick shower before heading into the autopsy suite. Stripping down in the shower room, I make the mistake of glancing in the full-length mirror to check out my new tan lines.

In a few days, Hurley and I will be traveling to Daytona Beach to attend a two-day educational seminar on advances in forensics, one of the requirements of my new job description. Though I failed to inherit my mother's tiny, trim figure, I did get her fair coloring, blue eyes, and blond hair. My normal skin tone is quite pale. Along with my height and my size-12 feet, it earned me the nickname of "Yeti" in high school. Given the warm weather and the sunny beach where we'll be staying for the seminar, I thought it might be prudent to spend a little time in a tanning bed getting some base color. I know the sun can be dangerous, but the idea of worshipping it a little is irresistible—especially since I'm in the midst of one of Wisconsin's infamously long, dark, snowy winters. Thanks to daylight saving time, I go to work in the dark and come home in the dark. Every day I check my canine teeth in the mirror, expecting to see that they've grown.

So an artificial sun is my only choice and I've had two sessions at the tanning bed so far. I got a bit impatient yesterday and set the timer for longer than I should have. As a result, I burned a little, leaving me cherry red instead of tanned. Fortunately, I kept my panties on and draped a small towel over my boobs so my more delicate parts didn't get hit. I'm not too worried about the red parts, because I know from past experience that they'll fade to tan in a few days, giving me an approximate two-week window of looking sun-kissed and healthy before giant sheets of my skin start peeling off like a sloughing leper's.

I planned it all out so that I'd look my best when we hit Florida. However, as I glance into the mirror and examine my backside, I realize I've made a fatal miscalculation. The curved tanning bed cradles me pretty tightly. As a result, I have a series of red-and-white stripes down both of my sides—red, where my skin was exposed to the tanning bed; white, where rolls of back fat kept certain areas tucked away and hidden. The end result is laughably hideous. I look like a mutant albino zebra.

Disgusted, I get into the shower and try to block the image from my mind, vowing to get back to the gym. A hugely overweight, semiretired detective by the name of Bob Richmond conned me into doing workouts with him a few weeks ago, but I've slacked off a bit as of late while he's been at home recuperating from a bullet wound. My idea of exercise is walking to the bakery rather than driving, and I'm convinced that the exercise machines at the gym were purloined from a medieval torture chamber.

Fifteen minutes later, I am cleaned of ash and my stripes are safely hidden beneath a set of scrubs. When I arrive in the autopsy room, Izzy informs me that he and Arnie, our lab tech, have already X-rayed the body—including a set of dental films—drawn vitreous samples, and obtained blood from the carotid artery. Hurley and another local cop, by the name of Junior Feller, are standing against the wall by the door. As I approach the table, the song "Bad Boys" from the TV show *Cops* starts to play. Looking a bit embarrassed, Junior takes out his cell phone and answers it, stopping the music.

"Are you kidding me?" Hurley mutters, with a roll of his eyes.

Junior says into the phone, "Not now, Monica. I'll call you later." He pauses and then says, "Yes, I can pick up some eggs on the way home. But it may be a while." He snaps the phone shut and drops it back into his pocket.

"Seriously, dude?" Hurley says, shaking his head. "You have the theme song for *Cops* as your ring tone?"

Junior looks sheepish and shrugs. "Monica likes it."

Monica is his new girlfriend and a committed badge chaser. I wouldn't be surprised to learn that she and Junior do it in the back of his cruiser while Junior keeps on his uniform and gun belt.

Izzy and I smile at one another, but say nothing. We turn our attention back to the task at hand. Jack's body is already laid out on the table and fully exposed. It's a bizarre sight. His limbs look like giant, burnt chicken wings; his torso is like a charcoal briquette. Yet, his face looks relatively normal.

Izzy starts his superficial exam at Jack's face, while I take a comb to what's left of his hair, searching for trace evidence. All I find are chunks of the asbestos insulation, ash, and some bits of ceiling tile. I collect it all on clean white paper and then bag and seal it as evidence.

Izzy steps up on the footstool he has to use in order to reach everything and opens Jack's mouth to look inside. "There's no sign of soot in his nostrils or in his mouth," he says. "That tells me he was likely dead before the fire started. I'll be able to tell better once I get a look at his lungs, and after Arnie runs the lab tests on the blood he sampled. But I'm guessing Jack's carbon monoxide level will be zero."

"Maybe not zero," I say. "He was a smoker."

"Good point." Izzy then explains the situation to the cops. "Smokers tend to maintain a carbon monoxide level anywhere from zero to ten, depending on what they smoke, how long ago they smoked it, and how often they smoke. But if he inhaled smoke from the fire, his level will be much higher than that."

Izzy peels back Jack's upper lip, then the lower one. "Hmm, this is interesting," he says, and both Junior and Hurley step up to the table to take a look. "He has some bruising here on the inside of his lips—something we often see when someone's been smothered."

Hurley asks, "Can it be caused by something else?"

Izzy thinks a moment before answering. "Yes, I suppose it could. The weight of the ceiling debris falling on his face might have caused it. But considering the amount of the bruising, I suspect he was still alive, with his heart pumping, when it occurred, and if that was the case, he'd have soot in his mouth. So I can only assume the bruising occurred perimortem, before the fire started and the ceiling came down. It's also possible he hit his face against the floor or some other object when he fell out of his wheelchair."

After Izzy snaps some photos, we examine the remainder of Jack's body surface, both in the room's normal light and again using our ultraviolet light. Aside from more ceiling debris, we don't find anything of interest, but we bag and tag what we do find, just in case.

Next Izzy hoses the body down and the resultant

gray water runs along channels on the sides of the autopsy table into a special filter and drain. The filter will be examined later for any additional trace evidence.

Izzy steps down from his stool and looks over at Junior and Hurley. "This next part is going to be a bit grim," he warns. "I need to straighten out his arms and legs." Izzy instructs me to hold Jack's shoulder and torso down while he takes hold of the lower part of the arm and pulls. He throws most of his weight into it—a considerable effort despite his height, since Izzy is nearly as wide as he is tall. His face flushes red and his bushy, dark eyebrows draw together and form a V over his nose as he pulls. Finally the arm gives way with a distinct *crack*. After a short breather, we repeat the procedure on the other side and then move to the hips and legs. By the time we have the body as straight as we're going to get it, bits of charred flesh have flaked off onto the table.

Izzy takes his scalpel and starts his Y cut. He has to work at it; burnt flesh doesn't cut as easily as normal tissue. Once he has the torso exposed, he goes to work cutting the ribs and removing the breastplate. The underlying organs are in better shape than I expected. They appear shrunken to some degree, but they are still identifiable and those in the upper part of the torso appear almost normal. The stench, however, is anything but. It smells like roasted, rancid meat and at this point, everyone in the room is mouth-breathing. The stinky aspects of this job do take some getting used to. Even Izzy, who I'd begun to think can't smell at all, since nothing ever seems to bother him, is wrinkling his nose.

"The organs are often protected to some degree by the outer layers of the body," Izzy explains, reading my mind and once again slipping into teaching mode.

"But if the fire burns hot enough, long enough, they'll eventually get thoroughly cooked and might even become charred."

When he dissects the lungs and trachea, the lack of soot verifies his theory that Jack died before the fire. Jack's stomach contents include some type of bread, bits of tomato, some soft, gooey white stuff, a thin, half-moon–shaped piece of what looks to be some type of meat, and a couple small chunks of something hard and white. I'm pretty sure I know what Jack's last meal was, and my suspicion is confirmed when Izzy crushes one of the small white chunks and the aroma of garlic wafts into the air.

Izzy and I exchange a look across the table and both say, "Pesto Change-o."

"Huh?" Hurley says.

"It looks like Jack's last meal was a pepperoni pizza from Pesto Change-o," I say.

"How can you be that specific?" Junior asks.

"Pesto is the only place in town that puts big chunks of garlic like this on their pizzas," I say.

I hold up the beaker with the stomach contents in it and point to one of the white chunks, which nearly makes Junior blow chunks. He clamps a hand over his mouth, prompting a muttered "Wuss ass" from Hurley. Izzy and I share a smile and then turn our attention back to the autopsy.

The fire burned much hotter near Jack's pelvis; and the lower down in the body cavity we go, the more distorted and damaged the organs are. Despite being shrunken and discolored from the heat of the fire, his liver appears otherwise healthy and non-cirrhotic. Apparently, his alcohol consumption hadn't been enough to destroy it yet.

By the time we're done removing and dissecting the organs, Arnie pops in with the results of the lab tests he's run. It's the first time I've seen him today, and I have to do a double take.

"You cut off your ponytail."

He looks back at me through his thick glasses and rubs the top of his head, where his skin is visible beneath the thinning brown strands. "It seemed a little too compensatory and pathetic," he says. "My hair is falling out, and it's about time I manned up and faced the fact."

Izzy, who has a superb bullshit detector, says, "Uh-huh." He stares at Arnie for a beat and then adds, "When are you going to tell us the real reason?"

"What do you mean?" Arnie asks.

Izzy stares back at him over the top of his specs; his left eyebrow arches in skepticism.

"Fine," Arnie concedes after several more beats of silence. "I lost a bet and had to cut the ponytail off as payment."

"Ouch," Junior says. "That's a pretty stiff penalty."

"Yeah, I guess," Arnie says, shrugging. "I bet a friend of mine who works for a certain government agency that the new big-screen TV he won in a company raffle had a hidden camera in it that allowed interested parties to spy on him."

This comes as no surprise to those of us who know Arnie. He's a conspiracy nut who believes homeless people are government spies, and all cell phones are secret monitoring devices created by aliens. "And there wasn't one?" I ask.

Arnie shakes his head. "We dismantled the entire TV and now we can't figure out how to put it back together." He shrugs again. "The ponytail seemed like a fair price to pay."

"The new do looks good on you," Izzy says. Then he quickly gets back to business. "What have you got for me?"

Arnie shows him the printouts he's carrying. "I didn't find anything too unusual, aside from his blood alcohol level, which was 402."

"Wow," I say. "Impressive. That's more than five times the legal limit."

"Would it be enough to render him unconscious, or kill him?" Hurley asks.

"Depends," I say. "When I worked in the ER, I once saw a couple of guys who were long-term practiced drinkers who were functioning quite well despite blood alcohol levels in the five hundreds. Over time you build up a tolerance."

"What was his carbon monoxide level?" Izzy asks Arnie.

"Six," Arnie says. "Typical for a smoker."

"Cyanide?" Izzy asks.

"Cyanide?" Hurley echoes. "Why would you test for that? Are you having flashbacks to that other case we had recently?"

"Certain types of foam and plastic give off cyanide gas when they burn, and the end effect is not unlike being in a gas chamber," Arnie explains.

Junior winces, and Hurley looks thoughtful. Arnie adds, "But that didn't happen here. The cyanide test was negative. Also, Jack Allen's dentist is local, so I sent over the X-rays we took and got a confirmation that the body is that of Jack Allen. The dentist said she'll send us over a copy of the corroborating X-rays later today."

"Thanks, Arnie," Izzy says. "And thanks for coming in today. I appreciate it."

"No problem." Arnie sets his printouts on a side counter. "I didn't have any big plans anyway." As Arnie leaves the room, I can't help but wonder how he spent his day. He's a transplant from L.A. and doesn't have any family here. I wouldn't be surprised to learn that he spent his time online in a chat room with like-minded conspiracy theorists, all of them wearing their protective tinfoil hats and discussing how the emphasis on holiday spending is a government plot to subvert religion.

We move on to Jack's head and our examination of the brain reveals nothing more, ruling out any brain injury from Jack's fall as a cause of death.

When we're done, Izzy looks over at Hurley with an apologetic expression. "I can't give you a definite cause or manner at this point," he says. "Nor can I give you a time of death. Hopefully, the stomach contents will help narrow that down, if we have any witnesses to when he last ate. If not, we might be able to get an estimate from the potassium level in the vitreous fluid. Though I know he died before the fire, there's no way to tell if his death was a homicide or an accident. As I said before, the alcohol level alone might have been enough. Though if he was a practiced drinker, that's less likely. He also might have succumbed to positional asphyxiation when he fell by landing in a position that blocked his airway. Or someone might have suffocated him."

"Well, whatever happened, we know arson was involved, and possibly robbery, too," Hurley says. "So for now, we'll treat this as a homicide, until we can prove otherwise."

"I think that's wise," Izzy says. "Those bruises inside the lips bother me. Based on the position of his body when we found it and the location of the nearby furniture, I find it hard to believe they were sustained in the fall, but I'll have to review the scene photos again to be sure."

Izzy has replaced the calvarium, or skullcap, and pulled Jack's scalp back into place. Then he pauses and stares at the body for a few seconds, his forehead furrowed with puzzlement.

"What is it, Izzy?" I ask.

He sighs and shakes his head. "There's something bugging me, something I feel I'm missing, but I can't put my finger on it at the moment."

"Well, if you figure out what it is, give me a call," Hurley says. "In the meantime, Junior talked with some of the neighbors and rounded up our first list of suspects." He nods at Junior, who takes out a small notebook and starts reading.

"It seems that Jack has a girlfriend, a woman named Catherine Albright, who conveniently appeared on the scene right around the time Jack won his money. I'm going to do a little research on her and see what I can dig up. There's also a housekeeper, who comes several times a week, and a nurse, who comes once a day. Jack never married, had no children of his own, and had only one sibling, an older sister named Megan Denver. The sister had one child—a son named Brian, who's now twenty—and the sister and her husband were both killed in a car accident a couple of years ago. That leaves the nephew, Brian, as Allen's closest surviving family member."

Junior closes his notebook and Hurley looks over at me. "We'll need to talk with all of these people, and there are more neighbors I want to canvass, too. I have names I can run, and I'll set up some interviews for tomorrow, if that's okay?"

I glance over at Izzy, who nods his approval. "That should be fine," I tell Hurley. "How about I meet you at the police station around eight?"

"That'll work," Hurley says. "In the meantime, do you have any plans for tonight?"

I'm puzzled by the question because it sounds suspiciously like a date request. But Hurley quickly adds, "I think we should visit the casino where Jack won his money and check out the employees who were on duty that night. Are you up for a little investigative gambling?"

"Tonight? It's Christmas. Are they even open?"

"You bet they are," Hurley says with a wink. He's very "punny" today.

"Okay, sure. I've never been to a casino before. It should be interesting."

"Never?" Hurley says, sounding skeptical. "You've never gambled?"

"Oh, I've gambled plenty, just not at a casino." I'm pretty familiar with most games of poker because one of my stepfathers—my mother's third husband—used to have a bunch of friends over once a week to play. I'd often sit in and watch, studying the facial expressions and body language of the players as they considered their cards. I'd ask questions whenever I didn't understand the rules, and sneak the occasional sip from my stepfather's alcoholic drinks.

"Well, you're in for a treat, then. How about I pick you up at your place at six?"

"Sounds like a plan."

"See you then." He turns to leave, but he hesitates and looks over at me. Then, with a sly grin, he walks over and whispers a parting shot in my ear: "Be sure you wear your lucky undies."

Chapter 3

I manage to escape from the office a little after five, which doesn't leave me much time to get ready for my trip to the casino with Hurley. After letting my dog, Hoover, outside to do his business, I top off the food and water bowls for both him and my cat, Rubbish, and then watch as Hoover lives up to his name by sucking his bowl clean in about a minute flat. I take another quick shower to wash away any lingering dregs of the "eau de formaldehyde" cologne that seems to permeate my workplace. Then I use the rest of my time trying to come up with something to wear. I don't have a whole lot to choose from. I didn't bring many clothes with me when I fled my marriage, and I only went back once to get more stuff. I didn't have far to go. Izzy has been my neighbor for the past seven years.

Any clothes I had left at the old house were destroyed in the fire, and I haven't spent much on new stuff because my funds have been a bit limited lately. When my marriage fell apart, I hid out in Izzy's cottage for two months, wallowing in my humiliation and misery, and putting on a few pounds as I became a preferred customer at all the take-out joints in town. In doing so, I spent most of my severance pay, and all the credit cards and accounts I had access to before I left were in David's name. Izzy giving me a job certainly helped; and while things are better now, thanks to my divorce settlement, I haven't had the time or the motivation to go out and do much in the way of clothes shopping. It's an activity I hate because finding stuff to fit a buxom, six-foot-tall, short-waisted woman, with arms that come frighteningly close to knuckle-dragger length, and legs that are not only long but full-bodied, is an exercise in frustration. Most of the pants and slacks I try on end up being capri length, not much fun in the winter.

As I contemplate the contents of my closet, I realize I have no idea what constitutes proper casino attire, not that I really care. What matters most is finding something that looks a bit sexy without making my butt look bigger than my house. After all, just because I can't have Hurley doesn't mean I can't tempt him.

The first outfit I try involves a pair of red slacks and a favorite black sweater I like because the sleeves are actually long enough for my arms. The red-and-black combo seems like a smart choice for a casino, where card suits and roulette wheels bear the same colors. But when I put my boots on and glance in the mirror at my backside, it looks like a baboon's ass. I peel off the red slacks and settle on a pair of blue jeans, instead. I have just enough time to put on a bit of makeup when I hear a knock on the door.

Hurley is standing on my porch, bearing three wrapped gifts. It triggers a moment of panic because I only have one present for him. "You shouldn't have," I say, eyeing the packages.

"It's not as good as it looks," he says, coming inside. "Only one of these is for you. I also got something for

Hoover and, against my better judgment, for that other beast of yours."

I'm touched. Hurley doesn't like cats, and his introduction to Rubbish was nothing short of a disaster. Not only had Rubbish stalked and killed an entire box of tampons, leaving the bodies all over my living-room floor, he then climbed Hurley's pant leg and tried to play a game of bocce ball with the Hurley family jewels.

"I have a little something for you, too," I say, closing the door.

Hurley hands me two of the packages, one bearing a tag with my name on it and the other with a tag that says simply, *For the beast.* He then goes over to Hoover, gives him a scratch on the head, and gets down on the floor with him.

"Here you go, boy," he says, offering the third gift to Hoover, who sniffs it as if he's a K-9 dog and the package is filled with drugs. Hurley gives him a prompt by ripping one corner of the paper wrapping and then teasing Hoover with it in a game of keep-away. It takes less than a minute for the two of them to decimate the wrapping, exposing a large, beef-basted rawhide bone. Hoover snatches it up and dashes off to one corner of the living room, where he settles down, nestles the bone between his front paws, and starts gnawing.

"I think he likes it," Hurley says, looking pleased.

"I'd say so. That was very sweet of you."

"I'll let you open up the one for Rubbish," he says, looking around the room warily. "Where is he, anyway?"

"Last I saw him, he was curled up on my pillow in the bedroom. I can get him if you want."

"No, that's okay," Hurley says quickly.

I set down the gift with my name and rip open the one for the beast. Inside is a package of catnip-filled mice toys. "He'll like these," I say. "And maybe it will distract him from my tree."

My Christmas tree—a small Charlie Brown–looking thing—is standing in one corner of the living room. Only the top half of it is decorated, as Rubbish made it his goal in life to bat everything within reach of his paws off the branches. I learned that decorating with breakable ornaments and those icicle tinsel things is not a smart idea when you have a cat. I've been cleaning up shards of glass for days now; and when I last emptied the litter box, I found little cat turds embedded with shiny tinsel.

I walk over to the tree and grab the only wrapped gift remaining beneath it. "Here you go," I say, handing it to Hurley.

Wearing a huge, little-boy smile, he takes my gift and shakes it. "It's big, but light," he says. "Interesting." He starts to rip at the paper, but he stops and says, "You first."

"Okay." I settle onto the couch and undo the wrappings. Inside I find a woolen scarf done in varying shades of blue and gray. "Wow, it's beautiful," I say. "Thank you."

"It's handmade," Hurley says. "A lady I know in Chicago makes them. I thought the colors would go nicely with your eyes."

I wrap the scarf around my neck, flipping one end of it over my shoulder with a bit of Hollywood flair. "How does it look?" I say, posing.

Hurley doesn't answer right away. Instead, he just stares at me with a warm look in his eyes, which makes my nether regions tingle. "I like what I see," he says finally.

I swallow hard; and after clearing my throat, I say, "Okay, now it's your turn."

Hurley finishes tearing off the wrapping paper on

his gift, revealing a large box. He rips the box open and pulls out tons of shredded paper packing before he reaches the envelope at the bottom. He looks at me with a goofy grin and a puzzled expression before opening the envelope. Then his expression changes to one of awe. "Are these for real?"

"Very much so. Two open tickets to a Green Bay Packers game, with seats on the fifty-yard line."

"How did you manage this?"

"I know someone," I say cryptically. Actually, it's Izzy who knows someone, a plastic surgeon with season tickets who is currently doing a two-month stint in Chechnya for Doctors Without Borders.

"Thank you."

"You're welcome. But there is a small catch. They're only good for this season, so you'll have to use them sometime in the next couple of weeks."

"Not a problem." Hurley stuffs the tickets into his wallet.

After I clean up the gift aftermath, we give Hoover one last pat on the head and head out. I'm wearing my new scarf, even though the outside temperature doesn't warrant it.

Since it's a half-hour drive to the casino, there is plenty of time to talk. Hurley fills me in on what he discovered after leaving the morgue.

"I spoke with Jack Allen's girlfriend. She's coming to the station at eight-fifteen tomorrow morning to talk to us."

"Why are you having her come to the station? I thought you preferred going to people's houses to get a better feel for what they're about."

"I do, but Catherine Albright doesn't have one. She was bunking at Jack's place most of the time. Now that

that's out of the question, she's renting a room at the Sorenson Motel."

"She sounds like a freeloader."

"She might be a lot more than that. I did some digging into her background. A little over four years ago, she married a well-to-do widower up near Duluth, who was twenty years older than she was. He died six months after the wedding, conveniently leaving Catherine all his money. Based on what the cops up there told me, Catherine went to work spending her inheritance as quickly as she could. She moved to Chicago, bought a million-dollar penthouse suite and a brand new Ferrari, ate out at the fanciest restaurants, got fitted with expensive new clothes, and took several trips abroad."

"Must be nice," I mutter. "Anything suspicious about the husband's death?"

"Possibly. The cops in Duluth said he died from injuries sustained in a fall down some stairs in his home. Catherine had an ironclad alibi and wasn't even in town when it happened, but the cops couldn't rule out a hired gun. Unfortunately, they couldn't come up with any evidence to support one, either."

"Interesting."

"And it gets more so. Turns out Catherine filed for bankruptcy two months ago. Apparently, she blew through nearly two million bucks in a year and a half, and ran up a staggering load of debt. She had to sell off the penthouse and the Ferrari, and these days she's tooling around in an old BMW."

"A BMW's not so bad."

Hurley scoffs. "Not to you. You drive a used hearse."

This is true. The hearse was the only thing I could afford right away after totaling my car, and before I knew David was going to give me any insurance money. I have to admit it took a bit of getting used to at first, but I've grown to like the thing. It runs well and has plenty of room. Plus, despite being nearly twenty years old, it has relatively low mileage. There is the issue of a lingering chemical smell I can detect when it's humid, but Hoover is in dog-sniffing heaven whenever he rides in the back. Also, I like the car's midnight-blue color; it complements my eyes.

"Anyway," Hurley goes on, "I think Catherine had plans to make Jack Allen her next sugar daddy."

"Except they weren't married. So how would killing Jack now benefit Catherine?"

"I suspect marriage may have been part of her original plan, but what if Jack did keep his winnings in his house? So far, we can't find any bank or investment accounts in his name to indicate otherwise—just one checking account, which has about twenty grand in it. If Catherine found out about Jack's stash, she wouldn't have to wait to marry him. All she'd have to do is steal the money and run."

"Then why kill Jack at all? Why not just take the money and head for South America or something?"

"Because Jack would know who did it and could report her to the police. By killing Jack and trying to make it look like an accident, Catherine might be able to get away clean with the money and not have to hide from the authorities for the rest of her life."

"Smart," I admit begrudgingly. "So this Albright woman might be both a serial marrier and a serial murderer."

"It's possible." There is a long moment of silence; then Hurley says, "Speaking of marriage, how does it feel to be single again?"

"Fine, I guess."

"You guess?"

I ponder the question seriously for a moment before answering. "To be honest, I'm relieved to have it all over and done with. I finally have some financial security, and David has found himself a new hussy to take my place. But I'm also a little saddened by it. Not because of David, per se—I'm long over him. But the whole thing seemed so . . . I don't know . . . anticlimactic. I never even saw David to say, 'Good-bye,' or 'It was great,' or 'Screw you for screwing someone else.' One minute I'm married, and then I sign a few forms and I'm not. Seven years of my life wiped away with little to no ceremony. It's definitely not the future I saw for myself. And now everyone looks at me with this pathetic expression on their faces." I sigh. "Sometimes I wish David had died so I could be a widow instead of a divorcée. It has much more panache, and you get sympathy instead of pity."

I glance over at Hurley to see if he's shocked by this revelation, because I have to admit I'm a little shocked at myself for thinking it. But if he's surprised by the black thoughts that cross my mind from time to time, his expression doesn't show it.

"Are you going to change back to your maiden name?" he asks me, smoothly segueing to a topic only slightly less volatile.

"Nah, I kind of like Winston. Besides, my mother changed her name every time she married and then changed it back again with each divorce. Fast-forward four marriages later, and you have Jane Elizabeth Odegard Fjell Odegard Nyland Odegard Carlisle Odegard Pulley. Even without the maiden name reverts, it reads like a roll call for the character Sybil. And, anyway, very few people know how to pronounce 'Fjell.' Most attempts sound like someone trying to spit out a loogie."

"And you have such a unique first name to go with it," Hurley says, reminding me that he now knows one of my best-kept secrets. "Whose idea was it to name you 'Matterhorn'?"

"My mother swears it was my father's idea. His last name, Fjell, means 'mountain' in Norwegian. And, apparently, his grandfather once climbed the Matterhorn. Hence, the name." I look at Hurley and smile. "That's family for you."

"Speaking of family, we found out some interesting stuff about Jack's nephew, Brian Denver. One of the neighbors told us he's a student at the U of Dub in Madison, and that Jack has been paying for his tuition and housing. But when we called the university to get contact information, they told us Brian dropped out of school last semester and hasn't been back since."

"Did you talk to him?"

Hurley shakes his head. "We don't know where he is. He's no longer at the last known address the university had for him, and his ex-roommates claim they have no idea where he went. We'll find him, but it may take a while. In the meantime, I have Catherine Albright coming in the morning, and then we have an eleven o'clock appointment at the home of Jack's house-keeper, a woman named Serena Vasquez. After that, we'll pay a visit to the nursing agency that employs Lisa Warden, Jack's home health aide."

"Wow, you've been busy."

Hurley shrugs. "Just a typical day, really, but I want to get moving on this case and cover as much ground as we can, as soon as we can. We've only got a few days before that seminar in Daytona Beach. I can turn the case over to someone else while we're gone, but I'd rather not. With a little luck, maybe we can solve it before we go."

"That would be nice." I sigh, gazing out at snow-spotted fields. With the warm temperature, the snow is rapidly retreating, turning the landscape into a barren, muddy mess. "I can't wait to relax with some ocean breezes, greenery, and sunshine."

"I'm afraid you won't have much time to enjoy the weather. We have two full days of sessions, and an early-morning flight out the next day."

"Yeah, but that still leaves two evenings to enjoy," I tell him. "Plus the lunch breaks are two hours long, and the hotel is right on the beach."

Hurley glances over at me with a faintly salacious grin. "Are you going to wear a bikini?" he asks, wiggling his eyebrows.

Over my dead, oddly striped body.

"Nope, no bikinis this trip," I say, like I'm a super-model who wears bikinis all the time. In reality, I don't even wear bikini underwear. "I have to be careful in the sun because my skin burns easily, so no bathing suit of any kind for me."

"None at all?" Hurley asks, sounding disappointed. "What if you want to go swimming in the ocean?"

"I won't. I don't want to drown. Plus there're sharks in the ocean."

I'm really not afraid of getting attacked by a shark, nor am I afraid of drowning. It turns out fat is very buoyant *and* I'm a strong swimmer. In fact, I'm a certi-fied scuba diver. But there's no way I'm letting Hurley, or anyone else, see me in a bathing suit until I can shed a few of my recovering-from-hubby's-infidelity pounds.

Hurley chuckles. "Hell, your chances of getting eaten by a shark are way less than your chances of get-ting murdered in Sorenson these days."

He has a point. I've heard comments from several people about how the murder rate in Sorenson seems to have quadrupled lately. It makes me wonder if the "black cloud" label I used to get slapped with when I worked in the ER has followed me to my new job. Our worst shifts in the ER always came whenever I was on duty, and it seems like the sharks in Sorenson have been very hungry since I started my new job. If anyone starts calling me "chum," I might have to find another career.

I hope that doesn't happen because there aren't many other jobs that put my best talents—nosiness and the ability to identify internal organs on sight—to such good use. Plus there are the side benefits. What other job could I find that would let me spend hours each day with Hurley?

Chapter 4

The North Woods Casino is a hopping place, with a packed parking lot and lots of people milling about outside. The inside is like its own little world, isolated from the cold, snow, and darkness, and filled with a cacophony of sounds. I hear people shouting, bells dinging, music playing, chimes going off, glasses clinking. And the lights! There are flashing lights of every size and color everywhere I look—an epileptic's nightmare.

As we walk through the main gaming area, I find myself drawn to the gambling going on. The hundreds of slot machines scattered throughout the place take everything from pennies to dollars. Interspersed with these are poker tables, blackjack tables, roulette wheels, and two craps tables. While most of the people look like they're having fun, a few of the slots players look like automatons as they robotically push buttons on their one-armed bandits.

"You've really never been to a casino before?" Hurley asks as I stare wide-eyed at the surroundings.

"Nope, never. But I've seen all the *Ocean's* movies. Does that count?"

"Hardly," he says with a snort. He reaches into his

pocket and takes out a five-dollar bill. "Ready to lose your gambling virginity?" he says, arching one brow suggestively.

I blush at the sexual innuendo and nod. A woman nearby abandons her penny slot machine with a kick and a look of disgust, and Hurley moves in. He slides the fiver into a slot and the machine sucks it up and displays five hundred credits. Hurley selects buttons that let us play five credits at a time and nine different lines. I watch as pictures spin inside the display window and stop.

"Nothing that time," Hurley says, stepping aside. "Why don't you give it a try?" As I step in front of the machine and hit the button to start a spin, he leans down and whispers in my ear, "You did wear your lucky underwear, didn't you?"

The little pictures spin rapidly. This time when they stop, alarms and bells start going off. Our credit display starts chiming off numbers, mimicking the sound of coins dropping into a tray. A light atop the machine is flashing and spinning like the cherry on a cop car, and people stop what they're doing to look over at us. Hurley hits a button that speed cycles the count, revealing the total amount.

"Wow!" Hurley says. "You *did* wear your lucky undies."

"I just won five hundred bucks?" I say, not believing it.

The woman who abandoned the slot machine right before we took it over is standing at a nearby machine. She looks over at us and mumbles, "Son of a bitch!" Then she stomps off.

I hit a button marked *Payout* and the machine spits out a printed ticket with a bar code and the amount of money printed on it—our winnings, plus $4.10 left from our original five. "This is kind of fun," I say to Hurley.

"Yeah, it is when you win, but most people lose much more than they win because they don't know when to stop. They take their winnings and gamble it again, losing hundreds or even thousands of dollars in the long run. Trust me, your experience tonight is the exception, not the rule."

"This should be yours," I tell him, holding out the ticket. "It was your money that won it."

"True, but it wouldn't have happened without your lucky undies."

Several people look over at us and smile.

"I don't have any lucky undies," I tell Hurley, leaning in close and lowering my voice, hoping he'll get the hint and do the same. "It was your money that won it, so you should keep the winnings."

Hurley looks down at me—something not many men can do when I'm standing—and his blue eyes darken. My hair is hanging in my face a bit, and he reaches up and tucks a stray lock behind my ear. "You're an amazing woman, Winston, you know that?" he says softly.

We share a pregnant pause, gazing into one another's eyes, a million things unsaid between us. Our bodies drift imperceptibly closer. Each of us leans into the other, but we stop shy of touching. For a few seconds, I can imagine how life might be if things were different— if Hurley and I could pursue our mutual attraction. But things aren't different. They are what they are, and Hurley and I have already discussed this.

I turn away first; and as I do so, Hurley lets forth with a long, deep sigh. "Tell you what," he says. "Why don't we split the winnings fifty-fifty, giving credit to both my money and your luck?"

"Okay, that sounds fair."

"Good. Let's go cash out so we can get back to business." He leans in close and finally drops his voice. "Don't forget why we're here. There might be a ruthless, conniving killer lurking in the wings."

I have to give Hurley credit; he sure knows how to sober up a moment.

Forty minutes later, Hurley and I are both $250 richer and we're standing off to one side of the cashier's area, waiting for the casino manager. It's been over half an hour since the manager was summoned; I'm starting to wonder if we're being purposely ignored.

I watch the gamblers closest to us, thinking how much fun it would be to play some more with my winnings. A blackjack table off to my right has two players and a couple of empty seats. Both players have a nice assortment of chip stacks in front of them. I'm about to tell Hurley that I'm going to take one of the empty chairs, when a tall, dark-haired man, who looks to be in his midthirties, approaches us. Judging from his jet-black hair, dark skin, and high cheekbones, I suspect he is Native American. He is my height and a little on the chunky side, though I wouldn't go so far as to call him fat. The word "sturdy" comes to mind.

"Are you the folks from Sorenson?" he asks.

Hurley nods and offers a hand. "I'm Detective Steve Hurley, with the Sorenson PD, and this is Mattie Winston, a deputy coroner with the Sorenson ME's office."

"Actually, the title is now medicolegal death investigator," I say.

The man shakes Hurley's hand. "I'm Joe White-horse, an investigator with the Indian Gaming Commission. Carl Sutherland, the casino manager, is unavailable this evening and he has asked if I would step in to see what you need." His voice is deep and very masculine, bordering on Barry White territory.

He lets go of Hurley's hand and reaches for mine. As we shake, he does a quick head-to-toe assessment before his gaze settles on my face. His brown eyes are so dark that they appear black, and I detect a hint of mischievousness in their inky depths. When he smiles, two adorable dimples appear, one on each cheek. I feel an instant sizzle of sexual tension as he squeezes my hand, and our handshake lasts a second or two longer than necessary.

I glance over at Hurley and see that he's scowling. At first, I think he might be jealous, but his next words quickly dispel that impression.

"If the manager is unavailable, why didn't the cashiers tell us that when we asked to see him?"

Joe Whitehorse shrugs and flashes those deep dimples in a tolerant smile. "I suspect the employee you spoke to didn't know," he says.

"And I suspect it's more likely the manager doesn't consider us worthy of his time," Hurley counters. "Would it make a difference if I told you we are here to investigate the murder of one of your recent big winners, and that robbery appears to be the motive?"

Joe's smile fades faster than a picture drawn on water. "Who is the victim?" he asks.

"A man by the name of Jack Allen. I understand he won around five hundred grand here, a couple months back."

Joe's brow furrows a moment. "Yes, I believe I remember him," he says. "He's confined to a wheelchair, right?" Hurley and I both nod. "If memory serves, he won the jackpot on a progressive slot. But why would you suspect any of the casino employees? He won that money a few months ago, so surely his winnings were banked long before now."

"It seems Jack didn't have much faith in banks and

kept a large amount of cash in a safe at his house," Hurley explains.

Joe frowns and his lips pinch together into a tight line. "One moment, please," he says, and then he moves a few feet away from us and makes a call on his cell phone.

I tug on Hurley's sleeve. "I'm going to try my hand at a little blackjack while we're waiting." Hurley looks like he's about to object, so I hurry over to a blackjack table and settle in before he has a chance.

"I'm new at this casino stuff," I announce to the dealer and the others at the table. "What do I need to do?"

The dealer assumes a put-upon expression, while the others at the table—three men—all sigh.

"Minimum bet is five dollars," the dealer says. I hand him a couple of twenty-dollar bills and he gives me eight chips. "Do you know how to play?" he asks with world-weariness.

"I do." And with the next five hands, I prove my claim, ending up twenty-five dollars richer. From the periphery of my vision, I see Whitehorse return to Hurley, and the two of them start talking. Part of me knows I should get up and join them, but I'm having too much fun. I lose on the next two hands, but then I split on a pair of aces, and score face cards on both.

Feeling flush with my winnings, I don't notice Hurley and Whitehorse approaching me until Hurley taps me on the shoulder.

"Ready to go?" he asks. "Mr. Whitehorse has promised to fax us a list of employees with their contact information."

"I'm on a winning streak here," I say, placing another bet.

"That's when you should quit, before you lose it all."

I detect a hint of annoyance in Hurley's tone; and

when I lose the next hand, I decide to give in. I gather up my winnings and take my chips to the cash-in window, with Hurley and Whitehorse on my tail.

"You seemed to be enjoying yourself," Whitehorse says as I'm stuffing my money in my purse. "How about a one-hundred-dollar voucher so you can come back and play on us?"

Feeling like I've hit the proverbial jackpot, I'm about to agree when Hurley speaks up.

"Thanks for the offer, but we can't accept any gratuities. It might be construed as a conflict of interest."

I realize Hurley is right and pout. Whitehorse shrugs and looks at me; his dark eyes are smoking. "Perhaps you'd like to come back sometime on your own dime, then. I'd love to show you around the place. Maybe even take you out to dinner?"

I'm flattered; but before I can answer, Hurley once again pipes up.

"I'm not sure that would be wise, at least until our investigation is over."

"Then we'll make dinner a part of the investigation," Whitehorse counters, undeterred. "I'll provide you with some insight into the overall operations of the casino, and do the same with any employees of interest. I'll even arrange some interviews for you. That way you can consider it an official part of the investigation." He looks at me and winks. "At least for now."

I like Joe Whitehorse. He's handsome, witty, affable, and the smoke signals in his eyes are hinting at a possible end to my sexual drought. "Thanks," I say, smiling at him. "That would be nice."

Hurley shifts uncomfortably, communicating his irritation. Then he says, "Fine. Where and when should we get together?"

Joe and I both turn to stare at him.

"Well, we're a team," Hurley says, pointing from me

to himself. "And we've been issued an edict to oversee one another's investigative efforts. So if you two are going to have dinner and discuss our investigation, I need to be there."

"I see," Joe says.

Hurley has clearly thrown down a gauntlet and I wait, curious to see if Joe will take the challenge. It's my own personal game of cowboys and Indians—and I'm kind of liking it.

"Okay, then," Joe says. "Why don't you two plan on returning here tomorrow evening and I'll bring the employee list and some files with me and go over them with you. We can meet at the restaurant next door. Does seven sound okay?"

"Seven will be fine," Hurley says. His eyes are the color of cold steel and he's wearing a smug smile, which irritates me.

We part company from Joe; on the way out to Hurley's car, I fume. As soon as we're settled inside, I let him have it.

"You don't think you're fooling anyone with that whole team speech, do you?"

"What do you mean?" he says, sounding all innocent. "It's true."

"I think you know damn well that Joe's original purpose for the meal wasn't to discuss the investigation."

"That's what he said," Hurley says, shrugging.

"Because you cornered him into it."

"If that wasn't his intent, then what was?"

"He was asking me out on a date."

"He was? I'm sorry. I didn't pick up on that."

"The hell you didn't."

I cross my arms over my chest and pout, staring out my side window. Hurley's jealousy is flattering, frustrating, and understandable. I can't deny that I'm attracted to him, and I remember my own feelings of jealousy as I watched Candy Kane flirt with him. But I also know that, painful as it may be, I have to find a way to let go of my feelings for him and move on. Hopefully, the sexual tension between us will evolve into a strong friendship over time. But if that's going to happen, I need to commit wholeheartedly to exploring other romantic relationships, and a dinner with Joe Whitehorse seems like a reasonable place to start.

"Look, Hurley," I say with a sigh of resignation. "I think we need to agree that we are free to see and date other people. It's going to be awkward at times, but I think it's for the best. Don't you?"

Part of me hopes he'll disagree, because I'm not totally convinced myself that this is the best thing to do. Or, rather, that it's the thing I want to do. But I realize it's what I *have* to do.

"I suppose you're right," Hurley says, scowling. His acquiescence relieves me, but it also leaves a tiny hole in my heart.

We ride in stony silence for the rest of the trip home. Along the way, an idea hits me. I suspect it will make Hurley angry, but it makes perfect sense.

Half an hour later, Hurley drops me off at my place. "See you in the morning," he grumbles.

I watch him drive off, saddened over the death of our romantic future but determined to move on. After letting Hoover out to do his business, I change into a flannel nightgown and toss a load of laundry into the machine in preparation for tomorrow's plan. When I finally sink into bed sometime later, I drift off quickly. It's a fitful night of sleep, and my dreams are filled with roulette wheels, blackjack tables, and a pair of lacy, lucky undies.

Chapter 5

The next morning dawns with the weathermen predicting a high of 56 degrees. This weirdly warm weather is highly unusual in Wisconsin, where many believe there are only two seasons: winter and road repair. Between the frost heaves and all the salting and sanding on our roads in the winter, spring often brings potholes big enough to swallow a car whole.

After a stop at the local coffeehouse—where I get stuck in line behind a woman who debates her coffee flavor decision as if it's going to affect the fate of the world—I arrive at the police station at seven forty-five, a full half hour before the scheduled interview with Jack's girlfriend, Catherine Albright. The day dispatcher, Stephanie, buzzes me through to the inner chambers and I make my way to the break room. Hurley is already there, seated at a table, reading the newspaper. He glances at me over the top of the paper and grunts, "Morning."

I have not arrived empty-handed; fortunately, there is no one else in the break room, since I only brought enough for Hurley and me. I walk over and set the two cups of coffee I have on the table. After digging around in the cabinets, I find a plate and set out the two cinnamon rolls I bought along with the coffees. "A peace offering," I say, smiling. "I even got the rolls with double frosting, the way you like."

Hurley lowers the newspaper and rewards my efforts with a tired smile. "Thanks. I suppose I owe you an apology for last night."

I shrug. "I suppose you do."

"I'm sorry."

"Apology accepted. You were right to remind me that we're a team."

Hurley makes a big production out of folding up the newspaper, even though it's only half the size of a normal city paper and all of ten pages long.

"Look," I say, taking the seat across from him. I grab the smaller of the two cinnamon rolls, figuring that going for the small one justifies the fact that I'm eating it in the first place. "Things like last night are bound to happen while we work through this new relationship of ours. What do you say we put it behind us and move on, okay?"

"Fair enough."

"So what's your plan with Catherine this morning?"

Hurley details some of the highlights he plans to hit with Catherine. As I listen, I peel my cinnamon roll, eating one sweet, doughy layer at a time. Several times I stop to lick my fingers, but when I see how it distracts Hurley each time I do it, I stop.

Hurley takes huge bites out of his roll and talks as he chews in true heathen-man style. I want to be disgusted by his behavior, but I find myself transfixed, instead. When he ends up with a little blob of frosting on his upper lip, I briefly fantasize about what it would be like to lick it off. But that takes my mind into very dangerous territory, so I gesture for Hurley to wipe the blob away by stroking my own lip in the corresponding spot.

* * *

At ten after eight, Stephanie buzzes over the intercom and informs us that our guest has arrived. *One point to Catherine for arriving early,* I think as I put a hatch mark in the "good" column of the mental tally sheet I'll keep for each of today's witnesses. I wait in the back hallway while Hurley goes up front to get her. Then I follow the two of them into the "interrogation room."

Since the Sorenson PD's interrogation room also does double duty as the station's conference room, it doesn't look anything like the dingy, sterile ones you see on TV shows. In fact, other than the two-way mirror—which is almost never used because the opposite side of it is in a large closet that is rumored to have been a regular trysting place for a very randy ex-cop and his stable of women—the only thing in the room that hints at its use for interrogation is the video camera mounted near the ceiling. The most intimidating thing in the room is the décor. The floor is covered with an industrial-strength plaid carpet in shades of "liver failure" yellow and "cyanotic" blue. The walls are a shade of green I've only seen in mental hospitals, and the furniture is basic IKEA. Four pieces of "art"— framed Wal-Mart pictures, which I'm pretty sure were bought for a buck and a half apiece—hang crookedly on the walls. Sitting on the floor at one end of the room is a three-foot-tall, irregularly shaped vase that is royal blue and looks like a Smurf on steroids. Rumor has it, the decorator for the room was the wife of the chief of police. Given some of the garish getups I've seen her in, I believe it.

Catherine Albright is a step or two above the chief's wife. She's a platinum blonde and her hair is perfectly coifed in a nice little chin bob tucked behind her ears. There is a shiny plastic look about it that makes me

suspect she has sprayed it into rigid obedience and it
wouldn't move if she was standing in a tornado. Her
ears are decked out with a pair of sparkly dangles bearing gems that I'm guessing, based on their size, are
made of cubic zirconia. She is a short, thin woman who
has a pinched face and a slightly snooty air about her.
I'm pretty sure her coat, boots, and gloves are expensive designer duds and the clothes underneath are tai-
lored and crisp. When she takes off her gloves, her
nails are impeccable—each one long, perfectly shaped,
and, perhaps appropriately, enameled in a blood-red
hue. They appear to be professionally done. In contrast, her makeup is so heavily applied that it empha-
sizes the lines in her face rather than hiding them. The
thick blue eye shadow clumped above her brown eyes
screams "street whore." The overall effect is that of a
woman trying desperately to cling to her faded youth
and a lifestyle of wealth and privilege. She is the quin-
tessence of a pampered, high-maintenance woman.
Given what we know about her last inheritance, I have
to figure that Jack was a definite step-down for her
moneywise. But it's understandable. She might have
been able to lure most men with her looks alone years
ago, but at this stage of her life I'm guessing she's
forced to set her standards a little lower.

Hurley steers her toward a chair. Once there,
Catherine puts her leather gloves on the table, slips her
coat a little ways off her shoulders, and then poses,
looking back with a coquettish tilt of her head as
she waits for Hurley to help her out of the coat. It's a
calculated move—one, I'm betting, she has practiced
and employed hundreds of times, no doubt success-
fully. So it's all I can do not to smile when Hurley ignores the gesture and turns away.

Catherine pouts demurely and opts to shrug her
coat back on before settling into her chair and placing

her laced hands on the table. I take the seat across from her, giving me an open, unobstructed view. Though she looks calm overall, a nervous tic in her left eyelid belies the outward appearance.

Hurley takes a seat beside me and hits the button located under the table that starts the audio and video rolling. After brief introductions, he gets down to business.

"I understand you were dating Jack Allen. Is that right?"

Catherine nods slowly and looks genuinely grief-stricken. When she finally speaks, I'm surprised to hear a British accent.

"He was such a sweet man," she says. "It's a terrible thing that happened to him." She hesitates, appearing lost in thought for a moment, before she adds, "I heard the fire was started by a burning cigarette. Is that true?"

Hurley nods, even though this theory isn't right. But it's the story we let out to the media, so for now we have to pretend it's the truth.

Catherine shakes her head sadly. "I told Jack to give up those damned cancer sticks."

"You're British?" Hurley asks, sounding as surprised as I feel.

"Oh, yes. Born and raised in London."

"What part of London?" I ask.

Her laced fingers start squirming. "Um, Notting Hill."

"That's a nice area," I say. "What part were you in? Were you by the London Bridge or the Tower Bridge?"

"London Bridge," she says without hesitation.

"And how long have you been here in America?"

"Nearly ten years. I came here because I fell in love with an American man, who had asked me to marry him. Sadly, he died six months later of a heart attack, but I fully embraced his country and my new life. I'm an American citizen now."

Hurley and I exchange looks over the news that there is yet another dead husband in Catherine's past.

Hurley asks her, "How long have you known Jack?"

"About three months. We kept bumping into one another at the coffee shop downtown, and over time we got to talking. Jack was fascinated with anything British. We would talk for hours while I told him about growing up in London." She shifts her gaze from Hurley to me and says in her most haughty voice, "I used to lunch with royalty on a regular basis, you know."

I'm pretty sure this is pure bullshit, but I say nothing. Instead, I just smile back, not willing to tip my hand yet.

"Were you and Jack living together?" Hurley asks.

As Catherine stares at my smiling, silent face, her arrogant expression collapses into a worried one just before she turns her attention back to Hurley. "We were living together for the most part, I suppose. I spent the majority of my nights at his place, but sometimes I preferred to be alone. When that happened, I stayed at the Sorenson Motel."

"It sounds like your relationship progressed rather quickly."

She smiles, revealing a set of teeth that are so perfect and white I figure they must be veneers. "We connected," she says.

"Yes, I'll bet you did," Hurley retorts. "Did you sleep at Jack's the night before the fire?"

Catherine shakes her head. "We had dinner together, a pepperoni pizza from Pesto Change-o." She pauses and flashes a flirty smile at Hurley. "Not the sort of fare my delicate constitution is used to, you understand. But Jack absolutely loved those pizzas, so I indulged him whenever I could." I glance over at Hurley, who looks utterly unsympathetic. Seeing that her feminine wiles aren't having the desired effect, Catherine's smile fades. "Anyway," she continues, "after dinner we watched a movie and then I went to the motel."

"What was the movie?" I ask.

"*National Lampoon's Christmas Vacation.* Jack said it's one of his favorites and that he watches it during the holiday season every year."

"What time did you leave?" Hurley asks.

Catherine scowls, tilts her head, and narrows her eyes at him. "What's with the third degree, Detective? I thought you said the fire was an accident?"

"Did I?"

Catherine looks from him to me, and back again. "Are you saying it wasn't?"

Hurley ignores the question and repeats his own, instead. "What time did you leave Jack's place the night before the fire?"

Catherine engages in a short-lived attempt to stare Hurley down, but she's no match for him. Finally she caves in with a shrug. "I think it was around ten or so, but I'm not sure. I'd have to ask the motel clerk what time I checked in."

"No bother, I'll do that for you," Hurley says quickly. "Where were you yesterday morning between the hours of seven and eleven?"

She gazes toward the ceiling and furrows her brow. "Let's see, I checked out of my room around eleven, and then I headed to the store to get some groceries for Jack. I planned to go to his place after that, but I couldn't even get close to the house because of all the fire trucks."

She looks back at Hurley and tries to assume an overwrought expression, though her efforts fall comically short. I'm disappointed; I expected better acting from such a practiced charlatan.

"The entire street was blocked off. I could see that it was Jack's house that was on fire and I kept asking people if he was okay, but no one would tell me anything." Her voice is escalating—no doubt trying to make up for her lack in expression. "Finally a woman firefighter named Kane talked with me. She told me they found a body in the house next to a wheelchair. She couldn't verify who the victim was, but I knew it was Jack."

I'm bummed to hear that Catherine talked to Candy. Hurley will need to verify Catherine's story, and that means he now has an excuse to see Candy again.

"Did you shop for Jack often?" Hurley asks.

Catherine nods and dabs at her bone-dry eyes with a linen hanky she pulls from her coat pocket. "God love him, Jack tried to stay as independent as possible," she says. "He used money from an insurance settlement to have his house remodeled to something more handicap-friendly, and he also got one of those wheelchair vans with the hand driving controls so he could get around. But he hated the way people stared at him whenever he went out in public. And he hated even more having to ask for help at the store when he needed stuff from the higher shelves. The minute he told me that, I knew I had to take over the grocery shopping for him. I've been doing it ever since."

"How sweet of you," Hurley says with no small amount of sarcasm. I suspect he's wondering, like I am, how much stuff Catherine skimmed for herself during her shopping sprees. "How is it you ended up here in Sorenson, Catherine? My research shows you were living in Chicago not too long ago."

"I was. But circumstance led to some hard times for me, and I had to leave. The cost of living there is outrageous."

"Really?" Hurley says. "I would have thought you were

pretty well off after you inherited your ex-husband's estate. Are you saying all of that money is gone?"

Catherine blinks twice in rapid succession—the only sign that she's surprised by Hurley's knowledge of her past life. "I made some bad choices," she says, avoiding a direct answer. She is clearly growing nervous and starting to squirm, so I decide the time is ripe to jump in and ratchet things up a bit.

"How often did you stay at the Sorenson Motel?" I ask.

Catherine turns to me, looking momentarily puzzled by the sudden shift in topic. "Once a week or so."

"That must have pissed you off, having him kick you out that often."

"He did not kick me out," she snaps. She straightens up, her back rigid and her eyes spitting sparks of indignation at me. "It was my choice."

"Really?" I respond.

Catherine opens her mouth to answer. Before she can get a syllable out, I ask, "Who paid for your room when you stayed at the motel?"

"I did."

"With what, may I ask? Do you have a job, Catherine?"

"I don't have any regular employment at the moment, if that's what you mean," she says, her voice tight.

"That's exactly what I mean. I'm trying to figure out if you were supporting yourself at all, or if you were freeloading off Jack for everything."

She narrows her eyes at me and shifts uncomfortably in her chair. "I resent your implication."

"I'm not implying anything, Catherine. I'm stating facts. It seems you have a bit of a history for hooking up with wealthy men who later end up dead. And you can drop the phony British accent. You no more grew up in London than I did."

Hurley turns sharply toward me. Catherine sputters for a few seconds and then says, "I most certainly did."

"No, you did not," I counter. "First of all, your accent is as phony as a three-dollar bill. One of my stepfathers was born and raised in London, so I'm pretty familiar with the way Brits talk. And, aside from your accent, which you lose when you get defensive, by the way, you possess none of the little dialectal idiosyncrasies someone raised in London would have. I know, because I've been there several times. When I was a teenager, my stepfather took us there once a year for five years running. That's also how I know that Notting Hill isn't anywhere near the London Bridge or the Tower Bridge—something that anyone who has ever been to London, much less someone who lived there, would know."

Catherine's lips constrict into a hard line and her stare turns flinty. She leans back, taking her hands from the table and dropping them into her lap. "Fine," she says, her accent suddenly gone. "So I embellish my history a little to make myself seem more appealing. Where's the crime in that?"

"That's what we're trying to figure out," I tell her.

"Jack and I were in love. We were planning to get married."

"I'll bet you were," I quip. "It worked out so well for you the last time."

Catherine's eyes narrow and the two of us stare at one another, waiting to see who will blink first. I can almost see the steam coming from her ears. After a few seconds, she turns to Hurley, pouts prettily, and says, "I don't like her."

Hurley grins.

I start to bristle. Though I try to contain myself, I can't. "I'm not here to be your friend, Catherine," I say. "And when you lie to us about your past, try to dupe us with your fake accent, and try to impress us with your expensive manicures and fancy clothes, it makes me suspicious."

"You're just jealous," Catherine fires back. "I can see why—what, with those chewed, ragged things you call nails. And I'll bet you don't have a single designer piece in your wardrobe, do you? Of course, you don't, because they don't make them in your size. And if you want to make that stuff you are wearing work better, take a little hint from me, honey. One word: Spanx."

I know that saying nothing at this point will be taking the high road. However, Catherine has managed to hit one of my most sensitive buttons, so I go crawling in the mud, instead. "Your designer duds won't do you much good in prison," I snap. "There everyone wears the same thing, an orange jumpsuit. It's a color that's really going to clash with that 'trailer park' eye shadow you're wearing."

Catherine looks at Hurley and sighs heavily. "I really, *really* don't like her."

"She does have a way of getting under your skin, doesn't she?" he says. And then, since Catherine's patience is clearly wearing dangerously thin, Hurley tries to placate her. "I apologize for my partner's impolite questioning. I'm sure she meant no offense."

The hell I didn't!

"And if you don't mind, I just need to ask you a few more questions about Jack's money."

"Like what?" Catherine huffs with impatience.

"Like where it is," Hurley says. "We know he won a large chunk of change at the casino a few months ago. But if he has any of it left, we can't find it. There's no money in his house, and the only bank account we can find has about twenty grand in it."

Catherine's expression of annoyance is replaced

with one of confusion. "His money is gone?" she says. Her voice quavers.

Hurley nods grimly. "Gone, as in 'missing' rather than 'spent'—at least as far as we can tell."

Catherine looks genuinely stricken for the first time during our interview. She grabs her gloves up from the table and starts pulling at the fingers, as if she's trying to milk them. After several long seconds of this figurative and literal hand-wringing, she fixes on Hurley and says, "I think I'm done here." She stands, dons the gloves, and asks, "Am I free to go?"

Hurley sighs and nods.

"If you have any other questions for me, you can direct them to my lawyer." With that, she struts from the room, slamming the door behind her.

Hurley and I sit there in silence for a moment before I say, "Interesting reaction."

"Yes, it certainly was."

"Sorry if I pissed you off by jumping in."

He smiles. "I'm not pissed, not at all. In fact, I'm rather pleased. You played a perfect round of good cop/bad cop. And it was fun watching the two of you go at it. Nice job on the London thing, by the way."

"Thanks." I bask for a couple of seconds and then say, "She looked genuinely shocked by the knowledge that Jack's money is missing."

"Or angry."

"Because we suspect she might have taken it?"

"Maybe," Hurley says, his eyes narrowing thoughtfully. "Or she's angry because someone else beat her to it."

Chapter 6

Next up on our list of interviews is Jack's housekeeper, Serena Vasquez. But thanks to Catherine's abrupt departure, we have some time to kill since it's just past eight-thirty and we don't need to be at Serena's until eleven. I call Izzy, and after filling him in on our aborted interview with Catherine, I ask if he needs me at the office. He informs me the morgue is thankfully empty of fresh bodies.

"I'm waiting on a few things from Arnie and catching up on some paperwork," Izzy says. "You can come into the office and spend time studying, or you can stay there at the station and hang with Hurley if you want, watch what they do with their investigations."

I've had plenty of opportunities to study lately. The office library has tons of tomes detailing the many ways people can die, and all the scientific ways we have of figuring it out. It's intriguing stuff and I've learned a lot, but there's only so much of it I can take. So the choice of being cooped up in the library or spending time with Hurley is a no-brainer.

"I think I'll hang here for now," I tell him. "I have

that seminar coming up in a few days. I don't want to OD."

"No problem. I'll call you if anything comes up."

I'm about to hang up when I remember something. "Oh, wait. I forgot to tell you something we learned from Catherine that might help. She confirmed that Jack ordered a pizza from Pesto Change-o the night before his death."

"Hmm," Izzy says. In my mind, I can see his eyebrows drawing together the way they do when he's puzzling out things. "What time did they eat?"

"We didn't pin that down, but it shouldn't be difficult to find out when the pizza was delivered. Catherine said she left Jack's place around ten that night, after they watched an after-dinner movie. So if we can believe her statement, my guess would be that they ate somewhere around seven or eight."

"Based on the condition of the food we found in Jack's stomach, he couldn't have died much more than an hour after he ate—two at the outside."

"Are you saying he was lying dead inside that house for twelve hours or more before the fire started?"

"No. If the food had been in his stomach that long, it would have been more fermented. Plus I have the results of the potassium level in his vitreous fluid, and that indicates his time of death was close to the time of the fire."

"Then how is it he still had food in his stomach from dinner the night before?"

"I don't think he did. The more likely scenario is that there was pizza left over and he heated it up and ate it not long before he was killed."

I slap myself on the forehead. "Of course," I say, feeling stupid. I look over at Hurley, who is watching me curiously and obviously listening in. I quickly replay the conversation in my mind, trying to discern if he can figure out my lapse based on my side of the conversation alone. If he can, I'll either have to admit to being dumber than a box of rocks, or admit that the idea of leftovers never occurred to me because whenever I order a pizza, I always eat the whole thing.

I thank Izzy for his insight, hang up, and then fill Hurley in on the highlights of our discussion, leaving out the part about how I'm a big fat pig when it comes to pizza.

I then watch over Hurley's shoulder as he does a computer search for Jack's nephew, Brian Denver, but I'm less focused on the computer than I am on the fresh, clean smell coming off Hurley's shirt. A man who not only does laundry but does it well is a very sexy thing. I find myself distracted. My mind keeps conjuring up mini porn flicks featuring me, Hurley, and a washing machine on the spin cycle.

A search of the DMV database offers up the apartment address where we know Brian is no longer living, and the make and model of his car, along with the tag numbers. There is also a picture of him—the one from his driver's license—showing a young man with longish black hair and a pimply face. A search on CCAP, the Consolidated Court Automation Programs, aka "the state circuit court site," and NCIC, the National Crime Information Center, turns up the same address and a prior conviction two months ago for cocaine possession. As we're reading the details of Brian's drug case, Junior Feller walks in.

"Hey, Hurley," he says. "Do you still have an ATL out for Allen's nephew?"

Hurley nods and then says to me, "An ATL is an 'attempt to locate.' It's basically the same as a BOLO."

I nod my understanding and Junior says, "Well, one of the county guys said he thinks the kid might be hanging with a group of squatters in an old abandoned farmhouse out on County Road P. He offered to meet us out there, if you want."

"I do." Hurley looks over at me. "Do you want to wait here or go back to your office?"

"Neither," I say, taking a nanosecond to weigh which option might bore me to death first. "I'm going with you."

"No, you're not. This isn't a social call, or a routine inquiry. There's no way of knowing what we'll find if the house is filled with squatters. It could be a drug house, for all we know."

"I'm not afraid of drug users," I insist. "I used to take care of them, all the time, when I worked in the ER."

Hurley gives me an impatient look. "I don't think you understand. This could get dangerous. There might be gunfire involved."

"Then give me a vest to wear."

Hurley's eyes rove down toward my chest, and the corners of his mouth turn up just a hitch. "I don't think we have one that will adequately cover your . . . assets," he says with a sigh.

I hear Junior snort back a laugh. I give him the evil eye as I say, "Then I'll just wait in the car while you do your police stuff and secure the place." Junior slinks off, muttering that he'll meet us out in the parking lot. I shift my attention back to Hurley. "Besides, I know you let civilians spend time with you guys on ride-alongs, so just pretend that's what I am, a ride-along."

I can tell from Hurley's expression that I've won, so I wait, knowing he'll want to save some face by not capitulating too quickly. Eventually he says, "Fine, but all ride-alongs are required to sign a waiver that absolves the department in case anything goes wrong."

"No problem. I'll sign whatever you want."

He rolls his eyes, walks over to a computer, searches for and finds the form, and then prints it. "Here," he says, handing it to me. "Sign where indicated and leave it on my desk. I need to hit the head before we go. I'll meet you out by my car."

Once I've watched Hurley long enough to make sure he really is going to the bathroom as opposed to sneaking out the door and ditching me, I shift my attention to the waiver. It's a frightening bit of work that says I run the risk of being maimed, raped, pillaged, plundered, or killed if I opt to ride along; and that in the course of said ride-along, I might encounter bullets, knives, riots, assaults, explosions, gas, electrocution, or the escape of radioactive substances. I find this last bit puzzling, since I'm not aware of any radioactive substances in Sorenson, but then I figure it's probably a reference to the biological issuances that might occur if the ride-along is stuck in a car with a cop who ate at the Peking Palace. Since Hurley is hitting the john before we head out, I hope I'm safe from this one.

The next paragraph of the waiver eliminates any and all liability for the police department, its officers, employees, board members, volunteers, commission members, and all other "respective sureties," which I suppose means anyone in the state of Wisconsin, or perhaps on the planet Earth.

I hear the faint sounds of a toilet flushing, so I scribble my name on the signature line and leave the form on Hurley's desk as instructed. I grab my coat and follow a silent Hurley out to the parking lot. Junior is waiting in his patrol car; and as soon as we're settled in Hurley's car, we follow him out into the country.

Hurley remains quiet for the entire trip, and I do the same. Through my side window, I watch the scenery roll by. There is no suburban sprawl here. Sorenson is surrounded by farmland; strip malls often back up to cornfields. If you blink long enough driving down Main Street, the GMCs and Hondas turn into Guernseys and Holsteins.

The house Junior takes us to is well outside the Sorenson city limits. Normally, it would fall upon the county sheriff's department to cover the area. But because of the small size of the police departments in this part of the state and the large size of the territories they cover, there is often a lot of overlap and mutual assistance.

The house looks long abandoned and there is no evidence of Christmas cheer here. Half of the windows are shattered, and the once-white wooden sideboards are rotted through in places and peppered with peeling paint, which makes the place look like it has leprosy. It's a fairly large structure built in a boxy Colonial style, and at one time I imagine it provided a cozy home to whoever owned the farm. Years of neglect have stripped it of any glory, however. Now it looks decrepit, old, and very unwelcoming . . . unless you happen to be homeless, a druggie, or both. Bedding down inside an abandoned wreck of a house is better than sleeping in a cardboard box in a store doorway downtown somewhere, and the social misfits in the area often do so, squatting until someone makes them leave.

Hurley pulls in behind Junior's patrol car, which has stopped behind the sheriff's car. We are about thirty yards from the house, alongside a grove of trees that protects us from view. Up ahead, I see two other cars parked near the house. One is a dented, primer-colored, run-down–looking Volkswagen Beetle. The second car—a black Hyundai with a few dings and dents, but in much better shape overall than the Beetle—is parked half on the lawn. A quick comparison of the plates on the

Hyundai to the info on the ATL sheet confirms that the car is Denver's.

"I don't suppose you'll reconsider and let me come with you?" I ask.

Hurley shakes his head. "Stay here in the car until we can scope the place out. There's no telling what these idiots might do, and you don't have a weapon."

"You could give me a gun."

Hurley snorts a laugh. "Hell no," he says. "I've seen the way you shoot."

"Hey, it was my shooting that saved your sorry ass not too long ago," I remind him.

"Yeah, thanks to a ricochet."

"How do you know I didn't plan it that way? Maybe I'm better than you think and I used one of my trick shots to take him down, like Annie Oakley."

Hurley's incredulous expression tells me what he thinks of that idea.

"Fine," I say, rolling my eyes. "Don't give me a gun. How about your Taser? Can I carry that?"

"Stay," Hurley says firmly, like I'm his pet dog. This should probably offend me, but my mind briefly goes off track as I imagine what it would be like to have Hurley pet me. By the time I shake it off, Hurley is out of the car, and he and the other two cops are disappearing through the front door of the house.

Time ticks by with all the speed of a snail, and I can't see or hear anything going on. After several minutes of impatient waiting, I dig my new key ring out of my purse, remove the tiny canister of pepper spray, which came with it, and climb out of the car. I position myself on the side of the vehicle farthest from the house, figuring I can duck down behind it if things get messy. But after several more minutes of nothing, my curiosity gets the better of me. I head across the lawn and up the stairs of the porch, which looks like it's trying to fall off the house.

The guys have left the front door ajar—not difficult, given that it's missing all its hardware except the hinges—and as I cross over the threshold into a small foyer, I pause, listening for any activity. There are stairs in front of me, and I can hear the sound of someone snoring loudly on the upper floor. Off to my right is an empty room, which I suspect was once the living room. There is another empty room to my left. Judging from the chair rail on the walls, I suspect it was once the dining room. I step into it and see another doorway on the far side leading into a room with cabinets. There is a faint hiss of whispers coming from this kitchen area and I tiptoe toward it, sliding the safety off my pepper spray canister and holding it in front of me at the ready.

I'm mere feet from the kitchen doorway when a hand clamps down on my shoulder. I yelp, spin around, and let the pepper spray fly.

Too late I realize that the person behind me is Hurley. As he starts bellowing like a cow about to drop a calf, I hear the pounding of footsteps overhead. Seconds later, Hurley and I are joined by Junior Feller and the sheriff, who come from the kitchen door behind me. In almost the same instant, several motley-looking characters charge down the stairs and out the open front door.

"Damn it!" Hurley yells. In an instant, his eyes are red and streaming. He coughs so hard that he retches. Junior and the sheriff take off after the squatters, and I can just make out the shouts above the sounds of Hurley trying to gag up his toenails. Hurley shrugs out of his jacket, undoes his vest, and then pulls his shirttails out of his jeans, using them in an attempt to wipe the pepper spray from his eyes.

"Don't rub it," I tell him. "It only makes it burn worse." I run into the kitchen in search of some water, but when I turn on the faucet in the sink, all I get is a loud clanking noise from the bowels of the house. There is a plastic cup on the counter and I grab it and head outside to fill it with snow, a task made difficult by the warm temperature and the rapid melting.

Over by the car that belongs to Jack's nephew, I see Junior and the sheriff handcuffing a young man. Based on the black hair and pimply face, I'm pretty certain it's Brian Denver. Two other young men—both of them filthy and unkempt—are lying on their backs on the ground, looking dazed. I dash back inside to Hurley.

"Here," I say, offering him the cup. "Use this snow to rinse out your eyes."

Hurley takes the cup and dumps some snow in his hand. He makes a fist to melt it for a second and then lets it dribble over his eyes. When the cup is empty, I run back out and refill it. Three trips later, Hurley appears to be a little more comfortable. Junior enters the house, pushing Brian Denver along in front of him.

"Sorry," I whisper to Hurley, "you startled me, and I didn't know it was you."

"If you'd stayed in the damned car like I told you, it wouldn't have mattered," he grumbles. "We'll discuss it later."

Junior wags a finger at me and then mimes a hanging, letting his eyes cross and his tongue loll.

Hurley turns his wet red eyes toward Brian Denver. "I take it that the reason you aren't in school is because you've developed a little drug habit?" he says irritably.

Denver is rail thin and short—just above boob height on me, the same as the boys in high school who always asked me to slow dance. His green eyes are huge and wary, making him look like a frightened child.

"I'm not a druggie," he says, his voice cracking. "I'll piss in a cup to prove it, if you want."

"Then what the hell are you doing out here with those other yahoos?" Hurley asks.

Denver shrugs. "I needed a place to stay, and a friend of mine told me about this place."

"According to our records, you already have a place to stay," Hurley shoots back. "Why aren't you there?"

Denver shuffles his feet and licks his lips, clearly nervous. "My roommates threw me out because I couldn't pay my share of the rent."

"What about the money your uncle gave you?" I ask.

His face flushes bright red. "I kind of spent it. I asked him to front me a little extra, but he told me no."

Hurley, Junior, and I all exchange a look. Brian just admitted to a stellar motive for murder.

"Is that why you killed him?" Hurley asks.

"Yeah, right," Brian says, with a scoffing tone and a tentative smile. His gaze shifts from Hurley to me, and then back to Hurley again, his smile slowly giving way to a look of dread. "Oh, geez, you're serious, aren't you?" he says, all wide eyed. He looks over at me and says, "Uncle Jack is dead?" I nod, and watch as Brian's face crumples. Tears form in the corners of his eyes and he looks stricken, but I can tell from the skeptical look on Hurley's face that he suspects the kid's reaction might be just a bit of clever acting.

"How did he die?" Brian asks, a hitch in his voice.

I start to answer, but Hurley beats me to it. "You should know," he says.

Brian looks back at Hurley with an expression of hurt confusion. Seconds later his expression shifts to anger. He crosses his arms in front of his chest, juts his chin at Hurley, and shifts on his feet as he goes into self-protection mode.

"I don't know how he died," Brian says through gritted teeth. "I didn't even know he was dead!"

Hurley stares at the kid for a few seconds and then says to Junior, "Take him back to the station. I'll talk to him more there."

Junior spins Brian and pushes him outside toward his patrol car. I see that the other two kids are in the backseat of the sheriff's car. I'm guessing they're headed for detox.

Hurley turns to me, his eyes swollen, red, and angry. He's drooling a little and his nose is running, making him look like a rabid dog. I brace myself for the tongue-lashing I'm certain is coming, even as the word "tongue-lashing" triggers lascivious thoughts in my brain.

"Mattie, your failure to listen to me is a serious matter."

"I know," I say, hanging my head. "Look, I'm really sorry. It's just that you guys were in here for so long. I was really afraid something might have gone wrong."

"And that is exactly why it is imperative that you listen to me from now on, without exception. You're *not* a cop. Your shooting is so bad you could be the poster child for a repeal of the Second Amendment, and you have no training on tactical maneuvers. What you did was stupid and careless. You risked our lives, as well as your own."

"I'm sorry. It won't happen again."

"It better not," he says, scowling. "Because if it does,

I'll be forced to take action, even if it means you lose your job. I'd rather see you get fired than see you hurt or killed."

I look up at him in surprise, touched by this statement. But my pleasure is short-lived.

"It would take me days to finish all the frigging paperwork," he continues. "*And* I'd have that sleazy brother-in-law of yours on my case."

Chapter 7

Hurley's mention of my brother-in-law is a sobering moment. Lucien is a lawyer—a pretty good one from all accounts—and well known in town. His notoriety doesn't come from his lawyering abilities, however, but rather from his reputation for being obnoxious, vulgar, and painfully honest. I suspect much of his career success has come about specifically because of these traits, and because his appearance is deceiving. He doesn't appear to be much of a threat with his strawberry blond hair, pale complexion, and rumpled clothes. But once he opens his mouth, it doesn't take long for most people to want to give in and run, or kill him and hide the body.

Aside from the fact that he's always shown a rather prurient interest in my private life, and never hesitates to flirt with me by making lewd and lascivious comments whenever he can, he seems to be a good husband to my sister, Desi, and a good father to their two kids, Erika and Ethan. For those reasons, I tolerate him—that, and because I suspect his crass demeanor is all an act designed to intimidate and keep his opponents and others off balance. It works well, but beneath all the bluster lurks a kindhearted, fair-minded man, however well hidden.

Nonetheless, the mere mention of Lucien's name in anything resembling polite company tends to make people turn pale and look frantically for the nearest exit. I guess that's why Hurley curses under his breath when the first thing out of Brian Denver's mouth once he arrives at the station is a request to call his lawyer, Lucien Colter.

Hurley shoots me a look.

"It wasn't me," I say, holding up my hands, though I can understand Hurley's suspicions. I've been known to solicit Lucien's help for folks in the past.

Hurley asks Denver, "If you don't have any money, how is it you think you can afford an attorney like Lucien Colter?"

Looking quite smug, Denver says, "I don't need any money. I did a favor for Mr. Colter a while back and he told me that if I ever needed anything, just to let him know and he'd help me out for free."

"What kind of favor?" I ask, bracing for the answer. With Lucien, the possibilities are frightening. I wouldn't be surprised to hear that bustiers and farm animals are involved.

"I set up a computer network in his office. It was right after my parents were killed, and I was staying with Uncle Jack for a while. Jack wanted to get a lawyer to sue the guy who hit him, and he took me with him when he went to see Mr. Colter."

I'm familiar with Jack's lawsuit, not because of anything Lucien told me, but because I spoke to Jack when he had his last surgery and heard his tale of woe. I share what I know with Hurley. "Jack's accident was caused by a drunk driver. After Jack's insurance topped out, he sued the guy for medical expenses. He won a decent chunk, too, if I recall, though I think a lot of it went to pay existing medical debts."

"Yeah," Denver says. "Mr. Colter did good by him in the end, but it's amazing he was able to do anything at all based on how old-school his office was. So I offered to help him out. I know a lot about computers. That's what I'm going to school for."

"You mean that's what you *were* going to school for," Hurley corrects.

"Yeah, whatever," Denver says, shooting Hurley a killjoy look. "Anyway, I helped Mr. Colter set up his office with new computers and a network, and I showed him how to use a bunch of software. I even wrote a couple of programs for his secretary to use to keep track of stuff. I didn't charge him for any of it, so he said he owed me one."

Hurley and I exchange looks of resigned dismay.

"And I plan to cash in on his offer," Denver concludes. When no one responds right away, he adds, "*Now,* please. And can I get something to eat? I'm starving."

Hurley sighs and steers Denver into the conference/interrogation room and gives him a phone and a phone book. Then he comes out, shaking his head. "I don't like that kid," he says. "He's a little too smug for my tastes, and the fact that he was so quick to ask for a lawyer seems suspicious."

"Maybe," I say.

We stand together in silence for a few moments, until Hurley says, "Think there's any chance your brother-in-law will renege on his offer?"

With that, my cell phone rings. When I look at the caller ID, I see that it's Lucien. "I guess we're about to find out," I say, and then I make the fatal mistake of answering the call on speakerphone.

"Hey, Lucien."

"'Mattiekins'! I hear from young Mr. Denver that you're hanging out at the police station with that detective you keep hoping to wrangle. Have you two done the 'tube-snake boogey' yet?"

"You're on speakerphone, Lucien," I warn, suspecting it's a waste of breath. Knowing he has a bigger audience is likely to only egg Lucien on to greater depths of depravity. I avoid looking at Hurley because while I doubt Lucien is capable of feeling embarrassed, I have no such limitations.

"I want you and the cops to wait until I can get there before you ask my client any questions. He says you think he's using drugs and he's responsible for his Uncle Jack's death?"

"Something like that," I say.

"I heard about Jack on the news last night. Awful thing. So I take it the fire wasn't an accident? You know, I just saw Jack not that long ago, right after he won a boatload of money at a casino. Wait, is that what you're looking at for motive, the money?" His words shoot out rapid-fire and unfiltered . . . classic Lucien.

I take a second to try to figure out which of his questions to answer first, but it seems it's unnecessary. Lucien says, "I'm pulling up out front and I'll be right in." With that, he cuts off the call.

I pocket my own phone, give Hurley a wincing look, and then brace myself for Lucien's imminent arrival.

We hear Lucien long before we see him as he greets Stephanie, the dispatcher, out front.

"Hey, Steph, how's stuff?" he says, fifty decibels louder than necessary. And a split second later, he adds, "Saw you chatting with that new English teacher in the grocery store parking lot the other day. I hear he's single. Has he knocked you up yet?"

There is a painful silence before Lucien barks out a laugh that sounds like it's coming from a demented hyena. "Aw, I was just poking fun with you, playing with words. Don't you get it, Steph? The guy is an *English teacher.*" He stresses the last two words very pointedly, as if he's talking to someone from another country, or maybe another planet. "And when *English people* are planning to go visit someone, they say they're going round to knock so-and-so up, you know? Do you get it now?"

Unlike Lucien's booming vocals, Stephanie's low murmur isn't enough to carry through the door that separates the front area from the back. It's probably just as well, for I suspect her words could melt steel. A second later, we hear the buzzer as she releases the door to let Lucien through. He looks as rumpled and disorganized as ever: his suit is threadbare and wrinkled, his hair is wildly out of control and long overdue for a cut, and he's carrying a tattered-looking briefcase that has dozens of sheets of paper hanging out of it as if they're trying to make an escape.

"Sheesh," he says when he sees us. He walks over to a nearby table and I notice his stride is a bit off. He's waddling more than walking and has a slightly bow-legged stance. "Steph sure has lost her sense of humor since the divorce, hasn't she?"

Neither of us says a word, knowing that Stephanie is probably sitting out front with a Lucien voodoo doll, savagely stabbing it with pins, or ripping its head off.

"So tell me about Jack Allen," Lucien says, smoothly shifting gears. He tosses his briefcase onto the table and opens it, revealing a heap of papers leaking from manila folders. "What happened? How did he die?" He takes out a small notebook and a pen, flips the notebook open, and stares at Hurley expectantly, with his pen hovering above the page.

"He was asphyxiated and his house was burned down," Hurley says.

Lucien's response is a total non sequitur. "Christ, Hurley, you look like hell. Have you been crying or something?"

"Don't ask," Hurley grumbles, shooting me a sidelong glance.

Lucien looks over at me. "You made him cry?" He gives me a head-to-toe ogle. "You are good, Mattiekins."

"Lucien," I say, tight-lipped and in my best warning voice.

"Okay, okay," Lucien says, holding up his hands in surrender. "Apparently, no one around here took their happy pills this morning. So . . . back to the subject at hand."

"Jack didn't die in the fire, though somebody tried to make it look like he did," I tell him. "The autopsy showed no soot in his trachea and lungs, so he was dead before the fire started."

Lucien digests this info for a few seconds, and then turns and shoots a questioning look at Hurley. "Motive?"

"It seems that Mr. Allen had an aversion to banks and opted to keep all his money in his house, instead. He had several hundred grand stashed there, as far as we can tell."

Lucien lets out a low whistle. "I told him he needed to put that money into something safe. I even referred him to Cal Worth."

Cal Worth is an aptly named investment counselor, the only one in town since Brady Harper absconded last year with both the life savings of dozens of Sorenson residents and the wife of the Episcopalian minister. This scandalous bit of hot gossip was made all the more juicy when folks discovered the message on the sign in front of the church when it happened: THE MOST POWERFUL POSITION IS ON YOUR KNEES.

Hurley says to Lucien, "You spoke with Jack after he won his money?"

"Yeah, he came to me to talk about drafting a will."

"And did he?"

Lucien shakes his head. "He said he wanted to think about it for a while. So unless he hooked up with another lawyer, I don't think he did. I can't recall what he won at the casino, but his settlement with the driver who hit him netted him half a mil. There were a few unpaid medical bills, and I know he used some of the money to make changes to his house and buy a wheelchair van. I think all of that was around two hundred grand, meaning there was still plenty left. If Jack had that kind of cash hanging around the house, your list of suspects is going to be mighty long." Lucien looks a bit smug and adds, "And that means reasonable doubt for my client."

"You're getting a bit ahead of yourself," Hurley says. "I haven't even questioned the Denver boy, much less filed any murder charges against him."

"What evidence do you have to suggest he might have killed Jack?"

"So far, all I have is motive and possible opportunity."

"Then why did you drag him in here? He said he was under arrest."

"He is, for B and E and the possession of drug paraphernalia," Hurley explains. "We found him shacked up in an abandoned house with a couple of other yahoos and enough syringes to stock the hospital's medication room. Frankly, I have no interest in pursuing either charge if I can rule him out for the murder. But I need to question him in order to do that, and he invoked his right to counsel before I could. He's dropped out of school, all his family ties are gone, and he's homeless, so I have no doubt he'll run if given half a chance. Given those facts, if I have to use the B and E and drug charges to keep him under wraps until we can sort things out, I will."

Lucien chews his lip in thought for a few seconds and then says, "Give me a couple of minutes to talk to him and I'll see what I can do."

Hurley nods and gestures toward the conference room.

"This is privileged until I say otherwise," Lucien cautions. "No turning on the recorder or eavesdropping until I come out."

"Understood," Hurley says.

Lucien gathers up his briefcase and disappears into the conference room, once again assuming his awkward stride. Hurley looks over at me and sighs. "I'm betting we won't get to ask the kid a single question."

"Maybe not," I agree. "But at the very least you ought to collect his clothes, scrape his nails, and comb his hair for evidence. He looks and smells like he hasn't showered or changed clothes in several days. So . . . if he did have anything to do with Jack's murder and the fire, we might find trace evidence on him to prove it."

Hurley cocks his head and smiles at me.

"What?" I say, glancing down to see if my blouse is gaping open.

"You've really taken to your new job, haven't you?"

I shrug. "It suits me. Plus I think it makes good use of my skills."

"And what skills are those?" There's a hint of a wicked gleam in Hurley's eye that leaves me unsure if he's mocking me or flirting with me—though it occurs to me that it might simply be the lingering effects of the pepper spray. My face flushes hot; and in an attempt to hide my fluster, I walk over to one of the wall cabinets, where I know there's a bottle of Mylanta stashed amidst the coffee mugs. It's been rumored that the station house coffee has been known to eat through metal; and if you drink it, you'll likely need to use Mylanta as creamer. I have another use in mind, however.

"Here," I say, handing the bottle to Hurley. "Dab some of this on your eyes. It will neutralize any remaining pepper spray."

He takes the bottle, rips a sheet off the paper towel roll by the sink, and proceeds to moisten a corner of the towel with the Mylanta. Then he starts dabbing it around his eyes.

"I'm still waiting for an answer about those skills of yours," he says.

"Well, my knowledge of anatomy and physiology, for one," I say, eyeballing his mighty-fine anatomy and wishing I could enhance my existing knowledge along his lines. Before I get too distracted, I add, "I'm also good at solving puzzles—something this job seems to have plenty of. And I think I'm good at reading people."

"Do you, now?"

"I do," I say, bristling at his tone. "In fact, I think I'm better at it than you are."

Hurley scoffs. "What gives you that crazy idea?"

"The fact that I've been right more often than you have when it comes to suspects."

"You hit a lucky streak is all," Hurley says dismissively.

"I don't think so. I've been a nurse long enough that I've developed a kind of sixth sense when it comes to reading people. I can almost always tell when someone is bullshitting me. And I have a skill for interpreting the subtleties in a person's tone of voice, mannerisms, body language, and words. For instance, I'm pretty certain little Miss Candy Kane"—I say her name in an ultrafeminine, lilting voice—"wants to jump your bones."

Hurley's eyes narrow at me. "You sound as if that bothers you."

"Nope, not at all," I lie.

"Good," Hurley taunts, "because I was thinking of calling her tonight and asking her out."

"Have at it," I say, shrugging. "Of course, you realize I'd be compelled to report your 'relationship'"—I couch this last word with little finger quotes—"to the higher-ups, since Miss Kane *is* involved in our investigation. Seems to me dating her might be construed as a conflict of interest, don't you think?"

I give Hurley a smug smile while he stares at me in silence for what feels like a gazillion beats of my heart. It's all I can do not to laugh since the dried circles of Mylanta around his bloodshot eyes make him look like something out of central casting for a brain-eating zombie movie.

"Besides," I continue, "I thought you were coming to dinner with me tonight to meet with Joe Whitehorse."

I see a tiny twitch of a smile tweak the corners of Hurley's mouth. "It would seem we are both in a holding pattern for the moment," he says.

"So it would seem."

"Okay, then, change of subject. What's your take on young Mr. Denver?"

"I'm not sure, but I'm leaning toward innocent. He's stick thin and starving hungry, still in the area, and living in an abandoned house that has no heat. If he had his uncle's money, he'd be holed up in a luxury hotel in Chicago, kicking back and ordering room service."

"Maybe," Hurley says, looking thoughtful. "Or maybe he's just putting on an act to make us think he's broke and starving. I'm banking on the killer being smart enough to know that he or she will have to lie low for a while in order to divert suspicion."

"Or maybe the killer is someone we haven't even identified as a suspect yet, and he or she is already on the way to Argentina."

"Argentina?" Hurley says, looking amused.

"Yeah, isn't that one of the countries criminals typically flee to, to avoid extradition?"

"Not if they're smart. All of the countries in South America have extradition treaties with the United States."

"Really?" I say, genuinely surprised. "I didn't know that. So where would I have to go if I wanted to escape punishment for a crime?"

"Why do you want to know? What crime are you planning on committing?"

Before I can answer, Lucien's booming voice interrupts as he exits the conference room, and what he says makes the crime of murder jump to mind.

"Hey, you two weren't trying to sneak in a little ride on the 'baloney pony' while I was in there, were ya?"

I shoot eye darts at Lucien, and Hurley, who is apparently reading my mind, says, "I'd go with Vietnam, or maybe Samoa."

Lucien looks from me to Hurley and back at me again. "Are you two planning a trip?"

"We might be, if you don't knock off the innuendo," I say.

Lucien tosses his briefcase onto the table again, and then he grabs the back of one of the chairs and leans forward, wincing.

"Lucien, are you okay?" I ask.

He shifts his stance and winces again. "Not really," he says. "My hemorrhoids are super inflamed today."

Hurley groans and rolls his eyes, while I look to the heavens and pray for a quick reprieve.

"They've flared up before, but never this bad," Lucien prattles on, oblivious to his audience's reaction. He shifts his feet and winces again. "They're killing me. And just why is it that they call them 'hemorrhoids'?" he asks. "Wouldn't it be more appropriate to call them 'asteroids'?"

"Lucien, please," I moan.

"Hey, I know you don't practice as one anymore, but you're technically still a nurse, right?" he says. Then he starts to undo his belt buckle. "I don't suppose you could take a look for me."

"I'd rather skin myself alive with a dull razor," I say.

A heartbeat later, Hurley adds, "If you drop your drawers in here, Lucien, I swear I'll shoot you."

Lucien pauses with his buckle and stares at the two of us with a half grin, thinking we are joking. Apparently, he realizes we aren't, because he shrugs, does his belt back up, and quickly changes the subject. "So the kid says he had nothing to do with his uncle's death. When exactly did the dastardly deed occur, if I may ask?"

"Sometime yesterday morning," Hurley says. "The fire call came in just before eleven, so we're guessing it was shortly before that."

"Well, my client says he has an alibi."

Hurley snorts a laugh. "What, his drugged-up buddies out at the abandoned house? I don't think we'll be taking their word for anything."

"No, it's a bit better than that," Lucien says. "He says he was at the North Woods Casino from ten o'clock on Christmas Eve until four o'clock yesterday afternoon. I'm sure the casino cameras will verify that."

Hurley scowls at this news.

"Are you going to press charges for the other stuff?"

"I don't know yet," Hurley says. "But I'm not going

to spring him on his word alone. I don't trust him to hang around."

Lucien shrugs. "He's agreeable to being jailed while you check out his alibi. Apparently, after a bit of a winning streak, the kid hit a major losing trend and lost everything he had. He says he's broke and has nowhere to stay. He was sleeping in his car prior to finding the house, so three squares and a bed is looking pretty good to him right about now."

"Fair enough," Hurley says.

"Let me know if anything new comes up," Lucien says, putting on his coat. With that, he leaves, and Hurley lets out an irritated sigh.

"What's wrong?" I ask. "I figured you'd be happy now that Lucien's gone."

"I am happy about that," Hurley says. "But I wish we'd known about this alibi earlier. We could have viewed the tapes at the casino when we were there last night and saved a lot of time."

"What difference does it make? We're going back there tonight anyway," I remind him. "Dinner with Joe, remember?"

Hurley frowns in a way that makes it clear he does.

"And I plan to wear my lucky undies."

"I don't think we'll have time for any gambling," Hurley says, still frowning.

I smile sweetly at him and wink. "What makes you think my lucky undies are for gambling?"

Chapter 8

Next on our agenda is a visit to Serena Vasquez's house, so Hurley hands off the jail duties for Brian Denver to Junior and we head to Hurley's car. Our journey is a short one, since Serena Vasquez lives in a small ranch-style home only a few blocks from downtown.

Though the house may have been cute at one time, it now appears worn and in desperate need of repair. There are several spots on the roof where shingles are missing, the double-paned windows are clouded from broken seals, and the paint on the clapboards is faded and peeling.

When Serena meets us at the door and invites us in, I can't help but think that she looks a bit like the house. Her auburn-colored hair has nearly an inch of dark roots showing, and the material in her shirt and blouse is worn and thin. However, her makeup is perfectly applied, her nails appear to have been recently manicured, and her hair is neatly styled, despite its color issues.

The inside of the house is cozy and welcoming. The hardwood floors gleam, and most of the rooms have been freshly painted in tasteful, neutral colors. Though none of the furnishings are part of any matched sets, they appear to be in good shape and well cared for. The entire place is spic-and-span clean. I suppose this shouldn't be surprising, given that Serena cleans houses for a living. The contrast between the inside and the outside makes me suspect Serena is renting the place.

Three kids are huddled around the TV in the living room, off to our left: two boys and a girl. The boys are identical twins, who appear to be about six years old and have the same dark hair, Hispanic complexion, and big brown eyes their mother has. The girl looks to be a year or so younger. She has blond hair, blue eyes, and a pale complexion, which all make me suspect she is either adopted, or someone else's kid.

In one corner of the living room is a Christmas tree, a live one, decorated with strung popcorn, strings of beads, and some baked clay and papier-mâché ornaments, which were clearly made by kids.

Serena leads us past the living room and into the kitchen, where the air smells good enough to eat. I detect the scents of butter and cinnamon seconds before my eagle eye spots a pan of what looks like snickerdoodle cookies cooling atop the stove. I can also smell fresh-brewed coffee. It's all I can do not to drool as Serena directs us to sit at the table. My stomach rumbles hungrily, and at an embarrassing volume, as I settle into my chair. Then Serena Vasquez moves to the top of my "I don't care if she did kill someone" list when she offers us samples of her wares.

"It is an awful thing that happened to Mr. Allen," she says as she sets a plate of warm cookies in the center of the table. "I saw it on the news last night." She shakes her head sadly. "He is a very nice man, and burning like that is an awful way to die, especially on Christmas."

I wince at this idiotic observation, as if burning to death could somehow be made worse simply because it happened on Christmas. I also make a mental note of Serena's use of the present tense when discussing Jack, and the fact that she seems to think Jack died as a result of the fire, though I realize the latter could simply be a clever bit of misdirection.

"Do you know what caused the fire?" Serena asks. "Was it his tree?"

Hurley shakes his head. "We aren't sure yet. When was the last time you saw Mr. Allen?"

"It was Christmas Eve day." She pauses a moment to think. "That was Monday, around noon. I clean for him every Monday, Wednesday, and Friday."

"How long have you known Mr. Allen?" I ask.

"I've been working for him for five years now. He is my steadiest customer."

"How did he pay you?" Hurley asks.

Serena's facial muscles flinch almost imperceptibly. She turns away, busying herself with fetching coffee mugs from a cabinet. By the time she turns back to us, she appears calm and composed, but that flinch has me watching her more closely.

"He writes me a check once a week," Serena tells us. "All of my clients do. And I am very careful to pay taxes on every cent of it."

I get a strong sense that Serena is lying, but I don't think Hurley cares that she might be sneaking a little money by the IRS, so I shrug it off. I grab a cookie from the plate and hold it in my mouth as Serena passes me a cup of hot, steaming coffee.

Hurley declines Serena's offer of a cookie, but he accepts a cup of coffee. "Did you know Mr. Allen very well on a personal level?" he asks.

Serena shrugs. "We chatted often, and sometimes I would sit with him for a while and share a snack, watch TV, stuff like that."

"I take it you knew about his big win at the casino,

then," Hurley says as I grab another cookie from the plate. They are exquisite, buttery, melt-in-your-mouth treats.

"Oh, yes," Serena says. "I knew. Pretty much everyone who knew him knew."

Hurley sighs, knowing that this makes our list of suspects frustratingly long. "Were you aware of any stash of cash Mr. Allen had in his house?"

Serena looks off to the side and hesitates a second before answering. "I know he kept some cash in the house, but I don't think it was any more than anyone else would keep around. He wrote checks for most things. He paid me with a check every week. He paid his bills with checks. He paid off his mortgage with a check. . . ." Her voice trails off and she shrugs.

"Did he pay for anything with cash that you know of?"

"He gives cash to Catherine from time to time so she can shop for groceries and such," she says. "That's all I ever saw when I was with him, but I don't know what he did the rest of the time. I suppose he might have given money to some of the folks who came begging."

"'Begging'?" Hurley and I both say at the same time.

Serena nods. "There haven't been as many lately, but he won some money in a lawsuit. And then shortly after that, he hit it big at the casino. Suddenly everyone was knocking on the door, or calling on the phone, or sending e-mails, dishing out a sob story of some kind and asking for cash."

I see Hurley scribble down some notes and suspect it's a reminder to check out Jack's phone records and e-mails.

"The whole thing made Jack pretty mad," Serena continues, "because some of the people who asked were people he hadn't seen or heard from in years."

Nothing like winning a ton of cash to enhance your following on Facebook.

"Jack told me he didn't mind giving money to—" She stops abruptly and looks away again. Her fingers are shredding a napkin she is holding. Hurley and I both stare at her, waiting for her to finish. After a few seconds, she obliges. "He said he wouldn't mind giving money to someone who really needed and deserved it."

"Did you personally witness anyone asking him for money?" Hurley asks.

Serena nods. "A neighbor of his—a Mr. Gatling, I think it was—wanted to know if Jack would front him the money to open up an auto repair shop in exchange for being made a partner in the business. And Jack's nephew stopped by and asked for more money recently, but that one is different because Jack is paying for his schooling. Also, I don't think it's a coincidence that Catherine Albright showed up when she did. I hope she doesn't get any of Jack's money."

"Why do you say that?" Hurley asks.

"I don't like that woman. There is something very sneaky about her. I don't trust her."

"Gut instinct, or did she do or say something to make you not trust her?" I ask.

"Both," Serena says. "She's always snooping around, and she's dropped some not-so-subtle hints to Jack about how he should spend some of his money."

"Such as?" Hurley prompts.

"Such as frequent discussions about what a nice car a Jaguar is." She gives us a look of disgust. "Can you think of a more inappropriate car for a man in a wheelchair?" She answers her own question with a little *pfft* and a can-you-believe-it look. When neither of us says anything, her eyes narrow, and it's as if I can see the lights turn on inside her head. "Wait a minute," she says. "Why are you asking so many questions about Jack? His death *was* an accident, wasn't it? And the fire? That was an accident?"

I decide to let Hurley field this one. Not only because I don't want to get in trouble for revealing more than I should to a potential suspect—something I've had issues with in the past—but also because my mouth is so crammed full of a snickerdoodle, I couldn't talk if I wanted.

"It appears Mr. Allen's death is a homicide," Hurley says.

Serena's dark complexion pales. She clamps a hand over her mouth and tears well in her eyes. "Who would do such a thing?" she says through her hand. "Jack never hurt a soul. This is so . . . wrong, so . . . unfair."

Hurley takes out one of his business cards and slides it across the table to Serena. I know this is our cue to leave, so I grab my coffee and take a big swig to wash down the sugary mass in my mouth. I relish the cinnamon flavor of the cookies as it mixes with the coffee. When I've swallowed, I get up from the table and follow Hurley, who is nearly to the door already. Seeing the kids again, I pause and look at Serena, who has followed me.

"Are they all yours?" I ask her.

She shakes her head. "The twins are mine," she says, with a sparkle in her eye. "But the girl is my neighbor's daughter. We trade off babysitting duties whenever we can. She is a single mother, like me."

"That must be tough," I tell her. "Is the boys' father in the picture? Do you get any child support to help you out?"

Serena's color, which had returned to near normal, fades again. She shoots a quick, wary look toward the kids, who are fully engrossed in *SpongeBob SquarePants*. "He is not around," she says just above a whisper.

Something in my gut tells me she is lying. But I also sense that if I try to push the issue, I won't get anything. So all I say is "I'm sorry," before I turn to follow Hurley out the door.

Chapter 9

When we're back outside in the car, Hurley dials a number on his cell and gives whoever is on the other end a laundry list of tasks: track down Jack's phone and Internet provider, pull a record of Jack's calls and e-mails for the past six months, look into the neighbor named Gatling, and check to see what company Jack's mortgage was with and if it is paid off, as Serena said.

As he disconnects the call and starts the car, he says, "If what Serena said about the mortgage is true, that would explain some of Jack's missing money."

"Not enough of it. Even at full price, I don't think his house would be worth more than two hundred grand."

"Still, it's a start. So what's your take on Serena Vasquez?"

"I'm on the fence. She wasn't being totally honest with us; and I suppose that as a housekeeper, she was in a good position to discover the speaker safe. But I'm having a hard time seeing her as a killer."

Hurley shakes his head. "You fall for those sob routines every time."

"I'm not falling for anything. Serena's emotions

seemed genuine to me. I think she was upset by the knowledge that Jack was cruelly murdered."

Hurley looks at me like I'm an ignorant child he's placating, someone whose wild but clearly uninformed ideas amuse him.

"What?" I snap, irritated. "Do you think Serena did it?"

"I don't know, but I'm not going to rule her out simply because she shed a real tear or two when we told her Allen was murdered. Those tears might have been triggered by something other than sadness," he says, still with the condescending tone.

"Like what?" I almost add "smarty-pants" to the question, but bite it back at the last second.

"How about shock or fear, triggered by the realization that her attempts to make Allen's murder look like an accident weren't successful?"

"No way. Those were sad tears."

"You might be right. Serena's realization that she might not get away with the murder she just committed would be enough to make her sad."

I roll my eyes at him. "God, you are a stubborn man."

"Pot, kettle," he says. "Which reminds me, I'm starving. We have an hour before our appointment with the nursing agency. Want to grab some lunch?"

Despite having a handful of snickerdoodle cookies in my stomach, I am hungry, not that hunger is a prerequisite for eating for me. "Sure. What do you have in mind?"

"How about Pesto Change-o? That way we can verify Catherine's pizza story while we eat."

My stomach gurgles happily at the suggestion, making Hurley smirk. "Sounds good to me," I say with stunning redundancy.

* * *

Ten minutes later, we settle into a booth with red seats, which remind me of how a high-school classmate, Cindy Clarkson, once launched a "Save the Naugas" campaign after Jimmy Nelson and Mark Holstadt convinced her that the creatures were being slaughtered into near extinction for their hides. Apparently, the campaign was unsuccessful, because I know dozens of Naugas in a variety of colors that have been sacrificed for this place in the years since.

In addition to their eat-in dining, Pesto Change-o does a thriving take-out and delivery business between the hours of eleven A.M. and midnight every day, except Christmas. I know this because I took advantage of their take-out service dozens of times in the months after I left David and moved into the cottage behind Izzy's house. If I'd had phone service in the place, I'm sure all of Pesto's delivery drivers would have had my address on autopilot after the first week.

Opting for delivery from Pesto means that you miss out on the full experience of the place, however, and it's worth the trip. The owner and founder, Georgio Conti, is not only an Italian immigrant and chef, he's an amateur magician. Ever since opening the restaurant, he has combined his passions for cooking and magic, providing a truly unique and entertaining dining experience. Georgio performs two kinds of magic. The first is with the foods he prepares: sauces that burst in your mouth with the flavors of garlic and spices, pasta cooked to al dente perfection, and pizzas with cheese that will stretch across a room when you try to take a slice.

The second kind of magic is the more traditional type. Each evening Georgio entertains his diners with a variety of illusions: everything from card tricks and vanishing coins to sawing waitresses in half.

For our lunchtime meal, the show would be a bit more sedate than the evening performance, but Georgio never disappoints. As soon as we are seated, he magically produces a beautiful bouquet of paper flowers from out of thin air and places them in a vase on our table. Then he lights our candle with a flame that seems to alight from his fingers.

Before Georgio can pull a rabbit out of his hat, Hurley halts the show with a question.

"Georgio, I need you to help me out with an investigation, a murder investigation."

"Murdah!" Georgio says with his Italian accent. "What an awful ting." He manages to look appalled and aghast, but I'm pretty sure I detect a bit of excitement in his voice. Hurley relays the specifics of the information we want, and Georgio provides an answer right away.

"I remember this order for Mr. Allen," he says. "I remember because he is a regular customer and usually orders himself, but the other night that new hussy staying with him ordered, instead. My driver say his tip from the hussy was only one dollar, and on Christmas Eve, too." He shakes his head and clucks his tongue in dismay. "Mr. Allen, he always tip five or ten dollars."

Hearing that Catherine is a cheapskate doesn't surprise me in the least.

Hurley says, "Do you remember what the order was for, what time it was called in, and when it was delivered?"

Georgio thinks a moment. "It was a pepperoni pizza, a large. I don't know the exact time of the order or the delivery, but I can check if you like."

"I like," says Hurley. "And I like even better if you can give me a copy of the slips with the times on them."

"That I can do," Georgio says with a smile. "Now, may I suggest a grilled portabella mushroom stuffed with feta and spinach for an appetizer, followed by some antipasto?"

I nod . . . vigorously.

"And for today's special, I fix fettuccini Parmesan with browned butter. Yes?"

Hurley says, "Sounds good, make it two." Then his cell phone rings.

Georgio heads off to work his gastronomic magic and I sit back, watching Hurley's face as he listens to whoever is on the phone. I wonder if antipasto and pasta work like antimatter and matter. Maybe if I eat both, they will cancel each other out.

Aside from a grunt or two, and one "Hmm, isn't that interesting," Hurley doesn't give me a clue as to who's on the other end.

When he's done, he hangs up, leans back, and looks at me with a self-satisfied grin. "Guess who just called the Sorenson police station to inquire about a local resident?" he says, looking annoyingly smug.

"Really? You're going to make me play twenty questions?"

"It was an immigration officer down in Texas. Want to guess who he was calling about?"

"Pancho Villa?"

"Very funny. It seems the officials down there pulled over a truck filled with illegals, and while several of them got away on foot, one of the ones they caught is a man by the name of Hector Vasquez. And Hector claims to be the husband of a legal immigrant by the name of Serena Vasquez. He gave the officials her address here in Sorenson."

I digest this info, but I can't for the life of me figure out why Hurley is looking so pleased with himself. "So?" I say, shrugging.

"Well, Hector also told the officials that he paid a coyote fifty grand to ensure his safe crossing and some papers once he got here. And he is insisting that he get them or get his money back. Want to guess where he says the money came from?"

Now I see the light. "Serena Vasquez?" I offer, hoping it's the wrong answer but knowing it isn't.

"Bingo," Hurley says. "Now, where do you suppose a single mother and housekeeper like Serena gets fifty grand in cash to send to Mexico?"

The damning info about Serena, coupled with Hurley's grating attitude, might be enough to ruin some people's appetites, but it doesn't faze mine in the least. To be honest, I can't think of much that has ever ruined my appetite—except for a bout or two of the stomach flu, and even that didn't kill it for long. And since I can never remember if you're supposed to feed a cold and starve a fever, or the other way around, I always just feed them both. Some people eat when they're depressed; others eat when they're happy. I eat for both. All my life, I've had this love-hate relationship with food.

I blame it on genetics, though clearly I didn't inherit my build from my mother, who is tiny in stature and has been fashionably thin all her life. No, I'm fairly certain my physique, along with my love of food, came from my father. He left us when I was five—something my mother never forgave him for. And if she has any pictures of him, she's never shared them with me. She never talks about him, either. So my only knowledge of him comes from my memories: vague images of a large man with brown hair, blue eyes, a deep, rumbling voice, and the underlying scent of apple-flavored tobacco for his pipe.

"What are you thinking about?" Hurley asks.

I shake off my nostalgia and focus on the here and

now. "I was just musing about life in general, and how unpredictable it is."

"That's what makes it interesting."

"I guess, though I can't help but feel like the whole thing is a bit of a crapshoot. I mean, look at Jack Allen. I'm sure his life's plan didn't include ending up as a wheelchair-bound paraplegic, or a murder victim."

"He probably didn't plan on winning close to half a mil at the casino, either," Hurley muses aloud, with a shrug. "Maybe it's some sort of karmic balance. Look at how many big lottery winners end up broke or plagued by tragedy after they win."

Georgio brings out our appetizer and antipasto, and Hurley and I dig in. After a few sumptuous bites, Hurley asks me, "What was your life plan when you were younger?"

"Ironically, I was more or less on track before David did what he did. I always imagined myself living in a big house, with a successful, handsome husband, a nice car, and a career that earned me both money and respect."

"What about kids?"

"Two, if I had a boy and a girl. Three, if the first two turned out to be the same sex. But I was definitely quitting at three."

"Wow, you really did plan it out."

I nod as I swallow a yummy bite of stuffed mushroom. "I was a victim of the 'Barbie and Ken syndrome,' so much so that I think I would have thought it perfectly normal if my husband had plastic hair and no genitals."

"Ah," Hurley says, with an evil glint in his eye. "That helps me better understand how you ended up with David."

I snort a laugh and nearly choke on my food.

Once Hurley is sure he won't have to perform the Heimlich on me, he asks, "Did you always want to be a nurse?"

"Hell no. Nursing wasn't on my radar for a long time. I went through phases where I wanted to be an astronomer, a veterinarian, a marine biologist, and a forest ranger."

Hurley chuckles. "I went through a forest ranger phase, too."

"I think most kids do."

"So when and how did nursing come into the picture?"

"I sort of fell into it because of certain . . . circumstances."

Hurley looks intrigued, and I can tell I've triggered his detecting radar. "What kind of circumstances?" he asks.

"Stupid ones," I say with a self-deprecating snort. "I was pretty idealistic in my late teens, and I had a crazy crush on this guy I knew in high school named Pete Nottingham. I was well into the throes of my 'Barbie and Ken syndrome,' and Pete actually looked a lot like a Ken doll, right down to his hair. He used some kind of cheap pomade product to try to tame it.

"Anyway, when I learned that Pete had plans to go to medical school and become a doctor, I opted to do the same so I could stay near him. I envisioned this romantic future with the two of us struggling through medical school and our residencies, then kicking back and enjoying the fruits of our labors once we were done. I went for the whole fantasy: the big house, two-point-five kids in a private school, matching Benzes in the drive, evenings spent at social events hobnobbing with the medical elite, and then nights of hot, torrid, fantastic sex."

Hurley's eyebrows rise.

"But during our second year in college, Pete changed his mind. He dropped both school and me at the same time. He said he wanted some time to experience life first before he committed to such a time-consuming career and a permanent relationship. Turned out that was code for 'I want to screw somebody else, but I don't have the guts to tell you.'"

"Ouch," Hurley says with a grimace.

"Yeah, ouch," I concur. "It's a pattern I seem destined to repeat. My second serious relationship ended the same way. I thought I'd broken the streak when I married David, but we both know how that turned out."

"I'm sorry your dream didn't work out."

I shrug. "It was unrealistic and stupid. I was young, naïve, and in lust. I'm smarter now, though that wisdom came at a steep price."

"What happened to your plans to become a doctor?"

"The same thing that happened to my plan to hide out for the rest of my life after David made a fool of me by schtupping Karen Owenby behind my back. I needed money. My school loans were mounting and I had rent to pay. I needed a career that would generate some quick income, so I switched to nursing. I found I liked it and was good at it. It turned out to be a good choice for me, one I've never regretted."

"For the record," Hurley says, "the only person David made a fool of was himself."

"I'm not sure I agree with you, but thanks for the sentiment."

Georgio arrives with our main course. For the next several minutes, the only sounds at the table are Hurley and I slurping fettuccini noodles and moaning with delight. I realize about halfway through my plate that

I'm sucking food in like my dog, Hoover, so I set down my fork to take a break and turn the tables on Hurley.

"So what about you? What was your life plan? Did you always want to be a cop?"

Hurley hesitates a moment so he can chew and swallow what he has in his mouth. "The cop thing, yeah," he says, twirling another forkful of pasta. "I love what I do. And with the exception of my forest ranger phase, I've wanted to be a cop for as long as I can remember."

"Why?"

He shrugs. "Because I like the uniforms?"

"But you don't wear one anymore."

He ponders a moment and then offers, "I like shooting things."

"Remind me not to piss you off too much."

"I also like the puzzle aspects of solving a crime, and the idea of bringing justice to the world." He pops some pasta into his mouth and nearly chokes when I ask my next question.

"Have you ever killed anyone?"

He manages to chew and swallow while I wait for his answer. Finally he says, "I have. Once. I did a brief stint in vice when I was in Chicago and I got involved in a shoot-out during a drug raid."

"That had to have been scary."

"Yeah, it was." There is a beat of silence and then he says, "Have you?"

"Have I what? Killed someone?"

Hurley nods.

"God, no . . . at least not that I know of. And if I had, I sure as hell wouldn't tell you. You're a homicide detective, for cripes' sake."

"Do you think you could, if you had to?"

I consider this a moment and nod. "I suppose I could, under the right circumstances."

"Such as?"

"Such as if my life was threatened and it was a matter of self-defense. Or if the life of someone I love was threatened and the only way I could save them was to kill someone else."

I pick up my fork, unable to resist the smell any longer. As I'm twirling up some fettuccini, Hurley asks, "Would you kill someone to save me?"

Talk about your not-so-subtle segues. Hurley's baby blues are like laser beams, boring into my brain and heart. I shove my forkful of pasta in my mouth and stare back at him, chewing slowly to stall for time, carefully gauging my answer. I'm well aware that, based on my last statement, a "yes" answer will imply that I love him. Do I? I know that I lust after him, and I know that when I thought he might be dying a while back, my heart felt as if it had been cleaved in two. But such thoughts are dangerous—because no matter how I feel about him, I can't have him.

Given all that, I decide to go with a vague answer, one that will leave things open to interpretation but not require a true verbal commitment from me.

"Of course, I would do whatever was necessary to save you, Hurley," I say, once I swallow. I see the corners of his mouth twitch into an almost smile right before I deliver my coup de grâce. "Because if you were gone, I'd be stuck working with Bob Richmond all the time."

Georgio appears with our check, which he then makes disappear in a flash of flame. Just as I start to feel excited about getting a meal on the house, he produces the real check, along with a copy of the bill for the pizza delivered to Jack's house on the night before the fire.

Hurley looks at Jack's receipt and says, "The pizza was delivered a little after seven. Assume an hour, give or take, for the actual dinner, then two hours for the movie, and so far the timeline Catherine gave us is holding up. We'll need to pay a visit to the Sorenson Motel to see if she'll let us search her room and to verify her check-in and checkout times."

"But even if she did check in or out when she said she did, it doesn't mean she couldn't have left the motel anytime in between those hours."

"True, but it's a start, and it's something we need to cross off our list." He pauses, assumes a cocky grin, and winks at me. "So what do you say, Mattie? Want to hit up a motel with me?"

Chapter 10

While a visit to any motel with Hurley sounds wonderful, our plans change when both of our cell phones ring at the same time. I grab mine and see that it's Izzy.

"We have a call," he says.

"What and where?"

"A farm out on Petersen Road. Apparently, the owners went out to fix a fence line along the river and they found a body near the shore. Their farm is just below the lake outlet, so I suspect it may be the fellow who went missing while fishing a few weeks ago."

Great. A floater. This will be a first for me, but I can't imagine it will be any worse than the advanced case of decomp I had to deal with a while back, or the crispy critter Jack Allen turned into. I recall the news story about the missing fisherman who, according to his wife, went out on the lake in his boat the day after Thanksgiving and never came back. The boat was found adrift the following day, filled with fishing gear but lacking any persons. The presumption at the time was that the gentleman fell overboard and drowned.

Izzy says, "All this melting with the warm weather

likely created enough current to bring the body to the surface and carry it into the river. Odds are he drowned, but we'll have to bring the body in and do a post to be sure."

I get the directions from Izzy and tell him I'll meet him there in fifteen minutes. Hurley disconnects his call about the same time. "The floater?" I say, and he nods. "Drop me off back at my office so I can change and get my car," I tell him. He does so, and I take a few minutes to run inside and change into a set of scrubs before getting into my car and heading out.

By the time I arrive at the farm, I see a couple of cop cars, along with our evidence van, parked by the barn. Izzy, Hurley, a couple of unis, and two other people I don't know are all standing beside the barn in front of a large fenced-in corral, which contains eight horses. The animals are staring wide-eyed at the humans. Their ears prick back and forth; their nostrils flare; their tails swish nervously as if they sense something is up. I wonder if they can smell the body, and that makes me wonder if I can. As I get out of my car, I pull a big breath in through my nose, testing the air. I smell mud, manure, hay, and a warm, sweaty scent that may be the horses' fears, but not much else.

"This is my assistant, Mattie Winston," Izzy says to the duo I don't recognize. "This is Troy Littleton and his wife, Jan, the owners of this farm."

We exchange murmured greetings, and then I turn my focus to my surroundings, looking for the river, where the body supposedly washed up. Izzy reads my mind and says, "The river runs along a field out behind the corral, about a mile or so. There isn't any road to access it, and they said the body is close to shore in a small inlet that would make using a boat awkward. We're going to take Troy's Gator to get there."

I look over at the ATV parked nearby, which has been

customized with lights at the top and an extra-long bed at the rear, bordered by six-inch-high panels. The front portion has two seats inside a metal frame, topped off with a roll bar and a retractable plastic windshield.

"Either that, or I can saddle up the horses for you," Troy says.

Hurley, who has been quiet up until now, says, "Actually, I don't see how we can fit all of the people and the equipment we need, not to mention the body, on the Gator. It will mean taking multiple trips. So if saddling up a couple of horses isn't too much trouble, it might not be a bad idea."

"Not a problem at all," Troy says. "How many?"

"I'll take the Gator," Izzy says quickly.

Hurley nods toward the horses and says, "I'd love the chance to ride one of those beauties."

Jan Littleton looks at me and says, "How about you, Mattie? Are you up for it? It's every girl's dream, isn't it? The sun warming your face, muscled flesh between your thighs, riding the wind like no one cares."

I swallow hard, wondering if she is talking about horses or if she's able to read some of the more lascivious thoughts in my mind. I'm guessing Hurley's thoughts are running along similar lines because he looks over at me with a grin and wiggles his eyebrows. Izzy coughs nervously and tries unsuccessfully to suppress a smile.

The pressure is on. I'm a little leery of riding out to the river on horseback. I've ridden before; in fact, I took lessons for a summer when I was eight or nine. But I haven't been on a horse since, and back then the horse was confined to a fenced-in arena. With a wide-open field to play in, I'm worried. Yet, there is something to what Jan Littleton just said. I remember the exhilarating sense of freedom and adventure I felt when I took hold of those reins so many years ago. I had that little-girl dream she spoke of, and the memory pulls at me now.

"I'm game for riding a horse out to the site," I announce. "But please make sure it's a well-behaved one. It's been a very long time since I rode."

"No problem," Jan says. "You can have Ellie, the chestnut over there by the gate. She's a sweetheart."

The uniformed guys both opt for horses, too. While we're waiting for the animals to get saddled up, Izzy and I load our gear onto the Gator. We're about ten minutes into this when we hear a car approaching. I turn to see Alison Miller pulling up in her SUV. She climbs out of her car, her ubiquitous camera hanging around her neck.

"I heard you found a body out here by the river," she says, looking around for some sign of the waterway.

I lean over and speak to Izzy, sotto voce. "How the hell does she always find out about this stuff?"

"Police scanner," Izzy says.

Seeing the Gator and the horses, it doesn't take Alison long to figure out what's going on. "Can I come along?"

Hurley looks annoyed, but he and I both know from past experience that Alison won't give up easily. Sometimes it's better to keep her on a short leash in hopes of having some control over what she sees, shoots, and writes about. "Fine," Hurley says, "but no pictures of the body."

"No problem," Alison says.

After a bit of discussion, it's decided that only one of the uniformed cops will ride out to the site with us. The second one will stay behind to wait for the funeral home Izzy called to come and transport the body for us. Alison opts to ride out on the fifth horse; and after another ten minutes, we are ready to roll. I spend a moment feeding Ellie some carrot bits Jan gives me, trying to make friends. Ellie's big brown eyes certainly look gentle, and her soft lips feel like velvet on my open palm as she takes the treats I offer. However, her demeanor is a little skittish, enough so to make me skittish as well. After Ellie is done with the carrots, I stroke her nose and talk to her in a low whisper, hoping to calm her. She responds by rearing her head back and letting forth with a gigantic sneeze, blowing carrot bits and horse snot onto my face and hair.

"I think she likes you," Jan says, chuckling.

"She has a funny way of showing it," I say, wiping loogies off my forehead. I hear the click of a camera and look over to see Alison already mounted on her horse, holding her camera, and sneering at me. I give her a dirty look just before Jan helps me mount Ellie.

After I get settled into the saddle, the horse seems to calm a bit. I take the reins, give a little kick to her sides, and practice riding her around the arena once while Jan and the uniformed cop get mounted. Hurley is already on his horse, a huge, beautiful jet-black stallion. He looks like the cover for a romance novel.

Troy starts the Gator and heads off across the field with Izzy in the seat beside him and our gear in the rear, leaving just enough room for us to load the body onto the bed once we get to it. Jan leads the rest of us, with Hurley, Alison, the uniformed cop, and me following in a line behind her.

The field is uneven and very muddy, thanks to the massive snowmelt, and the heavy Gator has to work to get through it. Troy takes a serpentine path, searching for areas where the mud isn't as deep or wet. Jan steers our little group along in the packed-down tracks the Gator leaves behind, giving the horses a more solid footing. The sun is shining warm on my shoulders and Ellie lives up to her reputation, following dutifully along behind Jan's horse for the first half mile or so.

But as we draw close enough to the river to hear it splashing along its banks, the horses all start whinnying and snorting—evidence they are growing more nervous. At one point, Ellie stops dead in her tracks, raises her head, and sniffs the air with her nostrils flaring. I give her a little kick in her ribs to try and urge her on, but she jerks her head to the side and looks back at me with a wide-eyed, are-you-kidding expression.

Hurley trots up beside me. "Need a hand?"

"I think she can smell the body and it's making her nervous," I say.

"Kick her a little harder," Hurley suggests.

I do so, and Ellie takes the hint by turning sharply right and breaking into a run. I nearly lose my seating as she takes off, but I manage to grab the saddle horn and hang on. Her footing is tentative in the loose, muddy field. I tighten my thighs and hang on for all I'm worth as she gallops across the field. Panicked, I pull back on the reins, yelling, "Whoa!" but all it seems to do is spur Ellie on. And then my worst fear comes true. Ellie stumbles, her front legs buckle, her shoulders drop, and her momentum comes to a dead halt. My momentum, on the other hand, continues unabated. I go flying ass over teakettle, over her head, and into the mud.

I roll a couple of times and end up flat on my back, with my legs sprawled. I'm staring up at the blue sky, trying to catch my breath, when I become aware of a commotion behind me. A second later, I watch stunned as Ellie gallops past me heading back toward the barn. I hear more activity behind me; then Hurley appears, followed by Jan. Hurley jumps off his horse and sloshes through the mud toward me, his horse in tow.

"Jesus, Winston, are you okay?" he says, looking down at me with a concerned expression. He squats beside me and gives me a quick head-to-toe visual exam. Jan appears behind Hurley and echoes his concerns.

"I'm so sorry, Mattie," she says. "Are you okay?"

"Just got the wind knocked out of me," I manage to say. "Give me a sec and I think I'll be fine."

Alison appears as well, looking smug and comfortable atop her steed. I glare at her as she lifts the camera and aims it my way, but she's not the least bit intimidated. I hear clicking sounds and whirs as she snaps off a couple of shots, making me want to snap off her head. I should have slipped a bur beneath her saddle back at the barn.

"I've never seen Ellie behave like that before," Jan says, sounding worried. "I swear she's the gentlest horse we've ever had."

I try to sit up and can't. At first, I'm convinced I'm paralyzed. Then I realize it's just the suction created by the gooey mud that's hampering my efforts. I finally manage to shake each arm loose with a wet, sucking sound. I roll my head slowly from one side to the other and say to Hurley, "Help me sit up."

He offers a hand, which I take. After a bit of a struggle, I manage to break loose from my muddy shackles and sit up. I look around me and realize I dug out a path in the mud when I hit, sliding a good eight feet. There is a huge heap of wet, soggy mud piled up between my legs. The stuff is clinging to every inch of my backside and a good portion of my front. After a tentative test of my legs, Hurley helps me to a standing position, a task made that much harder by the several pounds of mud clinging to me. My scrub pants threaten to fall down from the sheer weight of the mess. I hoist them up, pull the drawstring around my waist tighter, and tie it.

Troy and Izzy arrive in the Gator, stopping a few

feet away. I give them a thumbs-up and a smile—a sentiment I'm not convinced I feel.

"I seem to have lost my ride," I say, turning to see Ellie off in the distance, back by the farm buildings.

"She'll be fine," Jan says. "I can go and bring her back, if you want."

I shake my head. "No, that's okay. I'd rather walk than get on that beast again. Maybe I can hitch a ride on the Gator the rest of the way." Izzy and Troy both stare at me, looking horrified at the suggestion.

"Why don't you ride with me," Hurley suggests.

I eye him skeptically. "You mean two of us on one horse?"

"Sure," he says. "It will be tight, but we can do it."

"I don't think I want to get back on a horse again. Ever."

"Which is why you should do it now," Hurley says. "You need to face your fear head-on before it gets a chance to overwhelm you. There's a reason for that saying about getting back in the saddle."

"I don't know, Hurley."

"He's right," Jan says.

"I promise I won't let you fall again," Hurley says. "Besides, there won't be room for all of you on the Gator once we pick up the body. Someone's going to have to ride double on a horse, or ride in the back of the Gator with the corpse."

This argument settles it for me. Given my current mud-covered state, I'm pretty sure I know who will get to ride with the corpse, and I've done the riding-with-the-corpse thing before. It wasn't much fun. Plus it's obvious from the glare on Alison's face that she hates the idea of me riding double with Hurley, which means I have to do it. "Fine," I say, eyeing Hurley's horse skeptically. "How do we do this?"

Hurley helps me climb up into the saddle. After I

scoot myself as far forward as I can—a task made easier by the fact that his saddle is an English one, without a horn—Hurley climbs up and settles in behind me. He wraps an arm around my waist and takes the reins. Slowly we make our way over to the Gator and everyone falls into line again as we continue toward the river.

About fifteen minutes later, we arrive at the far edge of the field. The river is babbling along at a rapid clip, its currents enhanced by the extra water flowing into it from the snowmelt. When we reach the bank, I can see where a tree has fallen into the water, its roots loosened by the wet ground. There, tangled in the branches about ten feet from shore, is a body floating facedown in the water.

Chapter 11

We dismount from our horses and everyone stands on the bank for a few minutes sizing up our situation. The body is too far out to reach from land. Since we don't have a boat, I realize someone will have to wade out into the water to haul it in.

"The water out there is about four and a half feet deep," Troy tells us, reading my mind. I realize this rules Izzy out, since the water will be up to his chin.

"I'll go in," I say. It's a no-brainer, given my height.

"I'll help," Hurley says. His front side is covered with mud from my backside. While I suspect I look like a spa appointment gone horribly wrong, he looks like a hunky mud wrestler.

Troy produces a rope from the Gator; and after Hurley and I strip off our jackets and shoes and don Tyvek bodysuits, gloves, and waders from Izzy's site kit, we venture out into the water. We are carrying one end of the rope, while Troy hangs on to the other. The air may be uncharacteristically warm for this time of year, but the water hasn't followed suit. Despite the protection offered by the waders, I can feel the cold seeping

through to my body. It's slow going because the river
bottom is muddy, making for precarious footing.

As we inch our way along, I hear Alison's camera at
work back on shore.

"Remember what I said, Alison," Hurley hollers over
his shoulder.

"I'm doing scene shots," Alison yells back. "Nothing
with the victim showing."

Within a few minutes, we reach the body. I expect to
detect the nasty smell of decomp, but all I pick up, instead, is a brackish, muddy smell, like the river bottom.
Hurley and I work together to loop our end of the rope
around the man's waist and tie it. It's not easy. The
medical-type gloves we are wearing provide little protection against the elements and the cold water has
numbed our fingers to the point where neither of us
has much dexterity left. We manage to bump both of
the man's arms in the process, sending them floating
to the surface. Though the skin on his bare hands has
a wrinkly, waterlogged look to it, I don't see any evidence of decomposition. Apparently, the cold water
has forestalled the process. Once Hurley and I are
done fumbling through the rope business, Hurley yells,
"Okay, haul him in."

Troy and Izzy both start reeling in the rope from
shore and the body slowly makes its way toward the
riverbank. Hurley and I follow along behind it. When
the body hits the shoreline, Troy ties his end of the
rope to the Gator. He, Izzy, and the uniformed cop
come down to help Hurley and me out of the water.

Click, whir, click, whir.

As soon as I'm out of the water, my body starts shivering uncontrollably. My Tyvek suit, which normally
has me sweating like a pig, does little to warm me.

"You okay, Winston?" Hurley asks. He grabs one of

the blankets on the Gator and walks over to drape it over my shoulders as I step out of my waders.

"I'm fine," I say. "But damn, that water was cold!"

"Yes, it was," he says, grinning and looking pointedly at my chest.

I glance down and see that beneath my suit, which is strained to its limits across my ample chest, my nipples are standing at attention.

"Speaking of which," Hurley says, leaning in close to my ear, "when are you going to tell me about this nipple incident I keep hearing about?"

"When hell freezes over."

"I think it has," he says, winking.

I stand beneath my blanket, shaking, while Izzy and Hurley lay out a tarp on the shore by the body. Hurley steps out into the water and rolls the body onto the tarp, turning it faceup. It's our first glimpse of the victim's face, and it's a bit of a shocker. The body isn't in as good a shape as I thought. Part of the man's nose is gone, exposing the bony ridge beneath, and one eyeball is missing. The other eyeball is clouded over but wide open, its upper lid gone. The skin on the man's cheeks is abraded and pale white, like the underbelly of a fish.

"Looks like the fish started on him," Izzy says, grimacing.

The man's bare hands strike me as odd. When he went missing, the temperatures were in the 30-degree range—not enough to freeze all the water, but still cold enough that I would have expected him to be wearing gloves. The rest of his body is clothed appropriately with a heavy jacket, jeans, and boots. He has a full head of hair plastered close to his skull. As I look at it, something catches my eye. I take a step closer and see what appears to be a depression just behind his right temple.

"Is that a head wound?" I ask, pointing to the area.

Izzy bends down and moves the hair aside to examine the area. "It appears to be. Could be he fell out of the boat and hit his head." He probes the area and I see the skull move beneath his fingers. "His skull is fractured. It could be the cause of death, or maybe the blow rendered him unconscious and he drowned. Though it's odd there isn't any discoloration on the skin." He looks thoughtful a moment and then shrugs. "I'll be able to tell more once I get him back to the lab and open him up."

We get the body wrapped up, placed in a body bag, and loaded onto the back of the Gator. After rounding up our supplies, Hurley strips out of his waders and Tyvek suit. After helping me mount his horse, he climbs up behind me and I can feel his body heat radiating onto my back. I let myself sink into it gratefully, relishing the warmth. The gentle rocking of our bodies in the saddle is surprisingly erotic. With Hurley's arm wrapped around my waist, his breath warm in my ear, and the hard expanse of his chest against my back, I can't help but imagine what life might be like if we could be this close on a regular basis. Every fiber of my being wants to be snuggled up next to him any chance I get. How on earth am I going to be able to continue working with him this way, side by side, parrying his flirtatious comments, longing to feel his touch, wanting to be with him?

Maybe I'm going about this thing the wrong way. I do love my job, but is it really worth it? Am I making the wrong decision? Now that I have the money from my divorce settlement, is there a way to stretch it out, to live off it for years to come? Realistically, I know I can't. Without my job, I have no benefits. All it would take is one health disaster and I'd end up broke. I suppose I could go back to work at the hospital, but facing all those pitying, knowing eyes, day after day—not to mention David and his new love—is more humiliation than I can deal with right now. I could probably get away with a few years working at some lower-paying job, long enough to explore my relationship with Hurley. But then what? And what if the relationship doesn't work out?

My settlement, while generous, just isn't enough. But if I could somehow double the money, I might be able to make it work. That makes me think about the casino and Jack's lucky win. If he could do it, why can't I?

Our ride back to the barn goes off without a hitch, and the two uniformed cops help Izzy and me transfer the body from the Gator to the hearse that is waiting.

As Alison heads off to her car, Hurley hollers after her, "I want to see anything you write up about this before it goes to print! And no speculations until I give you something official!"

Alison rolls her eyes but nods her agreement. "I'll have something for you by tomorrow," she says. She climbs into her car, and moments later, she peels out.

I follow the funeral home hearse in my own. By the time we get back to the office, I am itching like crazy from all the mud. I head straight for the shower and scare myself so bad when I look in the mirror that I almost scream. With all the mud on my hair and skin, I look like the wife of Swamp Thing. I spend a long time under the hot spray, cleaning off and chastising myself for my foolish romanticism. Given the way I looked, I'm willing to bet Hurley had no such illusions. When I'm done, I put on a fresh pair of scrubs and head for the autopsy suite.

Izzy and Arnie have already done the preliminary processing on the body, including the weight, X-rays, and paperwork. The body bag has yet to be opened. It's laid out on the autopsy table waiting for our ministrations. Hurley isn't here yet—he's probably somewhere washing off the mud and stink of river smell.

Our autopsy proceeds along at a good clip and I monitor our progress with photos. I watch, fascinated, as Izzy degloves the victim's hands, removing the wrinkled, waterlogged outer layer to reveal skin beneath that is as smooth as a baby's bottom. The fingerprint ridges on this under layer are intact, which enables us to get a full ten-card. When we undress the victim, we find a wallet in the pocket of his jeans. It contains two dollars in cash, a driver's license, a debit card from a local bank, and a MasterCard. Despite their time in the water, the contents are all in surprisingly good shape. We set them aside to dry. The name on the license and cards is *Donald Strommen*. Izzy verifies this as the name of the man who went missing from his fishing boat a few weeks ago. His age is noted as thirty-six.

We also find a handful of photos in the wallet: two of a blond-haired girl, who looks to be in her early teens, and two of a towheaded boy, who appears to be eight or nine. The fifth picture is a family one, showing both of the children, Donald, and a smiling blond woman.

About the time we finish stripping off all of Donald's clothing, Hurley shows up. He is cleanly dressed, with his hair wet from the shower and his fresh, clean scent is a welcome respite from the smells of death and musty river water.

Izzy makes his Y incision and cuts out the breastplate so we can begin inspecting, removing, and analyzing the organs. He removes the lungs first. When he opens them, we find them filled with water.

"Does that mean he drowned?" I ask.

Izzy shakes his head. "Not necessarily. If a body is in

the water long enough, it will eventually get into the lungs."

"Then how can we know if drowning was the cause of death?" Hurley asks.

"There are a couple of clues that might help," Izzy says. "If a person inhales water, there is typically evidence of hemorrhaging in the sinuses and airways, and foaming in the lungs. The foaming might have dissipated by now, but a lack of both of these findings would suggest he was already dead when he hit the water. I'll also need to examine that head wound to determine if it might have been fatal. And there is one other way. We can look for diatoms in his blood and bone marrow."

"What are diatoms?" Hurley asks.

"They're microscopic, single-celled organisms found in most bodies of water. If Donald was breathing and his heart was still pumping when he went into the lake, he would have inhaled diatoms along with the water. The diatoms are then absorbed into the bloodstream and from there into the bone marrow. The types and amounts of diatoms existing in any given body of water will vary, based on how much light they get and what nutrients are available. Given that, we should be able to tell if the lake was the actual site of his drowning by comparing the diatoms we find in his body to those in the lake water. We might even be able to narrow down the specific part of the lake he drowned in."

Izzy takes a small sample of the lung water and drops it onto a microscope slide. After applying a cover slip, he puts it into the microscope on a side table, makes some adjustments, and then calls us over. "Those are diatoms," he says, gesturing toward the scope.

I step up first and look through the eyepiece. I can see a variety of tiny, transparent shapes shifting about on the field below: triangular, round, cigar-shaped, needlelike, and one that resembles a miniature piano keyboard. As I'm looking, another drifts into view. It resembles an oval-shaped rug with an undulating fringe around its edges.

I step back and let Hurley have a look-see.

"Wow," he says. "Who knew all that was in the water? Makes me never want to swim again."

We return to the autopsy table, where Izzy removes and dissects Donald's trachea, examining the inside of the breathing tube closely. The only finding of any consequence is a puzzling one: a small worm, about half an inch in length, caught up in the vocal cords. I photograph it and place it in a jar to send off to our entomologist in Madison for identification.

The rest of our work on the body reveals nothing of consequence, so we move to the head. Izzy cuts an incision over the top of Donald's scalp from one ear to the other. He then grabs the front end of this incision and pulls the skin back and down over Donald's face. He retracts the skin on the back of the scalp as well, revealing the skull. I cut a circular path through the bone with a special saw, taking care to avoid the area of the head wound. When I'm done, Izzy pries off the newly created skullcap and looks at Donald's brain.

"Well, the head wound didn't kill him," he announces. "In fact, he was already dead by the time this injury occurred."

"How can you tell?" Hurley asks.

I field this one. "If he was alive and his heart was pumping when the injury occurred, there would be evidence of hemorrhaging at the site, bruising, clots, that sort of thing. But there isn't any, not on the scalp, the skull, or the brain tissue."

"Which would make drowning the more likely scenario?" Hurley posits.

"I don't think so," Izzy says, frowning and examining

the man's sinus cavities. "There's no evidence of bleeding in the sinuses. Let's take a look at some bone marrow and see what it has to offer."

Izzy uses a special drill with a coring bit to drill a hole into Donald's pelvic bone. A few minutes later, he has a small sample of bone marrow prepped on a glass slide and positioned on a microscope. Hurley and I stand by, waiting, as Izzy adjusts the focus, moves the slide, and adjusts again, repeating these steps about a dozen times. Finally he steps back from the microscope.

"I don't see any diatoms," he says. "And that, combined with my other findings, means drowning is ruled out, as far as I'm concerned. Maybe the tox screen will give me something more when it comes back, but for now I can't give you a cause, or a manner."

Hurley nods solemnly, frowning. "Are you comfortable making an ID?" he asks.

Izzy thinks for a few seconds. "Given the damage to his face, I don't want to ask his wife to come down and identify him, but there is enough of it still intact to do a comparison with his driver's license picture. Based on that, I'm willing to make a preliminary identification. However, I won't make an official one until I have fingerprint or dental-record verification."

"Good enough for me," Hurley says. "When do you want to make the notification?"

Izzy looks grim. "I should have a definite identification by tomorrow, so we can do it then."

Notifying someone that his or her loved one is dead is never a fun task. It's even more difficult when the deceased is someone so young and there are small children involved.

"If you want, Hurley and I can do it," I say.

Izzy shakes his head. "Thanks, but I'll be fine."

I know he will be, but I can tell from the sagging lines in his face and the gloomy look in his eyes that this will be a tough one. You can only deliver heart-breaking news to people so many times before the weight of it all begins to wear you down. Izzy has been at this for over two decades. Even in a town as small as ours, that adds up to a lot of sadness. Most of the time, he bears the burden well; but at other times, like now, the cumulative effects begin to show.

I have a strong urge to walk over and hug him, to tell him I'll be there for him if he needs to talk. But I don't, for two reasons. One, Izzy doesn't respond well to coddling of any sort. And two, we discovered during the one and only hug we shared a few years ago that our disparate heights lead to near suffocation for Izzy, whose face ended up buried in my cleavage.

"It's late," Hurley says, glancing at his watch. I look over at the clock on the wall and see that it's after five already. "I think we should call it a day. I already called Joe Whitehorse and rescheduled our meeting for to-morrow night. The nursing agency, the motel visit, and our second talk with Serena can wait until tomorrow. We'll squeeze the notification in there whenever you're ready, Izzy."

"Sounds like a plan."

Chapter 12

The next morning dawns with a continuation of the wonky warm weather; everything outside is a muddy, wet mess. By the time Hoover returns from his morning bathroom rituals, his feet are encased in mud. It takes me half an hour to clean them off and wipe up the trail he left through the house.

After my shower, I inspect my body in the mirror, checking out the status of my tan. The redness from my burn is finally turning to brown, and that's when I discover that tanned cellulite looks like the top of a toasted English muffin—lots of nooks and crannies. Resigned to once again jump-starting my diet, I have berry yoghurt for breakfast, a choice made easy by the fact that it's the only thing I have to eat in the house that doesn't carry a pet food brand. I'm even out of ice cream, since I killed off the last of my Ben & Jerry's last night before going to bed. I consider it an omen, a sign that I need to revamp my eating habits. My conviction holds strong when I stop at the coffee shop on my way to work and order sugar-free flavoring in my skinny latte. But as I drive past the grocery store, the uncharacteristically warm weather seems to scream "ice cream" at me. I start thinking maybe I can switch to a lower-calorie brand instead of giving it up altogether. I spend the rest of my drive wondering how much Healthy Choice ice cream I can buy and eat before it ceases to be a healthy choice.

After checking in with Izzy and finding out that we are still waiting on test results for Donald, I give Hurley a call and meet him outside so we can go to the Sorenson Motel to check out Catherine's alibi.

The owner of the Sorenson Motel is a sixty-something curmudgeon by the name of Joseph Wagner, who is best known in town for his constant flow of "Letters to the Editor" criticizing the local government. Rumor has it that Joseph holds a long-term grudge against our current mayor, Charlie Petersen, because Charlie stole Joe's girl, Marla, some forty years ago. I find this obsession a bit odd, especially given that the mayor's wife looks like the red-haired troll doll whose head I kept on the end of my pencil in high school. This leads me to believe one of two things: either both men have odd tastes in women, or Marla Petersen has some serious bedroom talent.

Speaking of bedrooms, the Sorenson Motel is nearly as old as Joseph. Though he has done an admirable job of keeping things running and repaired, the place shows its age. The bedspreads and sheets are clean, if a bit threadbare, and the décor screams 1980s—the last time Joseph redid any of the rooms. The outside of the place looks like your typical 1960s-era roadside motel: a long, narrow building with two wings of units—front and back—divided by an office in the middle. Joseph does provide a few modern conveniences, such as free Internet access, cable TV, and pay-per-view porn, and the end units on both wings are suites that include a kitchenette and sitting area. It is in one of these units that my ex, David, has been living for the past few weeks, ever since our house burned down.

Hurley and I head for the office, where we find Joseph parked behind his desk, watching the Weather Channel. He has large, loose bags beneath his eyes, and his flannel shirt looks as threadbare as his bed-spreads. While the top of his head is nearly bald, his gray hair is thick and curly on the sides, making him look like Larry Fine from the Three Stooges.

On the TV, the Weather Channel reporters are predicting Armageddon in the form of a huge winter blizzard moving our way and due to strike late tomor-row before it cuts a swath through the southern states. The voices of the reporters are heightened and excited; their eyes are big with worry; their faces marked with concern. They cut from radar images of the national weather map to scenes in grocery stores down in Mis-souri, where the shelves are stripped bare. For some reason, snowstorms turn otherwise normal people into hoarders. Larders everywhere within the strike zone get filled to the brim with bread, milk, eggs, and the like . . . except here in Wisconsin, where people are more likely stocking up on beer, brats, and snowmobile gas.

Wisconsinites don't surrender easily to winter, and we are well used to the cold. I know people here in town who think any temperature above zero is warm enough to cook brats outside on the grill. When people south of the 42nd parallel are bundling up in wool hats, long johns, parkas, and mittens, Wisconsinites might throw on a flannel shirt. And when hell freezes over, Wiscon-sin schools might open two hours late.

Joseph—in classic Wisconsinite form—shrugs, clearly unimpressed with the trumped-up drama from the TV reporters. He shifts his gaze from the tube to us. "Bunch of idiots," he grumbles. "They're only calling for ten inches or so. Hell, that's nothing. It's just a snowstorm for Christ's sake." He dons a pair of glasses, which were sitting atop the desk register, and picks up a pen. "You two looking for a room?" he asks.

I wish.

"No, sir," Hurley says, whipping out his badge and holding it up. "I'm Detective Steve Hurley, with the Sorenson PD, and this is Mattie Winston, with the ME's office."

Joseph starts to scrutinize Hurley's badge until he hears mention of my name. Then he shifts his attention to me. "Winston? You're with that doctor down in suite twelve, right?"

I shake my head. "I'm not with him, no."

Joseph looks confused. "I thought you were married to him or something."

"Not anymore."

"So you're not here to help him move out?"

"No. He won't be moving out of here for a while yet. Not until his house gets rebuilt."

"I don't think so, missy," Joseph says, looking smug. "He gave me his notice two days ago. I assumed that blond woman helping him pack stuff into a car was you." He pauses, peers out at me over the top of his glasses, and does a quick head-to-toe perusal. After a few seconds, he says, "Yeah, okay. I didn't see her up close, 'cause they were down at the end of the wing, you know, and these old eyes ain't what they used to be. I thought it was you because of the hair, but I can see now that I was mistaken. She's got mosquito bites compared to you," he concludes, leering at my chest.

I feel my face grow hot and imagine myself bopping Joseph on his head a few times, nice and hard, Moe Howard–style. Hurley clears his throat and diverts Joseph's attention.

"We'd like to ask you some questions regarding a

customer of yours who's been staying here for some time . . . a Ms. Catherine Albright?"

"That fortune-hunting gold digger?" Joseph says with a snort of disgust. "What's she done?"

"We don't know that she's done anything yet," Hurley explains. "That's what we're trying to determine. I see you have security cameras here. Any chance we can take a look at your recent footage?"

Joseph shakes his head. "I don't believe in invading people's privacy like that. Those cameras aren't real. I just put them up so it looks like we have security monitoring. Helps keep people honest."

Hurley lets out a sigh of frustration.

Now that I've recovered from my homicidal thoughts toward Joseph, I ask him, "How much of your customers' ins and outs are you aware of? Do you watch people as they come and go?"

He swivels his head and looks at me over the top of his glasses again. "I see most of what goes on during the day and on most evenings, but every Friday night I go down to the VFW for the fish fry and polka fest." I make a disappointed face and Joseph seems to take offense at it. "Hey," he snaps, "don't underestimate the polka. When it's done right, it's a beautiful sight to behold."

"I don't care about the polka," I tell him. "I care about your ability to tell us of Albright's comings and goings."

"Then why didn't you ask that in the first place?" he grumbles. He flips back through his register and starts writing dates down on a piece of paper. "These are the nights that she's stayed here since coming to town. She was real regular at first, but I heard she was making a play for that paralyzed man who won all the money up at the casino, the one who died in that house fire the other night. And I guess she was getting somewhere with him, because she wasn't staying here much lately. Only about once a week or so."

"Did she stay here this past Monday night?" Hurley asks.

"Sure did. Let me see. . . ." He flips forward in the register and runs a finger down the page, then across it. "She checked in at ten-thirty that night and checked out at ten forty-eight the next morning."

"Any idea if she left the place between those two times?"

"Not before midnight, that's when I went to bed. And no one rang the bell after that, so I slept all night, until seven the next morning. What she might have done between midnight and seven is anyone's guess."

"How about Tuesday morning, before she checked out?" I ask. "Did you see her leave here at all?"

"Sure did. She was in and out of here a couple of times that morning. Went out and came back around eight, carrying a bag from McDonald's."

"Imagine that," I mumble under my breath, remembering her snobby claim that pizza was subpar to her usual meals. "Last of the big spenders."

"Then she left again, about an hour after that, and didn't come back until just before she checked out."

Hurley and I look at one another. "She lied to us," I say.

"Is she here now?" Hurley asks.

Joseph shrugs. "She checked back in on Christmas Day, just a few hours after she checked out. Far as I know she's still here, but I see her car is gone."

"Mind if we take a look at her room?" Hurley asks.

Joseph narrows his eyes at us. "Yeah, I kind of do mind. People have enough invasions of their privacy these days. I don't want to be adding to that crap."

Hurley starts to say something, but I beat him to it. "Is she paid up on her bill? Because she's a suspect in two murders, and if she hasn't flown the coop already, I suspect she will soon." This isn't exactly true—at least not that we know—but Joseph doesn't need to know that.

The gambit works. In a matter of seconds, Joseph's expression goes from worried, to doubtful, to angry. Apparently, a threat to his wallet is enough to make him toss aside his moral indignation. He grabs a key and leads the way.

It seems I'm an excellent predictor of behavior. Catherine's bed is neatly made, and the room is devoid of any personal items.

"Has a maid been in here?" Hurley asks Joseph.

"Naw, she said she didn't want maid service," Joseph answers. "Said she'd come and ask me personal if she needed towels or some such. Damn."

I gather from Joseph's reaction to the empty room that he did let Catherine slide on her room payment. No doubt she used her feminine wiles on him—the same way she did with Jack and every other man she'd ever met. Joseph is wilier than most, but even a crusty, old bachelor has to have a soft spot in there somewhere.

To be thorough, we search the room's drawers and closet, but Catherine is clearly a pro at covering her tracks. Even the trash cans are empty. When we're done, we thank Joseph for his cooperation and head back to Hurley's sedan.

I'm about to get into Hurley's car, when movement catches my eye from the end of the building to my right. When I look, I see David standing behind an SUV with its hatch up. Standing next to him is a trim woman, with blond hair. I recognize her as Patty Volker, our insurance agent.

"Can you believe that?" I say to no one in particular, though Hurley is the only one within hearing distance. "I'll bet he's moving in with her already."

Hurley responds with a total non sequitur: "I'm going to put out an ATL on Catherine."

"And to think I almost fell for his sad, little plea for reconciliation," I mutter.

"Ignore him," Hurley says. "He's not worth your time." With that, he takes out his cell phone to place a call.

I consider Hurley's advice and turn away from David and Patty, reaching for the passenger-side door. Something holds me back, though; and as Hurley starts talking into his phone, I let go of the car handle and look back again. The two of them are standing at the rear of the SUV, laughing, talking, and periodically touching one another with an unmistakable intimacy as they arrange items inside the car. Feeling like a lemming drawn to the cliff's edge, I start walking toward them, though I have no idea why I'm doing it, or what I'll do when I get to them. It's Patty who notices me first.

"Mattie," she says, looking very nervous all of a sudden. She has a hand on David's arm; and a second after she recognizes and acknowledges me, it drops down to her side. David turns to face me.

"Hello, Patty, David," I say. "What's going on?"

In true alpha-male surgeon style, David takes charge. "I'm moving out of here, and in with Patty, until we can get the new house built."

I hesitate a moment, wondering who the "we" is in this statement. Then I quickly decide that it doesn't matter. "You're moving in with Patty?" I say, looking at David. I shift my gaze to Patty. "I didn't realize you were renting out."

Patty shifts her feet nervously and looks up at David for help.

"She's not renting to me. We're a couple," David

says with the same level of nonchalance he might use to describe the weather. Then he adds, "I thought you knew that."

I had known it, but that doesn't make me want to let them off the hook without a little more squirming. "How would I know, David? You didn't tell me, nor did Patty."

"Well, given the way gossip spreads in this town, I just assumed. . . ." He trails off and shrugs.

Patty blushes and says, "I'm sorry, Mattie. You're right. I should have said something to you."

"You don't need to apologize, Patty," David says. "Mattie has made it very clear that I have no claims on her and she has no claims on me. We've both agreed that our romantic relationship is a thing of the past."

He's right, of course. So why does this little scene bother me so much?

Patty drops her gaze and stares at her feet, looking embarrassed. David turns to her, and in doing so, he effectively dismisses me. He lifts her chin with a finger, forcing her to look up at him. It triggers an odd, hollow sensation in my chest as I recall how sweetly romantic I thought that gesture was whenever David used it on me.

"You've got nothing to worry about," David says to Patty. "I think Mattie's feeling left out—that's all. It's hard to see happy couples, when you're not a part of one."

The hollow ache inside me quickly turns to fury. I open my mouth to defend myself, but then realize I don't have a defense. On some level, I know David has just hit a bull's-eye. All my other levels are trying to figure out how I can go all Lorena Bobbitt on his ass and make it look accidental. Then all the thoughts slip away as I feel a warm arm snake around my waist and find Hurley standing beside me.

"Hello, Doc," Hurley says, pulling me close. "Long time, no see."

"Hello, Steve." David's face darkens; I'm not sure if it's because Hurley is here, or because Hurley called him "Doc." It's probably both. These two have a complicated history—both as competitors for my affection and as doctor and patient. But even though David's face doesn't mask his true emotions very well, his voice is all professional and polite. "How are you?" he asks.

"I'm doing just great, Doc. Thanks for asking."

David's lips tighten almost imperceptibly, but it's enough for me to notice, telling me he doesn't like Hurley's little endearment. Hurley's next question makes me suspect Hurley noticed it, too.

"Who's your friend, Doc?"

David's cheek muscles twitch and he glares at Hurley for a second longer than necessary before making the introductions. "This," he says, gesturing toward Hurley, "is Detective Steve Hurley, with the Sorenson Police Department." Then he wraps an arm around Patty's waist the same way Hurley has done with mine. "And this is Patty Volker, my girlfriend and my insurance agent."

"Technically, she's *our* insurance agent," I toss out.

Hurley answers with a "Hmph"; then he says, "That must be awkward."

Patty smiles uneasily and says, "It certainly is at the moment."

"Well, then, we don't want to make things any worse than they already are," Hurley says. He looks at me and squeezes me tight before letting go and taking one of my hands in his. "Come on, babe," he says. "We need to get going."

As Hurley steers me back toward his car, leaving David and Patty in our wake, my mind momentarily turns to mush, unable to focus on anything other than our intertwined fingers and the fact that Hurley called me "babe."

"You can't let him get to you like that," Hurley says in a low voice, bringing me back into focus.

The sharp retort of the SUV's hatchback closing behind us makes me jump. "I know," I say. "I don't know why it irks me so much that he's jumped into someone else's bed already. I shouldn't be surprised, given our history."

"You're right, you shouldn't. So why does it bother you so much?"

"I don't know," I say, letting out a breath of exasperation. "I guess it's because it makes me feel duped, discarded, and insignificant."

We have reached Hurley's sedan when I hear both doors of the SUV slam closed and the engine start up. Hurley pulls me around in front of him and leans me back against the side of his car, locking me into place by positioning an arm on either side of me, his hands on the roof. He leans in close until his face is only inches from mine.

"What do you say we show them you couldn't care less what the two of them are doing?"

With Hurley's body hovering inches above mine, and his baby blues staring clear down to my soul, I can barely breathe. I manage to mutter, "How?"

Hurley bends his elbows, bringing us into full-frontal contact. His lips descend and settle on mine. For a second or two, I'm vaguely aware of the SUV driving by us very slowly. Then my mind is incapable of focusing on anything but the delicious sensations running through my body. Hurley is careful not to use any tongue, but he graces my lips with a dozen tiny butterfly nips and nibbles. Then he kisses the tip of my nose. My body feels like hot molten lava. I reach up to place my hand at the nape of his neck, determined to keep him right where he is, but he backs off before I can. Just then, the SUV guns its way out of the parking lot.

"That totally pissed him off," Hurley says in a self-satisfied tone.

I say nothing. I can't. My mind is mush. All the blood in my body seems to be centered on—and pulsating—between my legs. I stand there dumbfounded, grateful Hurley's car is behind me to hold me up.

Hurley, on the other hand, seems annoyingly unaffected by it all. As he walks around to his side of the car, he says, "What do you say, Winston? Should we go drill some more suspects?"

I have another kind of drilling in mind, but clearly I can't say so. When I have my wits about me enough, I push away from the car, open my door, and drop into the passenger seat.

I spend the time it takes us to drive to our next stop picturing Hurley and me, tanned and happy, tooling along the Florida coast inside our "Barbie and Ken Beach Cruiser."

Chapter 13

The nursing agency providing Jack Allen's home care is run out of a storefront office in a strip mall. Its overhead sign reads: FLETCHERNURSING. The interior is simply furnished with two desks—one of which is empty—a couple of file cabinets, a bookcase, and some fake plants. At the rear of the main room is a closed door, which I assume leads to a back area of the office.

Behind the one occupied desk is a man who is a prime example of the hazards of tanning beds. The skin on his face, neck, and hands is dark brown and fibrous-looking. While I guess his age to be somewhere in his mid- to late thirties, his skin and the gray in his dark hair make him look decades older. He's wearing a shirt with the sleeves rolled up and the collar open much lower than need be, and his neck and fingers are adorned with jewelry. Judging from the razor burn I see on his hairless chest, I'm guessing he's also into "manscaping." I see several travel brochures for the Caribbean mixed in with the papers on his desk, which might explain why his skin looks like worn leather.

"Hi, I'm Paul Fletcher," he says with a big smile,

flashing teeth that have been bleached into near transparency. "I'm the owner. How may I help you?"

"We're here to inquire about one of your patients, Jack Allen," Hurley says, flashing his badge.

Paul's smile fades, saving us from the blinding light of his teeth. "Oh, yes, poor Mr. Allen. What a horrible thing. How can I help you?"

"We understand one of your nurses visited Jack daily to provide care and saw him on the day he died."

"You mean Lisa Warden," Fletcher says. "She was Jack's home health aide. I was his nurse."

"Did you see Jack on the day of the fire?"

"No, I only visited Jack once or twice a week, to reassess his condition, update his care plan, and supervise Lisa."

"So when did you see him last?"

"I believe it was a couple of days before, but let me check." He gets up and walks over to one of the filing cabinets, opens the second drawer, and pulls out a file. "Yes, it was the twenty-third when I last saw him," he says upon opening the file. "Lisa saw him five days a week, sometimes six."

"Did you know about his big win at the casino?"

"Sure. Everyone pretty much knew. Jack didn't try to keep it a secret."

"What time was Ms. Warden there on the twenty-fifth?"

Fletcher consults the chart again. "According to her note, she was there from eight to nine that morning."

"May I ask where you were on the morning of the twenty-fifth?"

"Sure. I was here in the office finishing up some paperwork because I'm taking a vacation in a few days and needed to finish out my year-end billing. I got done around ten and then went home."

"Do you live alone?"

"Yes, I do," Fletcher says a bit irritably. "Why are you asking all these questions? I heard that the fire and Jack's death were accidents. Is that not so?"

"Do you have any knowledge of Ms. Warden's whereabouts after she left Mr. Allen's residence?" Hurley asks, ignoring Fletcher's question.

"I know she had two other patients she saw that morning, one at ten and one at eleven."

"On Christmas Day?" Hurley says skeptically.

"Illness knows no holidays," Fletcher shoots back.

Hurley sighs. "Can I have the names of those patients? We'll need to verify that Ms. Warden kept those appointments."

Paul shakes his head. "I can't give out that information. Privacy laws and all, you know."

Ah, yes, the ever-frustrating HIPAA laws. It's a set of rules that makes the provision of health care more of a secret than the location of CIA operatives. If bin Laden had been protected by HIPAA, he'd probably still be alive. But I've anticipated this objection.

"I understand that," I say. "I'm a nurse myself, so I respect the need for your patients' privacy. But what if you were to call them and ask them if they'd be willing to talk to us? If they give permission, that would cover you and your agency, no?"

Paul considers this, frowning. "I suppose that would be okay," he says finally. We stand there, waiting, and stare at him for a few awkward seconds, before he adds, "I'll give them a call and get back to you."

"I also need to speak with Ms. Warden," Hurley says.

"She's not in the office right now, but let me check her schedule." He pulls up a file on his computer and then says, "Today is her day off. Hold on and I'll see if she's home." He makes a call; and when Lisa Warden answers, he tells her why he's calling. He listens for a minute and then says to Hurley, "She said she can meet with you somewhere at one, if you like."

Hurley nods. "I'd like to meet her at her home."

Fletcher frowns and relays this information to Lisa. When he hangs up, he writes something on a piece of paper and hands it to Hurley. "That's her address," he says.

"One more thing, Mr. Fletcher," I say. "I'd like a copy of Jack's chart, please." Fletcher purses his lips, and I suspect he's about to throw HIPAA at us again. I head him off, though. "I'm with the medical examiner's office," I say, taking my turn to flash a badge. "If you check the state regs, you'll find that the ME's office is allowed complete access to the medical record of a deceased, when the death is suspicious. HIPAA doesn't apply."

Fletcher looks skeptical of my claim.

"I'll be happy to show you the actual regulation, if I can borrow your computer."

Finally he shrugs and says, "I'll need some time to copy it."

"I'll take it to my office and copy it for you," I offer. He doesn't have to let me take his original chart out of the office, but I'm hoping he either doesn't know that, or doesn't care. "By the time I bring it back, you should have some answers for us from those other patients."

Fletcher is clearly annoyed by this manipulation; but in the end, he capitulates, allowing Hurley and me to leave with the chart in hand.

Prior to hitting up the nursing agency, Hurley arranged for an officer to pick up Serena Vasquez and bring her to the police station. She is waiting there for us, along with her twin boys and the neighbor's daughter she is again watching. We discover Serena is in the interrogation/conference room with Junior, while the kids are hanging out by themselves in the break room, surveying the contents of the station refrigerator. When we walk in, I hear one of them say, "Are these bullets?" I dash over and drag them away, shutting the refrigerator door.

Hurley rolls his eyes and says, "Apparently, there isn't anyone else here to watch the kids. Do you mind staying with them until I can take over for Junior and send him out here?"

I look over at the three kids, who are all standing in front of a large wall poster that shows a teenage girl puffing on a joint with the caption *I'm not as think as you stoned I am.*

"Sure," I say, thinking, *How bad can it be?* I check my wallet for change and decide to herd the kids to the vending machine room down the hallway and treat them to some unhealthy snacks. "Come on, you guys," I say. "Who wants snacks?"

I'm answered with a chorus of "I do"; and like the Pied Piper of Hamelin, I lead the little rats out of town. When we get to the vending machines, the kids all line up in front of them. Their eyes are as big as saucers; their fingers are splayed on the glass.

"What's your name?" I ask the twin closest to me.

"I want Oreos," he says.

"'I-want-Oreos' is a silly name," I counter; at which point, he shoots me a dirty look.

Then his brother pipes up and says, "His name is Angelino."

Clearly a misnomer.

"And mine is Oro. That's almost like Oreo, so can I have some Oreos?"

Angelino shoves his brother and says, "I asked first." Oro shoves back. Before I know it, the two boys are engaged in an all-out brawl, while the girl backs into a corner watching them. She's clutching a Barbie doll in her arms. It's a vintage Barbie, the kind with ugly joints and a 1960s ponytail. I suspect it came from a yard sale. I'm tempted to warn the girl about falling for that whole "Barbie and Ken myth," but I don't. She's young yet; there's still plenty of time for her dreams to be shattered.

I ignore the boys, walk up to the machine, plug in some change, and buy a package of Oreos. Then I turn to the girl. "What's your name?" I ask.

"Susie."

"Do you like Oreos?"

She nods, looking shy.

I hand her the package. "Then this is your reward for behaving."

She takes the package, and the boys, sensing that something momentous has just occurred, break up their little tango and glare at me.

"We asked first," Angelino says. "We should get the cookies."

"Yeah," Oro chimes in.

"Well, neither of you will get anything, because you clearly don't know how to behave."

I'm feeling pretty smug until Angelino walks up and kicks me in the shin. Oro goes over to Susie, shoves her, and grabs the Oreos and the Barbie doll, though Susie's grip on her dream is much stronger than Angelino anticipated. All he comes away with are the cookies and Barbie's head. Susie is left crying in the corner as the two boys run from the room and down the hall to the men's room.

I'm sure they think this is a safe haven for now, that no reasonable woman would follow them into a men's room. They may be right, but it's a huge miscalculation on their part to assume I'm a reasonable woman.

I bang the door open and charge in after them, just

in time to see Angelino drop Barbie's head in the toilet. I also see Junior, who is standing in front of a urinal, finishing off his business.

Junior whips his head around and looks at me with a shocked expression. Unfortunately, other parts of his anatomy whip around as well. Clearly confused, he looks from me to the twins and then back at me again, before he realizes he's still holding his man muscle and has just dribbled pee on his shoes. Flustered, he quickly tucks things away and zips up. Meanwhile, his face is turning a shade of neon red. ·

I walk over to the boys, grab an arm on each of them, and start to yank them out of the stall. Angelino, who, I'm guessing, always has to have the last word, makes one final statement by reaching over and pushing down the toilet's handle. I shove him aside and make a desperate grab for the doll's head, saying a silent prayer of gratitude over the fact that whoever used the toilet last had the decency to flush it. Someone also felt the need to use a sanitizer in the bowl recently. Unfortunately, it's the type that turns the bowl water blue. I manage to grab Barbie's fake blond ponytail and pluck her head to safety just as it is about to be dispatched to goldfish heaven. However, it's not before the water has tinted her hair a lovely shade of royal blue.

"Everything okay, Mattie?" Junior asks, his face still blazing.

From off in the distance, we can hear Susie still screaming as if someone had ripped her head off rather than her doll's. The two boys are standing in the corner, staring at me all big-eyed, like I'm a crazy woman.

"Nothing a tubal ligation couldn't have fixed," I say, staring down the two hellions in the corner. "Those two are yours. If it was up to me, I'd just shoot them if they pull anything else, but I'll leave that decision for you."

Oro lets out a puff of a laugh at this; but when I narrow my gaze at him, his smile fades fast. He bites his lip and looks over at Junior nervously. Junior just shrugs at him, letting his hand fall casually onto the butt of his gun. Oro swallows hard and tries to shrink himself into the wall behind him.

I walk over to the sink and rinse Barbie's head, using a bit of hand soap to shampoo her hair. The end result is a very punk-looking Barbie. "I'll try to calm down the other one for you," I tell Junior as I dry Barbie's hair with a paper towel. Then, with one last glare at the hellions, I exit the bathroom and return to the vending room, where I find Susie slumped in a corner, still screaming.

I kneel down in front of her, take Barbie's body from her hand, and squeeze the head back onto it. "Here you go. Good as new," I say, handing it back to her.

"Her hair is blue," Susie whines, hiccupping sobs as she stares at the doll.

"Yeah, well, um, that's because she's secretly one of those people from *Avatar*," I say, praying the kid has seen the movie. Apparently, she has, because she stops crying and gives Barbie a thoughtful look.

Junior appears in the doorway with the two hoodlums in tow. "Hurley wanted me to send you into the conference room," he says.

Thank God. Parsing murder suspects is nothing compared to handling unruly kids. "Good luck with this bunch," I tell Junior. I start to leave, but then I turn back. "You might want to empty the ammo in your gun, just in case you're tempted." And with that parting shot, I head for the conference room.

* * *

Hurley is waiting for me outside of the interrogation room and we enter together. Serena Vasquez is sitting on one side of the table and she looks frightened out of her wits. Her eyes are huge and brimming with tears; her hands are trying to choke the life out of a wad of tissues; her entire body is rocking back and forth in her chair. Hurley and I take seats across from her and Hurley hits a button beneath the table that starts a camera rolling.

"I don't think you were totally honest with us when we talked to you before," Hurley says, leaning across the table and pinning Serena down with those laser-like blue eyes of his.

"No?" Serena says as a tear rolls down her cheek.

"No. Does the name Hector Vasquez ring a bell?"

Serena's flinch is so slight that it would be easy to miss. But I don't, and I'm pretty sure Hurley doesn't either. She stares back at him with a deer-in-the-headlights expression—clearly unsure of what, if anything, she should do or say at this point.

"This Hector Vasquez was involved in a very serious traffic accident down in Texas," Hurley pushes.

I suspect this is a lie, since Hurley said earlier that the van of illegals was pulled over, not involved in an accident. But I recognize the brilliance of him making the claim when Serena cracks.

"An accident?" she says, sounding panicked. "Is Hector okay?"

"He's fine," Hurley says, leaning back in his chair. "He's being held by the authorities down there pending his deportation back to Mexico."

When Serena hears this, her shoulders sag. Her expression changes to one of sadness and defeat. Recognizing the exposure of her underbelly, Hurley goes in for the kill.

"He's claiming to be your husband, Serena. Is that true?"

Serena nods, staring at her hands. Her tears flow freely now. "Yes," she says.

"He also told the authorities in Texas that you paid money to help him get into the United States . . . a lot of money . . . fifty grand, to be exact."

Hurley waits, letting the words hang. Serena's face contorts as she analyzes her position and the consequences of what she's just heard. The silence grows for a minute or more. When she finally speaks, it is with a surprising degree of anger.

"They cannot send him back there!" she spits out. "Please, you have to do something. We have worked too hard, waited too long for this. And I can never get that kind of money again."

"Where did you get it from this time?" I ask.

"Mr. Jack gave it to me."

"He gave it to you, or you took it?" Hurley retorts.

Serena turns and glares at him. "He gave it to me, I swear. Mr. Jack and I talked a lot about life in Mexico and how hard Hector worked to get me and the boys out of there. It is very dangerous there these days with the drug wars. Mr. Jack knew how much the boys and I missed and worried about Hector. So after he won big at the casino, he insisted that I take money from him and use it to pay a coyote to bring Hector here. He said we were good people, and because I never asked for the money, he wanted to help us out."

Hurley raises a skeptical brow. "You expect us to believe that Jack just gave you fifty grand out of the kindness of his heart?"

"I expect you to believe that is what he wanted to do," Serena says, looking a bit indignant. "But I insisted on paying him back."

"Sure you did," I say with no small amount of sarcasm.

"I signed a note for it," Serena insists.

I have to admit I'm impressed with how quickly she came up with a plausible lie, and I'm pretty sure I know what's coming next.

"And I'm betting that now you're going to tell us that note got lost in Jack's house fire," I say. "How very convenient for you."

If looks could kill, I'd be stretched out on Izzy's table right now, taking an eternal nap. I'm rethinking my position on Serena's guilt. If Oro and Angelino's temperaments are any indication of a genetic pass-along from their mother, it's not hard for me to imagine Serena killing for money, especially if it meant getting someone here to help her with the little demons. I'm thinking things are looking good for Hurley and me to crack this case and tie up most of the loose ends before we head for Florida. That is, until Serena makes her next comment.

"Mr. Jack's papers may have been burned up in his house," she says. "But I still have my copy. Take me back to my house and I will show it to you."

Chapter 14

Fifteen minutes later, Hurley and I are headed back to Serena's house, with Serena and all three kids in tow—though they are all behind us in Junior's cruiser, thanks to my description of how exciting it is to ride inside a real police car. This comment elicited a look of promised paybacks from Junior, but he accepted his mission with the courageous resignation of a soldier headed into battle. He turns on the lights and siren for a block or two, and I'm betting it's to shut up the kids, drown them out, or both.

"It's a bummer if Vasquez really has this note," Hurley says. "I thought we were close to winding this thing up."

"So did I."

"Guess that means we're still on for the casino tonight, then."

"Looks that way."

"What time do you want me to pick you up? Is six-thirty okay?"

I brace myself for what's to come. "I want to take my own car."

Hurley makes a face like he just tasted something disgusting. "You want to drive up there in a hearse?"

"That's what I drive these days, so yeah."

Hurley rolls his eyes and sighs. "Fine," he says. "Then *you* can pick *me* up at six-thirty."

"I don't think you understand," I say, looking apologetic. "No one needs to pick anyone up. I want to drive myself. Alone."

Hurley stares at me, unblinking, as several beats of silence punctuate the awkwardness of the moment. "You mean take separate cars?" he says finally.

I nod.

"That's a huge waste of gas. Why would you want to do that?"

"Because I'm thinking I might want to hang around there for a while once we're done with our official business."

Hurley's eyes narrow with suspicion. "Hang around? Why?"

I shrug. "I might want to try my hand at a little more gambling, just for fun."

"Gambling is a huge waste of money."

"Not if you win, and I did pretty well last time."

"Which makes it that much more dangerous for you," Hurley counters, clearly exasperated.

"I'll be all right. I'm thinking Joe Whitehorse will have some free time after our dinner and he can show me the ropes. I'm sure he'll . . ." I hesitate, searching for the right words. "I'm sure he'll keep an eye on me," I conclude, with a sly wink.

"You need to maintain a professional distance," Hurley grumbles.

"Don't worry. Everything will be strictly platonic . . . at least for now."

Hurley's grip on the wheel tightens almost imperceptibly.

"So meet you there around seven?"

Hurley's eyes are the color of a stormy sky. "Fine," he says.

We have arrived at Serena's house and he yanks the wheel irritably to the right to park, hitting the curb in the process. As soon as Serena and the kids are unloaded, Junior peels out. I can only imagine the hell he endured on the ride over and wonder if he'll ever speak to me again.

Once inside the house, Serena grabs a metal lockbox high on a shelf, opens it, and takes out two stapled pieces of paper, which not only contain a note for the fifty grand, identifying it as a loan with a set number of years for payback, but a notary seal for the signatures. I half-expect Serena to look smug as we examine the paperwork. Instead, she looks remorseful, sad, and a little bit frightened. I realize I may have misjudged her, perhaps because I based that judgment on my experience with the twins from hell.

Hurley takes the promissory note, telling Serena he will make a copy and return the original to her once he has checked out the notary. It will keep Serena on edge a little longer, but I can tell Hurley suspects, as I do, that everything will check out, which means we are back to square one.

Ten minutes before our scheduled appointment with Lisa Warden, Hurley and I leave Serena behind to fret and wrangle the kids. We head back to his car, and just as we get in, Hurley's cell rings. I can tell from his end of the conversation that it's Paul Fletcher calling with the names of the other patients Lisa Warden saw on the morning of Jack's death. Hurley writes the information down and tucks it into his pocket. The way things are going, I'm pretty sure we'll have Warden ruled out by day's end. That means we're going to have to start knocking on Jack's neighbors' doors. Not only am I beginning to think we won't solve this murder before we head for Florida, I'm starting to wonder if we'll ever solve it. So much of the evidence has been compromised because of the fire, and I fear the list of people with opportunity, means, and motive is growing frighteningly long.

As Hurley starts the car, he says, "Junior sure lit out of here in a hurry."

I fill him in on the kids' escapades back at the station.

"It sounds like they were quite a handful," he says.

"That's the understatement of the year. Five minutes with them made me rethink the whole idea of having kids."

Hurley shoots me a sidelong glance. "Don't say that. You have to have kids. They're in your plan, remember? Besides, I can just imagine a little Mattie running around with a head of blond curls and big blue eyes. I'm guessing she'll be in trouble a lot, but she'll get away with it because she's so adorable."

Hurley's words make my heart ache. It's ironic that he envisions a little me running around, because I've fantasized a time or two about having a dark-haired son with Hurley's baby blues. Yet, fantasy is all it can ever be. Between the kiss earlier at the motel, and this talk about kids and the future, I feel as if the lines demarcating our relationship are blurring dangerously.

There's no denying my attraction to Hurley, and I'm pretty sure he's attracted to me as well. And that makes me wonder if our current working arrangement is one we can live with for the long term. I enjoy his friendship and the chance to see him on a regular basis; and on some level, that fills a big need for me. But the way we get caught up in our need to flirt with one another is starting to mess seriously with my head. If we're going to make a success of this working relationship, the flirting stuff is going to have to cease.

"You've got to stop doing this, Hurley," I say.

"Doing what?"

"Implying things. Hinting at a relationship you and I can't have. Planting kisses on me when I least expect it, or kissing me at all, for that matter."

"I was just trying to help you out and piss off David."

"Really? Were you? Is that all that was behind that kiss?"

"Yes." He looks over at me; and as I stare back at him, his hands tighten on the steering wheel again. When he looks back at the road, his lips are pinched tightly. "Okay, maybe there was a little something else behind it, but you have to admit it was kind of fun." He shoots me a worried look. "Wasn't it?"

I smile. "It kind of was," I admit. "But that's the problem."

"Is that why you want to drive yourself tonight? Because if it is, I promise I'll be on my very best behavior."

"That's one reason," I admit. "But not the only one. I need to do more things on my own. I need to learn to *be* on my own. I have this newfound independence and I want to enjoy it."

Hurley frowns but says nothing more.

To fill the ensuing awkward silence, I say, "So what do you know about this aide we're going to talk to?"

"Her name is Lisa Warden. We did a background check on her and it came back clean."

"She doesn't sound very promising as a suspect."

"Probably not," Hurley agrees as we arrive at Lisa's address. "But maybe she can shed light on some of the other people in Jack's life, or on the timeline surrounding his death."

* * *

Lisa Warden lives in a small, one-bedroom apartment in an eight-unit building on the east side of town. It's the spreading end of town, where strip malls and fast-food chains are cropping up and slowly expanding the town's limits.

Lisa herself is spreading a bit, too—something I can empathize with. She looks to be in her late twenties and has short hair, which is spiky on top, in a shade of red not found in nature. Dishwater blond roots and eyebrows give away her natural coloring. Her apartment is furnished with what looks like garage sale purchases—nothing matches anything else—and a bookshelf in one corner is made out of cinder blocks and varying lengths of boards.

Lisa directs us to her couch, which is covered with a blanket. As I settle in, I can feel a spring poking me from somewhere below. She takes the only other seat in the room, a large overstuffed chair, which is also mostly hidden by a blanket. Parts of the underlying structure are visible and I can see that it's covered in a hideous floral weave pattern, which looks shredded. The source of the shredding becomes apparent when a large black cat with white paws, and a white patch beneath his chin, strolls into the room. In true cat fashion, he sits, eyes Hurley and me with disdain, and then proceeds to lick himself as if he's the only one in the room.

"That's my cat, 'Tux,' short for Tuxedo," Lisa says when she sees us eyeing the creature. Apparently, she notices Hurley's nervousness, because she then adds, "He's very friendly."

"I'm not fond of cats," Hurley says, inching closer to me and farther from Tux.

Tux seems to sense he's the focus of our attention, because he stops licking himself and eyes us again. Then he gets up and strolls straight over to Hurley, rubbing against his feet. I can practically feel the fear coming off Hurley—something that amuses me to no end. But in order to get things rolling, I figure I'll have to intervene.

"He really, *really* doesn't like cats," I say to Lisa. "Would you mind sticking Tux in another room until we're done?"

"Oh, sure. No problem." Lisa gets up and scoops Tux into her arms. She walks him over to her bedroom, which is just off the living room, and tosses him inside. When she shuts the door, Hurley shoots me a grateful look. But when he takes a pen and a small notebook from his jacket pocket, he starts clicking the pen over and over again—a sign of nervousness, impatience, or both.

"You said you wanted to talk about Jack Allen," Lisa says, once the cat is secured. "What a horrible thing for him to die like that." She plops back into her chair and rubs at her nose a couple of times, presumably to rid herself of errant cat hairs.

"How long have you been working for Mr. Allen?" Hurley asks her.

"A little over a year now. My agency assigned me to him last October."

"What, exactly, did you do for him?" Hurley asks.

"I visit him five or six days a week to help him with his skin care, his baths, his wounds . . . that sort of stuff."

"Wounds?" Hurley asks.

"He was prone to bedsores, as many paraplegics are. He had a large one on his coccyx that had to be surgically debrided last year. I've been working very hard on it for the past year, trying a variety of different salves and dressings. And I'm happy to say that it's now only about as big as a dime, when it used to be nearly three inches wide."

She smiles with pride as she says this, but then her face

falls. "Though I guess it doesn't make much difference now, does it?" She rubs at her face again, and this time I'm not sure if it's cat hair or tearful sniffles she's trying to abate.

As a momentary, awkward silence fills the room, the cat uses it to let us know he isn't getting the attention he feels he deserves. The bedroom door starts to rattle; and when I look over at it, I see a black-and-white paw in the gap between it and the floor, curled around the door bottom, shaking it. I feel Hurley tense up beside me, as if the creature could somehow tear the door down and come after him.

"Tux, knock it off!" Lisa yells. Amazingly, the door rattling stops.

"I used to work in the OR at Mercy," I say, hoping to draw Hurley's attention back to the topic at hand. "I saw Jack's decubitus when he came in last year. If your care got that monster healed down to dime size, you must be very good."

"Thanks," she says, giving me a wan smile. Then she shudders and adds, "Please tell me he died in his sleep of smoke inhalation or something like that, rather than being trapped and burned in the flames."

Hurley hesitates before saying, "I take it you knew about Mr. Allen's big win at the casino a few months ago."

Lisa frowns at his obvious avoidance, but she lets it go. "Most people knew. Personally, I think he should have been a bit more discreet, to keep all the greedy bastards at bay."

Hurley gives her a questioning look.

"Oh, you know how it is," she says. "When you come into a large chunk of money like that, suddenly everyone has a hand out. People were coming to him all the time, asking for help. And that Albright woman . . ."

She rolls her eyes, letting us know what she thinks of Catherine.

"I take it you don't like her," Hurley says.

"Well, could she be any more transparent?" Lisa snorts. "I mean, she just happens to appear right around the time he won his money, and she's all over him like he's some kind of stud or something." She winces, looking embarrassed. "I mean, it's not like he was ugly or anything, and he was a truly nice person, but come on. The guy was paralyzed from the waist down and required a ton of care and help. If you ask me, Catherine Albright is nothing but a gold-digging vulture. She was always asking him for money, and hinting around that they should get married. I'm sure if he'd ever given in and done the deed, she would have found a way to bump him off."

Hurley and I exchange a look before Hurley asks, "How did Jack handle all the money requests?"

"You mean from Catherine? Or all the others?"

"Both."

She shrugs. "He was generous to a point. He was always giving that nephew of his money for something, and I think he gave one of his neighbors some money to help him out when he lost his job and fell behind on his mortgage. But I'm only there for a couple of hours each day, so I don't know what went on when I wasn't around."

"Do you know the name of this neighbor?"

Lisa scrunches her face in thought. "I think it was George Smithers, or Smothers . . . something like that."

As Hurley scribbles the name in his little notebook, he asks, "When's the last time you saw Mr. Allen?"

"Christmas Day, the morning of the fire." She hesitates, looking off to the side. "We got into an argument and I cut my visit short as a result. If only I'd stayed there a little longer, maybe . . ." Her eyes tear up and she rubs irritably at her face.

"What time were you there that morning?"

"I got there at eight-thirty and left about an hour later," she says with a sniffle.

"Was anyone else there?"

"No."

"What did you argue about?" I ask.

"Jack's drinking. I kept telling him he needed to cut back, but he kept insisting that he only drank once in a while. I knew better, of course. I saw all the empties in his trash." She pauses and sighs heavily. "I suppose I understand it, given everything that happened to him. Life certainly has dealt him a shitty hand lately, what with his paralysis and his sister's death. The casino win seemed to be a turning point, but now I think it might have used up all the luck he had left."

Hurley says, "What made you think Catherine Albright would have tried to . . . How did you word it? Bump Jack off if he'd married her?"

Lisa gives him a *duh* look. "It was obvious to me that she didn't really care about him, only his money."

"Was their relationship sexual?"

"Not in the conventional sense. Jack had no sensation in his genitals, and I'm pretty sure he was incapable of sustaining an erection." She pauses and gives Hurley an irreverent arch of her eyebrow. "Of course, that doesn't mean he couldn't please a woman."

To my amusement—and Lisa's, if her sly smile is any indication—Hurley looks away, clears his throat, and blushes along the tops of his ears before asking his next question.

"Did you observe any behavior between Catherine

and him that would suggest something like that was going on?"

Lisa shakes her head. "Not when I was there. Catherine was all about spending as little time as possible with Jack himself, and as much as possible with his money."

"Speaking of money, how do you get paid? Did Jack pay you directly, or was it all handled through the company you work for?"

Lisa looks momentarily taken aback by the question, and curious as to why Hurley has asked it. "My agency pays me. I assume they billed Jack for my services."

"Is there anyone else you know of who might have tried to harm Jack for his money?"

She scrubs her face with her hands, hesitating before she answers. "I'm not sure I understand what you mean," she says finally. "How would hurting Jack gain anyone any of his money? Other than the nephew, of course, since he's likely to inherit. I mean, Catherine might have a claim if they were married, but I'm pretty sure they aren't." She pauses, and a look of enlightenment crosses her face. "Unless Jack left a will of some sort," she adds.

Hurley says, "We haven't found evidence of a will at this point, but it appears Jack kept a large sum of cash money in his house. Anyone who knew that could have taken the money and burned the house down to hide the evidence."

Lisa looks shocked by this revelation. "Are you saying the fire wasn't an accident?"

"We are looking into all possible scenarios," Hurley says vaguely.

"How large of a sum of money are we talking?"

"Big enough."

Lisa shrugs. "If he had a ton of cash lying around the

house, I never saw it," she says. "But it wouldn't surprise me if he did."

"Why's that?" Hurley asks.

"The guy was very antiestablishment. You know the type, always harping on about the ineptitudes of the government and how big corporations are out to screw the little guys. I wouldn't be surprised if he included banks in that group."

Hurley nods, closes his notebook, and stuffs it and his pen back into his pocket. "I guess that's all we need for now," he says, getting up.

It's my cue to do the same. But before we head out, my bladder prompts me to ask Lisa if I can use her bathroom.

"Sure," she says, gesturing toward the door.

I scurry in, shut the door, and relieve myself. As I'm sitting on the toilet, I can't help noticing how messy Lisa's bathroom is. I'm no great housekeeper, but by Lisa's standards, I figure I'm as much of a neat freak as my mother, who has a terrible case of OCD and whose house is more sterile than the OR where I used to work. The tub has a scum ring, which looks permanently etched into the fiberglass; there is mold growing on the shower curtain; the sink is littered with dried globs of toothpaste and myriad short, stubby black hairs. The grout in between the floor tiles is darkened with grime.

After flushing, I use toilet paper to turn on the sink faucet and rinse my hands, forgoing the bar of soap, which has a couple of short, curly, dark hairs dried into it. I wipe my hands on my pants when I'm done, since the towel looks like it's been hanging there for well over a year. I head back out to the living area.

I find Hurley standing by the door, looking impatient and wary: Tux is door rattling again, and it's clear Hurley wants to escape before the cat manages to claw down the door.

"I'm ready," I say, hurrying toward him.

Hurley opens the door. But before he steps out, he turns to Lisa and asks one last question. "Can you account for your whereabouts after you left Jack's house on the day of the fire?"

At first, I'm confused by this question, since we already know Lisa's schedule that day from our talk with Paul Fletcher. Then I realize Hurley is simply double-checking the information.

Lisa looks insulted by the question, and the tone of her answer confirms this. "I had two other patients I had to see that morning," she says, tight-lipped. "If you want specifics, you'll have to check with my agency. I can't share names with you because of the HIPAA laws."

As if to avenge his mistress's reputation, Tux steps up his efforts on the door. Now even I think he might manage to escape. He rattles it with the ferocity of a tiger and lets out a howl that makes my hair stand on end. I turn to Hurley to say, "Let's go," but he's already out the door in a half run to the car.

Chapter 15

"You ready to go talk to Jack's neighbors?" Hurley asks, once we're back on the road.

"Sure, but I need a bite to eat and a little more caffeine first."

We head for the coffee shop and order sandwiches: some fancy thing on weird-looking bread, with turkey and a sun-dried tomato paste for me, and a basic tuna on a hard roll for Hurley. I check in with Izzy while we eat and tell him I'll be back in the office sometime around three. He lets us know that the ID on Donald Strommen is still pending, but he hopes to hear from the dentist sometime in the next hour or two. Hurley calls the station and gets the proper name, address, and basic DMV information for Jack's neighbor, George Smothers, and to see if there is any more information on the neighbor named Gatling who Serena had mentioned the day before.

We leave the coffee shop with a sugar-free almond latte for me and a tall black coffee for Hurley. We also leave with two pieces of cinnamon coffee cake, an indulgence I justify by reminding myself of how good I did ordering the sugar-free flavoring in my latte. Since we don't have far to go, we sit in the car in the parking lot for a few minutes, scarfing down our cake and sipping our drinks.

When we turn onto the street for George Smothers's house, my eyes are drawn to what's left of Jack's. Blackened studs rise up from the ground on one side, looking like the ribs of a carcass, and the remaining siding is scorched and melted in places. Plywood covers the holes where the windows used to be, a blue tarp serves as a temporary roof, and police tape surrounds what's left of the building. There is a warning sign for asbestos posted near the front door.

The rest of the street is lined with modest homes—most of which are still cheerfully decorated for the holiday, providing a stark contrast to Jack's burnt-out shell. When we pull up in front of Smothers's home, it's apparent from the appearance of the place that the man has fallen on hard times. It's a small Cape Cod with white wooden siding that's badly in need of a paint job. The roof is missing a number of shingles, the front windows are cracked and have plastic sheeting stapled to the inside of them—the poor man's insulation against the winter cold—and the detached single-car garage beside the house is leaning at a precarious angle.

Mr. Smothers meets us at the door. After some quick introductions and a brief explanation of why we are here, he invites us in out of the cold. He is a small, balding man in his midforties, something I never would have guessed if we hadn't learned it from his DMV record. Despite the season, Smothers's skin is tanned into a dark, leathery state. That, combined with the rounded stoop of his shoulders, makes him look much older. The inside of his house is neat and sparsely furnished with worn but comfortable-looking items. The wood floors are scratched and long ago lost any sheen they might have had; the walls all look in need of a paint job. In the living room is an older-model color TV—no fancy flat screens here.

Smothers directs us to the kitchen, which, like the rest of the place, is old, worn, and cozy. A teakettle sits on the stove, with steam seeping out its spout.

"I was about to have a cup of coffee," Smothers says, pointing to a jar of instant granules on the counter next to a mug and a spoon. "Can I get either of you a cup, or some tea, or hot chocolate?"

I left my half-finished latte in the car, knowing it will likely be cold by the time I get back to it. Smothers's offer sounds good, but I loathe instant coffee. I'm also not much of a tea drinker. Yet, something about Smothers's demeanor strikes a soft spot in my heart. I sense that accepting his hospitality would matter to him.

"Hot chocolate sounds delicious," I say, smiling. "And it will be a nice hedge against the cold. Thank you."

I'm rewarded with a huge smile from Smothers, who takes a package of instant hot cocoa out of a cupboard and dumps it into a mug. Hurley passes, so Smothers adds the hot water to his mug and mine and brings both to the kitchen table, where Hurley and I are already seated.

As I stir my instant cocoa, Hurley starts the questioning. "Mr. Smothers, as I explained to you, we are talking to anyone who knew Jack Allen. What can you tell us?"

Smothers wraps his hands around his coffee mug and scrutinizes us for a moment. "I'm his neighbor and a friend. I've known him for about ten years. It's a shitty thing that happened to him—dying in a fire like that." He pauses and takes a sip of his coffee, while Hurley and I exchange looks. Once Smothers has swallowed, he continues speaking. "I'm guessing the fire wasn't an accident, or you two wouldn't be looking into his death this way."

"There are some irregularities," Hurley says. "But our investigation is still ongoing. You knew about Jack's win at the casino a few months back?"

Smothers shrugs. "The whole neighborhood knew."

"I understand that you approached Jack about a loan of some sort."

"So you know about that," Smothers says.

Hurley nods. I sip my hot chocolate, which is surprisingly good.

"Yeah, I asked him to loan me some money so I could pay up on my mortgage," Smothers says. "My wife, Carol, she got that ovary cancer last year. She died a couple of months ago. I run a lawn care business, and being self-employed . . . well, money gets tight and the only insurance we could afford didn't cover much."

"I'm sorry," Hurley says.

"Yeah, me too," Smothers says. "She was a good woman."

I feel sorry for Smothers, too. Individual policies often cost an arm and a leg in premiums and cover less than your average hospital gown. Most people who don't have a job that provides health benefits can't afford to get sick. At times I wonder if the government is supporting the labor market by keeping health care costs high, but those thoughts make me sound too much like Arnie's foil-hat conspiracy friends.

Smothers stares into his coffee cup for a few seconds, lost in whatever memories he has. "Anyway," he continues, "the medical bills added up, and before we knew it, the bank was trying to take away my house because we were behind on the payments. So I went to Jack to ask for help."

"And?" Hurley asks.

"And he loaned me enough to keep the bank at bay . . . for now."

"You say he loaned it to you. Were you supposed to pay it back?"

"We worked out an arrangement for me to earn it back by taking care of his yard for him, mowing and weeding in the spring and summer, snow and ice removal in the winter. Jack was keeping a record of each time I did something, and he attached a dollar amount to it, subtracting that from my balance."

"Do you have a copy of that?"

Smothers shakes his head. "I trusted Jack to keep track of things. To be honest, I was so grateful to him for helping us out that I would have kept doing his yard for him for the rest of his life for free. Jack was a good man, fair-minded, kind, and generous. He understood the pressure Carol and I were under, and I think he knew how hard it was for me to come to him in the first place. He said he would love to help us out more by paying some of our medical bills and such, but that he needed to keep most of his money for his own care. I understood that better than some might. Health care ain't cheap."

"How much did Jack give you initially?"

"Five grand. It was more than I asked for, but he insisted, saying he needed someone to tend to his property anyway, and to consider it a form of prepayment."

"And do you know how much you still owed?"

"Most of it," Smothers admits, looking sheepish.

"And your medical debts?" I ask.

He looks at me with an expression of betrayal, making me wonder if he's insulted by the subtle implication, or if he thought the hot chocolate was a bribe of some sort. "I still owe the hospital and the doctors a lot of money, if that's what you mean," he says testily. "But I've worked out payment plans, and I'm paying it off a bit at a time. I imagine I'll be paying it off for the rest of my life," he adds bitterly.

Hurley says, "Where were you on the morning of the fire?"

Smothers takes another sip of his coffee, staring at us over the top of his mug. "I was here, at home," he says when he's done. "And yes, before you ask, I was alone."

"Do you know if any of your other neighbors asked Jack for money?" Hurley asks.

"You'd have to ask them," Smothers says in classic, taciturn Midwestern style. "We're all friendly on this street, but people tend to talk only about the superficial stuff. It's a small town, you know. You got to mind your own business, or before you know it, everyone else is in it."

Don't I know it.

Hurley thanks Smothers for his time; and after I gulp down the rest of my hot chocolate, we leave. As we negotiate the crumbling stairs of Smothers's front porch, Hurley nods toward a gray ranch across the street and says, "Gatling's house is that one."

As we head across the street, Hurley says, "So what do you think about Smothers?"

"I don't know. He certainly has motive, but he seems broken and resigned to me rather than ruthless."

"You feel sorry for him."

"Yeah, I suppose I do. He's had a rough time of it lately."

"You can't let your emotions get in the way of the truth, Winston."

"What truth? We don't know anything for sure. Besides, he had little to gain by killing Jack—unless he knew the cash was stashed in the house, and there's no evidence of that."

"There's no evidence to say he didn't know, either. And killing Jack eliminates his debt," Hurley argues.

"Five grand hardly seems like much of a motive when you consider that he probably owes tens of thousands to the hospital and doctors. If he was suspected of blowing up the hospital's financial records, you might convince me. But otherwise, I don't see him killing someone in cold blood."

Gatling's house is in better shape than Smothers's. The yard appears well kept, though the overall charm is hampered by the three cars up on blocks in the driveway. I remember someone saying that Gatling talked to Jack about investing in an auto repair business. I wonder if he might have an off-site garage somewhere.

"Does this Gatling guy have a job?" I ask Hurley as we approach the front door.

"He was working at Gullen's auto repair shop until about a month ago, but they fired him for missing work and showing up drunk a couple of times."

We knock on the door and ring the doorbell, both of which produce no results. I head for a front window and peer inside. The house looks lived-in, but it's dark inside, and no one appears to be home. Hurley and I circle the house in opposite directions, looking through the other windows until we meet up in the backyard.

"Nothing?" Hurley asks me.

"No signs of life." Two trash cans are located at the back end of the driveway and I lift the lids on both to look inside. One contains nothing; the other is filled with empty beer and vodka bottles. "Interesting," I say.

"This looks like Jack's garbage. A sign of the economic times, I suppose. I've heard that people drink more when there's a recession."

"They do, and the current economic state means our list of suspects will just keep growing," Hurley says, shaking his head and sighing. "I'm beginning to wonder if we'll ever solve this case."

Chapter 16

Hurley and I head back to the police station. Once inside, he checks in with Jonas Kriedeman, the station's evidence tech and all-around guy Friday. Jonas is a twenty-something guy who at one time aspired to obtain a college degree in criminal justice, with an eye toward becoming a cop. However, because of his small build and a bad case of asthma, he couldn't pass the physical for the police academy. Then his girlfriend turned up pregnant and left a month after giving birth, leaving her baby daughter behind. As a result, Jonas became a single dad three years ago, forcing him to drop out of school and take whatever job he could get. His mom helps him with day care and such, and the local police department took him on in his current capacity. I've heard he's still pursuing a degree part-time; but for now, he's a valuable addition to our crime investigation team, helping to process scenes and collect evidence, some of which Arnie analyzes in our office, and some of which gets sent to the crime lab in Madison.

"Got anything for me?" Hurley asks him.

"I do. I searched Brian Denver's car and found a

bunch of extra clothes, which I sent off to the Madison lab just in case any of them might have been the ones he was wearing when he set the fire."

"*If* he set the fire," I say.

"Well, I also found a gas can in the car," Jonas says. "I sent it to the lab, too." He shifts his attention back to Hurley. "I checked on Jack Allen's mortgage, like you asked, and found that it was with a company down in Chicago. Jack owed just over a hundred and fifty grand on it when he won his big payday at the casino. He paid the whole thing off a month later."

"That accounts for some of the money," Hurley says. "But there's still a lot of it missing. Anything on the phone and e-mail records?"

"Yep, here you go." Jonas hands him a file. "I've identified some of the numbers for you. Not sure if it will help much, since they are all numbers we'd expect to find: the nursing agency, Brian Denver, the house-keeper, and some neighbors. There were no calls on Christmas Eve or Christmas Day. And his e-mails are pretty tame stuff."

Hurley takes the file and hands Jonas the agreement between Jack and Serena. "Do me a favor and check with the notary on this to see if it's legit. Then make a copy of it for our files and give me back the original."

"Will do."

As Jonas heads off, Hurley looks at me and says, "I'm going to look this stuff over to see if anything leaps out. You're welcome to help, if you want."

"Actually, I think I'll head back to my office and check in with Izzy. He was expecting a confirmation on Donald Strommen's ID. Then I'm going to copy and look over Jack's chart. I don't expect I'll find much—but if I do, I'll let you know."

* * *

I walk the short distance to the ME's office. After finding Izzy in his office, I fill him in on the day's findings and interviews.

"Sounds like you have your work cut out for you," he says when I'm done. "Arnie just told me that the hair combings and nail scrapings we took from Brian Denver didn't reveal anything significant. But given what Jonas found, it sounds like he's still on the suspect list anyway."

"Yeah, him and half the town, it seems. Looks like Hurley and I will be spending a lot of time together on this one."

"How is that going?"

Izzy is well aware of my feelings for Hurley. We have discussed the ramifications any romantic relationship might have on my position. It was a very serious discussion, as I gave Izzy reason to suspect my commitment to my job over Hurley on another, recent case. Because of this, I opt not to tell him about the whole kissing thing at the motel earlier today, since I don't want to mention anything that might make him question his decision to trust me again. Hopefully, he won't hear about it from someone else. Secrets are hard to keep in a small town, unless it's got something to do with health care.

"It's going fine," I assure him. He eyes me closely, and I know his bullshit detector, which is frighteningly well honed, is searching for manure. "We've had some frank and honest discussions about where the lines are, and the repercussions that might ensue if we cross them. We have an understanding, and we've settled into a nice, comfortable working relationship."

"Glad to hear it," Izzy says. While his tone supports his words, the narrowing of his eyes tells me he's still suspicious. "Want to come over for dinner tonight?" he asks.

"Dom is cooking beef tenderloin, with baby potatoes and asparagus."

I wonder if Izzy's invitation is merely an excuse to spend more time with me so he can better gauge my sincerity. Fortunately, I have plans, because Izzy is frighteningly good at reading me. Otherwise, I'd be tempted to give in and confess all, just so I could enjoy a meal prepared by Dom. Resisting food in general is not something I'm good at, and resisting Dom's cooking is tantamount to torture.

"Thanks, but I'll take a rain check. Hurley and I are heading back up to the casino tonight to look over some of the employee files there."

"I see," he says; and for one frightening moment, I think he does.

"Where are we on the ID stuff for Donald Strommen?"

"I expect to hear something shortly."

I leave Izzy and head for the library, which doubles as my office. I copy Jack's chart and then start reading through the various visit notes, doctor's orders, and summaries it contains. Lisa Warden's notes make up the bulk of the chart. It becomes apparent early on that her role was a dual one. In addition to the routine nursing stuff, such as baths, catheter care, wound care, and skin care, she also helped him with his meals and with the occasional errand. Her notes go back more than a year, with Paul Fletcher providing regular weekly supervisory visits. Everything is consistent time-wise with what we've already been told by Warden and Fletcher: Fletcher last saw Jack on December 23, and Lisa saw him early on Christmas Day.

Most of the notes in Jack's chart involve routine care you'd expect to find with any paraplegic, but there were a few bumps in the road: a hospitalization for the debridement of his bedsore, with a resultant infection that required IV antibiotics for several weeks; a bout of the flu, which led to a month of home respiratory treatments; and a recent problem with severe constipation, which required frequent enemas.

Izzy comes in, just as I'm finishing up with the chart.

"Strommen's dentist just called and confirmed, so we're good to go out there anytime," he tells me. "Given that I'm unsure of the cause or manner of his death at this point, we should probably invite Hurley along."

I call Hurley and put him on speakerphone. First I update him on Arnie's findings and my review of Jack's chart. Then he, in turn, informs us that the notary on Serena's note with Jack is legitimate, that the phone and e-mail records haven't turned up anything of interest, and that the two patients Lisa Warden supposedly saw on Christmas morning after leaving Jack's place have verified her alibi.

When I tell him we finally have an official ID for Strommen, the three of us discuss what to do next. We decide to have Hurley call Strommen's wife—both to make sure she is home, and to make the visit, at least initially, appear to be nothing more than another police inquiry into her husband's disappearance. Hurley puts us on hold to make the call and comes back a couple of minutes later to confirm that the wife is home and expecting him.

Izzy and I arrange to meet Hurley there. I decide to ride with Izzy in his car, figuring the arrival of a hearse at the Strommen house might be a bit impolite, considering our task. But riding with Izzy is a challenge, since his car is an old, restored Impala, with a bench front seat. Izzy can barely reach the pedals with the seat in its most forward position, which leaves me curled up in the passenger seat like a giant Baby Huey in utero. Unfortunately, the Strommens live on a farm at the edge of town, and the house is located at the end of a long, bumpy drive. By the time we arrive, I have a cramp in both legs, a bite on my lip, and the beginnings of a bruise on top of my head.

As I unfold myself from the car, I use a tissue Izzy gives me to wipe the blood off my lips and teeth. I look at the surrounding fields, which are now barren and plowed up, and the barn, which has huge holes in its sides and a missing door. Through the opening, I see a tractor and a combine parked inside, surrounded by a variety of farm attachments and an ATV that looks like it's seen better days.

The house looks to be at least a hundred years old. The clapboard siding is faded and peeling, and the window boxes on the front are filled with dead plants. A brick chimney on the roof, which is missing a large number of shingles, is crumbling. As we climb the front steps, I notice that the handrail is leaning precariously and the porch is missing a few boards in the floor. There is an older model Ford pickup with a dual cab parked beside the house, and given the towing unit I see on the back of it, I figure it was what Donald Strommen used to get his boat to the launch site. I wonder how long it was before the truck was returned to the family once it was determined that Donald was missing. Living out in the country like this, having some sort of vehicle is a necessity.

Charlotte Strommen—a tall, thin woman, with stick legs, almost no waist, and a face that is gaunt and wan— looks as tired and worn-out as her surroundings. She is wearing a tattered white housedress, a once-white cardigan sweater with holes in it, dingy white knee socks, and white tennis shoes. With her pasty complexion and bleached blond hair, the all-white combination makes her look like a ghost.

Hurley steps up and shows her his badge. "I'm Detective Hurley, with the Sorenson Police Department. I'm the one who spoke with you on the phone a short while ago." He then points to Izzy and me. "This is Mattie Winston and Dr. Rybarceski, with the medical examiner's office. I'm afraid we have some bad news for you."

Charlotte starts wringing the thin cotton dish towel she is holding in her hands. "You found him, didn't you?"

"Yes, ma'am," Hurley says. "I'm sorry. His body washed up along the shore of the river, near a farm on the other side of town."

"Are you sure it's Donald?" she asks, looking from Hurley to us, and back again.

"It's definitely Donald," Izzy says. "We verified the remains using his dental records."

Charlotte squeezes her eyes closed, and two fat tears roll down her cheeks. "I guess I knew it all along," she says. "The empty boat, the fact that he didn't come home . . . ." She sighs and her body sags, making Hurley step up and take her arm.

"Let's go inside and sit down," Hurley says. "Are Peter and Hannah here?" he asks, referring to Charlotte's two kids.

Charlotte shakes her head as Hurley steers her inside and to a nearby couch. "They're at a neighbor's house," she says. And then she starts to sob. "Oh, God. How am I going to tell them?"

As Izzy and I follow Hurley and Charlotte inside, I scope out the surroundings. Despite the warm temp outside, it's cold inside the house. And if the furnace is working at all, I'd wager the thermostat is set at around 50 degrees. There is a fireplace, but it's dark and empty. Based on the condition of the chimney outside, I'm guessing it's unusable. The walls are covered with faded, peeling paper; the furniture all looks like frayed and shabby rummage sale stuff; the wood floors are dulled, scuffed, and scarred from hundreds of feet wearing them down; the light fixture in the living room is hanging down from the ceiling by a cord that I suspect is old knob-and-tube wiring.

Off in one corner of the living room is a scragglylooking Christmas tree decorated with mostly homemade ornaments and two sparse strings of lights, none of which are lit. Clearly, the Strommen family has fallen on hard times. I wonder if Donald was out fishing in an effort to put food on his family's table.

Charlotte zeroes in on me for some reason—perhaps because I'm the only other woman in the group—with a stricken expression. "Did he drown?" she asks in a quiet, little voice.

"It doesn't appear so," I tell her.

Her eyes grow wide and she shifts her gaze to Izzy, then to Hurley, and back to me. "What do you mean, 'it doesn't appear so'? How did he die?"

Izzy jumps in. "At first blush, it looked as if he might have drowned, but the results of our subsequent examination ruled that out. He had a fairly significant head injury, but I don't think that was the cause of his death, either."

"Well, what else is there?" Charlotte asks, wringing her hands.

Hurley decides to take over at this point and deftly distracts her from the subject. "We're not done with all the tests. It would help us if you could go over what happened the day he disappeared."

"I already talked with the police about this," she says in an exasperated tone. "Don't you people share your notes?"

"We do," Hurley says with admirable patience. "But we like to go over the facts multiple times. Sometimes people remember things they didn't the first time, because they're too upset or emotional. I realize this isn't easy for you, but it would help us if you could just go over it once again."

Hurley takes out a notebook and pen and stands poised and waiting.

Charlotte sighs heavily and leans back into the couch. "Donald took the boat out to fish around two in the afternoon the day after Thanksgiving," she begins. "He liked going out at night because he said the fishing was better then. Usually, he came back by midnight, but that night he didn't come back at all. I didn't realize it until the next morning, because I was tired and went to bed around ten."

"Do you know where he fished?"

"He usually put in at the launch down by Riley's Corner. There's a bait shop there he likes."

A lot of folks like that shop because its name is a saucy double entendre: Bass Master Baits.

As Hurley scribbles some notes, I shift from one foot to the other, feeling the pressure of all the coffee and the hot chocolate I drank pressing on my bladder.

"Charlotte, would it be okay if I used your bathroom?" I ask.

"Sure. It's the door straight ahead at the top of the stairs."

I turn and leave the room, heading for the stairs. They creak loudly as I climb, plotting my progress for anyone who cares to listen. I find the bathroom, relieve myself, and wash my hands, noting that the only towel hanging in the room is as threadbare as everything else. When I'm done, I venture back out into the main hallway, pausing before I return to the living room. The stairway is located in the center of the house; and to the right of the landing down the hall, I see the doorways to two other bedrooms, one on either side, both of them closed. I move toward the first one and see the name *Hannah* painted on a piece of poster board and taped to the door. Under the name it says: KEEP OUT! in big red letters. The second door is plain and empty. Back toward the stairs, I see the entrance to a third bedroom, to the left of the landing. The door to this room is open and I can see the footboard for a double bed in the room. I assume this is the master bedroom. Curious, I tiptoe closer, grimacing as I hear the floorboards beneath my feet creak as loudly as the stairs had.

I step inside and stop short. The bed is neatly made and covered with an old-fashioned patchwork quilt. On top of the quilt are several piles of clothing—men's clothing from the looks of them, plaid flannel shirts, blue work shirts, jeans, and T-shirts. All around the bed are boxes; some of them with clothes inside.

I walk over to the closet. It's a small one, typical of these old farmhouses, some of which don't even have closets in all the bedrooms. Hanging inside it are a half-dozen housedresses, some slacks and blouses, and a woman's brown wool winter coat, which has a tiny slip of paper with a dry-cleaning number safety-pinned to the collar. On the overhead shelf are a dozen or so sweaters neatly folded and stacked, and lined up on the floor are six pairs of shoes—two pairs of women's sneakers, one basic pair of pumps, one pair of semi-dressy flats, a pair of clogs, and some everyday casual flats. The closet isn't overstuffed, but its tiny area is pretty much filled by what it contains.

I walk over to the bed and examine the clothes piled there and in the boxes. I see that my first assumption was correct; they all appear to be men's clothes. If Charlotte Strommen thought her husband was still missing, and she was supposedly hoping he might be alive, why was she packing up all his clothes?

By the time I make it back downstairs, I can tell that Charlotte has realized what I might have seen. She watches me warily as I reenter the room, fidgeting with a loose thread in her sweater.

I say nothing and avoid looking at her. Hurley closes his notebook and shoves it and his pen back into his pocket.

"I think we have enough for now," he says to Charlotte. "We'll keep you posted and let you know what we find, once we've concluded all our tests."

He thanks Charlotte for her cooperation, and then heads out the door with Izzy and me on his tail. When we reach the cars, I grab Hurley before he can get into his.

"Hold up," I say in a low voice. I glance back toward the house and see Charlotte watching us behind the thin curtains hanging in the living room. "I think we need to take a closer look at Donald, because something isn't right about this. Charlotte is lying to us. She knows more than she's letting on."

"What are you talking about?" Hurley says. Izzy leans in to hear what I'm going to say next.

"When I went upstairs to use the bathroom, I peeked inside Charlotte and Donald's bedroom. The bed was covered with his clothes, and some of them were packed in boxes next to the bed."

"Maybe she was just packing away the summer stuff," Izzy offers.

"I don't think so. There were heavy overalls, plaid flannel shirts, and a quilted vest packed in one of the boxes."

"Interesting," Hurley says.

"That's what I thought," I say. "Especially when I realized that the closet had only her clothes left in it.

Why would she be packing up all of her husband's clothes if she didn't even know he was dead yet?"

Hurley sighs. "I thought this was going to be an easy one," he says. "So much for buttoning things up before Florida."

Izzy says, "I'll put a rush on the tox screen."

"You know," I say, looking at Hurley, "with two kids in the house, I'm betting one or both of them might know something about what really happened to their father. Maybe you should talk to them?"

"Not a bad idea," Hurley says, "but I think I'll wait. Right now, Charlotte is cooperating with us, and I don't have any real evidence to suggest foul play. And if Charlotte is hiding something, she isn't likely to let us interrogate her kids. I could do it anyway, but it will just piss her off and make her less likely to work with us. So I think I'd rather hold off for now to see if you guys come up with anything new."

We climb into our respective cars. As we head back into town, Hurley's last words trigger an idea. Donald and Charlotte's daughter, Hannah, is close in age to my niece, Erika, and the boy, Peter, is around the same age as my nephew, Ethan. The Sorenson schools are small and the kids all know one another and gossip like crazy. If we can't talk to Charlotte's kids directly, maybe I can find out something by taking a more indirect route.

Chapter 17

I check out of the office around four-thirty and stop at the bank, where I pull out five thousand dollars in cash and get another ten grand split between two cashier's checks. My divorce settlement has me feeling pretty flush cashwise, and I figure I can afford to play a little at the casino tables tonight. After how well I did at the blackjack table last time, I'm eager to try my luck again with some bigger stakes. If I can grow my savings enough, maybe I can afford to live without a job for a while and pursue my relationship with Hurley.

I head home to tend to Hoover and Rubbish, and to dress. After mulling through the contents of my closet, I opt for a pair of black stretch jeans, topped off with a russet-colored sweater. The jeans are new—one of the few items of clothing I've bought for myself of late—and before putting them on, I carefully cut out the label that notes the size. Though I know the *W* on the label means "women's," I can't help but think it stands for "wide ass"; and I learned during my years working as a nurse in the ER that you never know when you might have some stranger stripping off your clothes.

Hoover seems to sense that I'm heading out again,

probably because he knows my usual at-home garb is sloppy sweats. He follows me around the house, watching me with his big, mournful brown eyes, sighing periodically. When I take him outside to do his business, he quickly waters a nearby tree, then runs over to my car and stands there, wagging his tail in a not-so-subtle hint that he'd like to come along.

My kitten, Rubbish, who is about five months old and growing faster than the federal debt, is even less subtle. While he initially feigns indifference by ignoring me as I try on a variety of outfits, he lets his true feelings shine through by thwacking me with a paw when I walk by the dresser he's sitting on.

Though it wouldn't surprise me to discover Hurley's car on my tail during the drive up, I don't see any sign of him. When I arrive at the casino, I feel the lure of the gambling tables tugging at me. I'm fifteen minutes early, so I decide to make a quick trip into the casino and try my hand at the slots before heading into the restaurant.

I find an empty dollar slot and plug in two dollars at a time. On my first six tries, nothing happens. But on the seventh, I hit a combo that pays out thirty bucks. Feeling flush with my success, I pocket my winnings and head for the restaurant.

The eatery is a bustling place and a hostess greets me as soon as I walk through the door.

"Are you on your own?" she asks after giving me a quick up-and-down perusal and a look that suggests pity.

"I believe there will be three. I'm having dinner with *two* gentlemen," I say, sounding a little smug as I emphasize the number. "Either or both of them may be here already: Joe Whitehorse or Steve Hurley?"

The hostess's pitiful expression disappears, like Georgio's flash paper, and is instantly replaced with a

cordial smile. "Ah, yes," she says. "Mr. Whitehorse is
expecting you. Follow me, please."

She leads me across a crowded room full of diners
and through double doors on the other side that have
the words WINNER'S LOUNGE stenciled above them
in huge, green letters. Two "hunkalicious" bodyguard-
looking types are standing at the doors, barring our
entrance.

"This is the party meeting with Mr. Whitehorse," the
hostess tells them. They nod, open one of the doors,
and make a sweeping gesture into the room in such a
smooth, coordinated rhythm, it's as if their bodies are
controlled by a single brain. But then, with bodies like
these guys have, a brain can be a frivolous accessory at
times.

I follow the hostess across the room and through a
second door into a smaller room that has a single large
dining table at its center. "Please make yourself comfortable," she tells me. "Mr. Whitehorse will be right
with you. May I get you a drink while you wait?"

"That sounds great." I think a moment, trying to
decide what to order, and the hostess jumps in with
some suggestions.

"We are known for our martini bar. Might I suggest
an appletini, or if you like chocolate, the Godiva martini is positively sinful."

Sin sounds intriguing, so I opt for the Godiva. The
hostess offers to take and check my coat. As soon as she
leaves, I scope out the room. It isn't opulent, but there
are obvious signs of wealth present. Mahogany wain-
scoting lines the walls; the carpet beneath my feet is
thick and cushy; the table setting features a richly em-
broidered tablecloth, crystal stemware, and fine bone
china. On the wall to my right is a large mirror with
an ornate, gilded frame. I walk over and give myself a
quick check, smoothing down a few flyaway hairs and

fixing an eyeliner smudge. Then, since I'm alone in the room, I also make a quick adjustment of the girls, shifting them inside my bra cups.

After several minutes perusing the art hanging on the walls, most of which is nature paintings, the door opens and Joe Whitehorse walks in, with Hurley on his heels.

"Good evening, Mattie," Joe greets, smiling broadly. His teeth appear stunningly white against his dark complexion. "You look lovely tonight."

"Thank you," I say, blushing. Hurley watches this exchange from just inside the door; there is a faintly amused smile on his face. I notice that he and Joe are both carrying drinks; Hurley's is already half gone.

Joe walks over to the near end of the table and sets down his drink. Then he shoves aside the place setting at the head of the table and sets down the briefcase he is carrying in his other hand. "Have a seat," he says, waving me over and pulling out the chair next to the setting he claimed with his drink. I walk over and settle in, letting him scoot my chair toward the table for me. "Has anyone taken your drink order yet?" he asks, settling into the seat beside me, while Hurley takes one across from me.

"They have. I'm about to experience my very first chocolate martini."

"Ah, you are a woman of indulgent tastes. I like that," Joe says. I see Hurley roll his eyes.

The door to the room opens and a waiter enters carrying a domed platter. He sets it down on the table—which seems ridiculously huge with only three of us sitting at it—and then removes the dome with a flourish, revealing an assortment of scrumptious-looking hors d'oeuvres.

"I have taken the liberty of arranging a meal for us tonight. I hope you don't mind," Joe says, looking from me to Hurley. "I think you'll find the food to your satisfaction. But if there is anything you don't like, just let me know and I'll see to it that you get something else."

"I'm sure anything you chose will be fine," I tell him. It's a pretty safe statement, given that I can count the number of foods I don't like on the fingers of one hand.

Hurley shrugs. "I'm not picky," he says, looking faintly amused in a way that makes me nervous.

Hurley and I back up our comments by grabbing at least two of everything on the platter: delicately fried butterfly shrimp, some kind of cheese and sprout stuff on toast points, melon and prosciutto on sticks, bagel chips with a chickpea and radish topping, crostini with tomato and feta cheese, and tiny puff shells stuffed with a crabmeat salad. Before we are done heaping up our plates, the waiter returns with a plate of fresh fruit.

While Hurley and I chow down, Joe takes a handful of grapes and eats them one at a time, watching us. "The food here is good, yes?" he says.

"So far, it's fantastic," I say.

"Superb," Hurley agrees.

"Good! I think you'll find the rest of the meal follows suit," Joe says, looking like a proud papa.

My chocolate martini arrives, and after one sip, I'm pretty sure I want to move out of my cottage and into the casino.

Joe opens the briefcase he had set on the table earlier and removes a stack of paper-filled folders. "I have information on the employees who were on duty the night Mr. Allen won his jackpot. We can look them over during dinner, if you like. Several of the employees are on duty tonight, as well, and if you want to talk with any of them, I will make them available to you."

"I appreciate that," Hurley says. "It's a start, but I might need to look at all of your employee files. The fact that an employee wasn't working the night Jack won his jackpot doesn't necessarily rule out that person. I'm sure word of something like that travels fast."

"Those files are the property of the casino, of course," Joe says. "But I can provide you with copies of any or all of them that interest you, just as we are doing with the tape."

"The tape?" I say between bites, looking confused.

Hurley says, "I called earlier and asked Joe to pull the security tape from the other night to see if Denver was telling us the truth."

"Oh, right," I say, recalling Denver's alibi. "How much of his time here will we be able to verify from the tape?"

"All of it," Hurley says. "There are cameras aimed at every square inch of this place, and they record everything that happens and everyone it happens to." Hurley points toward the ceiling. "See, they even have cameras in here. We were upstairs in the control booth watching things right before we joined you."

I look up where he's pointing and spy a small dome-shaped camera. A quick scan of the rest of the ceiling reveals three more of them. Then it hits me . . . the little adjustment I made in front of the mirror back when I thought I was alone in the room. I look back at Hurley, who is watching me with a self-satisfied grin on his face. I realize why he has looked so amused all along; my face blushes hot from my chin to the roots of my hair.

Joe says to me, "As I explained to Detective Hurley earlier, I went ahead and scanned our tapes this afternoon before you arrived. So far, it seems Mr. Denver was telling you the truth. But we're talking about a nearly twenty-hour period of time here. I can tell you he was in the casino from ten o'clock on the night in question until about four o'clock in the morning. But

I haven't had time to scan the hours between four A.M. and five P.M. on Christmas Day. You'll have to finish that on your own."

Over the next hour, Hurley and I wade through the employee information sheets we have, looking for anything that might scream "suspect!" while Joe keeps the food flow going. We enjoy a light squash soup, followed by a main meal of beef tenderloin, garlic and cheese-whipped potatoes, and broccoli florets bathed in a scrumptious herbed butter sauce.

By the time dessert arrives—an exquisite chocolate mousse, which I enjoy with a second drink, opting for a White Russian martini this time—we have waded through the stack of sheets Joe provided for us. And nothing out of the ordinary has popped up. In fact, all of the employees have been carefully vetted with extensive background checks and appear to have squeaky-clean reputations.

Frustrated, Hurley says, "I don't see anything here to raise any eyebrows. The casino seems to be very thorough."

"We take our responsibilities quite seriously," Joe says. "In fact, after talking with you last night, I authorized an investigation into the current financial status and recent activities for all of our employees. We have a stable of excellent private investigators we use who are discreet but thorough. I had them start with the folks whose info you have there," he says, gesturing toward our pile. "So far, nothing has turned up. But if it does, I'll be sure to let you know. And you have my promise that if something does point to one of our employees, we will deal with it swiftly and emphatically."

"Fair enough," Hurley says. "I appreciate your cooperation."

"My pleasure. And speaking of pleasure, may I invite

the two of you to enjoy some of our gaming tables tonight while you're here?"

"Sure," I say.

"No, thanks," Hurley says at the same time.

The two of us exchange a look, though a "stare down" might be a better term. Apparently, Hurley can sense my determination because he backs off first.

"I suppose a little fun is in order," he says. Then, more pointedly, he adds, "As long as the stakes aren't too high."

Chapter 18

Hurley and I head for the blackjack tables. In no time at all, we're settled in at a table with a five-dollar minimum. I buy a hundred dollars' worth of chips and start off betting five bucks at a time. I win several hands and decide to up my bet to twenty dollars. Hurley, who has lost some fifty bucks, raises his brows at my new bet, scrapes his chips off the table, and says, "That's it for me. Come on, Winston, you're up quite a bit. Now is when you should quit."

"I'm on a roll," I say, shaking my head. "I want to see how far it will take me."

"It will take you straight to the poor house," Hurley says irritably.

I dismiss his objection with a wave of my hand. "I'm fine. Besides, with the money I have from the divorce settlement, I can afford to gamble a little. I think I've earned some fun time."

"Fine," Hurley says, shoving back his chair and getting up. "Have your fun. I'm outta here."

Some small part of me is sad to see him go, but the pull of the table makes me quickly forget him. That, and the drinks, which keep on coming and get better with each new concoction I try. But though the drinks keep flowing my way, the money changes direction. I start losing, and in an effort to make up for each loss, I bet a little more with each hand. I win a hand, and then lose several more in a row. When my initial pile of chips is gone, I buy some more and keep on playing. To turn things around, I decide to leave my current table and move up to one with a fifty-dollar minimum and a maximum bet of a grand. Walking proves to be surprisingly difficult, however—no doubt from sitting so long—so I detour to the ladies' room, where I can pee and also splash some water on my face. While I'm at the sink, I wash the handful of chips I have left for good luck. I don't do much better at the fifty-dollar table and end up cashing in one of my cashier's checks. Hoping to make up for lost ground, I move again to a higher-stakes table—this time with a maximum bet of two grand.

The remainder of the night passes by in a blur of shuffling cards, cash draws, and shifting chips. When I finally decide to quit, I have spent both of my cashier's checks and have only one chip left. I shove it in my pocket and glance at my watch, startled to see that it's almost three in the morning.

I get up from my seat, grab my purse, and start walking toward where I think the main door to the casino is, but my legs don't seem to want to work right. Not only that, the room is spinning. I try to recall how many drinks I've had, but the only things I can see in my mind are cards and chips. Deciding that another cold splash to my face is in order, I switch directions abruptly and head for the bathroom. But my fickle legs clearly think this decision is a rash one. For a few seconds, I struggle to maintain my balance, but it doesn't take long for me to realize I'm going down.

As I prepare for the crash of hitting the floor, a strong arm wraps around my waist and pulls me back.

"Whoa, there," Hurley says as my body collides with his. "I think someone has had a bit too much to drink."

"I sink tho," I hear myself say. "I mean, I think so." The words come out slowly, carefully, as my tongue feels thick and clumsy. "Where ish my car? I need to go home."

"You're not driving anywhere," Hurley says. "You're drunk."

For some reason, I find this statement hilarious and start giggling.

"Come on," Hurley says. "I'll drive." He turns us in tandem as if we are dancing and steers my staggering legs in a different direction. I do my best to keep up, but I'm pretty sure that if Hurley's arm wasn't around me, I'd be flat on the floor . . . laughing hysterically.

A few steps later, the humor fades and I pick something new to focus on. "I thought choo were gone," I say, my alcohol-hazed brain recalling his earlier departure. "Did you come back?"

"I never left," he says. "I've been upstairs in the security area watching tapes and keeping an eye on you."

This strikes me as the most romantic and sweet gesture *ever* in the history of such gestures. My chest swells with emotion. All misty-eyed and fawning, I look up at Hurley. "You kept a die on me," I say. Then I frown, realizing the words didn't come out right, but I'm unsure exactly what is wrong with them.

"Something like that," Hurley grumbles.

We are near the front of the casino. Hurley props me up against a wall as he retrieves my coat and his jacket. He puts his on and then helps me with mine, a task that starts me giggling as I struggle to get my arms into the sleeves. When I'm finally dressed, he steers me toward the door, pushes it open, and hauls me through.

"You helped me with my coat. That is so shweet," I croon, making my best doe eyes at him. I focus—if the blurry mess my eyes see can be called a "focus"—on the parking lot and my feet, trying to stay upright. Finally we reach a car that, through the fog that is my mind, I recognize as Hurley's. He props me up by the back fender, while he unlocks and opens the front passenger door. I fall inside. When Hurley tries to help me get my feet in, my head ends up in the driver's seat, my body awkwardly draped over the center console. He finally manages to get my feet in enough to shut the door. A moment later, he opens the one on the driver's side.

I move my head on the seat a little and roll my eyes upward, until I can see him standing there. "Hi," I say with what, I suspect, is a goofy-assed smile. I want to sit up, but my body isn't cooperating.

Hurley reaches in and lifts my head from the seat, shoving me over into the passenger side. He drops himself in quickly, before I have a chance to slump over again. And slump I do. It's as if all of my bones and muscles have left my body, leaving me with the strength of a wet noodle. This time Hurley's broad shoulder stops me—that and his arm across my chest.

"You need to sit up and put your belt on," he says, pushing me upright. Both his tone and his expression are serious and solemn; he's making it clear he's brooking no humor of any kind. I burst out laughing, tip sideways again, and my head lolls forward, hitting the steering wheel.

"Ow," I say, putting a hand to my forehead as Hurley tries to push me back and straighten me up with his arm again. "That hurt." I look at Hurley; and for one second I, too, am serious and solemn as I frown and rub at the offending spot. We stare at one another for several seconds, and I think I see the corners of his mouth twitch upward just the tiniest bit. That triggers my hysteria again and raucous laughter bubbles up from my gut, spilling out into the car. The laughter is quickly followed by everything I ate and drank tonight, which also spills out into the car.

"Aw, damn it, Winston! What the hell is it with you wanting to puke on me all the time?"

I try to tell him that I'm sorry, but another wave hits me. I manage to keep this one down, but I don't dare speak. I'm afraid of what will come out if I open my mouth—and I'm not talking about words.

Hurley pulls a lever to pop open his trunk and then climbs out of his seat and heads to the back of the car. A moment later, he opens my door and hands me a towel. "Clean yourself up," he says, keeping a towel for himself and trying to do the same. I watch, mesmerized, as he rubs at his crotch.

"Where are your keys?" he asks me.

"In my pursh, I guess." I reach down to the floor at my feet, where he tossed my purse after tossing me into the car. I try to retrieve the keys, but I succeed, instead, in putting a dent in the middle of my forehead—compliments of the button on the glove box.

"Let me," Hurley says.

He reaches down between my legs and feels around for the purse, brushing the insides of my thighs with his arm. Even though I'm wearing slacks, I can feel the heat of his arm against my legs. It's almost as if his touch is 100 degrees hotter than my body; it's an incredibly sexy sensation. For one second, I imagine myself grabbing his arm and guiding it—and his hand—a little higher. I actually do grab his arm, but then I just hold it there, between my knees, looking up at him.

"We can't do thish," I say, while some distant part of my mind wonders, *Why the hell not?* Then I remember: my job.

"Do what?" Hurley asks, looking amused.

"This," I say, squeezing his arm. "You touching me like this. It makes me . . . it makes me crazy."

His lips broaden into a smile as he stands there beside me, bent down with his head in the car, his arm still in my grip. "Good crazy or bad crazy?" he asks.

"Oh, very good crazy," I say, closing my eyes and enjoying a slightly pornographic vignette. But then, things start spinning and I open my eyes in a panic, trying to focus. "No, thash not right," I hear myself say. "It's *not* good. It's not good to want you like I do."

"You want me?"

"I do." I smile, even as my brain struggles to convince me that this is a very serious moment.

"I think you're safe for now, Winston," he says. "The whole puking thing is a definite turnoff for me." He shakes my grip loose, grabs my purse, and pulls it up between my legs. After a moment of rummaging around inside it, he comes up with my keys. "Come on," he says, tugging on my arm and helping me out of the car. "I'm going to have to drive that monstrosity of yours home. You can lie down in the back and puke in it all you want."

I'm vaguely aware of Hurley dragging/walking me across the parking lot and tossing me into the back of my hearse. It's not so bad, I realize, being laid out in the back of a hearse. In fact, this incredible idea flashes through my brain as I lie on my back and stare at the fabric on the ceiling. Why not make caskets with windows in the lid so the people inside can see what's going on around them, and where they are. My mind senses that there is something a bit off with this idea, but I can't put a finger on what it might be. Then I remember that the dead don't see. Once again I'm struck by the hilarity of both my thoughts and my situation, and I start giggling uncontrollably. The echo of my maniacal laughter bouncing around inside the hearse is the last thing I hear for a while.

Chapter 19

When next I try to open my eyes, I'm hit with a white-hot pain that slices through my brain like the laser we used in the OR. I squeeze my eyes shut and curl in on myself, trying to block out the offending light. I wrap my hands over my aching head and hear myself moan. At least I think it's me I'm hearing; the sound seems awfully far away.

After a few minutes, I try again to open my eyes, doing it in small increments this time. Gradually I'm able to focus without the pain rendering me helpless and I recognize some of my surroundings: my quilt, my bedroom furniture, the picture on my bedroom wall.

My stomach churns threateningly and I swallow hard, trying to convince my peristalsis to move in one direction only. I manage to toss back the covers and sit myself up on the side of the bed. Every square inch of my body aches, though my head is definitely the worst, pounding away as if Thor himself is in there. My bladder feels like it's about to burst. When I look down at myself, I see that I'm in my bra and panties and struggle to remember how I got that way. The last thing I recall clearly is playing blackjack at the casino, then

Hurley, and cars, and laughing at something that was very funny. . . . Whenever I try to recall anything beyond that, I get nothing but blinding pain for my efforts.

I can hear faint noises coming from the main part of the cottage and I'm momentarily filled with fear, thinking that someone has broken into the place. But then I realize that Rubbish and Hoover aren't in the bedroom with me, so I figure that whoever is out there must be someone I know.

Slowly I stand, testing my legs and giving my body a minute or two to get used to being upright. Like Frankenstein rising from his table for the first time, I take one unsteady step, then another, repeating the process until I stagger my way out into the living room. I shuffle toward the kitchen, where I can smell the heavenly scent of freshly brewed coffee. There, standing in front of the counter, with a white apron neatly tied over his pressed black slacks and green sweater, is Dom. At his feet are Rubbish and Hoover, who are both staring up at him patiently as he pours a cup of coffee. Dom, with his fine reddish hair, slender body, and fair skin, looks like the perfect housewife standing there. Come to think of it, Dom *is* the perfect housewife—if you overlook the fact that he has a penis. He's a killer cook, has excellent taste in interior design, and loves to clean house. Izzy is a lucky bastard.

"Good morning," I mumble.

Dom turns around, holding the mug of coffee he just poured, smiling brightly. But as soon as he sets his eyes on me, the smile freezes and he gasps. "Oh, my," he says, looking a bit horrified. "Welcome back to the land of the living . . . I think."

Hoover glances my way and whimpers. Rubbish spares me a look of quiet disdain before dismissing me and starting to groom himself. I take a step toward

Dom and the coffee he's offering, but he stops me with a pointed look. "You might want to put on a robe or something."

I remember that all I'm wearing is my bra and panties. Blushing, I mumble an apology and shuffle my way back to my bedroom, where I have to dig around in the closet to find my robe. I slip it on and then head for the bathroom, where I catch a glimpse of myself in the mirror. My hair is matted down in some spots and sticking out in wild, tangled clumps in others, making me look like a long-haired cat with mange. The remains of my eyeliner and mascara are smeared and smudged zombie-style, and my lipstick has somehow spread well beyond the corners of my mouth, like some drunken clown. My zebra stripes have faded from flaming red to brown, but that hasn't made them any less noticeable. The overall effect is a frightening one. No wonder Dom gasped. I make a halfhearted attempt to rub away the makeup smudges and smooth the wilder parts of my hair, but I realize it's going to take more than some spit on my palm to fix this mess.

When I come back out to the living room, Dom hands me the mug of coffee, lightened with heavy cream the way I like it. I take a sip and then hold the mug close to my chest, as if it's the dearest thing in the world to me.

"How did I get home?" I ask, dropping onto my couch and nearly scalding my chest in the process.

"Hurley drove you in your hearse. Apparently, you turned his car into a giant barf bag."

I groan, both from the humiliation of this information and the persistent pounding in my head. "How did I get to my bed?" The hidden implication behind this question is clear, and I can tell from Dom's silly grin that he understands. He knows I don't really care how I got to bed. What I really want to know is how I got stripped down to my undies . . . and who did it. And did any other embarrassing things happen?

"Hurley woke up Izzy and me. Together, the three of us got you inside. Then Izzy and I stripped off your clothes and dumped you into bed. Your clothes, which were a bit barfy, are in the washer. I imagine you'll want to take a shower and throw your sheets into the washer next."

I wince, and not just because of my pounding head. "Oh, God, I'm so sorry, Dom. I don't know what the hell happened. One minute I was having a little fun playing blackjack, and the next thing I know, I'm here."

"Hurley said the casino was plying you with drinks the whole time. It's a ploy they often use to keep folks at the gambling tables and, hopefully, winnow away some of your common sense. Apparently, it worked, because according to Hurley, you managed to gamble away about fifteen grand last night."

I stare at him stupidly a moment, trying to parse the meaning from his words. "As in I *lost* that much?" I say, shocked.

Dom nods.

I hang my head in shame and embarrassment. "What must you all think of me?" I whine. Then it hits me. I snap my head up and look over at the wall clock. "Shit, it's after nine o'clock already. I'm late for work." I push up from the couch and feel both my balance and my stomach reel threateningly.

"Steady there," Dom says, hurrying toward me and grabbing my arm. "No need to rush. Izzy said you can have the day off."

"No, I need to go to work. I don't want Izzy giving me any special consideration, especially now that I'm trying to win back his trust."

"I don't think it's a smart idea, but if you insist," Dom says, shrugging. "Why don't you go take some ibuprofen and a shower. In the meantime, I'll fix you my special hangover breakfast."

Food doesn't sound very good to me at the moment—a highly rare event. Hoping Dom is right, I push myself up from the couch and head for the bathroom.

One hot shower, a thorough teeth scrubbing, four ibuprofens, three glasses of water, and a huge cup of coffee later, I emerge feeling at least half human, though my stomach is still threatening to stage a major coup.

Dom makes me sit and he shoves a plate with some kind of omelet on it in front of me. "Eat." I force myself to obey with one tiny forkful, then another. I repeat the process a few more times and realize my stomach is surrendering. Gradually I finish the entire thing. When I'm done, I feel tons better.

"Thanks, Dom," I say. "You are truly a lifesaver."

"You're welcome. Now, if I were you, I'd take it easy for the rest of the day."

"I can't. I have to go to the office, if for no other reason than just to see what progress Hurley has made."

"Can't you do that over the phone?"

"I could," I admit. "But I have some apologies to issue, too, and I want to do those in person."

Dom nods solemnly, making it clear how badly those apologies are needed. "Okay, but promise me you'll drink lots of water and take plenty of ibuprofen."

"I will. Thanks." Bracing myself for some humility and humiliation, I give Dom a kiss on the cheek, thank him again, and head out to my car.

Even driving as slowly as possible to postpone the inevitable for as long as I can, it only takes me five minutes to drive to the office. Fortunately, my car doesn't smell of barf. However, I do get a hint of just how wasted I was last night when I pick up on a strong tinge of alcohol in the air, enough to overwhelm the ever-present smell of formaldehyde that seems to cling to the hearse's interior. Something about that lingering odor bothers me, but my brain is still too murky to figure out why.

I find Izzy in his office. He's working on his computer, which sits on a credenza behind his desk. Since his back is to me, I knock on the door frame to announce my arrival. He spins around in his chair and stares at me for several seconds before he speaks.

"I didn't expect to see you here today," he says. "Didn't Dom tell you I gave you the day off?"

"He did," I say, struggling to gauge Izzy's tone. While he doesn't sound pissed exactly, his demeanor is definitely strained. He looks wary, almost wounded, and I feel a surge of guilt over being the likely cause of those emotions. Izzy is not only my boss, he's also my best friend. I can't believe I did something so stupid, jeopardizing our relationship like this. "I came in anyway because I'm supposed to be here," I tell him. "I'll stay late tonight to make up for the hours I missed."

Izzy leans back in his chair and eyes me for a moment, as if weighing the sincerity of my words. "There's no need to do that," he says finally. "Your position is salaried and you've put in lots of extra hours without any extra pay lately, so you have plenty of comp time coming. And you're entitled to a day off now and then. Besides, things are quiet here at the moment. I'm almost caught up with all my paperwork and there aren't any autopsies pending. So even if you did stay, I don't know what you'd do. And I'm sure you have stuff to do to get ready for your trip. What time is your flight?"

"We're taking a ten-thirty red-eye out of Milwaukee. Hurley and I are heading for the airport around eight."

Izzy nods.

"Do you have the Strommen file in here?" I ask, trying to shift the focus off me and back onto the work.

Izzy picks up a folder and hands it to me. "What do you want with it?"

"I want to make a copy of something." I leave with the folder and head for the library, where I make the copy I need, fold it up, and stuff it in my purse. I return the original to the folder and then return the file to Izzy. His back is to me again when I enter his office, so I make a great deal of noise to announce my presence and drop the file loudly onto his desk. My efforts are for naught; Izzy doesn't acknowledge my presence in any way.

Clearing my throat, which is strangling me with emotion, I say, "Since there's nothing going on here, I'll check in with Hurley and see how things are going with the investigations."

"It's up to you," he says over his shoulder.

Even though he's trying to hide it, I can tell he's disappointed in me. His calm dismissal of me is crystal clear, and wrenchingly painful. I'd rather have him yell at me, or fire me, or do anything other than turn his back on me. Tears burn at my eyes as my emotions tighten their stranglehold on my throat.

"Izzy, please believe me when I tell you how sorry I am," I choke out. "What I did last night was stupid and reckless."

He turns back to me finally; and though his initial expression is stern, when he sees the tears in my eyes, his face softens. "Yes, it was," he says quietly. "And not just because you drank yourself into oblivion. Hurley said you gambled away fifteen thousand dollars last night. I know you got some money from your divorce settlement, but that doesn't mean you can afford to be frivolous with it."

I nod. "I know. You're right. It won't happen again."

"See to it."

Finally, with these last three words, I detect a hint of emotion in his voice: a touch of anger tinged with disappointment and betrayal. And while it makes me feel like a child who is being chastised by a parent, it also gladdens me, in an odd way.

"I will," I tell him, swiping at the tears tracking down my cheeks. "I promise." I start to turn away from him, but he calls me back.

"Mattie, there's one more thing."

I look back at him, bracing myself.

"The tanning booth really isn't working for you. You should use an artificial tanner, instead. You know what horizontal stripes can do to your figure."

I burst out laughing; and to my delight, Izzy chuckles as well. I give him a salute and say, "Point taken"; then I head out.

My spirits are definitely buoyed by the return of the normal, no-holds-barred repartee that Izzy and I have always shared. However, my joy is tempered by the knowledge that my next stop is Hurley, where I expect the repartee to be a bit more humiliating.

Chapter 20

I detour to the library and pick up the original of Jack Allen's chart before heading out. I find Hurley in the police station break room with a bunch of papers in front of him. He is writing something on a notepad as I enter. When he looks up to see who has come into the room, I can tell from his expression that he is surprised.

"Didn't expect to see you here today," he says, confirming my thoughts. He leans back in his seat and studies me, wagging the pen in his hand. "You don't look too much the worse for wear."

"How I look and how I feel are two different things," I say with a wan smile.

"I'll bet."

"I understand I owe you both thanks and an apology for last night. So thank you, and I'm sorry."

"How much do you remember?"

"Everything up to my decision to call it a night. After that, not so much."

Hurley's mouth tightens, his eyes narrow, and he cocks his head to one side.

"Was I a complete idiot?"

"Not complete, no. But on a scale of one to ten, I'd give you a nine. Not only did you gamble away somewhere in the neighborhood of fifteen grand, you puked all over my car."

"So I heard," I say, wincing. "Is there anything I can do to make it up to you?"

He starts tapping the pen against his lips and looks skyward, deep in thought. "Actually, yes, there is. You can drive me up to the casino to get my car, since I had to leave it in their parking lot. *And* you can clean it out for me once we get there, since you were the one who messed it up."

It's a reasonable request—all things considered—though the thought of cleaning vomit out of his car after it's been sitting all night and half the day makes my stomach roil threateningly.

"Fair enough," I say. "When do you want to go?"

He glances at his watch and gestures toward the stack of papers. "I had Whitehorse send me a sheet on every employee at the casino. Our fax machine ran nonstop for nearly two hours and we went through two reams of paper. I figure I need another hour or two to finish. So what do you say to one o'clock?"

"Sounds good." I drop Jack's chart on the table. "I made a copy of this and looked through it all, but I didn't find anything unusual. I thought I'd let you look it over before I return it."

"Thanks, I'll have someone deliver it back to the agency when I'm done with it."

"Okay, see you at one."

I head out, intending to hit up a store to buy cleaning supplies. When I'm halfway there, it dawns on me that there is a much better place to get the kind of cleaning supplies I need. So, instead, I do a U-turn and head for the hospital.

* * *

The *swish* of automatic doors announces my arrival
in the ER waiting area. Stepping inside is like a trip in
a time machine. There's a saying that once you're an
ER nurse, you're always an ER nurse. I think it's true.
Of all the nursing jobs I've held, the ER was always my
favorite. I loved the variety, the camaraderie, the way
the workload could go from zero to sixty in a matter of
seconds, and the humor of the people who work there.
This last trait is one I've come to believe is necessary
for survival in a place where you may be witness to
some of life's worst tragedies.

At the moment, the place is calm; the waiting room
is empty. When I ask the registrar if I can sneak into the
back for a visit, she says, "Please do. It's been unnatu-
rally quiet today and they need something new to distract them back there. Last time I looked, they were
playing bedpan shuffleboard."

I find most of the staff inside the nurses' station.
While the patient flow might be quiet, the noise level
in the department isn't. There are only two patients—
a middle-aged gentleman with the sniffles, and a toddler with a leg wound—but they are both making
themselves known. The man is coughing, moaning,
and groaning loudly, and the kid, who is getting su-
tured, is screaming as if his leg is being cut off without
the benefits of anesthesia.

One of my old nursing pals, Phyllis "Syph" Malone,
is on duty, a definite coup for me. Since I'm basically
here to steal supplies, having someone I know and
trust—and who knows and likes me—is necessary. It's
been more than seven years since I worked in the ER
and the staff has seen a lot of changeover since then.

Amongst those on duty today are two new faces I don't recognize.

"Hey, 'Mets,'" Syph greets. "What brings you in here?"

"Thought I'd pop in and see how things were shaking, say hi to everyone."

Syph, who knows me well enough to know I'm here for more than a casual "hi" visit, cocks her head to one side and smiles. She watches me do a meet-and-greet with the rest of the staff; after which, she shares a retelling of my infamous nipple incident for the benefit of the two new gals. When one of the newbies asks about our use of nicknames, Syph fills them in on that, too. She explains how they were born out of boredom one evening years ago when a bunch of us nurses were making fun of the way we tend to refer to our patients by a diagnosis and room number rather than a name. We decided to give ourselves nicknames that resembled our real names and were also a disease or disorder. Clearly, Phyllis fared less well than the rest of us, and my nickname, a term often used to refer to metastases or the spread of cancer, isn't nearly as colorful. But the names have stuck, as has the habit, which is why the current patients are known as "The Man Flu in Room Eight" and "The Demon Spawn in Room Six."

When Syph is finished with her storytelling, she gets up and heads toward the back of the ER. "Hey, Mets, come on and I'll buy you a cup of our rotgut coffee."

As soon as we're ensconced inside the relative privacy of the ER break room, Syph says, "So what's up?"

"I need to borrow a few cleaning supplies, the strong biohazard stuff."

"Let me guess, you finally killed David and now you need to eliminate the evidence?"

I laugh. "No, nothing quite that serious. I've moved on from my homicidal rage to quiet acceptance."

"Ah, I see. You got your settlement."

"Bingo."

"Nothing like an infusion of cold, hard cash to cure the lovelorn," she says with a smile. "I hope you took the bastard to the cleaners."

"The settlement was a reasonable one. I'm satisfied."

"Good, though I have to tell you, no one here would blame you if you *had* killed him. I mean, it was bad enough that he was schtupping one of the nurses, but to do it right here in the OR? That was pretty low."

"Yes, it was. But I've moved on. I've decided David is a slinky."

"A slinky?"

"Yep, he isn't good for much, but it makes me smile when I think about pushing him down the stairs."

Syph chuckles and says, "So how's your love life going otherwise? Have you hooked up with that hunky detective yet?"

"No, our relationship is strictly a professional one."

"That's too bad."

That it is.

"And there's no one else?"

I shake my head. "Nope. Right now I'm enjoying my singlehood."

"Right," Syph scoffs.

"Being single has its perks."

"Yeah, like having no one to kiss at midnight on New Year's Eve."

"But I don't have to clean whisker hairs out of the bathroom sink," I counter. Something niggles at the back of my mind when I say that, but I'm too busy trying to defend myself to give it much thought.

"What about having someone to snuggle up to on these cold winter nights?"

"Two words: electric blanket. Plus I get the bed all to myself, and there's no one snoring next to me, keeping me awake. If I feel like I need a warm body, my dog, Hoover, does just fine."

Syph thinks for a few seconds and then says, "Okay, what about having someone to go out with, to the movies or dinner?"

I shrug. "No competition for the remote, so I can watch chick flicks all day long without having to suffer through football play-offs. And I can do it while eating ice cream for dinner, if I want."

"You have to sit at the singles table at weddings."

"As long as I get cake, I don't care. And speaking of sitting, I don't have to worry about whether the toilet seat is up or down," I say in my best smug *"take that!"* tone.

"What about sex?"

Damn it, she's got me there. I could always put on a disguise and head for the Garden of Eden, an isolated specialty shop a few miles outside of town that sells sex toys. But even if I buy a gas-powered, vibrating dildo with fifty attachments, I know it won't be the same.

"Fine, you win," I say, sulking. "If you're done point-ing out how miserable and lonely my life is, I'd like to get my cleaning supplies."

"I'll do better than that," Syph says with a sly grin. "I'll give you cleaning supplies and a phone number."

"A phone number? For what? 1-800-GIGOLO?"

"No, for this guy I know. His name is Mike. He's single, your age, and good-looking."

"Divorced?"

"Nope, never been married."

"So what's the catch? No, wait, let me guess. He lives with his mother and has a secret fetish involving WD-40, his sister's panty hose, and a weed whacker?"

"No," Syph says, laughing. Then she stops and looks seriously thoughtful for a moment. "Actually, I think he does live with his mother, but it's only temporary because he's new in town and looking for a house to buy. He seems like a really nice guy. Plus he drives a Beemer."

"I don't think so, Syph. The last blind date I had ended up sleeping with my mother."

"Oh, come on. Give it a chance. Put yourself out there. What have you got to lose?"

"You mean, besides my dignity, my sanity, or maybe even my life?"

She shoots me a give-me-a-break look.

"Fine," I say with a sigh of resignation. "How do you know him?"

"Al's been working with him to find a house," she says, referring to her Realtor husband.

"What does he do for a living?"

"He's a pharmacist at the drugstore downtown."

Resigned, I agree to let Syph give me the number, but when she calls her husband to get it, she goes straight to voice mail.

"I'll call you with the number when Al gets back to me," she says.

"Fine, but wait a few days. I'm heading to Florida tonight for a conference, so I won't be back until the thirty-first. And I'm not promising anything."

"Aw, come on, give the guy a shot."

"Why? Does he have an STD?"

"Very funny, but I'm serious. This could turn out to be fun. You know what they say about pharmacists."

Against my better judgment, I bite. "No, what do they say?"

With a sly wink, she tells me. "They like to do it over the counter."

Chapter 21

Five minutes later, as I'm stuffing my cleaning supplies into the back of the hearse, my phone rings. I half-expect it to be the pharmacist, but instead it's Hurley.

"Hey," I say into the phone. "Did you change your mind about the time?"

"Nope, we're still on for one, but I have some news. Guess what I just found out?"

"What?"

"The Strommens are in serious financial trouble. The bank started foreclosure proceedings on both the farm and the house, and the Strommens were using credit cards for their day-to-day living. They are up to their necks in debt and facing bankruptcy. Donald sold off all their livestock last year and has been selling off equipment, here and there, to try to keep them afloat. With the economy being what it is, well . . ."

"Ooookay," I say slowly, wondering why he sounds so excited about this information. "That's a very sad story and all, but what does it have to do with his death?"

"Want to guess what one payment the Strommens did keep up to date?"

I think a moment, but nothing leaps to mind that would cause the sort of self-satisfied tone I can hear in Hurley's voice—a tone I know from past experience means he's hooked into something big. Then it hits me. "A life insurance policy?"

"Bingo. And not just any life insurance policy, either. Donald Strommen was insured for half a million bucks."

"Wow!"

"Yeah, wow," Hurley echoes. "That translates into some serious motive for Charlotte."

"You think she killed him for the insurance money?"

"Why not? You saw how they were living. The creditors were going to put them out on the street. Charlotte saw only one way out and took it. You were the one who saw her packing away her husband's clothes before she was supposed to know he was dead."

"Yeah, I did." I frown because—despite what I saw, and my certainty that Charlotte wasn't being totally honest with us when we talked to her—I'm having a hard time seeing her as a cold-blooded murderer.

"I'm going to look into this insurance policy a little more. I'll let you know what I find out when I see you at one."

"Okay, see you then." I disconnect the call and glance at my watch. I still have a little over an hour left, so I head to my sister's house.

When I pull up out front, I find my niece, Erika, hanging out on her front porch. She's enjoying the unusually warm weather with a couple of girlfriends and two guy friends. She leaves the group and runs over to greet me as soon as I pull into the curb. Erika is going through a bit of a Goth phase, as evidenced by the blue-black hair surrounding her brown roots, a pair of black leather boots, which each have a dozen metal buckles, and makeup that includes kohl eyeliner and black lipstick. But beneath that grim appearance, Erika is really a sweet kid at heart. And given her fascination with blood and gore, I think she might make a crackerjack surgeon when she grows up. Still, while it's easy for me to imagine her someday saving lives, her current fascination is with death. Because of that, the hearse intrigues her.

"Hi, Aunt Mattie! Can I show my friends your car?"

So much for the social niceties.

The other kids hang back on the porch, watching us.

"Sure," I say.

"Cool! Hey, guys, come check this out. It's so rad! They used to put dead people in here." Erika's eyes grow wide with delight as she says this, as if a car for dead people were the coolest hangout on earth.

The other kids squirm and shift uncomfortably, looking at one another. Clearly, they aren't quite as enamored with the hearse as Erika is, though their expressions do indicate a certain level of curiosity. I suspect they are waiting for one person in the group to make the first move; it doesn't take long for a blond-ponytailed girl named Becky to take the plunge. The others wait a few beats and then follow, meandering over to us in that unrushed *"I'm cool"* manner that teenagers are so good at.

I stand off to one side and let the kids do their thing with the car. They open the tailgate and doors, run their hands over the leather seats, and check out the rails in the back, where the caskets used to lock into place. The two boys check out the gauges on the dash, while Erika climbs into the back and lies down between the rails, staring up at the ceiling, her hands folded on her belly in perfect repose.

"I'm dead," she says. "And you guys are my pallbearers. Can you carry me out?"

Nervous laughter follows, but no one makes a move. Erika is a spooky kid sometimes.

"Hey, guys," I say, deciding the time has come, "let me ask you something. Do you know Hannah Strommen?"

"'Charmin' Strommen'?" Becky says.

"Not so much these days," one of the boys comments.

Erika gives up on her pretend death and scoots out to sit on the back edge of the rear compartment. "Hannah's been kind of off lately," she tells me.

"How do you mean?"

"Well, ever since her father disappeared, she's been acting all weird and stuff. She won't talk to anyone, and her eyes are always red and puffy, like she's crying all the time. I guess that makes sense, since her dad is gone. But she doesn't ever eat anything at lunchtime now, and she keeps muttering strange things to herself."

"Like what?"

Becky says, "Well, like the other day, she was talking to herself about how she was going to burn in hell, and how her mother would be there with her. It was really creepy because she was saying it like she was talking to someone, but she was all alone. It was a total *Carrie* moment, you know?" she says, all wide-eyed and wary. "I mean, I'm sure it's a bad thing to go through, but seriously? The girl's creep factor lately is off the charts."

The other kids all nod in agreement.

"Is there someone at school Hannah is close to?" I ask them.

"Not anymore," Erika says. "She and Danny Olsen were a thing for a while, but they broke up. He said she's kind of demento lately. And she doesn't hang out with her usual girlfriends much anymore, either."

"I take it this is a change in her behavior?"

They all nod and Becky says, "Totally. It's like she doesn't care anymore. Hannah is kind of pretty, but lately her hair has been all stringy and greasy, and sometimes she wears the same clothes to school for days in a row." Becky pauses and wrinkles her nose. "She kind of smells."

With that, I thank the kids for their candor, leave them to explore the hearse, and head inside. I find my sister, Desi, in the kitchen; she's whipping up some kind of batter in a big mixing bowl. There is chili simmering on the stove, so I suspect the batter will be turned into Desi's mouthwatering corn bread.

"Hey, sis," she says when she sees me. She pours the batter into a glass baking pan and sticks it in the oven. "What brings you to our neck of the woods?"

"I missed my little sister," I say with a smile, settling onto one of the stools at the counter.

"I've missed you, too," she says. Then with a wink, she adds, "What's the real reason?"

"I wanted to pick the kids' brains about one of their fellow students. Something related to a case I'm working on."

"Lucien's case with that kid?"

I shake my head. "No, it's another one, not something I can talk about yet." I get up and walk over to take a spoon from the silverware drawer. Then I decide to risk my life for the greater good by doing a quick "poison test" on the chili. It's delicious, with just the right amount of spice.

"How is it?" Desi asks.

"Perfect, as usual. Clearly, you inherited cooking genes from your father, which I didn't get from mine."

Desi and I are technically half sisters. Though we

share the same mother, we each had different fathers—neither one of which is still married to Mom. Our mother goes through husbands faster than I can go through a pint of Ben & Jerry's. At least Desi's father, who was only married to my mother for a little over a year, is still somewhat involved in Desi's life, unlike my father, who escaped faster than Ellie the horse. Since our mother's idea of cooking involves nuking food into hard blocks of sterility to make sure it is free of both germs and taste, it's pretty obvious where Desi's cooking abilities come from.

"Is Ethan here?" I ask.

Desi nods. "In his room."

I toss my chili spoon into the sink. "I'm going to pop my head in and say hi."

Ethan is a peculiar kid in a different way from his sister. He's extremely bright, socially awkward, and a bit of a loner. It's probably just as well, since most folks don't take well to the hobby that is Ethan's greatest passion: bugs. The kid has a thing for insects of all kinds—the creepier and crawlier they are, the better. Fortunately, most of them are dead and pinned into cases, safely secluded behind glass fronts. But he has a few live ones. In addition to an ant farm, he has a terrarium that holds a tarantula, with the unfortunate name of Fluffy. Ethan is always quick to point out to anyone who mistakenly calls Fluffy a "bug" that he's actually an "arachnid." But few people hear this explanation because they are either running, screaming, from the room or passed out cold on the floor.

Ethan recently acquired a new pet: a Madagascar hissing cockroach. It's a hideous looking thing, a giant cockroach that measures about three inches in length and has an alarming habit of rearing back on its legs, waving its long antennae in the air, and hissing. Ethan bestowed the creature with the unimaginative but frighteningly apt name of Hissy. I don't know how the hell Desi does it. Living with Ethan and his pets would give me nightmares.

I find Ethan sitting at his desk, holding a magnifying glass, head bent over a display of beetles. Both Fluffy and Hissy are safely ensconced inside screen-topped terrariums atop a side dresser, so I venture in.

"Hi, Ethan," I say.

"Hi, Aunt Mattie."

"What are you up to?"

"Just studying some of my collections," he says.

His collections are all over the room: covered glass boxes that are filled with various creepy-crawlies, and flying bugs pinned onto white paper, with tiny, neat labels beneath each one bearing the critter's scientific name, the date it was obtained, and where it was found.

"I brought you something," I tell him, rummaging through my purse and pulling out the paper I stuck in there earlier. I unfold it, lay it on the desk, and smooth it out.

Ethan glances over at it, shrugs, and goes back to his beetle collection. "It's *Tineola bisselliella*," he says.

"Is it a grub for some kind of water bug?"

"Hardly," Ethan says in a tone that implies I'm an idiot. "It's the larva for the clothes-eating moth, though that's not a fair name because it's the larvae, not the moths that actually eat fabrics. I have an adult moth." He pushes back his chair, gets up, and goes to a shelf that holds dozens of display cases. He grabs one and brings it over to me.

"This is what the moth looks like. I've never found one of the larvae. Can I have this one?" He taps my picture.

"Sorry, but it's evidence in a case I'm working on."

"Did you find it on a sweater or something?"

"No, we found it in a body, inside the breathing tube of a man we think may have drowned."

Ethan looks up at me with a quizzical expression. "That's weird. *Tineola bisselliella* don't live anywhere near water. They like dark, dry places, like closets and trunks. Their primary food sources are fabrics and sometimes other insect parts, so I don't know how one would get inside a drowning person, or why it would. They aren't necrophagous, like the maggots of *Sarcophagidae* and *Calliphoridae,* the flies you typically find on decaying flesh."

Ethan's comfort level discussing this topic doesn't surprise me. He's had a fascination with bugs for as long as I can remember; not long ago, I arranged for him to spend some time with a leading forensic entomologist we had to consult on another case. Ethan was enthralled by the somewhat aptly named Dr. Beadle, and Dr. Beadle was equally fascinated with Ethan's knowledge and interest in entomology—enough so that he invited Ethan to attend the weeklong "Bug Camp" for kids Dr. Beadle runs every summer. Ethan is beyond excited about it, not only because it will give him a chance to learn more and collect new specimens, but also because he won't be one of the regular campers. Instead, Ethan will be functioning as Dr. Beadle's assistant, complete with pay in the form of a full camp scholarship and some rare bug with an unpronounceable name that Ethan gets to add to his collection.

Ethan says, "Was the drowned person wearing a scarf?"

"Not that we know of. There wasn't one on him

when we found him, but I suppose he might have had one, which came off in the water."

"What kind of coat was he wearing?"

I finally guess what Ethan is thinking. "I get it, you're wondering if that worm was on some of the clothing he was wearing. Am I right?"

Ethan nods. "It's possible that the larva was on his clothing. When he went into the water, it was knocked loose and he inhaled it, along with the water. That's the only explanation I can think of that makes sense."

I close my eyes and do a quick mental inventory of the clothing we removed from Donald Strommen's body during our autopsy. "He was wearing a parka, one of those fiberfill things with a nylon-type outer covering. Under that, he had on a flannel shirt and some thermal underwear. His pants were jeans. The socks might have been wool, but he was wearing heavy boots over them, and his long johns covered the cuffs. When we found him, he didn't have any gloves or hat, but they may have gotten lost in the water."

I open my eyes and see Ethan frowning. "What?" I say.

"The parka is definitely not moth material. The jeans, shirt, and underwear all could be, but those are items that are typically washed a lot and that should keep any larvae from settling or developing on them."

"Well, as I said before, he may have had a scarf or hat of some sort when he first went into the water. Those would be candidates, wouldn't they?"

"They would," Ethan says, nodding. "Don't you know what he was wearing when he was last seen?"

"I don't," I tell him, smiling at how keenly his mind is working along investigative lines. "But I can find out.

In the meantime, I need you to keep this to yourself for now, okay? It's top secret."

"No problem."

"You can't mention it to anyone. Not even your family or friends."

"Okay," he says with a degree of impatience.

I realize the risk of Ethan spreading tales is pretty low, since he tends to be a bit of a loner, preferring to spend time with his insects rather than other humans. So I decide to push a little further.

"Do you know Peter Strommen very well?" I ask.

"Not really. He hangs out with the other farm kids mostly."

"Have you noticed anything different about him lately? Or heard any rumors about him?"

Ethan thinks a moment and then shakes his head. "He's been a little sad since his father disappeared, but other than that . . ." He shrugs.

I reach over and tousle his hair, which makes him flinch. "Thanks for all your help, kiddo. Once our investigation is done, I'll let you know what we find, okay?"

"Do you think there's a chance I might be able to get that larva for my collection?" he asks, pointing to the picture that's still on his desk.

I grab the picture, fold it up, and stuff it back in my purse. "I don't know, buddy. I doubt it, but I'll see what I can do, okay?"

He shrugs again, and then he summarily dismisses me by settling back in at his desk and focusing on his beetle collection.

I head back out to the kitchen, where I steal a quick bowl of my sister's chili and a piece of hot-out-of-the-oven corn bread, which I promptly smother in butter.

As I scarf down the food, grateful that my stomach is finally back to normal, my sister fills me in on our mother's latest health complaints. Mom is not only a germophobe, but a hard-core hypochondriac. She recently became concerned that she might have cutaneous porphyria, a relatively rare disease that causes photosensitivity of the skin, resulting in blistering after sun exposure. Because of this manifestation, it is sometimes referred to as the "vampire disease," as its victims tend toward very pale complexions and avoidance of sunlight. Apparently, Mom was outside for all of thirty minutes yesterday. Despite the fact that she was wearing a sunscreen with an SPF factor of about 2 million, and not yawning at the sky the whole time, she is convinced the canker sore she developed in her mouth last night is a manifestation of cutaneous porphyria. With her naturally pale coloring, Mom fits the physical description of many who do have the disease. However, despite her ability to suck the life out of me at times, I'm as sure as I can be that she doesn't have it.

While I eat, I listen to Desi reiterate her conversations with Mom, and I nod or smile when expected. But I'm only partially focused as my mind ponders the puzzle of the inhaled moth larva. Maybe Charlotte really did kill her husband. Maybe she shoved a scarf or some other item into his mouth, choking him. I quickly discard that idea, because the size of Donald compared to the size of Charlotte makes it highly unlikely. But maybe she subdued him first and then choked or smothered him with something. Had she drugged him somehow?

The size issue makes me realize something else. If Charlotte did have something to do with Donald's death, then, in all likelihood, he died at home. How did she get his body to the river? Moving a man Donald's size when he's deadweight would be nigh onto impossible for someone of Charlotte's size. Someone had to have helped her. And given what I learned from talking to Erika and her friends, I'm betting that someone was Hannah.

There's no way right now to know if Donald was drugged, because the tox screen isn't done, and won't be for a day or two. But it occurs to me that the police might want to search the Strommen house to see what drugs they can find there, and to collect the items of clothing I saw Charlotte packing up before she has a chance to get rid of them. And I want to be there when they do it, to see and assess Hannah's frame of mind, even if her mother won't allow us to talk to her.

Chapter 22

When I pull up in front of the police station at one o'clock, Hurley is waiting for me out front, as promised.

As soon as he climbs into the hearse, I say, "I have a quick question for you. What clothing was Donald reported to be wearing when he disappeared?"

"The original missing persons report filed by Charlotte said he was wearing a hooded blue parka, blue jeans, a red-and-green-plaid flannel shirt, and brown boots. Pretty much what he was wearing when we found him. Why?"

"No mention of any scarf, or hat, or gloves?" I ask, ignoring his question.

"Nope. And now that you mention it, that's kind of odd, given the weather."

"Want to know what's odder than that?" I say.

"What?"

"You know that little worm we found in his trachea? It's the larva from a clothes-eating moth."

"You heard from the entomologist already? That's a pretty fast turnaround."

"Well, no, I haven't heard from the entomologist," I

say. "I showed a picture of the worm to Ethan and he identified it."

A long silence follows before Hurley says anything.

"Winston, look, I know you're proud of your nephew and his fascination with bugs and all, but I hope you'll understand if I opt to wait for an official report on this."

"I do understand, but I'm telling you, Ethan knows his stuff. So just keep it in mind, okay?"

"Yeah, okay," he says unconvincingly. "I have some news, too. We got a report back on the clothes Brian was wearing when we picked him up the other day. There are traces of gasoline on them. When I asked him about the gas can in his car, he said he used it in that house he was staying in to get a fire going."

"Do you believe him?"

"There's evidence that a fire was built in the fireplace there, so it doesn't really matter if I believe him or not. It's enough for reasonable doubt."

"I don't suppose there's any news on Catherine?"

"No, she's in the wind."

"No big surprise there. If she didn't kill Jack, she's probably moved on to find her next sugar daddy. Did you turn up anything in the files for the casino employees?"

Hurley shakes his head. "No, they're all well vetted by the casino, and there's nothing to suggest any of them had anything to do with it. My money's on Catherine, though Brian has a more logical motive."

"But what about the security tapes and his alibi?"

"Oh, I forgot to mention that. I finished going over those tapes last night while I was waiting for you, and it turns out Brian *was* in the casino until about seven in the morning. But then there's no sign of him for several hours. He appears again around noon. When I asked him about the missing time, he said he went out to his car and took a nap for a few hours so he could come back in and play some more. There is evidence of him leaving the building and walking through the parking lot. Unfortunately, his car was parked in an area that isn't visible to the cameras, so there's no way to verify that."

"Is he still in custody?"

Hurley nods. "It was agreeable to both sides. Sadly, I think the food and housing in jail is the best Brian's seen in a while. But to be honest, I don't know how much longer we can hold him if he wants to go. I spoke to the ADA and he says we don't have enough to make a case against anyone at this point."

"So where do we go from here?"

"We need to find the money."

"Maybe you should let Brian go then. If he's on the loose and has the money, maybe he'll start spending it."

"It's a thought. I'll see if we can hold him until we get back from Florida, and then we can spring him."

"So, switching cases, I talked to Erika and some of her friends earlier today about Hannah, the oldest of the Strommen kids, and they said she's been acting pretty weird ever since her father disappeared."

"Well, that's understandable, don't you think?"

"I don't know. They said she was talking to herself and saying things about going to hell and taking her mother with her."

"Hmm."

"I think we should go back out to the house and take another look around."

Hurley considers this idea, but he says nothing.

"And while I know you don't put much faith in Ethan's identification of that worm, I do. And I have a theory about how it might have ended up where it did."

"Do you now?"

"I do. What if Charlotte drugged him and then

stuffed something into his mouth to suffocate him? Something like a wool scarf? That sweater she was wearing looked moth-eaten, so maybe they have other clothing items in the same condition. And maybe one of those worms was on whatever she used."

Hurley nods. "Okay, maybe I can send Bob Richmond out there while we're in Florida."

"Is he back to work?"

"He said he can do some light duty."

"I suppose you could ask him, but, to be honest, I'd rather do it myself. I'm hoping the kids will be there. I think they might know something."

"Okay, I'll see if I can arrange for someone to keep an eye on the Strommen place while we're gone. It'll be a way to make sure Charlotte doesn't ditch any evidence."

"With all that land and the barn, there are plenty of places close by for her to hide something, if she wants."

"True, but I suppose that's a risk we'll have to take."

Huge clouds are scudding across the sky and it casts a dark shadow over the car as we drive, seeming like an omen. The temperature is dropping fast and I flip the heat on. For the rest of our drive, we talk about Florida, the conference, the classes we've signed up for, and our hope that whatever weather calamity is on the way will hold off until after our flight.

When we reach the casino parking lot, I pull into a space a few rows away from Hurley's car, the closest I can get. As I grab my cleaning supplies out of the back of the hearse, Hurley tosses me his car keys. "I need to go inside and use the can. Back in a bit."

Muttering curses to myself, I head for his car. When I unlock the door, I take a moment to brace myself, knowing what awaits me inside. Once I think I'm ready, I grab the handle and yank the door open.

The smell is awful, and I realize just how much I must have had to drink last night when I detect the scent of alcohol over and above the sour smell of old vomit. I put my hospital cleaning supplies to good use, and at some point during my scrubbing, Hurley returns to watch me. Twenty minutes later, the car is reasonably clean and smelling considerably better, though not perfect. I finish things off by hanging a new pine-scented air freshener from the rearview mirror.

Hurley does a quick visual inspection, and then he settles into the driver's seat and sniffs the air. "Not bad," he says.

"I used some heavy-duty industrial stuff."

He starts the engine and says, "I'll pick you up at seven forty-five. Warmth and sunshine, here we come." He closes the door, backs out, and takes off.

I'm feeling pretty upbeat for the drive home, so I throw some Beach Boys into the CD player to help me get in the mood. I've got just enough time before Hurley picks me up to take us to the airport to stop in and get my hair done. It's a visit long overdue, judging from Izzy's recent comment that I had bigger roots than the old oak tree in his front yard.

My current hairdresser, Barbara Moyer, is a bit outside the norm in that her main job is doing hair and makeup on dead people, and her salon is located in the basement of the Keller Funeral Home. She does some occasional side work on the living to help make ends meet, but it can be a little disconcerting because she only works on people who are supine. Like an artist who must have a certain light in order to envision a painting, Barbara must have a flat subject in order to envision her masterpiece. And she's very good, so as long as you don't mind having a dead person waiting in the wings as the next client, or the smell of formaldehyde hanging in the air, which to me isn't much worse than some of the color concoctions or permanent solutions regular salons use.

Today Barbara has two clients in her basement salon, one living and one dead, though it's hard for me to tell which is which at first. That's because the living one is an elderly woman with pasty, wrinkled skin, who is lying in perfect repose on one of Barbara's tables, hands atop one another just below her chest.

When Barbara sees me, she waves me in. "Hi, Mattie. Take a seat," she says, pointing to a chair against the wall. "I'm almost done with Irene."

When I hear the name, I realize who her other customer is. It's Irene Keller, the owner of the funeral home. Not long ago, I sort of fixed her up with a friend of mine, Bjorn Adamson, who, like Irene, is older than dirt. Like a character in a zombie movie, Irene opens her eyes and slowly turns her head to look at me. It's a bit creepy, because even with her eyes open, Irene doesn't look all that alive.

"Well, Ms. Winston," she says as Barbara puts some finishing touches on her hair with a curling iron. "Fancy meeting you again."

"Hello, Irene."

She eyes me from head to toe and clucks her tongue. "Have you got hepatitis or something?" she says.

"I've been using a tanning booth. I'm heading to Florida tonight and wanted to get some base color."

"Tan, schman," she says. "You should take better care of your skin if you want it to last your entire lifetime. If you're lucky, you'll end up with a creamy complexion like mine when you're older."

Not much of a sales pitch when you consider that Irene's face has so many wrinkles, it looks like a wad of crumpled paper; and her skin is so transparent that she's like a walking, talking anatomy class. And don't even get me started on her liver spots. Then again, last I knew, Irene had a boyfriend, which is more than I can claim. Granted, her boyfriend pees through a tube and forgets who and where he is several times a day, but I guess at Irene's age one can't afford to be too picky.

"How are things with you and Bjorn?" I ask her, hoping to change the subject.

"We're getting married next week," Irene says, beaming.

"Really? Well, congratulations." Considering that the two of them met only a few weeks ago, this seems a bit rushed, but then time isn't really on their side.

Barbara helps Irene sit up and gives her a mirror so she can check out the front view while Barbara works on the back. It proves to be a bit of a challenge, since Irene's hair is pretty thin. Barbara spends most of her time trying to cover the bald spots.

Irene surveys herself in the mirror and pats at the wattle hanging beneath her chin with the back of her hand. "I'm thinking of going braless for the wedding," she says, making Barbara and me both gape.

"Why?" Barbara asks, showing she's braver than I am.

"Well, watch," Irene says. She sets the mirror down, reaches under her blouse, and finagles around until her breasts suddenly drop several inches. "See?" she says. "The weight of my boobs hanging loose pulls all my skin down and minimizes this crap under my neck."

"I think you should wear a bra," I say.

"Whatever," she says, hoisting the girls back into place. "Have you picked out your funeral ensemble yet?" she asks me. "You know, it's never too early to arrange for your final sleep, and you want to make a good, lasting impression."

"Actually, I have," I tell her. "Barbara helped me pick

out my coffin and lining during my first visit here."
This is true, and it was an enlightening experience.
Also, a bit disturbing when I realized that I might look
better dead than alive. "I went with the mahogany."

"The mahogany is a nice choice," Irene says, "but we
have a whole new line of inventory available that you
might want to check out. There's this company that
makes very unique, personalized eternal beds."

Eternal beds? That's why I don't like funeral homes;
they all speak in "euphemese."

"Some lady had one made for her son that looks like
a skateboard," Irene goes on, "and an AT&T exec had
one made that looks like a cell phone."

"I'll bet the roaming charges are a bitch," I say, but
no one laughs. I try to think of a personalized coffin
for myself, but all I can come up with is one that looks
like a giant Ben & Jerry's container.

Ever the businesswoman, Irene hits me up with a
new pitch. "What about a plot? Have you purchased
one yet? We have some nice ones up on the hill, over-
looking the river. They offer a stunning forever view."

Her absurd funeral speak makes me laugh. "I don't
think the view will matter much," I tell her. "It will be
hard to see from six feet under."

"It's not all about you," Irene says. "You want your
visitors to have a peaceful, serene place when they drop
by for a visit. And who knows? Personally, I believe in
reincarnation, but until our spirits get reassigned, I
believe they hover over our burial place." She picks
up her mirror and starts examining her face again.
"I'm hoping to come back as a man," she says with a
sigh, perusing her upper lip. "At least then I can *choose*
to grow a mustache."

"I can bleach that, if you want," Barbara offers.

Irene considers this and then says, "Nah, that's okay.
Bjorn can't see it anyway. His eyesight's not so good."

She sets the mirror aside and looks at me. "I can make you a sweet deal on a plot if you buy now."

"Thanks, but I'm not ready yet."

Irene shrugs and says, "Suit yourself. But don't come bitching to me when you find out you have to spend your forever nap in view of the landfill."

Barbara announces Irene finished and helps her off the table. "You let me know if you change your mind," Irene says to me as she leaves.

Barbara pats the table and I get up and climb onto it, lying down in my own perfect repose. As Barbara's prepping my color application, I stare at the ceiling and think about Irene's spirit theory. "Do you believe in reincarnation?" I ask Barbara.

"I don't know. Some days I do. It's an interesting concept and a fun mind exercise when you try to figure out who, or what, you want to come back as."

I think about this for a second and the first thing that pops into my head is Hurley's jeans. Coming back as those would be a small slice of heaven. But I don't suppose an inanimate object is an option, so I think some more. "If we are reincarnated as animals, I think I'd like to come back as something symbolic and majestic, like an eagle. But with my luck, I'd probably end up as a dung beetle."

Barbara laughs. "I like to think that people who abuse animals come back as an animal that is then abused," she says.

"Ah, divine retribution," I say. "Like Sarah Palin coming back as a wolf, or Michael Vick coming back as a pit bull."

Our conversation continues as Barbara works her miracle on my hair. She's whip smart and a witty conversationalist, and our discussion touches on religion, philosophy, science, and death. By the time I'm done and look in the mirror, I'm starting to think reincarnation is entirely possible. Barbara has given my appearance a new life, and I bestow her with the nickname "the Reincarnator." With a Schwarzenegger-like "I'll be back," I head home, knowing that I'm about to spend a couple of days with Hurley in paradise looking my absolute best—as long as I keep my clothes on.

When I get home, I finish my packing and then head over to Izzy's house to talk to Dom, who has agreed to take care of Hoover and Rubbish while I'm gone. I go over Rubbish's food plan with him, and then start on Hoover's food and potty routines. Dom stops me short.

"Don't worry about Hoover. I plan to keep him over here while you're gone."

"Are you sure Izzy will be okay with that?"

Dom dismisses my concern with a wave of his hand. "Izzy pretends not to like animals, but I caught him sneaking Hoover some table snacks a couple of times, and he even petted him once." He pauses, frowns, and then adds, "Though I will have to make sure Hoover sleeps on the floor this time. When we took him to Iowa over Thanksgiving, he not only got into bed with us, he pushed Izzy right out onto the floor."

I grimace. "Sorry about that," I say. "That's my fault. I let him sleep in my bed with me all the time."

"You might want to rethink that," Dom says. "Just because you now have that bed all to yourself doesn't mean it will always be that way. Some guys might not like the idea of sharing your bed with a dog."

"There's plenty of time to worry about that," I say with a sigh. "I don't have any prospects on the horizon." Though I utter this with great nonchalance, my feelings on the subject are strong ones. On the one hand, I'm desperate to share some warmth, tenderness, and intimacy with someone, to satisfy both my emotional and my physical needs. But the person I most want to do that with is Hurley, and he is off-limits. So that means hooking up with someone new, someone who doesn't know me, someone who's never seen me naked before. Breaking in a new lover is never an easy task, and I'm not sure if I'm up for it.

"When is Hurley picking you up?" Dom asks. "I've got a pot roast on and it'll be ready in half an hour."

"Thanks, but I don't have time. I'll just grab a snack at the airport."

Dom tells me to have fun, but not too much—a reference to the night before, no doubt—and bids me adieu.

Hurley shows up on time. After a brief mutual admiration session with Hoover, he loads my suitcase into the car. By the time we're on the road, I'm feeling more excited than I have in months. Two days in paradise with Hurley! Can life get any better than this? But I'm also worried. The radio is filled with warnings for the coming storm, which is now arriving. Big, fat snowflakes are beginning to fall and the temperature outside has dropped dramatically. I'm cursing Mother Nature under my breath, praying that she holds back her full fury until after our plane takes off.

Hurley and I pass the time chatting about everything from the current political environment to the glacier-carved geography we're driving past. The only thing we don't discuss is work-related stuff. It's as if we have an understanding—a silent but mutual agreement to leave work behind us from this point on. There are periods of silence, too, unmarked by the awkwardness that can sometimes result from such pauses. To me, it's indicative of the level of comfort Hurley and I share with one another.

By the time we reach the airport, there is already an inch of snow on the ground. We park in the short-term lot and haul our luggage into the terminal, where we are relieved to see that our flight is still scheduled to leave on time. We get into line to check our bags and inch our way through the serpentine rope alleys, like cattle going to market. As each move brings us closer to the ticket desk, the silly-assed grin on my face grows bigger. Then, just as we reach the head of the line, I hear a familiar female voice behind us say, "Hurley! Mattie! Fancy meeting you guys here."

I turn around and see Candy Kane standing in line a few people behind us, a suitcase at her feet.

"Are you guys going to the forensics conference in Daytona Beach?" she asks.

"We are," Hurley says.

"Well, isn't that fabulous!" she says. "So am I!"

And suddenly I want to order a special casket in the shape of a fire truck.

Chapter 23

Though I'm determined not to show it, I'm mad enough to spit nails. I can't believe Candy has intruded on my time away with Hurley; and to make matters worse, she and Hurley chum up as soon as our bags are checked. They decide to hit up the airport bar for a drink while we're waiting. No one bothers to ask me what I want to do, so I tag along behind the two of them, like a fifth wheel.

When we arrive at the bar, Candy deftly maneuvers into place to take the stool on Hurley's left—damn, these tiny people are quick on their feet. Since there is a man on Hurley's right, I'm forced to sit next to Candy, who promptly turns her back to me to face Hurley, leaving my thoughts as dark as the sky outside. Hurley orders a beer and Candy goes for a screwdriver. Since I swore off booze for life when I got out of bed this morning, I opt for a wimpy club soda with lime.

For the next hour, I sit, watching, listening, and mentally fuming as Candy chitchats with Hurley about her family, her job, the weather, and other stupid stuff. Granted, it's the same stupid stuff I was so happy to chat about with Hurley earlier, but their easy camaraderie annoys me. I mean, they just met a few days ago! How is it Candy already has the same level of comfort it took me weeks to achieve with Hurley? I suffer through it by telling myself that once we're on the plane, I'll be the one seated next to Hurley and Candy will be somewhere else. . . . I'm thinking the wing might work.

When we finally board, Candy once again proves her dexterity by positioning herself between Hurley and me. She makes no effort, whatsoever, to look at the seat assignment on her boarding pass, leaving me to suspect she's going to try to edge in on my seat. Sure enough, when Hurley reaches our row, he settles into the window seat. I wait behind Candy, expecting her to move on. Instead, she turns to me and says, "Hey, Mattie, would you mind terribly if we traded seats? I'd like to finish my conversation with Steve."

"I don't think that's allowed," I say, trying not to sound as pissed as I feel. "With all the new security rules and such . . . you know."

"Actually, it's fine," says a female flight attendant standing nearby, "as long as we know about it ahead of time."

I give the flight attendant my best Death Star stare as Candy says, "See? There you go. My seat assignment is twenty-eight A, just a few rows back."

I appeal to Hurley with a look of desperation, but he's busy adjusting his seat belt and seems oblivious to it all as Candy settles into my seat. Furious, but unwilling to make a scene that might get me kicked off the plane, I make my way back to Candy's assigned row and cram myself into the window seat, feeling like I'm in Izzy's car. A moment later, a fiftyish-looking man in a business suit settles into the aisle seat next to me. He gives me a quick smile as he does up his seat belt, and then he opens his briefcase and takes out a stack of financial magazines: *Forbes, Bloomberg Businessweek, Kiplinger's, SmartMoney,* and *Barron's.* This bodes well for a quiet trip, but in case I'm wrong, I have an ace up my sleeve. Revealing what I do for a living, particularly if I do it in graphic detail, will typically put a damper on the most enthusiastic talkers.

My seat starts to bounce. At first, I think it's the luggage getting banged around below us. Then I realize it's the toddler behind me, kicking the back of my seat.

"Chandler, stop that," says the woman seated next to him, presumably his mother.

Chandler kicks a little harder; then the guy in the seat in front of me tries to recline, smashing my knees even tighter.

As I feel my feet start to go numb, the flight attendants shut the plane doors and begin their safety instructions, pretending that we all won't die a horrible death if something happens. It's only supposed to be a two-and-a-half-hour flight, but right now, Daytona Beach seems a long way off.

Our takeoff is a smooth one; and when the flight attendants come around with their drink cart, my seatmate opts for two of those cute little bottles filled with whiskey, and a soda to top them off. Judging from his red, bulbous nose and the fumes I've picked up coming off his breath, I'm guessing this is not his first drink, and he's no stranger to alcohol. I'm tempted to join him, but memories of this morning's hangover make me reconsider. I opt for a plain club soda, instead.

I spend the next hour and a half enduring my seat-kicking, knee-squashing torture. I am wondering what Hurley and Candy are doing. I keep peering over the seats in front of me, trying to see past the tops of all the heads to Candy and Hurley to make sure they are both still upright and in their respective seats. I decide that if Candy ever gets up to use the bathroom, I'm going to make a move to reclaim my seat. But she doesn't budge, leaving me to wonder how someone so small can have a bladder so big.

Just as my seatmate downs his second drink, the plane shudders and drops precipitously, triggering gasps from the passengers. The cabin lights are low and out the window beside me is a black void . . . until the sky lights up as a lightning bolt zigzags across the sky. The seat belt light comes on and the captain asks all passengers to take their seats in anticipation of a little turbulence.

Over the next ten minutes, it becomes obvious that the captain is a master of understatement as the plane bucks, drops, tilts, shudders, and shakes so hard it feels like the thing is going to come apart. The kid behind me starts to cry and the man next to me grabs for his barf bag. I grip the arms of my seat and turtle upward to scope out the cabin and find the closest emergency exits. Instead, my eyes settle on Hurley, who is also sitting bolt upright and looking back at me. Our eyes meet and Hurley mouths "Are you okay?" I shake my head, convinced we are all about to die. Then we go into a precipitous dive, and Hurley's head disappears from my view.

I'm frightened, but also oddly calm and thinking clearly. It's the hallmark of any good ER nurse, the ability to quash your natural adrenaline reaction and maintain your composure in the most frenetic and dire of circumstances. My mind starts pondering crazy stuff, like my appointment with Barbara earlier. I figure that if the plane does go down, there won't be enough of me left for even Barbara to fix, and the fact that her wonderful ministrations will go to waste saddens me more than my impending death does. Then I remember our discussion about reincarnation. Looking out my window and thinking about the distance between the ground and me, I decide I don't want to be an eagle anymore. I change my choice to a dolphin. Then I recall my conversation with Irene and realize how wise I was to avoid her attempts to sell me a plot. At this rate, my remains will likely fit into a peanut butter jar.

Outside my window, bolts of lightning flash everywhere, highlighting a menacing sky filled with black clouds. Rain and sleet pelt the plane, drowning out the frightened whispers of my fellow passengers. After a few more minutes of riding the flying, bucking bronco, the plane suddenly levels out and things settle down. My relief over death being a bit less imminent is quickly upstaged by my seatmate's stomach. Unlike our ride at present, his stomach is currently anything but settled. I watch as he pukes into his bag, and I wrinkle my nose as the smell of alcohol permeates the air.

A minute later, I look out my window and see the lights of a major metropolis below us. The captain comes back on the intercom to apologize for the mayhem and inform us that the plane has sustained some minor damage. This worries me, because if his definition of "minor damage" is as accurate as his definition of "a little turbulence," I can expect both wings to fall off the plane any second now. The captain assures everyone we can still fly just fine, but we are being forced to divert and land in Atlanta.

As we make our descent, everyone inside the plane is deathly quiet except for the seat kicker behind me, who is sobbing as his mother tries to reassure him. When the plane touches down and brakes, there is an audible sigh of relief and the cabin breaks into applause.

It takes another half an hour to reach our gate; and when the doors are finally opened, everyone disembarks in record time—no doubt fueled by the adrenaline surge of a near-death experience. I find Hurley and Candy waiting for me inside the terminal. Candy looks pale and frightened and, much to my dismay, is clinging to Hurley's arm.

"Well, that was certainly scary," I say as I approach them.

"I'll say," Hurley agrees. "Are you okay, Winston?"

"I'm fine, and glad to be back on solid ground."

Outside the terminal, more lightning bolts illuminate the sky, and a rumble of thunder shakes the building, making Candy jump. "Oh, my God," she says with an uneasy laugh. "My nerves are shot. And I need to pee something fierce."

Great. *Now* she has to go.

"I'll be right back," she says. She releases her death grip on Hurley's arm and heads for the nearest bathroom.

As soon as she's gone, Hurley looks at me with a worried expression. "Are you sure you're okay?"

"I'm fine," I say again.

"I'm sorry you had to go through that alone. I should have been there with you."

"I managed. My seatmate kept me distracted." Memories of the alcohol fumes emanating from him come back to me; and with it, some niggling thought that I can't quite suss out. "I don't think I'll be too eager to fly again anytime soon, though."

"I'm guessing that won't be an issue," Hurley says. "I don't think there will be any other flights leaving here for a while, thanks to the weather."

A nearby display of scheduled flights confirms this; *delayed* flashes beside each one. "We should try to rent a car," Hurley suggests, "but I imagine everyone else will have the same idea. We need to get to a rental stand before all the cars are gone. It's about eight hours to Daytona Beach from here. If we drive all night, we should be able to get to our hotel in time to still make most of the conference."

Candy returns from the bathroom, looking a little better, but still visibly shaken. When we fill her in on the new plan, she eagerly agrees. "Driving sounds like a good idea to me," she says. "I don't care if I never get on another plane again."

"Let's get going then," Hurley says. Candy and I follow his lead, heading for the main terminal. When we reach a juncture that shows the baggage area to the right and the rental car section to the left, Hurley hands me his luggage check ticket. "I'll go see about getting us a car. You guys go and get our luggage."

"That was one of the scariest things I've ever been through," Candy says as we part company and hustle toward the baggage carousel. "I was frightened to death!"

"Yeah, it was scary," I say, thinking uncharitably that if we had died, she would have at least had Hurley to hang on to. I, on the other hand, would have been dispatched to the netherworld with a puking alcoholic as my eternal companion.

"I've never been a fan of flying, and this just confirms it for me," Candy says. "Toss me into a burning building anytime over an airplane."

Don't tempt me.

When we reach the baggage area, the carousels are still and quiet, and there's a large crowd of people milling around. It's a good half hour before our luggage starts to arrive, and it doesn't take me long to find my suitcase and Hurley's. Candy's, however, proves a bit more elusive. After waiting another half an hour, the carousel is stopped and empty, with no sign of Candy's luggage.

"That's just great," Candy says irritably.

"Maybe it got misplaced. Let's see if we can find someone to help us."

We take off in the direction of the main terminal area, and halfway there we run into Hurley.

"Good news," he says, holding up a handful of papers. "I got us a car."

"Bad news," I say, gesturing toward Candy. "We've lost some luggage."

It takes us another hour to find someone to search unsuccessfully for the lost luggage and for Candy to then file a claim. She's clearly mad about the situation and does her best to intimidate the airline staff; her anger is no doubt fueled by her lingering adrenaline. But in the end, she resigns herself to the situation and says, "I'll just pick up some stuff when we get to Daytona Beach."

By the time we finally get to our rental car and leave the airport, it's after two in the morning. Hurley offers to drive; and after a little negotiating, Candy opts for the backseat so she can lie down and nap. That leaves me in the front with Hurley.

Thirty minutes later, we are on a major highway, and the worst of the storm is behind us. Candy falls asleep in the backseat almost immediately; and though I'm feeling quite tired myself, I'm determined to stay awake to make sure Hurley does the same. But the rhythmic lull of the tires on the road, combined with the exhaustion left behind by my earlier adrenaline surge, gets the better of me. My eyelids grow heavy; and after a few minutes of struggling to keep them open, I give in to the bliss of sleep.

I'm awakened to a loud *pop*, followed by an ominous shaking. For one horrifying moment, my mind thinks I'm back on the plane, plummeting toward certain annihilation. I sit bolt upright, see a stretch of highway in front of me highlighted by morning sun, and register the *thud-thud-thud* sound of a blown tire.

"Damn it!" Hurley mutters. He lets off on the gas and carefully pulls the car off onto the shoulder. "I swear this trip is jinxed."

Candy is awakened by the noise, too. As the two of us sit there, rubbing the sleep from our eyes, I ask, "Where are we?"

"About half an hour from the Florida state line," Hurley says as he shifts the car into park. He gets out to survey the damage, and I decide to join him and stretch my legs a bit. Our rear passenger tire is flatter than the proverbial pancake. After sighing heavily and raking a hand through his hair, Hurley opens the trunk and rummages around. He comes up with a spare, a jack, and a lug wrench, and heads for the damaged tire.

Fortunately, the shoulder on this part of the road is wide, and beside it is a large field that is mostly dirt, with a few clumps of grass. I've seen those TV shows with footage of inattentive drivers hitting cars that are on the side of the road, like ours is. So I stand safely off to one side in the field, where I can watch the two lanes of traffic coming at us and warn Hurley if anyone appears to be veering our way.

Despite the flat tire setback, I'm buoyed by the warm air, a breathtaking sunrise, and the knowledge that I'm not about to die a horrible death aboard a crashing plane. I raise my face to the sun and close my eyes a moment to enjoy the warmth.

When I finally open my eyes again, I see that Candy has also gotten out of the car. She's standing behind the trunk, watching as Hurley loosens the lug nuts on the wheel. I start to say something to her, to warn her that she should move, in case some idiot does rear-end us. But before I can utter a word, my entire body starts to burn like it's on fire, and the only thing that comes out is a scream.

Chapter 24

The next few seconds are a collage of pain and confusion. The skin on my torso, arms, and legs is on fire. As I look down at my chest, I'm horrified to see hundreds of tiny red ants crawling on me. They're on my arms, too; and when I pull out the waist of my pants, I can see them crawling down there as well. The fire on my skin grows hotter and the pain morphs into panic as I look down at my feet and realize what's happening. I am standing atop an ant nest and the buggers have swarmed up my legs, inside my jeans, under my shirt, up my back, and down my arms. And now that they are all in position, they are biting.

Frantic, I scrape at the ones on my arm and pull my shirt away from my body to try to brush those away. But the fabric keeps getting in the way and the burning sensation is growing more intense by the second. Desperate to rid myself of the ants, I peel off my shirt and jeans and start swatting, jumping, swiping . . . doing a crazy spasm dance in an effort to get them off me. Though my eyes are focused on the army of ants swarming over me, some distant part of my mind becomes aware of both Hurley and Candy staring at me with bewildered expressions. I hear Hurley say, "What the hell? Why is she dancing in her underwear?" He and Candy both hurry toward me. A trio of semis drives by and blasts their air horns, and then cars start adding to the cacophony.

I hear Candy say, "Fire ants"; then she and Hurley are brushing and swatting at me. They keep yelling at me to hold still, but I can't. The pain is too great.

After several minutes of swatting and swiping, they have dispatched the ants, but my skin is still on fire. I can see dozens, maybe hundreds, of fiery red wheals on my body, and I realize I'm standing on the side of a major thoroughfare in my underwear.

Candy steers me back toward the car, while Hurley scoops up my clothes and shakes and examines them to make sure there are no remaining ants in them. Candy opens the front passenger door and sits me down on the seat. Hurley hands me my clothes and goes back to changing the tire. As I struggle to put my clothes back on, the wheals on my skin continue to burn. And now my throat feels like it's growing tight. I realize I'm having a reaction to the bites. I tell Candy, "I'm having . . . trouble breathing . . . and I need . . . to get to . . . a hospital."

Candy takes out her cell phone and yells at Hurley, "Hurry up, Steve! I think she's having a bad reaction."

Massive itching sets in, along with the burning, and I can see the wheals on my skin spreading into hives. I'm vaguely aware of Hurley cussing, banging, and clanging things by the flat tire; then I feel the car sink down as the jack is let off. Candy gets in the backseat, while Hurley jumps behind the wheel and takes off. I can hear him and Candy talking back and forth frantically, calling 911 and looking for an exit that has one of those blue signs with an *H* on it. I can barely suck any air through my throat, and the world around me is rapidly closing in. Then it all goes dark.

The next thing I know, I'm flat on my back staring up at a ceiling with four fluorescent panel lights in it and a large exam light on a swivel arm. I blink and make out the top of an IV pole with a bag of IV fluids hanging from it on my left. I raise that arm and see tubing snaking its way into the bend of my elbow, where a transparent dressing is covering an IV catheter. My nose feels dry and I realize there are oxygen prongs poking into each nostril.

I hear a strange female voice say, "Look, she's awake."

Suddenly Hurley's worried face is above mine, staring down at me.

"Winston? Are you okay? Can you hear me?"

I nod, and then I try my voice. "I can hear you," I croak through a raw, parched throat. "What happened?"

"You stepped on a fire ant nest back along the interstate when we stopped for the flat tire. They stung you all over your body. The doc said you had a flax reaction . . . or something like that."

I smile. "Anaphylaxis," I say.

"Yeah, that's it," Hurley says. "You were barely breathing when we got you here." He sighs heavily and swipes at his brow. "You scared the crap out of me, Winston."

The curtain, which is surrounding my bed, parts, and a dark-haired, ponytailed, short woman enters. "Welcome back to the land of the living," she says. "I'm Dr. Tennyson, and your friends told me that you're an ER nurse."

"Used to be," I say.

"Do you remember what happened?"

I shake my head. "I remember the ants, and I

vaguely remember getting shoved into a car, but after that . . . nothing."

"I'm not surprised," Tennyson says. "You were bitten several hundred times by fire ants and you went into anaphylactic shock. I damn near had to intubate you, but the epinephrine and Benadryl kicked in fast enough to turn things around."

"Thank you," I say.

"I think you'll be fine now, but I want to keep you here for another hour or so to make sure you don't have any rebound."

I nod my understanding.

"I'll check back with you in a little while," Tennyson says, and then she's gone.

I look over at Hurley and ask, "What time is it?"

"A little after nine."

I wince and close my eyes. "I'm so sorry."

"You don't need to apologize," he says. "It wasn't your fault."

"But the conference . . ."

"Screw the conference," Hurley says. "This whole trip has been jinxed from the get-go. First the plane nearly crashes, then Candy's luggage goes missing, and now this." He shakes his head in dismay. "The only place we're going when you get sprung out of here is home."

"We could still make tomorrow's sessions," I say.

Hurley shakes his head again. "No way. I'm taking you home."

"Where's Candy?"

"She went to make some phone calls. She should be back anytime."

As if on cue, Candy appears. "Mattie, thank goodness! Are you okay?" she asks.

"I will be," I say, scratching away at my skin. "But these damn bites still burn like a bitch."

Hurley fills her in on the doctor's report and his plans to call off the trip and head home.

"That's fine by me," Candy says, "but I'm not getting on another plane. If you two are planning to fly home, I'll drive the rental car back."

This plan momentarily buoys my spirits, since it means I might finally get Hurley to myself, but then Hurley says, "We should stay together. I'll call the rental company and tell them we're changing our plans. I'm sure it won't be a problem."

As I listen to this conversation, it's all I can do to keep my eyes open. My eyelids feel like they have tiny weights on them, pulling them down, down, down. No doubt, it's the effects of the Benadryl I was given.

"How long will it take to drive back?" I ask.

Hurley says, "It's somewhere around eighteen hours, I think. If we take turns behind the wheel, we should be able to do it all in one day."

"I don't think I'll be able to drive for a while because of the drugs."

"That's okay," Candy says. "Steve and I can handle it."

Though I know she is trying to reassure me, the implication that the two of them are a team annoys me. But the drugs have my brain so fogged up, I can't drum up any real ire. Instead, I give in to the enticing pull of a drugged slumber and let myself drift off.

A little over an hour later, I am awake, disconnected from my IV, dressed, and ready to check out. My skin still burns in spots, so the doctor gives me a prescription for Vicodin, which Hurley gets filled at the hospital pharmacy. He decides to take the first shift behind the wheel. When we get to the car, I still feel groggy from the drugs, so I opt to take the backseat this time. My intent is to stay awake and keep an eye on the twosome in the front seat, but fatigue wins out over my jealousy, and soon I'm fast asleep.

At some point later, I'm jolted awake by a bang and shaking; I think I'm back in the plane again, riding the storm to certain death. I sit bolt upright and realize I'm in the car when I see Candy in front of me in the driver's seat, and Hurley in the front passenger seat. I breathe a sigh of relief, wondering how much longer the plane ride from hell will continue to haunt me. I look out the windows and see we are parked next to a pump at a gas station/convenience store combo. Outside, the sky is dark and ominous. Tiny icicles are hanging off the carport roof above us, and sleety snow is pinging against the car. Judging from the wet spots on Hurley's head and shoulders, I'm guessing he's the one who pumped the gas.

"Well, hello there, Sleeping Beauty," Hurley says with a smile. "How are you feeling?"

"Groggy," I say, wiping the sleep from my eyes. "But otherwise okay." I look at my arms and see that while the dozens of bites I have are red and itchy, the hives are in full retreat. "Where are we?"

"Somewhere in Tennessee," Hurley says as Candy starts the car.

"Wow, how long was I asleep?"

"About eight hours. We had to stop to gas up and we're going to grab a bite to eat. There's a pizza place just up the road. Are you hungry?"

"Starving." I'm glad to hear we're not hitting the road right away, because I also have to pee.

When we arrive at the pizza place, we discover our food plans are dashed when the staff informs us they are closing early because of the weather, though I manage to convince them to let me use the bathroom. The weather outside is getting more ugly by the minute. By the time I return from the bathroom, frozen rain is pelting the roof, and small hailstones are bouncing in the parking lot.

Before we head back outside, Hurley says, "Candy, why don't you let me drive. This weather is going to make for treacherous roads."

Candy squares her shoulders, dons her feminist armor, and says, "I'm fine. I've driven the fire engine in stuff worse than this."

Hurley looks like he's about to object, but he purses his lips, instead, and stays quiet. The short trip to our car is a nasty one. Walking atop the hailstones in the parking lot is like trying to walk on ball bearings, and everything is covered in a thin sheet of ice. Hurley takes my arm as we negotiate the distance, but it's small comfort. The stuff falling from the sky stings as it hits, and the air is bitterly cold.

Once we're settled inside the car, the windows steam up from our radiating body heat. We have to wait a few minutes for the defroster to defog and melt the ice on the windshield. No one volunteers to get out and scrape.

The next hour is a white-knuckled drive for Candy, and an equally white-knuckled ride for Hurley and me. I can feel the tension radiating off all of us as we creep down the road with minimal visibility, passing dozens of cars off in the ditches. Candy seems to be playing it safe and sensible, going slowly and leaving plenty of room between our vehicle and the cars ahead.

The precipitation turns to snow and comes down hard and fast, sticking to everything in sight. The fact that it's no longer ice that's falling seems to give the drivers a false sense of security because the speed of the traffic inches up a notch.

And then disaster strikes.

A semi in front of us brakes; and in a flash, it starts to skid. Its cab turns to the left, while the trailer continues its forward momentum. Candy, who is a good ways behind the truck, hits the brakes as well. I feel our car start a sickening slide. Candy pumps the brakes, trying to break out of the skid, but it has little effect. We all stare at the truck in front of us, which is now jackknifed across the road and looming ever closer. For several terrible seconds, it looks like we aren't going to stop in time. But at the last moment, Candy turns the wheel a hair to the left and she's able to stop the skid and come to a halt with us sideways in the road.

And then a pickup behind us crashes into Candy's door, sending our car spinning across the road, down a small embankment, and into a huge rock wall.

Chapter 25

When we come to a stop, I see that the driver's side of the hood is crumpled beneath a large rock outcropping. Smoke or steam—I can't tell which—is spewing from the engine. I do a quick self-assessment, find everything in working order, and then focus on the other two.

"Hurley? Candy? Are you two okay?"

Hurley answers first. "I think I'm okay." He undoes his seat belt and moves his legs tentatively. "I'm a bit banged up, but everything seems to be working." He looks over at Candy, whose face is pinched with pain.

"I think my leg is broken," she says.

I peer over the backseat and see that the engine compartment has been pushed back into her knees.

I undo my own seat belt and try to open the door to my left. It's stuck, so I shift to the other side and try that one. It opens and I carefully climb out of the car and make my way around to Candy. Hurley gets out, too, and joins me. Together, we try to open Candy's door, but it is buckled and dented so badly it won't budge.

"Shit!" Hurley says.

We hear the sounds of other crashes behind us as two more cars collide with the stopped traffic. The road is impassable, thanks to the jackknifed truck. As far as I can see, there's a nightmare of stopped cars and wreckage, all of which is rapidly getting buried in snow.

Hurley takes out his cell phone and looks for a signal. "Damn it, I got nothing," he mutters.

I try mine and get the same result. I see the driver of the semi climb out of his truck, apparently unhurt. "Go and see if that trucker can call for help on his CB." Hurley nods and starts to climb up the small incline to the shoulder. "But be careful," I tell him. "There's no telling how bad this might get."

I watch as Hurley carefully makes his way up onto the shoulder and across the road. The night sky is alight with falling snow and the beams from dozens of headlights, creating an apocalyptic landscape. I make my way back around to the passenger side of the car and climb in through the front door. Candy looks pale, and her face is frozen into a grimace.

"Candy, tell me where you hurt."

"My leg."

"Okay, I'll get to that in a minute. How about your neck?"

"No, it's fine," she says. Her eyes are pinched closed in pain. I run my fingers gently down her spinal bones, feeling for any deformity. Then I palpate her head, looking for scalp injuries. Next I open her jacket and push on her sternum and ribs. "How about here?" I ask. "Any pain?"

"Just the leg," she says irritably.

"Okay, good." I palpate her belly, which feels soft, and then I lift her shirt, looking for bruises. Fortunately, I don't see any.

"Candy, everything else looks okay for now, so I'm going to try to get a peek at your legs, okay?"

She nods, but says nothing; her lips are tight with agony.

I kneel on the floorboard and maneuver my head behind the steering wheel, which has been pushed back a few inches. There I see the underside of the dash resting atop Candy's left leg, and the front of it is pushed into her right knee. The right leg below the knee appears relatively straight, but the left one has a bend in the middle of the calf, and the left foot is turned at a very unnatural angle. I manage to palpate the right leg with one hand, and everything feels proper and intact. Then, as gingerly as I can, I pull up on Candy's left pant leg, trying to expose the injured area.

She lets out a yelp of pain, making me wince.

"I'm sorry, Candy. I don't want to hurt you, but your left leg is definitely broken. I need to check it to make sure there's no bleeding and that your circulation isn't compromised."

"Okay," she says through gritted teeth.

Inch by inch, I work her pant leg up, until I have all of the injured area exposed. It's a bad break—two of them, in fact, as her ankle appears to be broken, too—but the skin is intact, warm, and pink.

I wiggle my way back to a sitting position just as Hurley returns.

"Did you ask the trucker to call for help?"

"He already had, but they told him it might take a while for anyone to get here. Fortunately, none of the folks up there on the road have anything more than minor injuries."

"She's in an awful lot of pain," I say, nodding toward Candy. "I think her left leg is pinned."

"Is she going to be okay?"

"I think so. The leg seems to be the only injury, but she's in a lot of pain."

"What can we do?"

"We need to make sure she stays warm and doesn't go into shock. Get some clothes out of the suitcases so we can use them to cover her."

Hurley does as instructed, while I zip Candy's jacket back up. Candy moans, and then I remember the Vicodin prescription I have. I climb into the backseat, find my purse on the floor, and dig out the bottle of pills. There is also a bottle of water on the floor, so I grab that, too. When Hurley returns with his arms full of stuff from the suitcases, we wrap Candy up in a clothing burrito. I give her two of the Vicodin pills with some water to wash them down. Then we do the only other thing we can. We wait.

Hurley climbs into the backseat, leaving me in the front next to Candy. Minutes turn into half an hour, then an hour, then two. The pain pills kick in and Candy stops moaning, but they also make her drowsy. I have to check her pulse and shake her every so often to make sure she's still okay. The weather outside continues its furious assault; up on the road, everyone is inside their vehicles, huddled against the maelstrom. I keep rousting Candy and reassessing her situation every ten minutes. So far, she's proving to be a trouper by maintaining a positive attitude, but her growing lethargy worries me. I feel a twinge of guilt for all the mean thoughts I've had about her.

Fear, cold, and desperation color my thoughts, and I find myself going off on weird tangents. How long might we be stranded here? Could it stretch into days? Is there a chance Candy might die? My stomach growls hungrily, but I'm not very worried for myself. I figure I can outlast a lot of other folks based on reserves alone. My fat will not only provide extra insulation against the cold, but it will provide a source of nourishment for my body for a good while before I start seriously digesting myself. Then I start thinking about the rugby team whose plane crashed in the Andes years ago, forcing them to cannibalize the dead passengers. I look over at Candy and figure we're screwed. She's much too skinny to sustain us for long.

I give myself a mental shake, chastising myself for such idiotic thoughts and wondering if I'm losing my mind. When I see a flashing light up on the road, I'm not sure if it's real or if my mind conjured it up out of hope.

But then Hurley sees it, too, and he's out of the car and climbing up to the road. Moments later, he returns with a police officer in tow; the two of them skid and slide their way down to our car.

"Help is here," I tell Candy. "Hang in there." I get out of the car and brace myself against the howling wind and snow, yelling over the top of the car to the policeman. "We need to get her to a hospital right away. She's pinned inside and has multiple leg fractures."

The officer nods and yells back, "Fire and rescue are on the way! We'll get on it as soon as they get here."

I nod my understanding and get back inside the car with Candy as Hurley climbs back up to the road with the policeman. "We're going to get you out of here," I tell Candy. "Just a little bit longer."

She nods weakly and turns her head to look at me. "Thank you for helping me."

"I haven't really done anything."

She reaches over and takes my hand, giving it a little squeeze. "But you have. You made me feel safe," she says. "And you helped me deal with the pain."

The guilt her words trigger is so overwhelming that I'm about to confess that I was not only eyeing her like a rib roast a short while ago, but I also found her lacking. I'm saved from myself when I see men dressed in snow gear sliding down the hill toward us and carrying the "Jaws of Life."

* * *

By ten P.M., Hurley and I are warm, fed, perked up
with coffee, and sitting in a hospital waiting room. I put
in a call to Izzy to let him know what's going on; he up-
dates me on our cases, telling me that the tox screen
on Donald Strommen is still pending and that the cops
haven't found Catherine.

I hang up, and as I'm sharing this information with
Hurley, an ER nurse comes out to us and says, "Your
friend is fine. She has a comminuted tib-fib fracture
and a dislocated ankle, but we've made her comfortable and we're prepping her for surgery. You can go in
and see her, if you like."

We find Candy propped up on a hospital stretcher
with her leg splinted, IVs snaking into her arms, and a
glazed look in her eyes. "Hey, guys," she says with a
slightly slurred voice. "It looks like I'm going to be here
awhile."

"Looks that way," I say. "How are you feeling?"

"Much better." She flashes us a goofy smile and rubs
her palm over her nose. "The meds they gave me are
good ones. I don't have any pain anymore, but my face
itches like crazy."

"That's the narcotics," I tell her. "They trigger a
release of histamine."

"You guys might as well head on home," Candy says.
"I'll be fine. I called my family and they're flying in
from California as soon as the weather clears."

"We'll stay long enough to make sure your surgery
goes okay," Hurley says. "It's going to take a while,
anyway, for the weather to clear, plus I've got to rent
another car and file a claim for the wrecked one. And
I think we can all use a good night's rest."

A few minutes later, the nurses whisk Candy off to
surgery, and Hurley and I head back to the waiting

area. After an hour with a phone book and our cell phones, it becomes clear that there isn't a motel within a twenty-five-mile radius of the hospital that has a vacancy, thanks to the weather. But a kindly registration person who overhears our dilemma comes up with a solution by calling the hospital supervisor, who arranges for us to sleep in an unused patient room, a semi-private with two beds in it.

Hurley and I kill time reading magazines, pacing, and drinking hospital coffee. By the time we are notified that Candy is in recovery, it's after two in the morning. We head for the patient room, which has been so kindly offered to us, and drop, fully clothed, into our separate beds. I'm so exhausted I barely have time to register the fact that I'm sleeping in the same room with Hurley. I fall instantly into a deep, dreamless sleep.

Chapter 26

It's noon the next day before Hurley and I manage to get ourselves up and going, check on Candy, take care of the car issues, and get back on the road. The storm has blown through, leaving behind a winter wonderland of bright sunshine and sparkling snow. The remainder of our trip is uneventful and largely silent, and we are able to drop off the rental car at the Milwaukee airport and retrieve Hurley's a little before eleven at night. By the time we arrive at my cottage, it's after midnight.

The place is dark and, with the curtains all pulled closed, it looks empty and abandoned. I unlock the door and flip on the lights, but it does little to dispel my feelings of isolation and loneliness. Hurley carries my suitcase inside, drops it in the living room, and looks around the cottage expectantly. I guess what he's thinking.

"Hoover is probably over at Izzy's," I say. "Dom took care of him while I was gone."

Hurley looks disappointed, and I have to say I'm feeling a bit letdown as well. There's something about that wagging tail and warm nose rushing to greet you when you come in the door that's kind of nice. I don't know if dogs really are man's best friend, but Hoover is definitely mine. He's always happy to see me; he doesn't care if I don't shave my legs; plus he's the only living creature I know who likes my cooking.

On the heels of our trip and my close proximity with death—twice—I feel an overwhelming need for company, affection, and an affirmation of life. Suddenly I'm dreading being here alone, and then I feel sorry for myself when I realize that Hoover is the closest companion I have in my life right now. It all seems rather pathetic.

My pity party is interrupted when Rubbish saunters out of the bedroom, eyes the two of us, and then sits and starts to groom himself. I walk over and pick him up, holding his soft, purring body close to my chest. It's a comfort, but not much of one.

"I guess I should feed the beast," I say to Hurley, carrying Rubbish into the kitchen. I set the cat down on the floor and take a can of cat food out of the cupboard. Rubbish weaves himself in and around my feet as I dish up his food. But as soon as the bowl is on the floor, he's on it, his affection for me forgotten.

When I turn around, I'm startled to see that Hurley has followed me into the kitchen. He's leaning against the doorjamb, watching me.

"It was a hell of a trip, Winston, wasn't it?"

"I'll say."

"Funny, even with all my years as a cop, this trip may be the closest I've ever come to dying."

"Me too."

"I don't know what scared me more—the thought of dying, or the thought of losing you."

I'm not sure what to say to this, so I just stand there, looking back at him. Emotions well up inside me and I feel the sting of tears in my eyes. Embarrassed, I look down at the floor and try to make a hasty retreat from the kitchen. But Hurley grabs my arm and stops me when I try to walk past him. Against my better judgment, I look up at him.

"Look, Mattie, I know you've made it clear that there can't be anything between us, but damn it, I can't help what I feel. I've been trying to ignore it, but this trip and all the close calls we had made me realize just how much I want to be with you."

"But you *are* with me, nearly every day."

Hurley's eyes darken. "You know what I mean."

Boy, do I.

Hurley gently turns me so I'm facing him, but he does nothing more. I know he's waiting for me to make the next move, to close the gap between us. And every inch of my being wants to, but I keep thinking back to my talks with Izzy, and the ramifications there might be if Hurley and I get together. One of us would have to quit our jobs, and it seems obvious that it would have to be me. There isn't much else Hurley could do here in Sorenson, but I have options. I could go back to work at the hospital, though I don't want to. I know I'd be the subject of pointed stares and whispered gossip, and I don't want the humiliation. And while I couldn't have anticipated how much I'd like my new job, the fact is, I do like it. A lot. And I'm good at it.

As I weigh all these options in my mind, we stand there, mere inches apart, staring at one another with a soul-exploring intensity. Hurley finally breaks the spell by swallowing hard, releasing my arm, and diverting his gaze.

"Okay," he says, sounding resigned.

I want to shout out that it's not okay, but the words stick in my throat.

After a few seconds, he looks at me again and smiles

warmly. "I'm glad you're all right, Winston. Get some sleep and I'll see you in the morning."

With that, he leans down and kisses me on the forehead. I close my eyes, resigned to our status and relishing his touch as a confirmation of life, our friendship, and our basic humanity. But then his kiss becomes something more when his lips linger a little longer than necessary. Eventually he pulls away, but not very far; I can feel the warmth of his breath on my face.

It's a pivotal moment, and some distant part of my mind recognizes this and warns me to back away. But the majority of my mind is still recalling how close we both came to dying, and my body is overcome by a need for closeness—a yearning for touch—that affirmation of life.

Our hands touch, and I'm not sure which one of us made the move. Maybe we both did. Whichever it is, it's enough to push me over the edge.

"Stay with me," I whisper, my eyes still closed.

I hear a hitch in his breath, and he says, "I don't think I can without taking this thing to the next level."

"I know," I whisper.

His breathing speeds up and his fingers lace themselves with mine. "Are you sure?" he asks, his voice low.

I open my eyes then and look deep into his, knowing this is my last chance to back out. But I get lost in the dark blue depths of his eyes and my own burning need. "I'm sure."

He needs no further coaxing. His lips descend on mine, soft yet crushing in his need. He pulls my body into his and wraps his arms around me. One hand cradles the back of my head as his tongue gently parts my lips and traces over my teeth. My loins are on fire, and not in a bad, fire ant way. I grind my hips against him in feverish need, feeling the hardness of him.

Our lips part and Hurley backs up enough to undo

my jacket and slip it off. I do the same with his, and we let them fall to the floor. We start sidling our way toward my bedroom as Hurley grabs the bottom of my sweater and pulls it over my head. He tosses it aside as I attack the buttons on his shirt.

And then there's a knock on the door.

We freeze, both of us panting with desire. Exasperated, I holler out, "Who is it?"

"It's Izzy. I have Hoover. Can I come in?"

"Just a minute." I thrust Hurley back away from me, grab my sweater up from the floor, and hastily pull it on. Hurley clutches his shirt closed, looks down at the impressive pup tent in his pants, and beelines for the bathroom, shutting himself inside. I take a few seconds to smooth my hair, grab our coats, and toss them on the couch. I gather myself together before heading for the door.

"Hello, Izzy," I say. Hoover lets out a muffled woof and runs over to me. I squat down and wrap my arms around his neck, letting him lick my chin while his butt wags in delight.

"Sorry to pop in like this, but I couldn't sleep and I heard you guys pull up," Izzy says. "So I thought I'd come over and see how you were."

"We're fine," I say. "Tired, but okay."

"Where's Hurley?"

"He's in the bathroom. It was a long trip."

Izzy nods. "I take it you managed to avoid any further disasters?"

"Fortunately, yes," I say, thinking that his arrival helped me to avoid a big one. "Everything good at the office?"

"It's been quiet. I'm still waiting on the results of the tox screen on Donald Strommen, but the Madison office is backed up because of the holiday. I'm hoping we'll have something in the next day or two."

Hurley comes out of the bathroom then and I'm relieved to see that evidence of our recent encounter is no longer visible.

"Hey, Steve," Izzy says. "Thanks for delivering our girl here back home, safe and sound."

"My pleasure," Hurley says. He gives me a look laden with innuendo.

"I'm glad I caught the two of you together," Izzy says, making my heart skip a beat. Hurley lets out a nervous, little cough. "Dom and I are planning a small party tomorrow night for New Year's Eve and I wanted to invite you both. Dom plans to serve drinks and hors d'oeuvres and we'll have champagne to toast at midnight. Can I count on you both to be there?"

"Of course, I'll be there," I say.

"Me too," Hurley says. "What time?"

"We're planning to start around nine, but you're both welcome to join us earlier for dinner, if you like. Say around seven?"

"I'd love to," Hurley says.

I smile and shrug. "You know me. I rarely pass up a chance to eat Dom's cooking."

"Sadly, neither do I," Izzy says with a laugh, patting his belly. "Well, I'm sure you both want to get settled, so I won't keep you any longer." He looks at me and adds, "See you in the morning at the office?"

"Bright and early," I say, giving him a snappy salute.

"Okay, then. Good night."

I see Izzy to the door. As soon as he's gone, I close the door and lean back against it, with a sigh. "That was close," I say.

Hurley grins wickedly. "It sure was. I felt like I was back in high school." We stare at one another across the room for a moment before he adds, "I guess I'll be going home?"

Izzy's arrival has had the effect of a cold shower on

me, squelching my hormonal hot spot faster than the fire hoses squelched the fire in Jack's house. "I think that's best," I say, wondering if it's true. "I'll call you in the morning."

He looks disappointed, but he nods, gets his coat from the couch, and puts it on. Hoover waddles his tail-wagging butt over to the couch and sticks his nose in Hurley's crotch, making me sigh. Hurley gives him a scratch on the head and a pat on the rump, making me even more jealous of my dog. Then, as Hurley approaches the door, I step aside to put a safe distance between us.

"See you in the morning," he says. And then, sadly, he's gone.

Chapter 27

I wake to the screech of my alarm clock the next morning at seven sharp. My head feels logy and dull. Every time I blink my eyes, it's as if they're lined with sandpaper. A shower helps minimally, but two cups of strong coffee make things better, as does the sugar jolt I get from the gigantic pastry I buy from the local bakery, Swedish Sweets. It's New Year's Eve and I resolve to get serious about my diet, but that starts tomorrow. I decide that today I'm going to indulge myself one last time.

The meteorological Armageddon that's been all over the news for the past couple of days has left its mark here as well. Outside the temperature is 19 degrees, with a predicted high of 23. And that's without the windchill. Sharp gusts of cold, stinging wind howl from every direction, sculpting the foot of snow on the ground into artistic drifts. I drive past a house that has a snowblower parked on the roof and a snowman built atop a bench, a noose around its neck tied to an overhanging branch. The sky has an odd yellowish gray tint to it, which reminds me of the skin color on a renal-failure patient, and I can't help but wonder if there's more nasty weather on the way.

When I check in at the office, I'm delighted to discover that the entomologist in Madison we consulted has faxed his report to us, making the same identification of the worm we found in Donald's trachea that Ethan did.

There isn't much going on in our office—so far, no one is checking out on the last day of the year—and because tomorrow is a holiday, I figure Hurley will want to tie up as many loose ends as possible today. I head over to the police station a little before nine, where I find him holed up in the break room with the newspaper.

"Great picture of you on the front page," he says. He hands me the newspaper and chuckles. There I am, in full color, front and center, just above the fold, on the edge of the river, wearing my waders and the underlying Tyvek suit. My hair and face are smeared with mud, and my body is bent over at a slight angle that makes the waders billow out around me. I look like a grubby Teletubby.

Alison Miller may have given up on her pursuit of Hurley, but she's clearly still holding a grudge. The headline reads, BODY FOUND IN RIVER; and as I scan the article, I see that Alison has remained true to her word. There is no speculation on the cause of death or the identity of the body, outside of a mention of the gender. Nor is the body visible anywhere in the picture. It's of little consolation.

I toss the paper onto the table in disgust. "I have some news," I tell Hurley. "The entomologist in Madison faxed his report over and he identified the worm we found in Donald's throat."

"Judging from the smug expression on your face, I'm guessing he agreed with Ethan?"

"That he did."

"Well, good for Ethan. But what does it mean in terms of our case?"

"I'm not sure. Maybe nothing. Or maybe my theory about Charlotte drugging Donald and shoving a scarf in his mouth to suffocate him is right. I want to go back out to the house and look around some more."

"Can do. Thanks to the storm, my officers reported that Charlotte didn't leave the farm at all until yesterday, when she went grocery shopping and then returned home."

"Are they still watching her?"

"They are."

"So we know she's home. Let's drop in for a visit. Should we give her a heads-up or just surprise her?"

"I like surprises." He gets up and grabs his coat; but before he puts it on, he turns to me and says, "Listen, about last night—"

I hold my hand up to stop him. "Let's just put it behind us for now, okay?"

He frowns at that, but nods. "Okay."

As usual, Hurley insists on driving. He cranks up the heat as we head out of town. By the time we pull up outside of the Strommen house a few minutes later, it's snowing and a stiff wind has blown in. When we get out of the car, I pull my collar close to me, against the cold; but out here in the open country, the gusts that blast us are hard and frigid.

Charlotte Strommen opens the door as we approach, and she doesn't look all that surprised to see us. She doesn't look happy, either, and I suspect there won't be any kindly offers of a hot drink at this stop.

"What now?" she asks, exhaling one of those weight-of-the-world sighs.

So much for the country welcome.

Hurley says, "We need to talk to you some more about your husband's death."

"This isn't a good time," Charlotte says. "My kids are here."

All the better, I think. I'm already plotting a way to get Hannah Strommen off to myself so I can talk with her.

Hurley quickly clamps down on any more objections by saying, "We know about the life insurance policy."

I half-expect Charlotte to play dumb, but to her credit, she doesn't. Instead, she goes on the offensive. "So? Just what do you think that proves?"

"It proves you had a motive to kill your husband," Hurley says.

"You've got to be kidding me," Charlotte says, her voice rife with skepticism. "You want to take the only piece of dumb luck I've had over the past few years and use it to frame me for something I didn't do?"

"Dumb luck?" I echo.

Charlotte shifts her angry gaze my way, her eyes ablaze. "Yes, dumb luck," she snaps, stepping out onto the porch and letting the screen door close behind her. "Don's father died of a brain aneurysm when Don was only fifteen, leaving him and his mother, who was handicapped from multiple sclerosis, destitute because Mr. Strommen didn't have any life insurance. As a result, Don's mother ended up in some rat house of a nursing home, where she died five years later. Because of all that, my husband was a firm believer in life insurance. We argued many times about that damn policy and what it cost, but Don refused to cancel it. I thank my lucky stars that he didn't, because now my children and I have a future. You people trying to make that into something sinister is just cruel."

By the time Charlotte is done with her rant, she has closed in on us; both Hurley and I have backed up to the edge of the porch steps. Charlotte's rage is intimidating—and given what I've seen, I have a new-found respect for Donald Strommen. If he managed to hold out against this woman's wrath, he had to have been a man of strong character and immeasurable patience.

I force myself to step forward, moving into Charlotte's space. She looks surprised by my action; but before she can back away from me, I take one of her hands in mine.

"I'm sorry, Charlotte," I say in my best calming voice. "It isn't our intent to upset you. But we found some irregularities when we did Donald's autopsy and they raise some questions. We're here to try to find out the answers. We didn't come with any preconceived notions about anything. We just want to get to the truth. If you have nothing to hide, then helping us will only make things easier for you."

Charlotte's angry expression relaxes a smidge, but not enough, so I deliver my coup de grâce.

"Please understand that we are simply trying to do our jobs here. And until we can come up with some sort of satisfactory explanation for the unanswered questions surrounding Donald's death, we can't complete a death certificate. And without a death certificate, any insurance settlements that are pending will be tied up for an indefinite amount of time."

I'm not sure if this is true, but it sounds good, and has the desired effect on Charlotte. Her angry expression evaporates, and both her body and her face sag. "Fine," she says in a defeated tone, turning back toward the house. She grabs the screen door, pulls it open, and waves her arm. "Go on in."

We step inside and immediately I notice a small, pale face peering out at us from the kitchen. It's Hannah Strommen and the poor child looks like death

warmed over. Dark circles surround her eyes; her skin
has the pasty, waxen look of a long-term shut-in; her
hair is a tangled mess that looks like it hasn't been
combed in weeks. She's dressed in a flannel nightgown
under a worn cardigan and wearing a pair of old
mukluks on her feet.

I turn and give Hurley a pointed look, gesturing
ever so slightly toward Hannah as Charlotte shuts the
front door. Hurley acknowledges my gesture with a
slight nod of his own and moves in on Charlotte.

"Mrs. Strommen, I need to examine some of your
husband's things, and I'd like to start with his clothes."

Charlotte looks from him to Hannah—who retreats
into the kitchen—and then at me. I can tell she isn't
comfortable with the arrangement, but she doesn't
object. Seeming resigned to whatever fate awaits her,
Charlotte says, "Follow me"; then she heads up the
stairs.

Hurley falls in behind her, while I make a beeline
for the kitchen. Hannah is seated at the table pushing
a few soggy, flaccid cornflakes around in a tiny puddle
of milk at the bottom of a cereal bowl.

"Good morning, Hannah," I say, taking the chair
across from her. "I'm Mattie Winston. I think you know
my niece, Erika Colter?"

She doesn't answer right away; and when she raises
her eyes from the bowl to look at me, I'm shocked. Several years back, I took care of a guy in the ER who had
been involved in a bombing over in Iraq that killed
most of his fellow soldiers and left him deaf in one ear,
missing one eye, and minus his left arm. Even worse
was the invisible damage he incurred. He was suffering
from PTSD and plagued with depression, insomnia,
numerous somatic complaints, paranoia, and anxiety.
There was a haunted, resigned, dead look in his eyes—
the look of a mortally wounded animal that has lost its

will to fight. I never saw that look again, until today. Hannah Strommen has the same haunted, dead-eyed expression.

"I take it your mom told you about your dad," I say to her.

"Yeah, I guess you could say that," she says with a sarcastic snort. She drops her gaze back to her bowl and pushes the cornflakes around some more.

"Where is your brother?"

Her hand freezes midstir and she looks up at me again—this time with a spark of life in those eyes. "What do you want with Peter?"

"I want to talk to him."

"Why? He doesn't know anything about this."

"Your mom hasn't told him yet?"

"Why would she do that?"

"Well, sooner or later, your brother's going to need to know that your father is dead, isn't he?"

I watch confusion play across Hannah's face; and then, as if someone flipped a switch, the deadness returns.

"What aren't you telling me, Hannah?"

She drops her spoon into the bowl and it clatters loudly. Then, without another word, she gets up and leaves the room. I hear her thumping her way up the stairs—even her gait sounds defeated—and then I hear a door slam closed above me.

Left alone, I decide to check out the kitchen, opening drawers and cupboards. Many of the shelves are bare; and the fridge, an older model with a tiny freezer that's nearly closed due to ice buildup, yields similar results.

Next I head out into the living and dining area to scout around. In the dining room, there is an old credenza along one wall, with a large drawer in the middle. I open it and find a mini office supply catchall:

a partially used notepad, some pens and pencils, a handful of rubber bands, a box of paper clips, stamps, envelopes, and a stapler. Just as I close the drawer, my cell phone rings.

"Hello?"

"Mattie? It's Syph. I just wanted to let you know that I got that phone number for you."

Great, the blind date. I briefly consider trying to beg off again, but I know Syph won't let it go. Besides, sooner or later, I need to start dating again, and I suppose a pharmacist is a reasonable place to start. At least we'll have something in common. "Hold on. Let me get a pen and some paper." I reopen the credenza drawer and grab a pencil and the notepad. "Go ahead."

She gives me the number and I write it down at the top of the page, along with his name, *Mike*. Then I rip the sheet off, fold it in half, and stick it in my purse. "Thanks," I say, wondering if I mean it. "I'd love to chat, but I'm in the middle of something."

"No problem. I'll catch up with you later. Oh, and I should probably tell you that I also gave him your number. Good luck!"

Before I can gasp and cast several nasty curses on Syph's soul, she disconnects the call. So I curse myself, instead, because I should have known she'd push the issue. When I worked with her years ago, she did more matchmaking than the hospital's blood bank.

I slip my phone back in my purse and head upstairs, where I find Hurley in the master bedroom with Charlotte. She has made no effort to hide the boxes of clothing I saw when we were here before. I see Hurley gloved up and sorting through one of them.

He looks up at me and says, "Charlotte was explaining to me that her husband has always kept his clothes in boxes because they only have the one dresser and the closet is so small."

"I see," I say. As explanations go, it's not a bad one, but I suspect Charlotte may have dreamed it up since the last time we were here, once she realized that I likely saw the boxes. After seeing and talking with Hannah, I'm more convinced than ever that not only is there something more to Donald's death, but that Hannah knows something about it.

"I'm going to go check out the bathroom," I say.

Charlotte shoots me an exasperated look. "Just what are you searching for?"

"Answers."

"To what?"

"To how and where your husband died."

Charlotte shakes her head in disgust, and plays with a strand of her hair. I see her make a quick, nervous glance toward the bed, and decide to postpone my search of the bathroom for a moment.

"Which side of the bed do you sleep on?" I ask Charlotte.

"Why? What difference does that make?"

I don't answer; I just stare at her, instead.

With an irritated sigh, she points to the closest side of the bed. "I sleep on this side," she snaps.

I walk around the foot of the bed past Hurley, who is still milling through the clothing boxes, and approach the far side of the bed closest to the window. My suspicion is confirmed when I see Charlotte watching me with an anxious expression, chewing on one side of her thumbnail. The bed is neatly made, with layers of blankets beneath the old quilt that serves as a bedspread. The mattress looks lumpy and there is a definite hump in the middle, a raised no-man's-land.

I pull back the blankets and examine the sheets beneath. They are as threadbare and worn as everything else in the house. I pull the sheet off the mattress and look at its surface. No big stains to indicate anything nefarious happened on it. Next I lift the mattress and look at its underside. Nothing there, either.

I let the mattress fall back into place and make it up again. Then I leave Hurley to his boxes and head for the bathroom. My first stop is the medicine cabinet above the sink. Here I find two bottles of prescription medications—a sleeping pill for Charlotte and an antibiotic script for Donald, which has three pills left in it. The date on the antibiotic is from a year ago, telling me that Donald, like many others, decided to stop the medication once he felt better rather than finish it off. Charlotte's sleeping-pill bottle is dated three months ago; when I count the contents, it is only one short of the quantity listed as dispensed on the front, making it unlikely that she used any of them to knock out her husband. The rest of the cabinet contains some shaving cream and razors, toothpaste, a can of cheap hair spray, and the usual over-the-counter medications found in most homes: laxatives, stool softeners, cough and cold medications, and a bottle each of the generic versions of acetaminophen and ibuprofen.

There is a small built-in cabinet containing washcloths and towels and a couple of bars of deodorant soap. Disappointed with my findings, I head out of the bathroom and glance toward the master bedroom to make sure Charlotte is still in there. I see her busily refolding clothes in one of the boxes Hurley has gone through, so I decide to venture a little farther. The door to Hannah's room is closed and I hear the sound of a Britney Spears song playing, so I make my way to Peter's room. His door is open and I find him inside, sitting on his bed, reading a library copy of a Harry Potter book.

"Hi, Peter," I say. "I'm Mattie. I'm working with the police and we're trying to figure out what happened to your dad. Can I ask you a couple of questions?"

He eyes me with curiosity over the top of his book. "He's dead," he says, his voice flat and dull.

"Yes, he died," I say. "That must make you very sad. I'm sorry."

He sets the book aside, tented open to the page where he left off. His eyes tear up and he folds his arms over his chest. "Harry Potter's parents both died," he says.

"Yes, they did. But that's just a story, make-believe."

His eyes well up even more and he looks away from me toward the window.

"You must miss your dad a lot."

He sniffles, but he says nothing.

"Do you want to talk about it?"

"What the hell are you doing?" says someone behind me. I whirl around to find Charlotte standing there, looking mad as hell. "I did not give you permission to talk to my son." She shoves her way past me into the room, goes to the bed, sits next to her son, and gathers him to her. Peter buries his face in her chest and starts to sob. "I think it's time for you to leave," Charlotte says. Her eyes shift to something over my shoulder. "Both of you."

I sense Hurley standing behind me, and a quick glance confirms it.

"Mrs. Strommen," he says. "I'm sorry if we upset you, but—"

"But nothing," she snaps. "If I understand things right, you can't search my house without my permission, unless you have a warrant. Is that right?"

"It is," Hurley says, "but in the spirit of cooperation—"

"And do you have such a warrant?" she demands.

Hurley hesitates before answering. "No, we don't," he admits.

"Then get out. Now."

"Charlotte, please," I try.

"I said, *get out!*"

Hurley takes my arm and tugs me out into the hallway. "Come on," he says. "Let's go."

As we head down the stairs and out the front door, I can feel Charlotte's glare burning into my back like a death ray.

Chapter 28

Hurley and I slog our way to his car through falling snow, which is coming down sideways. I wait until we are safely ensconced inside before I say anything.

"I'm sorry, Hurley. I should have waited before talking to Peter."

"Yeah, you probably should have."

Silence follows as Hurley negotiates the newly fallen snow, going down the driveway at a frightening speed. "Slow down," I tell him. "The roads are slick."

He pulls onto the main road and the rear end of the car fishtails dangerously before he manages to straighten it out.

"Hurley, please. One accident a week is enough, okay?"

He sighs and lets up on the gas, slowing the car to a more reasonable speed.

"What's wrong?"

"Both of these cases are making me crazy," he grumbles. "I feel like all I'm doing is spinning in circles."

"We just have to keep plugging along the best we can," I say. "If at first you don't succeed—"

"You probably shouldn't try skydiving."

After a couple of beats, we both chuckle, providing some much needed relief to the tension inside the car. "If it's meant to be, we'll figure it out," I say.

"I'm not that fatalistic. And I don't like it when things don't go the way I want them to." He glances over at me with a pained expression, making me suspect he's referring to more than the topic of our conversation. "It's damn depressing."

"Do I need to go to your house and hide all your bullets and razor blades?"

I'm rewarded for my question with a glimmer of a smile, but no answer. Instead, he says, "Did you have time to look in the bathroom?"

"I did, but I didn't find anything of significance."

"What about the daughter?"

"I'm pretty sure she knows something." I relay my conversation with her, and then add, "It was obvious to me she was afraid we might tell Peter something other than the fact that his father is dead. I'd bet money that Hannah is hiding something. And based on her demeanor and the way she looks, it's eating away at her. But she walked off mad before I could get anything out of her."

"I'll see if we can keep an officer on to watch the place tonight to make sure Charlotte doesn't leave or try to dispose of any evidence. And, hopefully, by tomorrow, I can get a search warrant for both the house and the barn, though it's not going to be easy with the holiday looming. People tend to take off early, and most places right now are staffed with skeleton crews."

My cell phone rings and I answer it without looking at the caller ID, assuming it's Izzy. "What's up?"

"Is this Mattie Winston?" a strange male voice asks.

"It is. Who is this?"

"Michael Landon."

"Is this a joke?"

"No, it's not. I know, the 'Michael Landon' most people know is dead, but I'm not him. I just have the same name. I got your number from Phyllis Malone?"

"Oh, right," I say, remembering the pharmacist Syph wanted to fix me up with. "Sorry."

"Don't worry about it. It happens a lot."

"I'll bet."

"Anyway, I was wondering if you might be interested in having dinner with me tonight. I know it's short notice, and New Year's Eve. So if you already have plans, I understand. It's just that I'm new in town and don't know many folks, so . . ."

I can see Hurley eyeing me curiously, wondering who's on the phone. I do a quick mental debate of my options, grateful that Michael was kind enough to give me an out, if I want one. But Hurley and I have waded into some treacherous waters here recently, and maybe having a built-in buffer is a good idea.

"I do have plans," I tell Michael, "but you're welcome to join me, if you'd like. I've been invited to my boss's house for dinner and a party, and I know he won't mind me bringing a guest."

"Are you sure?"

"I am." Then, in the interests of full disclosure, I add, "Syph did tell you what I do for a living, didn't she?"

"She did."

"And you're okay with that?"

"Why wouldn't I be?"

"Okay, then, why don't you plan on meeting me at my boss's house at seven." I give him the address; and when he asks, I tell him the dress is casual. "See you then," I say, and hang up.

"What was that all about?" Hurley says, scowling.

"I have a date for tonight."

"With whom?"

"Michael Landon."

"Isn't he dead?"

"He is, but given what I do for a living, my choices are kind of limited."

"Very funny," Hurley says in a tone that suggests otherwise. "What does this guy do for a living?"

"He sells drugs."

"So you have a date with a dead drug dealer?"

"Sounds about right," I say with a smile. "I think my social life is looking up, don't you?"

Hurley doesn't smile back. A few minutes later, he pulls up in front of my office. "Later," he says without so much as a look my way.

Realizing I'm being dismissed, I get out of the car and head inside.

I find Izzy in his office reading something on his computer.

"Need any help?" I ask.

"No," he says, spinning around in his chair to face me. "But I'm glad you're here. I was just about to call you."

"Why?"

"We got the tox screen back on Donald Strommen. It was negative for all of the usual drugs, but they did find traces of something unusual." He smiles at me and waits, drawing out the suspense.

"And that would be . . . ?"

"Ether."

"*Ether*? Why the hell would he have ether in his system?"

"You got me."

"And how would he get it?"

"You got me there, too. That's what I'm researching."

"Well, that certainly makes things more curious, doesn't it?"

"That it does. How did things go out at the Strommen place?"

I fill him in on our visit and Hurley's plan to get a search warrant; but as I relay the facts, my mind keeps going back to Hurley and his foul mood. Is it really just the cases we're working on that have him frustrated? Or is it me?

That reminds me of Michael Landon, so I tell Izzy about my planned date. Though in an effort not to sound too presumptuous, I make it sound as if things are still up in the air. "Is it okay if I bring him along to your party tonight?"

"Of course," he says. "The more, the merrier. I'm glad to see you getting back into the swing of things."

Knowing that the results of the tox screen will provide a stronger probable cause for the search warrant, I head for the library and call Hurley to fill him in. He listens politely, thanks me, and hangs up. His cold attitude toward me leaves me feeling melancholy, and I'm still rattled by the near-death experiences of the last few days. If this job has taught me anything, it's taught me that life is often much too short and we need to live every day to its fullest. When my time comes, I don't want to have any regrets. But at the moment, Hurley is starting to look like he might become one.

Once again I weigh the value of my job against the value of my love life. I could go back to working at the hospital and eliminate the whole conflict-of-interest problem, but I love what I'm doing now. And I really, really don't want to go back to work at the hospital, though I can't think of another job I can qualify for that doesn't require me to ask, "Do you want fries with that?" Not that a fast-food job would be horrible, but I know that easy access to that kind of food won't be good for me.

Then my mind goes all *Ozzie and Harriet* on me and I start fantasizing about a life with Hurley where I don't have to work at all. I could stay at home, keeping the house, eating the occasional bonbon, and preparing fabulous meals for when Hurley comes home at the end of his workday. My imaginary scenario screeches to a halt, because even my most fantastical mind can't buy into that last part. So, instead, I mentally amend the scene to include me getting fabulous take-out meals for the two of us.

I shake off the image, because I know I could never do this. The financial dependence I had on David has taught me a valuable lesson. From here on out, I want to be earning, and controlling, my own money. My divorce settlement offers me some freedom, but it's not enough to live off and provide me with some sort of retirement fund.

The obvious answer is to increase my little nest egg. Given the volatility of the stock market lately, and the dismal interest rates available for savings accounts, I only see one way to do this.

Around noon, Izzy interrupts my thoughts by popping his head in and informing me that he has arranged for coverage with the neighboring county's coroner from now through the morning of January 2. We covered Christmas for them; so in return, they are taking the New Year's holiday.

"Let's close up shop for the day," he says. "I'm going to head home and help Dom prep for tonight's party. Take the rest of today and tomorrow off, and we'll start fresh on the second."

This seems like a sign to me, so I head out and make a beeline for my bank, where I take out twenty grand in cash and cashier's checks. If I'm going to have a chance at increasing my nest egg, I'm going to have to take big risks, I decide. Feeling lucky, I head for the North Woods Casino.

Over the next four hours, I bet big and take those huge risks at the poker tables. I hit it big early on, winning a cool five grand at Texas Hold 'em, so I start increasing the bets even more and taking bigger risks than before, counting on my luck and skill to hold out. But neither one does. The river turns in more ways than one and I end up giving it all back, and then some. By the time I head home, I have managed to set a new record for myself; my total losses so far are at a little over thirty thousand dollars.

So much for Ozzie and Harriet.

Chapter 29

I head home in a funk to get ready for the evening's events. I go through the usual ministrations to prep for my blind date, trying on a half-dozen outfits before I finally settle on a lavender sweater and my ever-ubiquitous, supposedly slimming black slacks. Though I have no intention of "getting lucky," I go the extra mile and shave the winter fur from my legs.

I head over to Izzy and Dom's place a little early and offer to help with the preparations, but Dom, as usual, has full control of the kitchen and insists that I relax. I join Izzy in front of the TV in the living room with a glass of wine and the evening news.

Ten minutes later, the doorbell rings and Izzy gets up to answer it. I hear an unfamiliar male voice and assume it's my date, so I set aside my wine and head for the door. But instead of my date, I find a priest and a nun standing in the foyer. For a second, I wonder if Izzy has plans for an exorcism. But then the woman speaks and I recognize the voice as belonging to Cass, our part-time office secretary/file clerk/receptionist and all-around gal Friday. She and Dom are both members of a local thespian group, and Cass typically rehearses her roles on a 24-7 basis, showing up in costume and in character whenever she comes to work. As a result, I'm not sure I've ever seen the real Cass, and it appears that tonight will be no exception. The priest, whose name is Charles, turns out to be Cass's date, as well as one of the other actors in the play they're currently working on. As we are making introductions, the doorbell rings again. When Izzy answers it, I see Hurley standing on the threshold, along with a tall, bespectacled, short-haired brunette woman, who looks vaguely familiar. Hurley introduces her as Christine Carter, or "CeeCee." As soon as I hear the nickname, I recall how I know her. She is our local librarian.

I feel an instant spark of jealousy, but I bury it and try to put on my best front. Another ring of the doorbell interrupts the introductions; this time when Izzy answers, there is a single man standing there.

"Hi," he says, proffering a bottle of champagne. "I'm Michael Landon."

Izzy invites him in and the introductions resume. It turns out Michael Landon doesn't look anything like his famous namesake. He is about my height, with reddish brown hair, green eyes, and a dimple in each cheek that deepens when he smiles.

As Izzy takes and hangs coats, Dom joins us, and introductions are made all around. Then Dom announces that dinner is ready and herds us into the dining room.

Izzy settles in at the head of the table, and Dom takes the seat to his right, leaving the rest of us to sort out what's left. Hurley takes the seat to Dom's right, with CeeCee next to him, and Charles and Cass take the seats to Izzy's left. Michael claims the other end of the table, leaving me with the seat to his right, next to Charles and directly across from CeeCee.

Dom's meal is his usual stupendous creation. He has

prepared Cornish game hens, wild rice, and baby peas. We all dig in with gusto, and soon everyone is eating and chatting—about current events, the crazy weather, and, inevitably, thanks to Cass and Charles, religion. Michael proves to be a bright and witty conversationalist, who entertains us with tales about living in New York City for the past ten years. I'm starting to feel hopeful about this first date, but then I notice how he and CeeCee keep bowing their heads together and engaging in private, hushed conversations. I try to engage Michael a few times with questions; but after brief but polite answers, his attention keeps going back to CeeCee. Then they start the full flirtation dance: she twirls her hair; he finds an excuse to touch her arm; they exchange several shyly flirtatious glances.

So far, my first-date experiences post-David have been a huge success—for other women.

After dinner I offer to do the cleanup and insist that Dom kick back and relax. I start clearing the table and Hurley joins me as the others depart for the living room. Izzy breaks out a Trivial Pursuit game, and within minutes we hear raucous laughter coming from the other room. Hurley and I silently clear the table and meet up in the kitchen when we're done.

"Well, it would appear that you and I are quite the matchmakers," I say a bit bitterly, scraping plates and loading them into the dishwasher. "You'd think they could at least *try* to be subtle about it for tonight and wait until tomorrow to hook up."

"It's just as well," Hurley says with a sigh. "CeeCee has been hinting around for months that she'd like a date, but I kept making excuses. I only asked her out tonight because I didn't want to be a fifth wheel. That midnight-kiss thing can get kind of awkward when you're the only one without a partner." There are a few seconds of awkward silence before he continues.

"Truth is, the only person I wanted to be with tonight was you."

I squeeze my eyes closed. "Hurley, we—"

"I know, I know," he says, stopping me. "I get that we can't be together, and I get why. That doesn't mean I have to like it." He shoves a dish of leftovers into the fridge, slams the door, and storms from the room.

I tiptoe into the dining room and eavesdrop as he enters the living room.

"I hate to be a party pooper," Hurley says to the group, "but I think I'm coming down with something. I'm going to head home."

I hear CeeCee say, "No problem. I'll get my coat."

Then Michael chimes in, "If you want to stay, I'll be happy to give you a lift home."

"Um, well, I guess that would be okay," I hear CeeCee say. "That is, if you don't mind."

I'm guessing this last part is directed at Hurley, and I'm proven right when I hear him say, "Please stay. There's no reason for anyone else to have a bad night just because I am."

"Okay," CeeCee says. "Thanks, and I hope you feel better soon."

"Yeah, me too," Hurley says.

I hear the rustle of moving bodies and duck back into the kitchen. I go back to the dishes, but I do them as quietly as I can, listening to what's going on in the rest of the house. I hear Hurley and Izzy talking at the door, the opening and closing of the coat closet, and then the opening and closing of the front door. Moments later, I hear the sound of a car engine start up and then fade off into the distance.

I finish loading the dishwasher and close it up. When I turn around, I see Izzy standing behind me. "Good Lord, you scared me," I say, clapping a hand to my chest. "Don't sneak up on me like that."

"Sorry. Are you okay?"

"As good as can be expected, considering that my date is hitting it off with Hurley's date better than he's hitting it off with me." I lean back against the counter and sigh.

"So I noticed. What was Hurley upset about?"

"He wasn't upset. He said he wasn't feeling good."

Izzy arches a skeptical brow at me. "Did you two have a fight? Is that why he left?"

Busted again. I can never hide stuff from Izzy. To him, I'm as transparent as the wrap Hurley used on the leftovers. "Yeah, we had a bit of a disagreement," I admit. "It's hard sometimes, you know?"

"I do." He leans against the counter beside me. "Look, it's obvious that you and Steve share a strong attraction for one another, and we've talked about why it might be a problem if you acted on those feelings."

"I know. And we haven't acted on them." I'm staring straight ahead and glad Izzy is, too, so he can't read my face as I tell this tiny white lie. "But it hasn't always been easy."

"Then maybe it's time for you to weigh your options and decide what's most important to you in life."

I finally risk a look down at him. "What are you saying?"

"I'm saying that if you decide you want to go back to nursing, I'll understand. You're very good at this job, and I love having you working with me. But if your allegiance to me is figuring into this equation in any way, eliminate it now. I'll survive without you, and all I really want is to see you happy."

His words bring tears to my eyes; on an impulse, I push away from the counter and grab him in a giant bear hug. "You truly are a good friend," I say.

He lets me hold him for all of two seconds before his

muffled words and the warmth of his breath between my breasts make me let him go. "Sorry," I say.

He blushes and mumbles, "No problem."

"Look, if it's all the same to you, I think I'm going to cut out early, too. Will you make up an excuse for me to the rest of the group?"

"Don't you think they'll find it suspicious that you and Hurley both cut out around the same time?"

I shrug. "I really don't care. And I doubt that Michael and CeeCee will, either."

"Are you going to go talk to Hurley?"

I shake my head. "No, you've given me a lot to think about and I need some time to sort things out. But if and when I reach a decision, I promise I'll let you know."

"Fair enough."

He walks me to the door and gets my coat for me. After trying to hold it so I can slip it on, and watching me contort myself into a back bend, we both laugh. He hands me the coat and I put it on myself. I give him a quick kiss on top of his balding head; and as I'm walking out the door, he stops me.

"Mattie?"

"Yeah?" I say, looking back at him.

"Be careful, okay?"

"I will."

"And whatever you decide, you know I'll support you."

"I do. And I can't tell you how much that means to me, Izzy. Thank you."

I walk the short distance to my cottage and let Hoover outside to do his business, while I think about everything Izzy said. I realize that one of the main things holding me back at this point is my allegiance to Izzy. I owe him big-time for helping me out when I was at my lowest, but I also helped him out to some degree by stepping in as a ready and willing assistant as soon as the old one quit. Given that, it would be inconsiderate

and ungrateful of me to abandon him just because I'm
back on my feet—except it sounds like he's now giving
me permission to do so, and with his blessing, no less.

I don't really want to go back to the hospital to work,
but I can feel my resistance to the idea weakening beneath the power of my attraction to Hurley. What I
need is financial independence; and once again, I feel
the lure of that one big win pulling at me. If Jack Allen
could do it, so can I. I take Hoover back inside, grab my
debit card, and head out.

Chapter 30

Forty-five minutes later, after negotiating some dicey, snow-covered roads, I arrive back at the North Woods Casino. I head inside, and after deciding to switch up my game, I make my way to the first high-dollar blackjack table with an empty seat. I start off with some fairly conservative bets. But after suffering a lengthy losing streak, and watching one of the gentlemen at my table win huge by betting huge, I change my strategy and start betting larger amounts. At first, it pays off, and I win a couple of hands. Then I lose ten in a row and decide to get up and try a different table. When that fails to trigger a steady winning streak, I carry my chips to the bathroom, wash them for good luck, and change tables yet again. I employ a series of mental chants, and even try to exert my mental powers on the cards—all in an effort to change my luck.

I keep playing—taking advance after advance with my debit card—until I'm forced to quit when the tables close at four in the morning. I'm shocked at the hour. I'm also shocked at the outcome, as I have lost close to thirty thousand dollars. I have a little over a grand left in my wallet; and, still thinking that the Fates have to turn my way soon, I hit up a progressive slot and manage to go through the last of my money before the sun comes up.

I drive home, bummed and exhausted, and spend half the time bemoaning my stupidity, and the other half convincing myself that I simply had an off night. Lady Luck aside, simple mathematical odds say things should turn my way at some point. One good day is all I need to recoup my losses, and then some.

I drop into bed at six in the morning and fall asleep almost immediately. I dream about hitting a big jackpot the same way Jack did; and in the dream, all of my friends and family are around when it happens, cheering me on. Lights are flashing and bells are ringing, and suddenly I realize that the bell sound is actually my cell phone ringing. I ignore it and try to go back to sleep, but to no avail. I stumble out of bed, see that it's afternoon, and put on a pot of coffee. While the coffee is brewing, I check my cell, see that it was my mother who called, and that she left me a message. I dial into my voice mail and listen as she wishes me, "Happy New Year." I briefly consider calling her back, but then decide against it. I'm depressed enough already.

When I take Hoover outside, I half-expect to see Dom or Izzy come out, but the party must have gone on late into the night because their windows are all darkened and there's no sign of life.

I keep flashing back on my dream, on Hurley, and my future, and on the entire day stretching out ahead of me with nothing planned. Before I know it, I'm on the road again, heading back to the casino.

After pulling another ten-grand advance with my debit card, I settle in at a big-stakes blackjack table next to a young bleached blonde who is wearing a lot of makeup and jewelry, and little else. Despite the frigid temps outside, the only clothing she has on is a skimpy tube top and a tiny, very short leather skirt. The makeup, while heavy, is skillfully done, and she has the figure for the clothes. If I was to wear that tube top, I fear the weight of my boobs would turn it into a belt. She, however, wears it very well and has just enough bosom to create some enticing cleavage. It has the male dealer at the table well distracted. I feel rather frumpy in my black jeans and heavy sweater; but when the skimpily clad woman wins several hands in a row, I figure it's worth the humiliation if some of her luck rubs off on me.

Once again, a cocktail waitress appears out of nowhere the minute I settle in; and, still wary of the evil drink, I order a club soda. My tablemate has no such compunction and she gulps down the martini in front of her and immediately orders another.

"You should try the martinis here," she says to me as the dealer doles out another hand. "They're quite good."

"I know," I say. "They go down a little too easily for me."

She smiles and nods. "My name is 'Cin,' short for 'cinnamon,' not a vice." She rolls her eyes. "My mother liked the spice." She extends a hand and I shake it, surprised at its strength.

"My name is Mattie," I say. "It's short for something you don't want to know."

We both laugh and then turn our attention back to our cards. Cin ends up with two 10's and I get a queen and a nine. We both stay, and the dealer turns over fourteen followed by an eight. We high-five one another over the dealer's bust; after deciding my table choice was a good one, I up my bet.

Over the next two hours, I watch as Cin cleans up with one hand after another, rarely losing. But my luck seems to have stopped with the first hand, because nearly every one after that is a loser.

I bid Cin adieu and decide to play the dollar slots for
a while, betting multiple credits and multiple lines. But
the cards keep calling to me; and when the slots stop
paying out, I cash out and get a credit slip for eighty
bucks. Then I settle in at a poker table, eager to try out
some different strategies. I look for patterns in the flow
of the cards, and I try to keep track of what's been
played, but the dealer's shoe has multiple decks in it,
making it impossible. I win a few nice hands, but it
doesn't take long before I've lost the last of my cash.

I still have the eighty-dollar chit in my purse, so I
leave the table and circle the huge room, checking out
all the slot machines and trying to decide which one to
use. Given that none of my other strategies have
worked, I finally settle on a machine that has the most
colorful lights. There are black lights running up each
side of it, and a rainbow of neon lights below and
above. It has a buried treasure/beach theme, and I
consider that a good omen, since I'm owed a beach
experience.

I dig into my purse and feel around for the credit
slip. Instead, I pull out a folded piece of paper. At first,
I have no idea what it is. But when I unfold it, I see it's
the paper from the Strommen house that I used to
write down Michael Landon's phone number. I start to
put it back in my purse, when something catches my
eye. When I hold the sheet up close to one of the black
lights, it reveals a page full of impressions left over
from whatever was written on the sheet above it. I angle
the paper this way and that, until I can make out
the words.

I read them, stunned by what they reveal, and suddenly everything about the Strommen case starts to
make sense. Excited, I grab my coat and head for the
main entrance at a fast clip. I'm startled to discover
that it's dark outside; when I glance at my watch, I

realize I've been at the casino for nearly eight hours. I'm struggling to put on my coat as I step through the doors and into the parking lot. In my distracted state, I step on a patch of snow and ice.

My right foot slides and my ankle rolls outward, painfully. I manage to remain upright, but there are a few moments of deep-breathing, eyes-squeezed-shut pain before I am able to gimp my way to my car and head home.

I pull up in front of Hurley's place half an hour later and limp to his front door. I knock and then ring the doorbell, but I get no answer. His car is there, so I start pounding, instead. I'm about to give up, thinking Hurley is either sleeping or at a neighbor's place, when he opens the door. His hair is mussed, and his eyes are bloodshot. There is a day's worth of beard on his face. His clothes are wrinkled, and I notice they are the same ones he was wearing last night.

"Happy New Year, Mattie," he says, and the smell of alcohol on his breath nearly knocks me over.

"Oh, great," I say. "How long have you been drinking?"

He thinks for a second; then he smiles and says, "Since last year."

"Very funny." I push past him into the house, gimping my way into the kitchen and dropping my purse on the table. On my way past the living room, I notice a drink glass and a nearly-empty bottle of Jack Daniel's on his coffee table, along with a half-dozen empty beer bottles. There's also a throw tossed aside; so I guess from this tableau that Hurley spent the night on the couch.

Hurley closes the front door and shuffles along behind me, dropping into a kitchen chair as I start rummaging through his cabinets, looking for coffee. I find it, and the necessary filters, and start a pot brewing. While it's dripping, I dig out a plastic bag and fill it with ice cubes; then I take the chair across the table from him and use a third chair to prop my foot on. My ankle doesn't look very good; it's turning shades of blue and purple, and it's swollen to twice its size. I drape the ice over it, wincing, and shift my attention to Hurley.

"I need you to sober up," I say.

"Why?" he says, wearing a goofy grin. "Sober makes me think, and I don't want to."

His words confuse me. "You don't want to get sober, or you don't want to think?"

"Both."

"But I need you to do both. I've cracked the Strommen case." I reach over and take the folded piece of paper out of my purse.

He looks at me through squinted eyes for several seconds and then says, "Okay, I'll try to think, but I'm *not* going to feel." He punctuates the word "not" by jabbing his finger in the air at me.

"Fair enough," I say. I unfold the paper, impatient to reveal my discovery. "You don't have to feel."

"But I do, damn it," he says, looking hound dog sad. "When I'm with you, I feel, and I don't want to."

Great, Hurley, of all the times for you to get emotional. "We'll talk about us later. Right now, I need you to focus."

He frowns and says, "Okay, I'll be serious." He narrows his eyes at me again and tries to look stern, but the end result is comical, and I burst out laughing.

"Maybe you should take a shower while the coffee is brewing," I say.

He raises his right arm and sniffs his pit. "Do I stink?"

"Probably," I say, not willing to find out. "But more important, you're drunk."

He smiles and drops his arm. "Yeah, I kind of am. Happy New Year!" He shouts this, making me jump. Then he takes on his ridiculous serious look again and says, "Would you take a shower with me?"

In a heartbeat.

I gesture toward my ankle. "I'm a bit handicapped at the moment. Can you make it upstairs on your own?"

He sighs heavily. "Okay, but you have to take a rain check. Or maybe it should be a shower check?" He laughs at his own joke as I roll my eyes. "Okay," he says, once he's done laughing. "One shower coming up." He pushes away from the table, gets up, and shuffles his way toward the stairs. I listen as he climbs them, bracing myself for the worst, but he makes it to the top without falling. After a few minutes, I hear the water come on and the shower door close. For a moment, I imagine myself tiptoeing up the stairs behind him and sneaking a peek at him naked in the shower, but my throbbing ankle convinces me otherwise.

After twenty minutes, I start to worry. I haven't heard any loud thumps, so I don't think Hurley has fallen in the shower, but I wonder if he might have passed out or gone to sleep. Just as I've resigned myself to having to climb the stairs to find out, the water shuts off.

Ten minutes later, Hurley reappears. His eyes are still bloodshot, but he's dressed in clean clothes and his damp hair smells fresh and wonderful. I get up and limp over to the counter to pour us each a cup of coffee.

"Do you want something to eat?" I ask him.

He eyes me skeptically and swallows hard. "Not if you're going to cook," he says.

Well, at least we're back to reality.

We sip our respective cups of coffee in silence for a few minutes. When he seems a bit more recovered, I slide the sheet of paper over to him.

"What's this?" he asks, staring at the page. "Why are you giving me the phone number of some guy named Mike?" Before I can answer, he narrows his eyes suspiciously and adds, "Wait a minute, is this the number for your date from last night?"

"It is, but—"

"You're not going to suggest some kinky three- or four-way thing, are you?"

"Ignore the phone number."

"Then why did you give this to me? Do you want me to write 'I won't drink anymore' one hundred times?"

"No, though that's not a bad idea," I say, smiling. "I gave it to you because it's the top sheet from a pad I found in the Strommen house. There's a note on it."

He stares at the paper for a while, blinking several times and squinting.

"You can't see it now, but you will," I tell him. "First we need to go to Nowhere."

He looks up at me with a confused expression. "And you think I'm the one who's drunk?"

"The bar," I explain. "We have to go to the No-where bar."

Three of the bar owners in town got together years ago and decided to name their bars the Nowhere, the Somewhere, and the Anywhere. It's easy to end up in the middle of a "Who's on first?" scenario when talking about them. Given that Hurley's already in a flummoxed state of mind, I'm determined to avoid that.

Hurley's expression turns even more confused. "You want to go drinking? I thought you were trying to sober me up."

"I am. I don't want to go there to drink. I want to go there for the ambience—in particular, the lighting."

I watch as Hurley tries to puzzle this out, but he can't. Finally he shrugs and says, "Okay, Winston. I have no idea what the hell you're talking about, but I'm yours."

Maybe soon, I think. *Maybe soon.*

Chapter 31

I load Hurley into my hearse and drive us to the Nowhere bar. It's pretty packed inside and it takes a few minutes to work our way over to the bar. There are no empty seats, but that's okay. What I want doesn't require one. The bartender on duty is a guy named Richie. When he sees us, he heads our way and asks what he can get for us.

"We're not here to drink," I say quickly, lest Hurley be tempted. "I need to borrow something for a few minutes. Do you have that black light you use to scan hand stamps when you have live music with a cover charge?"

Richie eyes us like we're crazy, but he's too busy to worry long about it. "Just a sec," he says. He disappears into the back and returns a minute later with a small lamp. I take it and lead Hurley back over to the door, where I know there's an electrical outlet. As soon as I plug it in and turn it on, I take the paper out of my purse, open it up, and shine the light on it.

"Here, look at the paper now," I say, handing it to Hurley and shining the light just so. He scans the empty page for a second and suddenly his eyebrows arch. I wait impatiently as he reads it all.

When he finally looks up at me, he says, "You found this at the Strommen house?"

"I did. It was in a drawer in the credenza in the dining room. My friend Syph called me when I was looking through the drawer to give me Mike's number, so I used the pad to write it down. I had no idea what was on it until I saw it under the black light at . . ." I hesitate, not wanting to admit I was back at the casino. "Anyway, it explains everything, Hurley—the worm we found, the lack of diatoms in his bone marrow, and Hannah's strange behavior, because I'm sure she had to help her mother move the body. That had to have been traumatic for her."

"Where has this paper been all this time?"

"In my purse."

Hurley sighs and rolls his eyes. "Great," he says with heavy sarcasm. "So much for a chain of evidence."

"I know. I'm sorry. But I had no idea what it was until now."

"We'll never be able to use it."

"Maybe not as evidence, but we can use the knowledge, can't we? We can confront Charlotte with what we know, and maybe she'll admit to everything."

"Maybe," Hurley says, looking deep in thought. "But what about that head injury Donald had? Nothing in this note explains that."

"No, but I think I can. We know from the lack of bleeding in the tissue that the injury occurred post-mortem. I think it happened while Charlotte was trying to dispose of the body. Donald was a big guy, and even with Hannah helping, he had to have been a handful because he was deadweight. Literally. My guess is they dropped him."

Hurley nods thoughtfully. "Makes sense," he says.

"Let's run it past Izzy and make sure everything is in keeping with the autopsy evidence. Then I guess we'll need to pay Charlotte another visit." He starts to turn away, but I grab his arm and pull him back.

"Wait, what are you planning to do?"

"What do you mean? I just told you what I'm going to do."

"I mean, what are you going to do to Charlotte? She's had a pretty rough time of it already, and the fact that we discovered this isn't going to make her happy. But I don't want to compound that by arresting her for what she did. Those kids need her, now more than ever."

Hurley looks askance at me. "Are you saying you think we should just let her get away with it? She's committed at least two felonies I can think of, and I'm sure I can come up with more."

"I know, but I just hate to see that family torn up any more than it already is. Isn't there some way we can minimize the aftermath?"

Hurley stares at me for several long seconds, and then says, "You're serious."

"As a heart attack."

He lets out an exasperated breath. "I need a drink."

"I think you've had plenty already," I say, but he ignores me, flags down the bartender, and orders a beer.

"You want anything?" he asks me.

I shake my head. "I'll try to get hold of Izzy while you do more damage to your liver."

I limp my way through the crowd and step outside, where there is less noise interference. I take out my cell and dial Izzy's number. He answers on the third ring.

"Hey," I say, "I think we've had a bit of a break regarding the Strommen case." I tell him about the paper, the contents of the note that was written, and my theory about Donald Strommen's death.

"It all makes sense," Izzy says when I'm done. "Though it's too bad the note wasn't recognized and handled as evidence right away. Have you told Hurley yet?"

"I just did. He's here with me now."

"Where is here?"

"We're at the Nowhere bar. But don't worry, the only one getting snockered is Hurley."

"Should I ask?"

"Probably not."

"So what's Hurley plan to do now?"

"That's still a bit up in the air at the moment."

"Okay," he says slowly. "Then I guess just keep me posted."

"Will do." I end the call and head back inside. My ankle is swelling more with each passing minute, and the pain is increasing as well. I need to get Hurley out of here and back home so I can get off my feet. I find him standing where I left him; half of his beer is gone already.

Someone has put money in the jukebox and loud music is adding to the cacophony of voices, making it hard to hear. I get up close to Hurley's ear and say, "I just got off the phone with Izzy, and he agrees with our interpretation of things."

We do a little head jog that puts Hurley's lips at my ear. "We can't just ignore this, Winston," he says.

"I know. But why don't we go home and sleep on it. Then we can regroup in the morning and discuss what to do."

Hurley shakes his head, takes a swig of his beer, and then leans into my ear again. "I know you're not going to give up," he says. "You're too damn stubborn." He punctuates the comment with an attempt at a laugh, but it comes out as a belch, instead. "Shit, sorry," he says. "That's what happens when you have a gut full of booze."

His words, and the boozy smell of his breath, turn on a lightbulb in my head. And in a series of mental flashes, I recall the smell of my barfy seatmate on the plane, and the lingering odor of alcohol when I cleaned up Hurley's car. My eyes grow huge and I grab Hurley by the shoulders. "That's it!" I say loudly. "That's what was bothering me!"

Hurley looks confused. "My belching?"

"No, no, not that. The smell of alcohol. Or, rather, the lack thereof."

Hurley shakes his head as if he's trying to rattle something loose.

"Come on," I say, grabbing him by the arm. "We need to get out of here."

We manage to get to the car, despite the fact that neither of us is walking very well. I start the engine to warm us up and try to call Izzy back on my cell. It flips over to voice mail and I leave a message for him to meet us at the office ASAP.

"Where are we going?" Hurley asks as I pull out of the lot.

"To my office. I need to take another look at the file on Jack's autopsy."

"Why?"

"Do you remember me telling you about the guy I was sitting next to on the plane?"

"Look, I said I was sorry you had to be alone through all of that, but it—"

"Yeah, yeah, I got it. It's not important right now."

Hurley gives me a wounded look.

"What is important is that this guy had a lot to drink. When he started puking into his airsick bag, I could smell the alcohol he'd consumed. It permeated the air. Something about it nudged at my brain, but I couldn't figure out why at first. The same thing happened when

I smelled lingering alcohol fumes in both my car and yours after my . . . indulgence."

Hurley's brow furrows as he tries to follow my logic, but our conversation stops because we've arrived at the office.

Slowly we make our way inside—Hurley because his step is still a bit unsteady and I because my ankle is killing me. I head for Izzy's office and dig through the files on his desk until I find Jack's. Opening it, I thumb through the paperwork, searching for what I need. I find it, read it, and then show it to Hurley.

"This is the report on Jack's stomach contents."

Hurley squints as he reads it. "Yeah, so? We already know about the garlic."

"Never mind what the report says *was* in his stomach. Focus on what isn't there. That's what was bothering me—what I *didn't* smell during the autopsy."

"I'm not following you," Hurley says irritably.

"Think about it, Hurley. If Jack drank enough to get his blood level as high as it was, how come there's no alcohol in his stomach contents?"

Chapter 32

Hurley frowns and rakes a hand through his hair. "Of course," he says. "I can't believe we missed that."

"Missed what?" says a voice behind us.

We both turn around to find Izzy standing there. I hand him the report and say, "Why isn't there any alcohol in Jack's stomach contents?"

Izzy frowns, too; then he gives himself a slap on the side of his head. "Oh, hell," he says. "I knew something was off when we were doing the autopsy, but I never figured out what it was."

Hurley runs his hand through his hair again, making it stand up like a cockatoo comb. "But the alcohol had to get into his system somehow. Could it have moved into the intestines already?"

I shake my head. "No, he still had food in his stomach, and that would have delayed emptying to some extent. And with his blood alcohol as high as it was, he had to have consumed a large amount that same morning, just prior to his death."

"Then how did it get into his blood?"

Izzy and I exchange a look. "Intravenously?" I pose.

Hurley looks askance. "You can give that stuff in an IV?"

"Sure," I tell him. "Years ago they used to use alcohol in an IV to stop premature labor in pregnant women."

Izzy adds, "And there were some controversial studies done years ago using intravenous ethanol on acutely ill alcoholic patients to forestall dangerous withdrawal symptoms. The right dose of IV alcohol could have rendered Jack stuporous without killing him."

"Wouldn't that leave a mark?" Hurley asks.

Izzy nods. "Normally, it would. But remember, Jack's arms were burned so badly it would be hard or even impossible to find such a mark. I might be able to find some inflammation in the underlying tissue; but other than that, we may be out of luck. I'll take another look at Jack's body, but don't hold your hopes up too high."

Hurley looks thoughtful and I can tell he's sussing out the implications. "If this theory is right, and there was an IV involved, would Lisa Warden know how to do it?"

I shrug. "Possibly. Anyone with a medical background might know how. EMTs are often trained to do them. Veterinary assistants can do them. I suppose even a layperson could learn how." I add this last bit in, because I'm feeling a little defensive of my kind. As a nurse, I don't want to believe that another person in the medical profession would commit such a heinous act, even though a rogue mercy killer or an occasional adrenaline-seeking psycho who kills patients for the excitement of a code situation crops up in the news now and then.

"I suppose we should take another look at Jack's body," Izzy says.

We nod our agreement; and half an hour later, we're gathered in the autopsy room with Jack's body laid out on the table. With magnifying glasses, Izzy examines what's left of Jack's arms, but he shakes his head after several minutes. "There's too much damage to the tissue. I can barely find enough to examine, and what I do see is so charred that I'm afraid it's useless. I'm sorry."

While Izzy goes about closing up the body bag and returning Jack to the morgue's cold storage, Hurley and I step out into the hall and lean against the wall. Hurley closes his eyes and rubs his temples.

"Headache?" I ask.

He nods.

"I'm not surprised. You had quite a bit to drink today. Want some ibuprofen? I have a bottle in my locker and I could use some myself for this damned ankle of mine. It's killing me."

"That's okay," he says. "I have some at home. And I think that's where we should both go for now. I'll look into getting search warrants for the nursing agency and Lisa Warden's apartment and we can start fresh in the morning. Maybe we'll get lucky and find some evidence to support the IV theory. We can head back to the Strommen place then, too, to deal with Charlotte."

"Okay. Where and when do you want to meet up?"

"It's going to take me a little while to get the warrants. Why don't we plan to meet around noon? I'll come by your office and pick you up. If there's any change to that, I'll call you."

We tell Izzy good night and I drive Hurley back to his house, dropping him off out front. By the time I get back to the cottage, my ankle is swollen beyond recognition and throbbing like a toothache. I let Hoover outside to do his business. When he's done making yellow snow, I lock the front door and go for some ibuprofen. When I open my medicine cabinet, I see the bottle of Vicodin that was prescribed for me by the doctor in Georgia. Thinking my pain is big enough to warrant the stronger med, I take one. After changing into my jammies, I hobble out to the couch and settle in with the remote in hand, my phone on the end table, a throw over my body, and a pillow beneath my foot.

The next thing I know, my phone is ringing. I start awake and glance at my watch; it's one in the morning. I grab for the phone, nearly dropping it on the floor.

"Hello?" I answer irritably.

"Mattie, it's Izzy. We have a call."

"I thought we were off duty until morning."

"We were, but the covering coroner already has two other cases at opposite ends of his own county, so he called to see if we could pick up a little earlier than planned."

Crap. "Okay, give me five minutes?"

"Meet me at my car."

The pain medication seems to have helped. But when I toss back my throw and look at my foot, I'm horrified to see that it's still grossly swollen and the skin around it contains nearly every shade in the visible color spectrum. The bulk of it is blue and purple, but there are also hints of green, yellow, and red. At first, I think I'm going to have to call Izzy back and tell him to go on without me. However, when I give the injured foot a tentative road test, I discover that the Vicodin I took earlier did its job. The foot is still tender and the ankle is a bit wobbly; and while I won't win any prizes for grace, I can walk on it.

I dress as fast as I can and find Izzy outside with the motor running, waiting for me. I ease into the front seat, wedging myself in behind the dash. At least this way, I can't see my foot anymore. Despite the fact that the heater outlets are only inches from my face, Izzy's old car never seems to warm up very well. As a result, a blast of frigid air hits me full on.

"What do we have?" I ask, shivering against the cold and rubbing at my face. My nose itches like crazy, and I assume it's because of the air blowing at me.

"The cops said it appears to be a drug overdose."

As soon as Izzy says this, I realize that my itching has less to do with air than it does the Vicodin in my system. And in the interests of professional responsibility, I decide that I better tell Izzy what I took.

"Speaking of drugs, I took a Vicodin a while ago because my ankle was really throbbing."

"Thanks for telling me. Did it help?"

"It did." I rub at my nose again.

"Do you feel like you can function okay?"

"I think so. To be honest, I don't feel much of an effect from it, other than the fact that my ankle feels a smidge better and my face is itching like crazy."

"Good. When we get to the scene, I'll do the bulk of the hands-on stuff and you can handle the pictures."

"Sure, but if you see me do anything stupid, promise me you'll tell me, okay?"

"I'm not worried. I trust you. You've got a good eye and a sharp mind for this work, Mattie. You're a natural at it. Catching that bit about Jack's stomach contents was brilliant."

"Thanks."

"Have you given any more thought to what we discussed, about you and Hurley?"

"I have," I say, thinking that so far my plan for financial independence isn't going very well. "I'm still thinking about it."

"You really are good at this job, and I know you don't want to go back to work at the hospital. But if that's what it takes to give you and Hurley a chance to see if whatever it is you two have can turn into something bigger, maybe it would be worth it. If there's one thing this job has taught me, it's that life is all too short. *Carpe diem* and all that, you know?"

"I do. And thanks for being so understanding about it."

Izzy turns onto a residential street and I see a bunch of cop cars and an ambulance up ahead. As he pulls in behind the ambulance to park, I realize where we are. I start to get a sick feeling in my stomach. We get out and Izzy opens the trunk, handing me the camera while he grabs his site-processing kit. We then follow an officer's directions inside to the victim's apartment.

There are several cops standing around a couch in a huddle, and I see that Hurley is among them. He turns and sees us enter. From the look on his face, I know my worst fears are about to be realized. I hobble up closer to the couch and push my way through the moat of people there.

The victim is lying on her back; her open, dead eyes are staring at the ceiling; a froth of white foam is drying on her lips. She's wearing a sweater, and the left sleeve is pushed up to above the elbow. Embedded in the crook of her arm, hanging there like some deformed, bloodsucking tick, is a needle and syringe.

"Well, this is one less search warrant I'll need to hunt down in the morning," Hurley says to no one in particular.

Looking confused, Izzy turns to me and asks, "What does he mean? Who is this?"

I raise my camera and snap off my first shot before I answer him. "It's Lisa Warden, our prime suspect in the Jack Allen case."

Chapter 33

I snap several pictures of Lisa's body and then of the room in general. Izzy makes the cops move out of the way, gloves up, and gets closer to Lisa to do his exam. Carefully, using only two fingers, he removes the syringe and needle from her arm, dropping it into a plastic sharps container, which he then seals with evidence tape.

"We'll dust that syringe for prints and I'll do an analysis of the contents when we get back to the lab," he says. "But based on my preliminary exam, I have to say that everything appears consistent with a narcotic overdose: the foaming of the mouth, the pinpoint pupils, and all these track marks on her arm."

Hurley says, "I guess this answers the question of whether or not Lisa knew how to start an IV. If she was practiced at finding her own veins, I'm guessing it wouldn't have been hard to find Jack's."

I rub at my nose again; and when I do, it triggers a memory. "Damn," I say. "I should have picked up on that when we were here before."

"Picked up on what?" Hurley asks.

"Lisa kept rubbing at her face all the time, the same

way Candy did when we saw her in the ER, remember? It's a classic sign of narcotic use. The histamine release triggered by the narcotic makes your face itch. I didn't realize that's what it was. I thought she was itching at cat hairs. Which reminds me, where is Tux?"

"The cops who got here first found him on top of Lisa's body. They've got him locked in the bedroom for now," Hurley says.

As if to confirm this fact, the bedroom door rattles and we all hear a plaintive meow. I look over and see one of Tux's black-and-white feet poking out from beneath the door.

"I'm going to go check on him," I say, heading for the bedroom.

"Don't let it out," Hurley says in a panicked rush. Everyone in the room turns to look at him, reacting to the tone in his voice. Seeming to realize that he's revealed more than he meant to, he gives everyone a "What?" look and comes back with a quick cover-up. "Well, there might be evidence on him."

"That's true," I say. "Do you want to check him out for that, or shall I?"

The room is perfectly still, waiting for Hurley's answer. Torn between facing his fear and saving face, he vacillates a moment before caving in. "You can do it," he says.

I snap a few more pictures of the living area, and then I head into the kitchen for a quick look. The sink is filled with dirty dishes; the refrigerator shelves are covered with various spills, but are otherwise pretty bare; the cupboards don't contain much in the way of food or dishes. Other than that, I don't see anything of significance; so after taking a few shots of the room, I head for the bedroom.

Before opening the door, I squat down in case Tux decides to make a run for it. But he patiently waits as I enter the room and shut the door behind me, and then he makes friends by rubbing up against my legs and weaving around my feet. I bend down and give him a little scratch under the chin and he starts to purr. Near the door is a large, enclosed litter box filled with fresh litter, and a bowl of food and water. It looks like the same one I saw in the bathroom on my last visit, albeit cleaner. Occupying the bulk of the room is a queen-sized bed, which is unmade. There is also a dresser in the corner. After snapping some pictures of the overall room, I head that way to search the drawers, Tux on my tail.

The dresser contains the usual suspects: an assortment of clothing, some belts, and a small box containing several pairs of cheap earring studs. I sift through the clothes, squeezing all the paired socks and feeling the folded items for anything that might be hidden. I also take each drawer out of the dresser and examine the back and undersides, but I come up empty. On top of the dresser is a music box. When I open it, a little ballerina pops up and starts to spin as the box spews out "Nadia's Theme." Tux jumps up on top of the dresser and bats at the ballerina, and then he mashes it down, causing a small hidden compartment in the bottom of the box to pop open. Inside I find an assortment of pills, some of which I recognize as hydrocodone and oxycodone. I wonder how Lisa got her hands on the pills and whether she stole them from the patients she was caring for.

I take photos of the pills and then move to the closet. Here I find a couple of men's shirts and a man's suit hanging with Lisa's clothing. To be thorough, I look under the bed, where I find some prehistoric-sized dust bunnies, but nothing else. I give Tux a few more pets and then head back out to the main part of the apartment, keeping the cat locked away. I report on my findings and no one seems inclined to enter the bedroom to verify things, so I move on into the bathroom.

Fortunately, it's been cleaned some since the last time I saw it. I recall the dark, short hairs that were in the sink the last time I was here. Given Lisa's own lighter hair color, I figure they must have been a boyfriend's. Based on that and the clothing in the closet, I'm guessing he and Lisa had some sleepovers. I proceed to take the usual general photos of the room and then head for the medicine cabinet. Here I find an assortment of over-the-counter meds and one prescription bottle with an antibiotic label on it. The pills inside aren't antibiotics, however; they match those I found in the music box.

The only place left to search is a small built-in cabinet. I open it and find shelves of towels, washcloths, cosmetics, and personal-hygiene products. After taking a picture of it as is, I start searching through the items. It's not until I look inside a large economy-sized box of tampons that I hit pay dirt. There, stashed among the handful of tampons left, are a dozen or so syringes.

After taking a picture, I carry the box out to the living room and show it to Hurley, along with the bottle of narcotic pills.

"I didn't find any IV supplies, but they would have been easy enough to get rid of," I tell him. "Given Lisa's drug habit, and the fact that she had all these syringes, it certainly seems feasible to think she could have given Jack an IV."

Hurley nods. "And that would close this case up with a tidy bow," he says.

"Except for one thing," I say, frowning.

He nods again and then, in perfect sync, we both say, "Where's the money?"

Izzy decides to join in on our speculations. "If Lisa

had a drug habit, she might have been using the money to buy whatever she was shooting up. Maybe she flashed too much green in front of the wrong persons and they decided to come back and help themselves. Maybe her overdose wasn't an accident." He looks at Hurley. "How did you guys come to find her?"

"We got a call from a neighbor, a woman named Tonya Collier, who found Lisa's cat out loose. She knew Lisa never let the animal out, so she caught the cat and brought him back to Lisa's apartment. When she went to knock on the door, she found it ajar and pushed it open. She saw Lisa on the couch and realized she was dead. After tossing the cat inside and shutting the apartment door, she called the police."

"Was Lisa alone?" I ask.

One of the uniformed cops answers, "Yeah, why?"

"I'm pretty sure Lisa had a boyfriend who slept over from time to time." I explain about the clothing and the hairs I saw when Hurley and I were here before. "So the boyfriend might have found and taken the money. Or maybe the neighbor?"

Hurley shrugs. "It's possible, I suppose. Why don't we go talk to her and see if she'll let us search her place?"

I look over at Izzy, who says, "Go ahead. I'll finish up here with the body and arrange to get it to the morgue. Let's plan on doing her autopsy later in the day, say around noon?"

Hurley and I both nod. I give Izzy the camera and follow Hurley outside and across the stairwell to the apartment opposite Lisa's. Hurley knocks and, a moment later, a woman answers. And not just any woman, either. Tonya Collier is a knockout. She's tall and lithe, with a gorgeous mane of wavy red hair, crystal blue eyes, and porcelain skin.

"Yes?" she says, her voice sultry. She looks straight at Hurley, and it's as if I'm not even there.

Hurley does the introductions and then says, "We'd like to talk with you about your neighbor. May we come in?"

"Of course." She steps aside and waves us in, her gaze pinned on Hurley.

I follow him in, noting that Tonya's apartment is a mirror image of Lisa's in the general layout. Beyond that, it couldn't be more different. The place is clean, neat, and tastefully decorated.

"May I get you something to drink?" she asks. "I can make coffee or, if you prefer, a bottled water?"

"No, thank you," Hurley says. I shake my head, but it hardly seems necessary. Tonya and Hurley have an obvious connection and it's as if the two of them are the only people in the room. We settle in on the leather couch Tonya indicates, and she perches on the edge of a matching chair across from us. Her legs, which are encased in snug skinny jeans, are demurely slanted to one side; and her top, a cowl-necked mohair sweater in shades of purple and blue, sets off her eyes beautifully. "What do you need to know, Detective?" she asks.

I'm annoyed by the way she is ignoring me, so I jump in and say, "Why is it you're fully dressed at this time of night?"

Her eyes drift slowly my way. I suspect I've managed to make a tiny dent in that perfect façade, based on the way she narrows her eyes at me, but her smile remains firmly in place. "I just got home from work," she says coolly. "I'm a bartender at the End Zone."

The End Zone is the requisite sports bar in town, done up in Packer green and gold. I swear every town in Wisconsin has one. They do a thriving business year-round, but they're particularly busy during football season. The typical customer tends to have more than his fair share of testosterone, and I'm betting Tonya does very well there, raking in the tips.

"How well did you know Lisa Warden?"

Tonya shrugs. "Not real well. We exchanged the usual pleasantries when we saw one another, but we weren't friends or anything." She turns toward Hurley, dismissing me. "I saw that syringe in her arm. I had no idea she was a drug user," she says, pouting prettily. "She was a nurse or something like that, wasn't she?"

"Something like that, yes," Hurley says. "We have reason to believe she may have had some cash in her apartment, a lot of it. Did you see anything like that when you went in there?"

"No, not at all," she says, her brow gently furrowed with concern. She claps a hand to her chest and I note her French manicure. "Do you think she was robbed?"

"Possibly," Hurley says. "Did she have any regular visitors, or a boyfriend of any kind?"

"There was one guy that came by from time to time, but I don't know his name."

"What did he look like?"

"Dark hair, average height . . . I never got a very good look at him. Do you think he took this money?"

"We don't know, but we'll look into it. In the meantime, since you had access to Lisa's apartment before any officials arrived, we'd like to do a search of your premises and your car to make sure the money isn't here. We aren't implying or accusing you of anything, just tidying up the loose ends. It's an unfortunate but necessary step so we can rule you out."

"Of course." She gives him a dismissive wave of her hand. "You can look at anything I have, Detective," she says flirtatiously. "Where would you like to start?"

The woman is a master of innuendo. Before she can snag Hurley and drag him into her lair, I speak up. "I'll start with your bedroom," I say. "Why don't you show me the way?"

She turns and looks at me again with that narrowed-eye expression. "I'd be happy to," she says in a way that suggests otherwise. She looks back at Hurley and gives him a dazzling smile. "Would you care to join us, Detective?"

Like someone under a spell, Hurley smiles back at her, all glazy-eyed, and says, "Sure."

Tonya gets up; and when her back is to Hurley, she flashes me a smug look. "Right this way," she says, and we follow her into her bedroom.

Like the main room, the bedroom is neat and perfectly organized. Unlike my own bedroom, there isn't an article of clothing out of place; the bed is neatly made and absent of pet hairs; the air is scented with the subtle smell of just-laundered sheets. Since I'm not about to let Hurley go through her drawers and handle her underwear, which I'm betting comes from the hooker section of Victoria's Secret, I make a beeline for the dresser. My suspicions are confirmed with the first drawer I open, and I sift through the lacy, skimpy underthings, feeling both annoyed and envious. The second drawer reveals neatly folded nightwear: slinky, skimpy gowns, lustrous loungewear, and a pair of long underwear made out of satin. I flash on my own collection of flannel nighties and cotton tights and make a mental note to do a wardrobe upgrade as soon as possible.

Hurley and Tonya are at the closet, and I pause between drawers to look over and check out the contents. The closet is like everything else here: organized, neat, and chic. On the floor are a couple of dozen pairs of shoes, everything from fashionable pumps and high-heeled, sling-backed sandals, to designer running

shoes and stylish flats. This display makes me even
more envious. With my size-12 feet and my six-foot
height, I not only shy away from heels, my choices are
often limited to shoes that require license plates.

I turn back to the dresser and go through the rest of
the drawers, where I find stacks of neatly folded
sweaters, jeans, and T-shirts. When I'm done, I head for
the bedside stands. The first one contains socks in one
drawer, and a collection of notepads, books, pens, and
magazines in the other. The second stand is a shocker.
When I open the first drawer, I find a collection of
sex items: a vibrator, bottles of various lotions, several
packages of condoms, and a pair of fur-lined pink
handcuffs. I shut it quickly and glance over my shoulder toward the closet. Tonya is watching me with an
enigmatic smile on her face. Fortunately, Hurley is
distracted elsewhere, searching through some boxes
on the closet's upper shelf.

I'm afraid to open the second drawer, wondering
what it will contain. It's a bit tamer, but not much. It
contains several packages of sheer stockings, a garter
belt, a couple of teddies, and a sleep mask, which I'm
betting has never been used for sleep.

Shutting the second drawer on the sex supply cabinet, I drop down to my hands and knees and peek
under Tonya's bed. The only thing I find is a large box.
I pull it out and open it up, half-expecting to find a
collection of porn videos. But, instead, it's filled with
memorabilia: loose photos, yearbooks, picture albums,
and some miscellaneous items that I'm guessing have
some emotional significance for Tonya.

Hurley finishes with the closet just as I'm pushing
the box back under the bed, and we head out to the
main room, with Tonya following. I make quick work

of the bathroom and a small second bedroom Tonya
uses as an office, while Hurley and Tonya search the
kitchen and dinette area.

We finish up in the living room, where Tonya hands
a set of keys to Hurley and says, "My car is the blue Ford
Escape parked out front. That other key is to my apartment." She pauses and gives him a sly wink before
adding, "You can make a copy, if you like."

Chapter 34

Our search of Tonya's car comes up empty, too, and I manage to get the keys from Hurley and return them to Tonya myself. She is clearly disappointed when she opens the door and sees me standing there. However, she takes it in stride, wishes me good night, and shuts her door.

Izzy offers to take Lisa's body back to the morgue and do the preliminary intake, and Hurley agrees to drive me home. He has someone at the station run a DMV profile on Lisa and we find her car, unlocked, parked in the lot. Our search of it doesn't turn up anything of interest, and Hurley calls to have someone come pick it up and drive it to the impound lot. But when the driver shows up, we can't find a key to the car. Our search of Lisa's body, purse, and apartment turns up a single key chain, with two house-type keys on it, one of which proves to be for the apartment door. But it's one of those double-sided, detachable rings, and half of it—presumably the half with the car key attached—is missing. Hurley has the car towed, instead. After another hour or so of bagging and tagging evidence, we are ready to head out. Hurley is about to lock the door and seal it with crime scene tape when I remember Tux.

"What about the cat?" I ask him.

"What about it?"

"We can't just leave him here."

"Put down some food and water for him. He'll be fine. I'll call animal control later today and they can come and pick him up."

"But they'll just take him to a pound."

Hurley shrugs. "Probably."

"Let me take him. If he goes to the pound, he'll probably end up dead. Let me keep him until we can figure out if Lisa has any family who want him."

Hurley shrugs. "It's your funeral."

I head back into Lisa's bedroom, where I find Tux curled up on the bed. I walk over and sit next to him, petting him until he starts to purr. I scoop him up and carry him out to the living room. "Okay, I'm ready," I say. I stroke Tux, who is propped on my shoulder like a baby being burped.

Hurley looks at me, kind of buggy-eyed. "Don't you have a cage or something to put him in?"

"I didn't see one anywhere, did you?" It's a rhetorical question; we've searched the place from top to bottom and we both know there is no carrier here.

"You plan to let that thing loose in my car?"

"No, I'm going to hold him, just like I'm doing now."

Hurley bites his lip; and he looks so sexy doing it, it makes me want to bite it, too. I can tell he wants to say no to me; but after a few seconds of indecisiveness, he relents. "Okay, but make sure you have a tight hold on him."

We head out to the car and I climb in. Tux is happy to be where he is, getting petted, and he purrs loudly. Then Hurley gets in and starts the car and all hell breaks loose. Tux flexes every muscle in his body, digs his claws into my shoulder, and bolts for the backseat.

"Shit!" Hurley yells. He scrambles out of the car and stands there with his door open, looking panicked. "I knew this was a bad idea," he says.

Fortunately, the thickness of my clothes and jacket has kept Tux's claws from doing any serious damage. I turn around in my seat and find him sitting in the back window, his eyes as wide as Hurley's.

"Tux, kitty, come here," I coo. "It's okay."

Tux stares back at me, clearly frightened, and then his sides start to heave.

"Oh, hell, what's he doing?" Hurley asks, backing up a step. "He looks like he's going to blow or something."

And blow he does. After a few more heaves, Tux barfs up a giant ball of hair and slime that slides down the backseat.

"Great," Hurley says, rolling his eyes. "That's just great."

"Aw, he's just scared. That's all," I say, reaching over and turning off the engine. "Close your door before he runs out."

Hurley reluctantly does as I ask. I pull the keys from the ignition, get out of the car, and shut my door behind me. "Let me go back inside the apartment and I'll get something to clean it up," I say.

"And leave him in there unattended?" Hurley asks. "What if he shreds my seats, or craps in there or something?"

"He won't," I say, hoping I'm right.

Together, we head back into the apartment and I round up some paper towels, a garbage bag, and some cleaning spray, which I find under the kitchen sink. Then a thought hits me and I hand the cleaning supplies to Hurley. "Hold these. I'm going to get his litter box from the bedroom and bring that along, just in case. Okay?"

Hurley looks ill at the idea, but he takes the stuff I hand him and waits while I get the litter box. Then we head back to the car after resealing the apartment door. It takes me a few minutes to clean up the hair ball, but Tux appears settled now and he sits quietly in the rear window while I work. When I'm done, I hand the garbage bag to Hurley, who walks over and tosses it into a nearby Dumpster. I set the litter box on the backseat and Tux eyes it a moment, but he stays put. I close the back door, open up the driver's-side door, and get in. Then I start the engine. Tux flinches a hair, but he refrains from any more theatrics. I get out and climb into the backseat, leaving the engine running. I pet Tux and talk softly to him for another minute or so, and then I take him off the window ledge and hold him again, stroking his fur.

"He's fine now," I tell Hurley. "Let's go."

Hurley looks skeptical, but he slowly gets into the car, keeping an eye on Tux and me the entire time. Five minutes later we pull up in front of my cottage. I hand Hurley my keys and say, "Go unlock the door and let Hoover out. I'm not sure how comfortable Tux will be around a dog, and I don't want to spook him again."

Hurley is more than happy to get away from the cat; and when I see the joyful way Hoover greets him, it makes me rethink the reincarnation thing. Maybe I should come back as a dog. Their lives are so simple and uncomplicated.

As soon as Hurley and Hoover are a ways away from the house, I get out and carry Tux inside. I plop him down in the middle of the living room and go in search of Rubbish. I find him curled up, asleep, on my bed. I decide to let sleeping cats lie and go back out to the living room and watch Tux warily explore his new surroundings. Eventually he finds Rubbish's food dish, which is empty—Hoover never leaves any food around for long—and starts sniffing. I open up a can of tuna-flavored food and scoop it into the dish for him. He starts to purr immediately and digs in, but either the sound or the smell has aroused Rubbish and he comes scampering into the kitchen.

Rubbish immediately comes to a halt, flattens his ears, and stares at the interloper, who is oblivious for the moment. I take a second dish out of the cabinet and scoop some cat food into it, setting it down about a foot away from Tux. This catches Tux's attention; and when he turns toward the new bowl, he sees Rubbish.

The two cats face off, both of them with their ears flattened and their hackles raised, and they start circling. It's like the standoff at the "Kitty-Cat Corral"; but after a few minutes of this macho posturing, Tux does the equivalent of a shrug. He turns his back to Rubbish and resumes eating.

Rubbish approaches warily and sniffs at Tux's butt. When this action fails to get a rise, he heads for the other bowl. As soon as the two of them are eating, side by side, I head outside to find Hurley.

"So far, so good," I tell him. "Let's toss Hoover into the mix and see what happens."

Hurley hands me the leash, and then he bends down to talk in Hoover's ear. "Be strong, buddy. And whatever you do, don't turn your back on it." Then he looks at me. "Can I loan Hoover my Taser, just in case?"

"Very funny."

"I'm not kidding," he says, looking all serious. "Facing down a pissed-off cat is like facing down a ninja armed with a dozen throwing stars. I'm afraid poor Hoover will end up with a three-dimensional bar code on his face."

"Well, there's only one way to find out."

I take Hoover inside and lead him over to the two cats, who are still focused on their food. Hoover gets excited the minute he sees Tux and lunges, yanking the leash out of my hand. Tux hears him coming, whips around, arches his back, and hisses. Hoover puts on the brakes and drops to the floor in front of Tux, exposing his underbelly in a classic doggy surrender.

"Oh, for Pete's sake, Hoover," Hurley grumbles. "Man up."

"Look who's talking," I counter.

Tux turns sideways, his back still arched and his body rigid. Then he does a series of side hops toward Hoover. Hoover winces, as if preparing for the blow, but he maintains his position. Tux closes in and gives Hoover a little bitch slap on the nose with a front paw. This makes Hoover bark and roll back to a standing position, which sends Tux six feet straight up off the floor. When Tux comes back down, he takes off running, with Hoover hot on his tail.

We find them in the bedroom: Tux backed into a corner, his tail twitching; Hoover with his shoulders to the floor and his butt up in the air, tail wagging. When he sees us standing there, Tux switches gears and becomes suddenly indifferent. He sits down, extends one hind leg, and starts to lick his crotch, completely ignoring the dog.

Hoover cocks his head to one side, whimpers, and then drops his butt down to the floor. He lays there watching the cat tend to his personal hygiene for a moment, and then gets up and goes over to offer some help. He sticks his nose into Tux's crotch and sniffs hard a few times. Surprisingly, the cat tolerates it.

"See there?" I say to Hurley. "A couple of butt sniffs and suddenly they're friends."

Hurley looks over at me with a sly half smile. "Works for me," he says.

We share an awkward moment, staring at one another, as the innuendo hangs between us like a curtain waiting to be pushed aside. But no one crosses the line.

"Okay, I'm out of here," Hurley says finally, his gaze breaking off. "What time do you want to visit Charlotte Strommen?"

I glance at my watch and see that it's after four in the morning already. "Izzy said he wanted to do the post on Lisa at noon. Do you want to visit Charlotte before or after? I can be ready to go by ten."

"Ten it is. That will give me time to see about the search warrants. But let's plan to get Charlotte out of the way first. Should I pick you up here or at the office?"

"Here."

"Okay, see you then." He sees himself out.

After shrugging out of my coat, I walk over to lock the door. Before I can, there's a knock and my heart skips a beat. I am scared and excited, certain that Hurley has decided to push that curtain aside, after all. I decide I'm going to go for it, and will let whatever happens, happen. I whip open the door, and just as I expected, Hurley is standing on the threshold. I have a nanosecond to feel the thrill of impending adventure before I realize that he's holding Tux's litter box.

"You forgot your feline Porta-Potty," he says, handing it to me.

"Oh, right. Thanks." I take the box and set it down beside the door, wondering if Hurley is taking advantage of it as an excuse to return. But by the time I straighten up to look back at him, he's already in his car, shutting the door. The engine starts and he pulls away. I stare at the red glow of his taillights fading over the snow, feeling as if my hopes are locked inside them.

Chapter 35

Knowing I have only a few hours to sleep leaves me edgy and restless—a state helped by the fact that Hoover, Tux, and Rubbish spend the rest of the night having races and playing hide-and-seek. My cottage has become a pet play station. While I manage to doze off for a few short periods of time, I spend most of the night tossing and turning. My mind reels as I try to sort out my feelings for Hurley. By the time my alarm goes off at nine, I have made a decision.

Clearly, I have feelings for the man, and it seems pretty obvious he has feelings for me, too. And if all of my jobs have taught me anything, they've taught me that life is just too damn short and love is too damn rare to let either one slip away. If Hurley and I are meant to be together, I need to know that. I need to give us a chance, and if that means humbling myself and returning to my hospital job, so be it. And judging from the way my casino trips have gone, that seems to be my only remaining option.

I shower, dress, and take Hoover outside to do his morning rituals. I'm feeling pretty jazzed about my decision; and when Izzy pulls out of his garage and drives over to where I'm standing with Hoover, I smile and mime rolling down his window.

He does so and I greet him with a chipper "Good morning! I was going to call you as soon as I got done out here."

"What's up?"

I inform him that Hurley and I are heading out to the Strommen place and that we'll both be in the office by noon for the autopsy on Lisa Warden.

He nods, but he looks confused. "You seem rather happy for someone who's about to deliver devastating news."

"Well, the Strommen thing won't be fun," I admit, "but I've reached a decision on the other matter."

"You mean the working-for-me matter?" he says, frowning.

"Yes."

With that, we hear a car approaching and Hurley pulls into the drive alongside Izzy's car. Izzy says, "We can talk some more later." He waves at Hurley, and then pulls away.

Hoover runs over and jumps up on the driver's door of Hurley's car, tongue lolling, tail wagging. I know how he feels. Hurley rolls down his window and gives him a few pats on the head.

"Let me put him in the house and I'll be right out," I tell him. I take a reluctant Hoover inside and head back out to the car. I'm tempted to tell Hurley about my decision, but I figure there isn't enough time, and I don't want to tell him before I tell Izzy. Hurley has brought me a cup of coffee, light with cream—the way I like it. I take it gratefully; my mind is filled with images of more mornings like this, the two of us riding somewhere together, comfortable and happy with one another. It's both a scary and an exciting proposition.

"Are you ready for this?" Hurley asks me.

For a second, I think he's read my mind, but then I realize he's talking about the Strommen thing.

"I'm not looking forward to it," I admit. "Have you given any more thought to what we discussed the other day? About Charlotte, I mean."

Hurley sighs heavily. "She's broken several laws, Mattie. And unless Izzy is willing to lie on the death certificate, my hands are tied. The best we can hope for is a lenient judge."

"What about Hannah?"

"I don't see us filing any charges against her. She's been through enough already."

Hurley has arranged for two officers to meet us, and they pick up our tail at the bottom of the Strommen drive. We all pull up in front of the Strommen house and park. Charlotte is at the window. When she sees us, her shoulders sag. There is no need to knock once we climb the steps to the front porch; Charlotte opens the door before we get to it.

We all head inside: Hurley and I, a female officer named Brenda Joiner, and a new rookie officer named Kevin Masterson. Charlotte doesn't pretend this is a welcomed or social visit. She doesn't offer to take our coats; she doesn't invite us to have a seat. I'm pretty certain she won't be offering us any refreshments. I doubt she has much to offer anyway.

We stand in the foyer; everyone is shifting awkwardly for several seconds before Hurley speaks. "Charlotte Strommen, you are under arrest for insurance fraud and evidence tampering. You have the right to remain silent." As Hurley finishes reciting Charlotte's rights, Masterson walks over to Charlotte with a pair of handcuffs. He slaps one on, pulls that arm behind Charlotte, and then goes for the other arm.

"You're arresting me?" Charlotte says, clearly shocked. "What about my kids?"

Hurley, who has finished reading Charlotte her rights, says, "Officer Joiner here will take them to the station. We've arranged for Child Protective Services to meet them there. They'll be placed with foster care for now, until we can get you arraigned."

"No," Charlotte whines, tears brimming. "Please don't do this."

I'm betting Charlotte isn't going to be able to raise bail, and that means her kids are likely to be shuffled around for a while.

"Where are Hannah and Peter?" I ask her.

"Upstairs in their bedrooms. Do you really have to do this?" she asks. Her voice is bordering on hysteria. "Please, they've been through so much already."

"I'm sorry, Charlotte," I say, meaning it.

We hear a commotion from the top of the stairs. When I look up, I see Hannah and her brother standing there, staring down at us. "What's going on?" Hannah asks, looking angry.

"Your mom is being taken down to the police station for questioning," I tell her. "I think you know why."

Hannah says nothing, and Peter looks up at her, his expression curious. Finally Hannah turns around and stomps down the hall. We hear her bedroom door slam shut seconds later.

"I got them," Joiner says, heading up the stairs. Peter starts to cry.

Masterson asks Charlotte if she has a coat, gets it, and drapes it over her shoulders. He then steers her out of the house to his patrol car.

"This is awful," I say to Hurley.

"Yeah," he admits, looking glum. "It is."

* * *

Ten minutes later, we are all at the police station. Masterson takes Charlotte into the interrogation room, removes the cuffs, and has her sit down at the table. Charlotte does as directed, looking scared, lost, and desolate. Hurley and I head into the room, and Hurley takes a seat across the table from Charlotte. He turns on the switch for the audio- and video-recording device as I settle into the seat next to him.

Hurley starts by reminding Charlotte that her rights have been read to her and asking her if she understands them. She nods solemnly, so he continues to speak. "Charlotte, we found something when we did your husband's autopsy that was confusing at first; but in light of other evidence we've uncovered, we've since figured out how it came into play."

He pauses, no doubt waiting for Charlotte to ask what this evidence is, but she's not playing. She folds her arms over her chest and stares him down, the muscles in her cheeks twitching like crazy.

"We know your husband committed suicide," I say softly.

She shifts her gaze to me and her eyebrows arch with surprise.

"We also know how he did it," I add. "We found a small worm stuck in his throat and it was identified as a clothing-moth larva, like the kind you might find on a wool coat. My guess is that it was stuck to the coat hanging in your bedroom closet, and your husband inhaled it when he put the plastic dry-cleaning bag that was on that coat over his head. Normally, that would be a nearly impossible way to die. It's been done, but it's very rare. Most people can't resist the urge to pull the bag off their heads once they begin to suffocate. But your husband found a way around that by putting

ether on a washcloth and putting it in the bag before
he put it over his head, effectively putting himself to
sleep."

Charlotte bows her head and sighs.

"How did he get the ether?" I ask. "Do you have any
in the barn? I know sometimes farmers use it on their
livestock."

Charlotte's whole body sags, and I know she has
given up. I breathe a small sigh of relief because without the paper bearing the impressions from Donald's
note, all we have is speculation. And thanks to me, that
evidence is inadmissible. If Charlotte doesn't confess,
we don't have a case.

"Donald learned how to make his own ether years
ago, back when we had cows," Charlotte says. "It's actually quite easy. All he used was some water, a plastic bag,
and a certain type of starter fluid."

Hurley says, "We found the note he wrote to you."

Charlotte looks up at him, confused. "You couldn't
have. I burned it."

"But you kept the notepad he wrote it on," I say. "We
were able to see what he wrote from the impressions it
left on the sheet beneath. We read his apology to you
and his explanation that it was the only way he could
see to provide for you and the kids. Despite all your
financial troubles, he kept up the payments on his
life insurance policy, and that was the only real asset you
had left. The only problem was, the policy wouldn't pay
for a suicide. So he instructed you to remove the bag
and washcloth, destroy them, and put his body in his
boat. Then you had to drive your ATV into the back of
the pickup, hook up the boat and take it down to
the landing. Once you got the boat in the water, you

motored out a ways and tossed your husband's body
overboard."

Fat tears drop from Charlotte's eyes onto the tabletop.

"After that," I continue, "you brought the boat back
to the landing, aimed it out at the lake, revved up the
motor, and let it go. Donald told you in his note to
empty most of the gas in the motor so it wouldn't go
far. He figured someone would find the boat adrift and
assume he'd fallen overboard and drowned. Then you
drove yourself home in the ATV, using fields so you
wouldn't be seen. Donald planned it out well, except
for one thing."

Charlotte looks up at us with red, watery eyes and
nods. "He didn't realize how hard it would be for me
to move his body alone," she says. "When I found him
in our bed that way . . ." She hiccups a sob and I recall
the nervous look on her face when I examined her
bed a few days ago. Now I know why. "I tried to move
him," Charlotte groans, "but I couldn't do it. I had to
get Hannah to help me. And even then it was a struggle. When we tried to . . . put him in the water, we
dropped him, and his head hit the side of the boat."
Her eyes take on a haunted look. "I think that was
when Hannah broke."

She looks so pathetic, so wounded, it breaks my
heart. I want to reach out to her, but I don't because I
suspect she'd only pull away.

"I shouldn't have done it," she says, hiccupping sobs.
"I should have just called the cops when I found him.
But I didn't want his death to be for naught. If I'd
known how much it would affect Hannah . . ."

Her voice drifts off and she puts her arms on the
table and drops her head onto them, crying. I feel like
crying myself. Hurley gets up and leaves the room,

and Masterson comes in. He walks over to Charlotte and takes her arm. "I need you to come with me, Mrs. Strommen," he says.

Charlotte obliges, shuffling like a zombie as Masterson steers her along. I follow them out and watch as Charlotte is led past her kids, who are in the vending room with Brenda Joiner. The kids watch their mother walk by, but no one says a word. It's a portrait of a family completely and utterly broken.

Chapter 36

I have nearly an hour before the autopsy on Lisa Warden is scheduled to start. I ask Hurley to drive me home so I can check on the animals to make sure they haven't killed one another, and to get my car. We make the trip in silence, both of us depressed over the morning's events. Hurley doesn't say a word when I get out of his car, and he takes off before I'm in the door.

Inside all is relatively quiet. As usual, Hoover greets me at the door, tail wagging, and I let him outside to do his business. I find Tux curled up on the sofa, grooming himself, and he barely spares me a glance as I come in. Rubbish is in the kitchen sprawled atop his food bowl, sound asleep.

Happy to see everyone is living together amicably, I head back out and drive to the hospital. There I make my way to the human resources office, where I find the hospital's HR director, Paula Wren.

"Hey, Mattie, what brings you back here?" she says. "Have you decided to stop cutting up dead people and go back to cutting up live ones, instead?"

I suspect she's merely making a joke and this is confirmed when I say, "Actually, yes, I am."

She arches her brows in surprise. "Are you serious?" she asks. "Because we have several openings: one in the OR and two in the ER. And given your experience, I suspect you'd be a shoo-in."

"I'm not interested in going back to the OR. But I'm very interested in the ER positions."

She nods sagely. Little explanation is needed, given that everyone knows my history with David, who is currently the hospital's only general surgeon. Working with him again would be a bit too awkward for everyone involved.

"I'm sure Molinaro will be thrilled to hear you're coming back," Paula says. "We haven't had many qualified applicants."

Nancy Molinaro is the director of nursing for the hospital. She is often referred to as "the Don" because of this title. It's a fitting nickname, given her scary appearance and ruthless reputation.

"Can you give me an application?"

"Of course, though it's really just a formality in your case." She gets up from her desk and walks over to a basket on top of a file cabinet. "Here you go," she says, grabbing an application and handing it to me.

I thank her and leave, heading for the ER and taking a back hallway into the department that will lead me right past the office of Collette "Colitis" Morgan, the department manager. I find Collette at her desk, where she is, perhaps serendipitously, working on the staff schedule.

"Hey, Collette."

"Mattie! What brings you around these parts?"

"Actually, I'm looking to come back here to work."

She looks confused. "I thought you were working at the ME's office now."

"I am, but it's not working out quite the way I hoped. Paula said you have some openings here in the ER?"

"I do—two of them, in fact. Both are full-time; one is three twelve-hour night shifts a week, and the other is five P.M.'s. Are you looking for something here in the ER?"

"I am. This was always my favorite place to work, and going back to the OR at this point would be . . . well, you know."

She nods.

"And I'd be most interested in the night position." Twelve-hour shifts are tough sometimes, but it means only working three days a week as opposed to five, giving me more time to spend with Hurley. And if I work the night shift, I'll be less likely to run into David.

Collette looks delighted and relieved. "Well, if that's the case, you can pretty much consider yourself hired." This isn't surprising. Nights are the least popular shifts, and the hardest to fill. "How soon would you be able to start?"

"I need to check with Izzy. I don't want to leave him in the lurch. But I'm thinking something like two to four weeks."

"Fantastic! Get your paperwork started and we'll get working on it. And welcome back."

"Thanks."

I leave, feeling comfortable with my decision. Yes, there will be some awkward moments to deal with; and yes, I'll probably be the subject of whispered conversations in the hallways, lounges, and cafeteria for a while, but it feels like the right thing to do.

I head back to the office to prepare for Lisa Warden's autopsy, feeling upbeat and positive. By the time I get changed into my scrubs and head for the autopsy room, Izzy is already there and has Lisa's body on the table.

"I went ahead and started on the preliminaries," he says. "Hurley called and said he won't be able to make it, but to let him know if we find anything. He said he had some business to take care of."

As always, I'm disappointed that I won't get to spend time with Hurley, but I console myself with the knowledge that we have our whole future ahead of us.

"It's just as well," I tell Izzy. "I need to talk to you anyway. I've decided to go back to work at the hospital."

He looks at me with a sad expression. "I figured as much from what you said this morning. Can't say I'm not disappointed to lose you, but I'm also happy for you, if it's what you really want."

"They have openings there in the ER and I can start whenever you're ready to let me go. But I told them I wouldn't leave you hanging. I'll stay on until you can find a replacement."

"I appreciate that. As luck would have it, I have someone who's interested."

"Really? Who?"

"Jonas Kriedeman."

"The evidence tech?"

"One and the same. He told me some time back that he had thought about applying when I had the opening you took. But by the time he decided to go ahead with it, you were already on board."

"Well, that's great."

Even I can hear the lack of enthusiasm in my voice, and Izzy eyes me curiously. "You don't sound very convincing," he says.

"It *is* great," I say. "I'm happy to know you have a ready and willing replacement waiting in the wings. And Jonas is a great guy. I'm sure he'll do a good job."

"I sense a 'but' in there somewhere," Izzy says.

The man reads me like a book. "I guess I wasn't

expecting all of this to happen quite that fast. It makes it so . . . real all of a sudden."

"Is that a bad thing? Because I'm more than happy to keep you on."

"No, it's a good thing. It's just that I do like this job, Izzy, more than I ever expected to. I like what I do, I like the people I do it with, and it's going to make me a little sad to leave it. I thought I'd have a little more time to get used to the idea, that's all."

"Well, if you really miss it all that much, you can always come for a visit."

"I just might do that."

With the difficult stuff out of the way, we get down to business. Two hours later, Lisa Warden's autopsy is done. Unfortunately, we haven't found anything other than evidence of the narcotic habit we already knew she had. Arnie pops his head in to let us know that the syringe we found in her arm tested positive for morphine and had only one set of prints on it: Warden's.

"Well, based on what we have so far, I can't rule out an overdose, though I can't tell if it was accidental or intentional." He looks over at me. "Do you want to deliver the news to Hurley, or should I?"

Since I'm anxious to let Hurley know about my work decision, I say, "I'll do it."

It takes me another half hour to clean up the autopsy room; and when I'm done, I head back to the locker room to change out of my scrubs. I discover a voice mail message on my cell phone and play it back, half-expecting to hear Hurley's voice. But I hear the whispery, slight lisp of Nancy Molinaro, instead. All she says is "Call me." I figure she wants to welcome me back to the hospital fold. I try to call her back, but her secretary informs me she has left for the day and won't be back in until the morning.

Next I try to call Hurley, but I get his voice mail. Rather than leave a message, I hang up, figuring I can try again later. By the time I head out to the main office area, it's going on three o'clock. Since our day started in the middle of the night, and we're now back on call, Izzy decides we should both head home for the day.

Back at my cottage, I try calling Hurley again. Again I get his voice mail and I leave him a message about our findings on Lisa's autopsy. I don't mention anything about my job and life decisions, however, because I want to do that in person. Instead, I simply end my message with "Call me."

Feeling groggy from my lack of sleep, I decide to lie down for a while. I manage to doze off for what feels like a short while. When I wake up, it's dark outside. I look over at my clock and see that it's almost six. I stumble out to the living room and dig my cell phone out of my purse to see if Hurley called back. But the phone is deader than Lisa Warden, because I forgot to charge it. I put it in the charger; and after freshening myself up a bit, I walk over, knock on Izzy's door, and let him know about my phone situation.

"I'm headed over to Hurley's place, so you can reach me there if a call comes in. Though, I imagine, I'll find out when Hurley does."

"No problem," he says. Then, with a wink, he adds, "And good luck."

I thank him, hop into my hearse, and head out.

I pull up in front of Hurley's house a few minutes later and see his car in the drive and the lights on inside, telling me he's home. Feeling both nervous and

excited, I head for the front door. Halfway there I'm
brought to a sudden halt.

The drapes on Hurley's front window are open a
crack and I can see him sitting on the couch, watching TV.

Cuddled up beside him is Tonya Collier.

Chapter 37

I stare at the tableau before me in disbelief, feeling as if someone has just stabbed a shiv through my heart. When I look back toward the street, I belatedly notice Tonya's car parked on the other side.

Feeling crushed, I head back to my car and drive to the closest convenience store, where I purchase a frozen mac-and-cheese for dinner and a pint of Ben & Jerry's Cookie Dough ice cream for dessert. When I get back to the cottage, I toss the mac-and-cheese into the microwave and treat myself to an appetizer of cookie dough chunks while the meal cooks.

I'm stress eating, and I know it, but I don't really care. The animals seem to sense that I'm in a funk and they all keep their distance, watching me warily as I pace and mutter to myself. I can't believe my crappy luck. Just when I make the decision to change my life in a huge way so I can be with Hurley, he hooks up with someone else.

I turn the TV on and plop down in front of it, scarf down my mac-and-cheese, and then finish eating all the cookie dough chunks out of the ice cream. There is a sitcom on, but what little of it my brain is following doesn't seem at all funny. My mind keeps circling around the fact that Hurley has hooked up with Tonya. But then, what did I expect? How many times lately had I told him that nothing can go on between the two of us, that he had to move on? Well, now he has, damn it.

It's just a first date, I tell myself. Maybe it won't go anywhere. Maybe when I tell Hurley that I've quit my job and decided to submit myself to the humiliation of hospital gossip just so I can be with him, he'll drop Tonya like a hot potato and hook up with me, instead. Or maybe he'll look at me like I'm crazy and take out a restraining order.

I can't focus on the TV, so I turn it off. I can't do the same with my mind, however, and I sit there torturing myself, wondering what Hurley and Tonya are doing now. It occurs to me that I could go back to his house and break things up by dropping in on the two of them. Then it also occurs to me that I could go back to his house and simply spy for a bit, to see where things go. This last idea feels wrong, but irresistible. Before I know it, I've changed into dark pants. I dig out my black coat and hat and some dark blue mittens, and tuck my hair up inside the hat to hide it. Disguise in place, I grab my half-charged cell phone from the charger, in case Izzy calls, and head back to Hurley's neighborhood.

The hearse is a dark midnight blue, but hardly inconspicuous, so I park a block away and then walk toward Hurley's house. The living-room drapes are still cracked open in the middle; but as I skulk my way across the lawn, cursing the streetlights, I see that the couch is now vacant. Cripes, had they hit the sack already? They have to be inside, because both cars are still here. So where are they?

I creep around the side of the house, until I reach

the kitchen window. There are no curtains here, so I have a full view of the room, which is fully lit. Tonya and Hurley are standing at the kitchen counter, side by side, talking and sipping beers. I feel a brief sense of relief that they aren't upstairs in the bedroom, but it doesn't last long. As I watch, Tonya sets her beer bottle aside and comes around to face Hurley. She leans in close to him and his free arm comes up and snakes around her waist. And then my cell phone rings.

I duck down because the ring sounds frighteningly loud in the quiet night air, and I'm worried Hurley and Tonya might have heard it. I reach into my pocket and clamp my hand over the phone to try to muffle the noise. Afraid of getting caught, I hop and hobble as fast as I can back toward my car. My injured ankle is still a significant impediment to any fast getaways.

I answer the phone on the fifth ring, just before it switches over to voice mail. I assume it's Izzy; but after I say hello, I hear Nancy Molinaro's distinctive voice.

"Mattie, do you have a minute to talk?" She doesn't bother with any greetings, or even say who it is. She is a woman who is used to being treated with awe, fear, respect, and deference.

"Sure," I say, a bit winded. I'm half a block away; and after a quick glance over my shoulder to make sure Hurley and Tonya aren't outside looking for or following me, I slow to a walk.

"I understand you talked with Collette today about coming back to work at the hospital."

"I did. She said there are a couple of openings in the ER."

"Yes, well, there is a small problem."

"What?"

"Your husband."

"David? Technically, he's not my husband anymore. We are divorced now."

"And therein lies the problem."

"I don't follow you," I say, coming to a stop as if the brainpower needed for walking might be enough to stump me. "What problem?"

"David said he doesn't want you working here anymore."

This momentarily stymies me. "I'm not asking to come back to the OR; I want to work in the ER."

"I know."

Silence follows for several seconds as I digest this. "Well, David will just have to tough it out," I say finally.

"He was rather insistent. He said it would be too awkward to have you working here at all. It *is* a small hospital."

"Are you saying you won't hire me?"

"I'm sorry, Mattie. My hands are kind of tied."

"You can't do that, Nancy. It's illegal."

"We don't have to hire you back, Mattie. You did leave with no notice when you were here before."

"For a good reason," I say, feeling myself grow angrier.

"And if need be, we can find enough issues in your old file to justify not hiring you back. Like that nipple incident, for instance."

"That happened more than seven years ago," I say in disbelief. "I can't believe you're doing this to me."

"I'm sorry, Mattie. But your husband holds all the power at this point. And today he told me that if we hire you, he'll leave. With Sydney Carrington gone, David is the only general surgeon we have on staff. We've been looking for a second one, but so far there aren't any takers."

"He's bluffing, Nancy," I say, thinking that the "MD" after David's name stands for "Major Dickhead."

"Perhaps, but it's a risk I'm not willing to take

right now. The hospital can't afford to lose that kind of revenue."

"That son of a bitch," I seethe.

"I'm sorry, Mattie, I really am. It's unfortunate that you and David couldn't work things out. Best of luck to you."

And just like that, she's gone, taking my life with her. I stand there, staring into space, my mouth hanging open, my breath creating giant steam clouds in the air. My first reaction is a screw-you-I'll-sue-you attitude. But when I think about the logistics of it all, I know it would be a lost cause. Molinaro would never admit to saying the things she just told me, and David would never admit to his ultimatum. It would end up being my word against theirs, and Molinaro could easily say that the reason they didn't hire me back was because I quit without notice last time. She'll use that and a few other minor transgressions I had over the years, and put it all together as a legitimate excuse. I'm screwed. And I'm mad enough at David right now that I could kill him.

I get in my car and start to pull out, when I see Hurley and Tonya come out of Hurley's house and get into his car. At first, I'm relieved, thinking he is taking her home, but then I remember that Tonya's car is here. Why wouldn't she just drive herself home? As they pull out, I follow, keeping back a ways. Hurley drives to the Peking Palace, where they both get out and head inside. Great, they're having dinner together.

Pissed, I drive home and drop onto my couch in a state of stunned disbelief, wondering how my life could have gone so wrong, so fast. I quit a job I know I love, so I could be with the man I think I love, but now he's with another woman. I'm unemployed, unattached, and unloved.

I need to call Izzy and tell him I've changed my

mind. I grab my cell phone, speed-dial his number, and he answers on the second ring.

"Izzy, hey, it's Mattie. Listen, I've been thinking about this whole job thing, and about Hurley, and I think I made a hasty decision earlier. I've changed my mind about quitting."

There's an uncomfortably long pause on his end before he says, "Your timing is astoundingly bad. I called Jonas this afternoon, right after you and I talked, and offered him the job. He accepted and he's set to start in two weeks, maybe one if I can convince the PD to cut him loose early."

I say nothing back to him at first. I can't. I'm too stunned. After a long silence, he says, "Mattie, are you still there?"

"I'm here," I manage to reply.

"Why the change of heart? Do you want to talk about this?"

God, no. I'd rather stab myself blind with a dull fork. How the hell did I manage to screw everything up so spectacularly in such a short amount of time? The last thing I need right now is someone feeling sorry for me. I don't want Izzy to know how utterly devastated I am, or how utterly stupid I've been. So I pull myself together and say, "No, I don't need to talk. I was just having second thoughts, some last-minute jitters and doubts. It will be fine. And we can talk about it tomorrow."

"Are you sure? Dom and I are out for dinner, but we can come home if need be."

"No, I'm sure. I'm fine."

"Call me if you change your mind."

"Thanks, Izzy. I'll see you in the morning." Before he can say another word, I disconnect the call.

Chapter 38

I drop my cell phone back into the charger and sit on the couch, staring at the wall, trying to digest everything. I'm angry as hell at David, at Hurley, at myself, and the whole frigging world. I'm angry at Barbie and her implied promises of a perfect life with Ken, and at Harriet for having such a good life with Ozzie. Somehow I've become a tragic figure in the soap opera that is my life, and I've hit an all-time low. I mean, what the hell else could possibly go wrong?

No sooner do I think this than there is a knock at my door. I'm afraid to answer it, thinking I've just tempted the Fates a little too much and a cloaked figure with a scythe will be waiting on the other side. I realize I'm overreacting and it's most likely just Izzy; but to my surprise, I find Paul Fletcher standing there.

"Hi," he says. He smiles, flashing those pearly whites at me. "I know this is a bit strange, coming to your house and all, but I understand that you have Lisa's cat, Tux, here."

"I do," I say, wondering where this is going.

"Oh, good. I was worried about him."

"He's doing fine."

"Good, good." He shuffles his feet for a few seconds. "It's a terrible thing that happened to Lisa," he says. "She was a good employee, and a good friend."

Maybe not as good as you think.

"Anyway, I thought I'd come by and offer to take Tux off your hands. I'll be happy to take him home with me. I think it's what Lisa would want."

Great. I haven't had nearly enough losses tonight. I want to tell him no, but I really don't have any grounds to do so. Tux isn't my cat; and while he isn't Fletcher's, either, he probably has more of a claim to him than I do.

"Yeah, all right," I tell him. "Come on in."

Fletcher steps inside and I shut the door. Hoover walks over and tries to sniff Fletcher's pant leg, but Fletcher pushes him away with his foot and mumbles, "Get off me, dog."

I call Hoover over and he scurries to my feet and sits.

"I think Tux is in the bedroom. Hold on and I'll get him for you." I call to Hoover to follow me and he does so. I find Tux asleep on my bed on one pillow, Rubbish on the other. I scoop Tux up and he settles into my arms and starts to purr. I tell Hoover to stay and carry Tux out to the living room, holding him out to Fletcher. "Here you go."

Fletcher is hesitant at first, looking as if he'd rather do anything than take the cat, but he finally reaches for him. As soon as he touches him, Tux tenses up, hisses, and wriggles himself loose, scratching Fletcher's gloved hand in the process. Tux hits the floor, running, and dashes back into the bedroom.

"Sorry about that," I say. "He's been through a lot. I think he's just spooked. Let me get the carrier I use for my cat. If I can get Tux into it, you can use it to take him home, and I'll get it back from you at a later date."

Fletcher nods and I head for my bedroom again. The carrier is in the back corner of the closet. I drag it out and leave it open and ready before approaching Tux again. He is now sitting between Hoover's front legs. Talking softly in easy, sibilant tones, I pet Tux for a minute or two before picking him up. He is complacent in my arms and lets me slip him into the carrier without any further ruckus. Remembering how he freaked out in Hurley's car, I realize I should have had the carrier with me when I took him from Lisa's place.

Then it hits me. How did Fletcher know Tux was here?

I pick up the carrier and head back out to the living room. Fletcher is standing in the middle of the room, with his gloves off, rubbing at a nasty-looking scratch that is bleeding slightly. "Here you are," I say, holding Tux out to him.

He takes the carrier, walks over toward the door, and sets it down on the floor. Then he turns back to me. "I'll need his litter box, too," he says.

"How did you know I had him?"

"What?"

"How did you know Tux was here?"

"Oh, um, I went by Lisa's place right before I came here and talked to one of her neighbors, a lady named Tonya. She told me you took him in."

My first thought is that Tonya seems determined to ruin my life tonight. My second thought is that I think Fletcher just lied to me. Even if he has the time wrong and he talked to Tonya some time ago, how would she know I took the cat in, as opposed to taking him to the pound?

"You just saw Tonya?" I say.

"Yeah, like ten minutes ago."

"She was pretty shook-up the other night. How is she doing?"

Fletcher shrugs. "She seemed fine."

Yes, she did, damn it.

Clearly, Fletcher is lying to me. The question is why? Why does he want Lisa's cat?

"Um, the litter box?" he says.

"Oh, right," I say. "It's in the bathroom. I'll get it for you." I head into the bathroom, look inside Tux's litter box, and see a rock-hard, dry-looking turd inside. I use a scooper to remove it and toss it into the toilet, thinking that Tux might need a kitty enema soon if this is what his output looks like.

And with that thought, I realize Jack Allen didn't have to get his alcohol through an IV; he could have gotten it via enemas. The rectal mucosa absorbs medications and nutrients just as well as, if not better than, the gut. And when I think back to the condition of Jack's body, the lower part of his torso was burned much worse than the upper. At the time, I thought it was just because of where the fire was in relation to his body, but now I realize it might have been the flammability of the alcohol in his intestines that caused it.

I also remember from reading Jack's chart that he received a lot of enemas lately, and Lisa wasn't the one who gave them. Paul Fletcher was. That realization leads me to another. It's not Tux that Fletcher wants; it's the litter box.

I look at it again. It's a large, bulky thing with two halves that clamp together, and the bottom half has a plastic bag liner in it, making it easier to change. I glance over my shoulder to see if Fletcher is watching me; and to my chagrin, he is. I smile at him. "Just cleaning it out for you," I say, waving the scooper. I turn back to the box and stick the scooper in again, even though there is nothing left to remove. I dig around through the litter, poking the scooper as deep as it will go. It doesn't go far. Despite the fact that the bottom half of the box is about ten inches deep, the litter inside it is only a couple of inches thick. Either the box has a false bottom in it, or there is something beneath the liner. I'm pretty sure it's the latter.

I make a show of scooping something more into the toilet, leaning to block Fletcher's view so he can't see that the scooper is actually empty. My mind is reeling, trying to think of a way to stall Fletcher, when he speaks right behind me. I hadn't heard him approach.

"What are you doing?" he says. I jump and look up at him as my heart pounds in my chest.

"I was just cleaning out the box for you."

"You seem nervous. Why is that?"

"You startled me, is all."

The muscles in his cheeks are twitching and his eyes narrow at me. I can tell he's weighing the truth of my statement. I see blood oozing from the scratch on his hand, and, thinking fast, I say, "Cat scratches are notorious for causing infections. I have some antiseptic in the medicine cabinet. Let me clean that wound up for you before you go."

I stand and take a couple of steps toward the medicine cabinet over the sink, thankful the door will swing open toward Fletcher. I know I have a pair of sharp scissors in there; and if he can't see inside it right away, I might have time to grab them. But just as I'm about to open the door, Fletcher stops me by splaying his hand on the mirrored front.

"You know, don't you?" he says.

"Know what?" I say, trying to prolong the charade, even though I'm pretty sure my goose is cooked.

"The money," he says. "You know about the money."

"I don't know what you're talking about."

Clearly, my denial isn't fooling him. He drops his hand from the medicine cabinet, reaches into his pocket, and pulls out a scalpel, retracting the protective cover on the blade. He points it at me and says, "Take the lid off that litter box."

I do as he says, unclamping the top and lifting the lid, which I set aside. "You killed Jack, didn't you?" I say, knowing any further pretense is useless.

"I didn't mean to," he says. "It was an accident. He got drunker than I expected, and I guess he tipped his chair over reaching for another piece of pizza. His head got wedged between the chair and the coffee table, and either he passed out or he didn't have the strength to move. I didn't hear him fall, because I had turned up the volume on the Christmas music he had playing to cover up the sounds of me opening the safe. By the time I found him, he was already dead from asphyxia."

"You got him drunk with the enemas," I say.

He smiles at me. "I'm impressed. How did you figure that out?"

"There was no alcohol in his stomach. If he'd drunk himself into oblivion, it should have been full of it."

"A miscalculation on my part," he says, with a shrug. "I just wanted some of that money he was hoarding. I wasn't going to take it all, just enough to keep the agency going and give me a little boost. Lisa told me she saw him with a big wad of cash once, and he had this key that he wore around his neck all the time. So I started snooping around and found that fake speaker safe. One day when I was there to give him an enema, I had just come from the liquor store and I decided to put some alcohol in the enema to see what happened. Within an hour, he passed out in his chair, so I took the key and opened the safe. He had wads of money in there, and I only took a few hundreds that first time. The next day, he was confused about what had happened, and I blamed it on a new med he was taking.

"I only meant to do it that one time, but my agency

hasn't been doing too well lately because the insurance payments we get are ridiculous. So I went back for more a few times. I never wrote those visits up, and I always parked over on the next block and came through Jack's backyard to avoid being seen. But it all went wrong that last time. I was just going to take the money and leave; but I figured if someone found Jack dead, with a butt full of alcohol, it would look suspicious. So I set the fire to destroy the evidence and make it look like it was an accident."

"What about Lisa? Was she in on it? Did she know what you did to Jack?"

"Not at first. But she started asking questions about why Jack was so drunk some of the time because she didn't see any evidence of him drinking that much. I knew the guy across the street was an alcoholic and that he checked himself into some fancy out-of-state rehab facility a couple of weeks ago, so I raided his trash cans and stashed the empties in Jack's trash."

Ah, the mysterious missing Mr. Gatling.

"After you guys showed up at my office the other day, I was afraid you'd come to my house next. Once you went and talked to Lisa, I figured her place was safe, so I took the money there. I told her what happened to Jack and how I decided to take the money. I offered to give her some to pay for her habit if she let me stash it at her place temporarily. She's been hooked on narcs for a long time now. As long as I supplied her, which is easy enough to do, since I can steal a couple pills here and there from my home care patients, she did anything I wanted."

"Why not just take the money and run?"

"Because if I disappeared, I knew I'd be suspect number one. I didn't want to be looking over my shoulder for the rest of my life. I planned to wait things out for a few weeks and then quietly close up shop and disappear. But Lisa hid the money and told me I had to take her with me when I left or she wouldn't tell me where it was. Apparently, she was under the misconception that there was something romantic going on between us just because we had sex a few times."

"So you overdosed her?"

He shrugs again. "I have a couple of hospice patients who are on morphine pumps and it's pretty easy to siphon off a little here and a little there. She was doing heroin anyway, and I couldn't very well have her going to the police, could I? But that stupid cat of hers screwed me. I searched her apartment; and when I didn't find the money, I got her car keys and went to look in it. That damn cat ran out when I opened the door, not that I cared, but then that neighbor came home, saw the cat, and took it to Lisa's apartment. I hid across the street and watched her call on her cell after she tossed the cat inside. And I stayed and watched when the cops showed up. That's how I knew you had the cat. I heard you talking about taking him home. At first, I figured Lisa had stuck the money in a safe-deposit box or something; and when the cops found it, they'd figure she was the one who took it. But I never found a key for a safe-deposit box; and when I saw you walk out with that litter box, I realized that was the one place I hadn't looked. So I followed you."

He chuckles and shakes his head. "I gotta give the girl credit. It was a brilliant hiding place. She knew I hated that damn cat and its nasty, smelly litter box. Speaking of which . . ." He gestures toward the litter box. "How about taking that liner out of there?"

The scalpel blade catches the light and glimmers menacingly. I swallow hard, bend down, grab the sides of the liner, and lift. It's surprisingly light, considering what the box weighed. And in the next second, I see why. Underneath it, neatly stacked in several rows, are bundles of hundred-dollar bills.

I stand there, holding the bag of litter and watching Fletcher. His eyes grow wide at the sight of the money; a little smile breaks out on his face. Then he looks back at me and the smile fades.

"Just take the money and go," I tell him. "I won't do anything, and I won't tell anyone."

"Do I look that stupid?" he says. "Look, I'm sorry this all got so out of hand. It wasn't what I wanted. I didn't want to hurt anyone."

"Then don't."

"It's too late. I'll try to make it as painless as I can for you." He lifts the scalpel and looks at it. "One quick cut on the carotid and you'll be unconscious in a minute or two. I've heard it's not a bad way to go."

"Really? And just who was it who told you that?"

He sighs and says, "I'm sorry."

I'm not about to wait for him to come slashing at me with that scalpel, so I make my move. I toss the bag of litter at his head and score a direct hit. Half the litter flies out of the liner and hits his face full on. The rest of the bag hits him in the neck, and it's enough to knock him off balance. I leap forward and shove him, making a mad dash past him and out of the bathroom. His arm flails out and a hot burn rips along my neck, making me holler out in both terror and pain, but I keep on going, heading for the door.

Hoover appears in front of me, growling and baring his teeth. I know he's there to protect me, but my momentum is too great to stop or sidestep him and I run into him, instead. My feet tangle with his and I fall forward onto the floor. Behind me I hear Hoover growling and snapping and I try to get up. There is a pool of blood on the floor beneath me and on my hand. Panicked, I reach up and feel my neck, wondering if

I'm already pumping blood from the wound Fletcher inflicted. But some distant part of my mind, the nursing part that I've trained to stay rational and calm in the direst of circumstances, tells me it's okay. There isn't enough blood on the floor, or any arterial spray. I hear Fletcher yell; I hear Hoover growl; then I feel a cold wind on me. I look toward the source of the cold and see Hurley standing in the doorway, his gun drawn. I hear Hoover yelp behind me and watch as Hurley charges across the room toward the bathroom.

I hear Hurley yell, "Hoover! Down!" Then it's followed by "Drop it or I'll shoot you where you stand!"

I manage to get to my knees and stand, but I feel woozy. I stumble over to the couch and drop into it. I see Hurley in the bathroom doorway, his gun pointed into the room. "Mattie, are you okay?" he asks over his shoulder.

My fingers probe the wound on my neck. It's long, but not deep, and the blood is oozing, not pumping. "I'm cut, but I'm okay," I tell him.

He moves to one side, still keeping his gun aimed, and Hoover comes limping past him. There is blood dripping from his face and one of his front legs.

"Oh, no, Hoover!" I push myself off the couch, my wooziness forgotten, and hurry over to my dog. He, too, is cut, in two different places: one on his foot and the other on his cheek. The one on his cheek is nearly two inches long. The one on his foot is between his toes and it's nearly half an inch deep.

Hurley takes out his cell phone and calls 911, requesting both police backup and an ambulance.

I head for the kitchen, with Hoover limping along behind me, and grab a towel. Then I set about cleaning Hoover's wounds.

The first cop shows up in a minute or two, and soon the place is swarming with cops and EMTs. Hurley hands Fletcher off and comes into the kitchen to hover over Hoover and me. The EMTs quickly determine that I'll need stitches; and while it isn't an emergent problem, they offer to take me to the ER.

"I won't go, unless my dog comes with me," I tell them. "He saved my life."

"I'm sorry, Mattie," one of the EMTs says. "We can't take a dog in the rig. You know that."

Hurley says, "That's okay. I'll take her."

He loads Hoover and me into his car, leaving the other cops to haul Fletcher off to jail. Along the way, I fill him in on my visit from Fletcher, and the details I now know. "Thank goodness you showed up when you did," I tell him as all three of us get out of his car and walk into the ER. "Why did you come by?"

"Izzy called me after he talked with you on the phone. He was worried about you. He told me that you quit your job and then asked for it back."

"He already offered my position to Jonas. I thought I had a job here at the hospital, but Molinaro called me tonight and told me she wouldn't hire me back because David said it would be too awkward."

Hurley mutters a few colorful adjectives for David.

"So now I'm unemployed," I finish.

We're at the doors to the ER and I'm about to go in when Hurley stops me. He places a hand on either shoulder and turns me to face him. "Izzy also told me why you quit," he says.

I smile awkwardly. "Yeah, well, sorry about that. I was stupid."

"What do you mean?"

"I know it's too late, Hurley. I came over to your house tonight, to tell you about the job and all, and I saw Tonya there. And I saw the two of you head out for dinner at the Peking Palace."

"Tonya called me. And I only agreed to see her

because you said the two of us could never be. I drove her back to her car and dropped her off as soon as Izzy called me. Why didn't you tell me you were thinking about quitting your job?"

"I didn't want to say anything to you until I had a chance to talk to Izzy. And I only told him this afternoon."

Hurley's eyes rove over my face and hair. One hand comes up and touches the bandage the EMTs put on my neck. "I nearly lost you again tonight, Winston. And that scared the crap out of me."

Hoover chooses that moment to whimper at our feet, reminding us that we're not alone. Hurley's hands drop to his sides, but then he takes one of mine in his and opens the ER door. "Come on," he says, holding my hand tight. "Let's get the two of you fixed up, and then you and I are going to talk some more."

Chapter 39

Nearly two hours later, both Hoover and I are patched up and ready to head out. The doctor on duty, Allan Connor, kindly agreed to stitch Hoover's wounds, along with mine. Knowing it might get him and others on staff in trouble if we took Hoover into the ER proper, Connor set up a sterile field in the ambulance bay and stitched Hoover up there.

Not long after we arrived at the hospital, Izzy called Hurley on his cell phone, panicked because he and Dom came home and found a bunch of cops in my cottage and a bunch of blood on the floors. Hurley filled him in on what happened, assured him he would take care of me for the night, and promised to update him in the morning.

After thanking Dr. Connor and the ER staff for their help, Hurley, Hoover, and I head back out to Hurley's car. As Hurley pulls out of the lot, I look over at him and say, "What am I going to do for a job?"

"You have the money from your divorce settlement," he says, making me wince. "That should hold you for a while."

I debate telling him that I've lost a big chunk of my

settlement money at the casino, but decide not to. There's still enough to hold me for a little while; but sooner or later, I'm going to have to find another job.

"Don't worry about it tonight," Hurley says. "You can start fresh in the morning."

I decide he's right. There's nothing I can do about it tonight anyway. So I sit back and try to relax. That's when I notice the route we're taking.

"Where are we going?" I ask him.

"My place. You and Hoover are spending the night with me so I can keep an eye on the two of you. If you go back to your place, I'm afraid you'll be haunted by what happened there and you'll never get any rest. Besides, your place is a mess. Tomorrow I'll take you over there and help you clean it up."

"But I have to go back. Tux is stuck inside that cat carrier. I can't leave him there all night like that. And what about Rubbish? He's probably all freaked out by what happened."

"When I spoke to Izzy earlier, he said he and Dom had both of the cats at their place. They'll be fine."

Hurley pulls into his driveway and shuts off the car. We get out and head inside, where I see two empty beer bottles sitting on the coffee table, a reminder of Hurley's earlier guest. He sees them, too, and quickly grabs them up and tosses them in the kitchen trash. "Do you want something to eat?" he asks. "I can fix you up a sandwich."

"Sure." I settle in at the table and Hoover makes himself at home by curling up on the rug in front of the sink. Hurley tosses him some slices of ham while he's preparing the food and then sets two sandwiches on the table. He goes over to a cabinet, takes out a couple of wineglasses, and then grabs a bottle of Chardonnay from the fridge.

"It will take the edge off things for you," he says, filling both glasses.

The sandwich tastes wonderful; and as we eat, we discuss the night's events some more. Somewhere in that process, my wineglass gets emptied and refilled twice. After I drain it for the third time, Hurley says, "Come on upstairs and I'll get you something to sleep in so you can get out of those bloody clothes. You're welcome to take a shower, if you want."

"Thanks. I think I will." I get up from my chair and follow Hurley upstairs. He digs out a baggy old T-shirt and some sweatpants, and then he fetches me a towel from a hall linen closet.

The shower feels wonderful; I emerge tired but feeling renewed. The issue of my job keeps trying to take the lead in my thoughts, but I act like Scarlett O'Hara and push it back, thinking tomorrow is soon enough to worry about it.

When I come out of the bathroom, Hurley and Hoover are both waiting for me in the upstairs hallway.

"Feel better?" Hurley asks.

"I do."

"I've made up the guest bedroom for you." He turns and heads down the hallway and I follow him to the first door on the right. He stops just outside and extends his arm through the doorway. I step into a simple bedroom with a double bed, a nightstand, a dresser, a closet, and a large color picture on the wall of the Chicago skyline at night. A lamp on the bedside stand warms the room with a cozy glow.

"Mattie?"

Hurley is standing right behind me and I can feel his breath on the back of my neck when he speaks. "Yes?" My heart is pounding in my chest and I dare not turn to look at him.

"You don't have to sleep in here, if you don't want to."

There it is, the line drawn in the proverbial sand. Do I cross it? I've given up so much to be able to do so. I turn to face him, looking up into those deep blue eyes. "Where else would I sleep?"

"With me." He reaches up and tucks a stray hair behind my ear.

He takes my hand and leads me down the hall to the master bedroom. Hoover gets up to follow, but Hurley stops at the door of the bedroom and gently tells him to stay. We head for the bed; and when we reach it, Hurley turns to me, pulls me close, and kisses me. And from that moment on, I'm a goner.

Later, Hurley and I are lying in his bed, mostly naked, side by side. Both of us are staring up at the ceiling, panting slightly, and wearing goofy grins. My brain struggles to wrap itself around what's just happened, because the sensations Hurley awakened in me were mind-numbingly awesome. I'm also keenly aware of the line we just crossed. My mind-body argument is abruptly interrupted when I hear the ring of Hurley's doorbell.

Hurley scowls and glances at his watch. "It's nearly eleven at night," he says. "Who the hell could that be?"

The doorbell rings again and Hurley sighs, clearly annoyed. He gets out of bed, pulls on his jeans, and heads toward the stairs, with Hoover on his heels. I reluctantly roll out of bed, pull on the shirt and sweatpants I was wearing earlier, and follow Hoover, stopping at the top of the stairs as Hurley opens the door below. Standing on the front stoop are a woman and a teenage girl.

"Hi, Steve," the woman says.

Several beats pass before Hurley says, "Kate?"

"Yep, it's me. Quite the blast from the past, eh? You're a hard man to find."

Apparently, not hard enough.

"What are you doing here?" Hurley asks.

"We need to talk. Can we come in?"

Though he's clearly annoyed, Hurley nods and waves them into the foyer. He sees me standing at the top of the stairs and does a perfunctory introduction.

"Mattie, Kate. Kate is an old friend of mine."

"I'm a bit more than that," Kate says as Hurley shuts the door. "I'm his wife."

For a moment, I think I'm delirious and hallucinating. My legs start to tremble and I sit down on the landing so I won't fall down the steps.

Hurley whirls on Kate and says, "You *were* my wife, many years ago. We're divorced."

"Actually," she says, looking apologetic, "we're not."

"I signed the papers."

"I never filed them."

I squeeze my eyes closed as I feel my world crumble around me. Could this day possibly get any worse? Apparently, it can. Kate proves there is no end to my misery with her next words.

"And this," she says, putting an arm around the teenage girl who is with her, "is your daughter, Emily."

Chapter 40

More than anything, I want to escape from Hurley's home and return to my cottage. However, I don't have a way to get there unless I walk, and I'm not about to head out at eleven at night in the bitter cold for an hour-plus stroll. Hoover and I stake out the living room, while Kate, Emily, and Hurley huddle in the kitchen. I can't help but eavesdrop on the conversation.

"I didn't know where else to turn," Kate says. "I lost my job, my house is in foreclosure, and we have nowhere to stay."

"What about your parents?" Hurley asks.

"Dad passed away a couple of years ago after a heart attack. And Mom has early Alzheimer's. I had to put her in a home last year."

"Your brother?" Hurley says.

"I haven't heard from him in years. Even if I knew where he was, I doubt he'd be much help. The last time I saw him, he was hooked on coke and hanging out with a seedy bunch. For all I know, he may be dead."

I hear Hurley sigh. "Why didn't you go ahead with the divorce?"

"I meant to, but right after you sent the papers back to me, I found out I was pregnant."

"Why the hell didn't you tell me?"

"I didn't want you to feel trapped. I thought I could do it on my own." With that, Kate bursts into tears and I hear Emily consoling her.

I hear a chair push back and then Hurley appears in the living room. He looks at me with this awful expression that says it all.

"Mattie, I'm so sorry," he says. "I can't turn them out into the cold."

"I want to go home."

He looks crushed, but he nods and heads back to the kitchen.

"I need to take Mattie home," I hear him say. "The two of you can make yourselves at home here, for now. There's a spare bedroom upstairs you can share."

I grab my coat, and Hoover and I are waiting by the door when he returns. We walk out to the car in silence.

"Why didn't you tell me about her?" I ask him, once we're under way.

"I didn't think there was anything to tell."

"You didn't think the fact that you were married— still *are* married, apparently—was worth mentioning?"

"I didn't know Kate never filed the divorce papers. And we were only married for a few months. We were young and stupid, and we both knew it was a mistake right after we did it. I'll get it sorted out. Please just give me a little time."

"Take all the time you want," I say irritably.

"Look, you're mad, and I get that," Hurley says. "I'm none too happy about this, either. But it can be dealt with. It's not the end of the world."

Not the end of your world, maybe, but mine is looking pretty grim at the moment.

We pull up into the drive in front of my cottage and I get out with Hoover. As I'm about to shut the door, Hurley again says, "I'm sorry, Mattie."

"Yeah," I say. "Me too."

I head inside, with Hoover on my heels. When I close the door to the cottage, I can't help but feel as if I'm also closing the door on a chapter of my life.

The place is a mess. There's dried blood on the floors and litter spread all over the bathroom. I set about cleaning it up, my mind numb. When I'm done, I drop into bed, exhausted, depressed, and spent. I make one final curse at the Fates, who seem determined to keep me and Hurley apart; and then, with Hoover curled up at my side, I cry myself to sleep.

If you like the Mattie Winston mysteries,
keep reading for a special preview of
Murder on the Rocks,
the first in the new Mack's Bar Mysteries series
by Allyson K. Abbott.
Coming August 2013!

Chapter 1

Stumbling upon a dead body before I've finished my first cup of coffee is not my idea of a great way to start the day. Not that anyone would think it was, but the discovery was more complicated for me than it would be for most people.

For one, I'm not and never have been a morning person, thanks to a biological clock dictated as much by nurture as nature. I own and run a bar in downtown Milwaukee, Wisconsin, which means I keep some odd hours. It takes a couple of cups of coffee every morning to wake me fully and get me thinking clearly. As a result, my senses are dulled and sluggish when I first get up. Turns out this is a good thing, because my senses aren't always kind to me.

The bar is called Mack's, after my father. He bought it the year before I was born and hoped to have a namesake son who would take over the business someday. I came along, instead; and while I may not have had the right genital equipment, I did have my father's red hair, fair complexion, and, it seemed, his gregarious nature. According to him, the nurses who cared for me after I was born were fascinated with me because they said I was more interactive than any other new-born they'd ever seen. In hindsight, it may have been my condition that accounted for that, but no one could have known it at the time.

Anyway, Dad was not a man easily deterred; and he managed to pass along his name by putting *Mackenzie* on my birth certificate and calling me "Mack" for as long as I can remember. Over time we became known as "Big Mack" and "Little Mack," and Dad's future plans for the bar moved along.

My mother died right after I was born, so my father brought me to work with him every day, sharing my care with any number of patrons who came into the place. As a result, I now have a handful of "aunts" and "uncles" who have no claim to me other than the occasional diaper change or play session. I've lived my entire life in the bar. I took my first steps there, uttered my first words there, and did my first pee-pee in the big girl's toilet there. I knew how to mix a martini before I knew how to spell my own name. During my school years, I spent every afternoon and evening doing my homework in the back office, and then helping Dad out front by washing glasses or preparing food in the kitchen. He always sent me to bed before the place closed . . . easy to do, since we lived in the apartment above, but the bar itself was the place that really felt like home to me.

It has been my home for thirty-four years, thirty-three of them very good. Dad died eight months ago, so it's just me here now. It's been a struggle to go on without him, though he prepared me well by teaching me everything I'd need to know to take over running the bar. Everything, that is, except what to do with a dead body in the back alley.

Milwaukee is no stranger to dead bodies turning up

in unexpected places, but my neighborhood, which is
located in a mixed commercial and residential area
built up along the banks of the river that runs through
downtown, isn't a high-crime spot. Despite that, this
isn't the first time someone has died in the alley
behind my bar. My father has that claim to fame after
being mortally wounded by a gunshot just outside our
back door this past January; though if you got right
down to it, I couldn't say for sure that anyone really
died in the alley. My father's death occurred in the hospital a short time after his attack, and I had no way of
knowing where this second person died. All I knew for
sure was that there was a body next to my Dumpster.

It was a little after nine in the morning on a hot and
humid August day, and I'd gone down the private back
stairs to toss my personal trash before readying the bar
for opening. Because it was pickup day, the Dumpster
was overflowing and extremely ripe in the stifling heat.
The smell hit me as soon as I opened the back door
and I had to force myself to mouth breathe. As I drew
closer to the Dumpster, the stench grew, becoming a
palpable thing—something I not only smelled, but saw.

The combination of the heat and the olfactory
overload triggered a reaction that might seem strange
to most people, but is all too familiar to me. My mouth
filled with odd tastes and I heard a cacophony of
sounds: chimes, bells, tinkles, and twangs . . . some
melodious, some discordant. My field of vision filled
with flashing lights, swirling colors, and dozens of
floating shapes. I struggled to see past this kaleidoscope
of images and that's when I saw the arm—small and
pale—sticking out from under a pile of torn-down
boxes beside the Dumpster.

My first thought was that it wasn't real, that perhaps
someone had tossed out a mannequin. After blinking
several times in an effort to see past the weird stuff, I

realized that thought was nothing more than blissful denial. The arm was real. Then it occurred to me that it might belong to someone who was sick or injured. It wouldn't be the first time I found a drunk passed out somewhere outside my bar. Just in case the person was more than ill, I grabbed a plastic bag from my personal sack of trash and used it to raise a corner of the cardboard without actually touching it.

I tried to see what lay beneath; but my visual kaleidoscope swelled into something so big and encompassing that it blinded me to all else, forcing me to drop the cardboard and stumble-feel my way back into the bar.

Once I was inside with the door closed, the smell dissipated and the air cooled. The images, sounds, and tastes began to fade. I made my way down the hall, past the bathrooms to the main lounge area, where I normally would be getting things ready in preparation for opening the doors to my lunch crowd: my neighborhood regulars and the hard-core drinkers who provide a source of steady income for me at the expense of their own livers.

I grabbed the bar phone, since my cell was still upstairs, and dialed 911.

"Nine-one-one operator. Do you have an emergency?"

I felt weak in the knees and leaned against the back bar. "There is a dead body in the alley behind my place," I said. I relayed my name and address to the operator, who instructed me not to touch anything. *Too late for that.*

"I'm dispatching officers there now," the operator said, and then she started asking questions, some of which I couldn't answer. "You said the body is outside?"

"Yes, it's on the ground beside the garbage Dumpster."

"Is it male or female?"

I hesitated, struggling to interpret what I'd seen when

I lifted the cardboard. I knew the arm was small and not muscular, and I thought I recalled a hint of femininity in the edge of a sleeve. "I think it might be female," I told her.

"But you're not sure?"

"No."

"Is the body mutilated?"

"I don't know. There's cardboard piled on top of the body, so I couldn't see the whole thing, just part of an arm." This was a tiny lie; but with any luck, no one would know I'd lifted the cardboard.

"I see," said the operator in a tone that suggested otherwise. Realizing our conversation was likely to get more confusing if it continued, I prayed the cops would arrive soon.

And just like that, my prayer was answered. Someone pounded on the front door and a male voice hollered, "Milwaukee police."

I hurried over and undid the locks, letting in two uniformed male officers. "The police are here," I told the operator. I relocked the doors, disconnected the call—thus ending my inquisition, though there would be plenty more to come—and switched my attention to the officers.

"You have a dead body here?" said the taller one, whose name pin read *P. Cummings*.

I nodded. "It's out back in the alley, by the garbage."

"Male or female?"

"I'm not sure." I repeated my covered-with-cardboard lie as I led both cops to the alley door. As soon as I stepped outside, I switched to mouth breathing to try to forestall another reaction. I stopped several feet from the Dumpster and pointed to the pile of cardboard, where that one pale arm protruded.

Both officers were wearing gloves and Cummings's partner, whose name pin read *L. Johnson,* walked over and lifted the cardboard. Instinctively, I clamped a hand over my mouth, a fatal mistake since it forced me to breathe through my nose.

The smell hit me full force, triggering a cacophony of sound. The kaleidoscope of images blinded me again and some weird tastes followed. I found myself wishing for a drink as alcohol tends to minimize my reactions. And with the way things were going, this was starting to look like a four-martini day.